D1562412

ALSO BY ANTHONY GIARDINA

Norumbega Park

White Guys

Recent History

The Country of Marriage: Stories

A Boy's Pretensions

Men with Debts

REMEMBER THIS

REMEMBER THIS

A Novel

ANTHONY GIARDINA

FARRAR, STRAUS AND GIROUX
NEW YORK

Farrar, Straus and Giroux
120 Broadway, New York 10271

Frontispiece photograph by James Andrews1 / Shutterstock.com.

Library of Congress Cataloging-in-Publication Data
Names: Giardina, Anthony, author.
Title: Remember this : a novel / Anthony Giardina.
Description: First edition. | New York : Farrar, Straus and Giroux, 2025.
Identifiers: LCCN 2024035178 | ISBN 9780374611347 (hardcover)
Subjects: LCGFT: Novels.
Classification: LCC PS3557.I135 R46 2025 | DDC 813/.54—
dc23/eng/20240802
LC record available at https://lccn.loc.gov/2024035178

Designed by Gretchen Achilles

Our books may be purchased in bulk for promotional,
educational, or business use. Please contact your local bookseller or
the Macmillan Corporate and Premium Sales Department at 1-800-221-7945,
extension 5442, or by email at MacmillanSpecialMarkets@macmillan.com.

www.fsgbooks.com
Follow us on social media at @fsgbooks

1   3   5   7   9   10   8   6   4   2

To Jim Magnuson

and to Anais

Yet it pleased the Lord to bruise him

ISAIAH 53:10

What should be true of the remembered life
is a freshness of detail: this is how it was—

the almond's smell from a torn almond leaf,
the spray glazing your face from the bursting waves
—DEREK WALCOTT, *TIEPOLO'S HOUND*

CONTENTS

ONE: How to Be This Age (2012)   1

TWO: The Politics of the Understudy (2014)   63

THREE: Days Without Rules (2016)   191

FOUR: The Remembering Animal   335

Acknowledgments   369

ONE

HOW TO BE THIS AGE
(2012)

I.

The young woman—young, though nearly forty—stood with her head bent slightly toward the window of McNally Jackson bookstore on Prince Street. She had stopped mid-stride, was on her way somewhere—was, in fact, late—and to see her father's image in a bookstore window was not anymore such a new thing. This particular book had been out three or four months, and had become prominent enough that to catch it as she'd just done—his face on the cover, his peculiar, slightly hostile smile—was not so unusual, even in a city as emptied of bookstores as New York had lately become. Still, she never lost the startled feeling she felt now. It was as if her footsteps were drawn toward it by a complex loyalty of their own.

Two weeks before, they'd sat around a table, celebrating, at a restaurant not far from here. Celebrating what? There was almost too much. He was about to turn seventy, his book had lately reached the middle rungs of the nonfiction bestseller list, he was leaving for Haiti on what he termed a "do-gooder mission." A group from his church in western Massachusetts was going to the post-earthquake island to rebuild the roof of a parish deep in what he called "the Haitian bush." ("Though from what I'm told, there *is* no more Haitian bush.") "Something mildly noble," he called it, flush with self-mocking irony, on his third or fourth glass of one of the higher priced selections on the restaurant's wine list. Then he had embarrassed her, deliberately. "Do you know who I am?" he'd asked their waitress, the actress or NYU student or budding first novelist who had made the mistake of treating him as though he were a man she *should* know. The question, though tossed with a humorous spin to the waitress, was actually directed at her, his daughter, Miranda, as though her wish to simply be present, celebrating him, sitting

3

between her mother and her cousin and surrogate brother, Philip, was something he felt the need to complicate. They'd shared a moment, eye to eye, while the waitress understood the question begged no response. He had had to register for his daughter's benefit, even at the risk of the kind of embarrassment ("teasing," he would have called it, "*fond* teasing") he had lain on her from adolescence onward, that he took none of his new fame seriously. That she must see this about him. That she must, above all—the essential part of their bond—see *him*.

The image of his face on the cover of the book took up the entirety of the available space, shared only with the words *How to Be This Age*, and his name, Henry Rando. It had been a kind of publisher's folly, thinking that a book of this type would sell, and then, miraculously, it had. Henry had been as astonished as anyone to learn that somewhere deep in the culture, underneath the appetite for style wars, for the dreary memoirs and novels of lost empires and washed-ashore refugees, the endless slop and wash of the political moment, lay a desire, on the part of thousands of readers, to learn how to be *seventy?* Six brief chapters, thirty pages each. Love. Sex (or what is left of it). Friendship. Community Service and Political Engagement. Solitude. A pause, and then, God. Here's how to do it. Here's how to face the abyss cut into existence by all that has been neglected during the incomplete years of youth and middle age. Here's how to broach the loss of will, of power, of *force*. You can buy this book and slip it in your pocket. It was that small. Twenty-five dollars. Outrageous, yet not really. At another celebratory lunch, this time with his publisher, Henry had been told, "It's your face that did it, I think. On the cover. You look like you're putting one over on us in a way that makes us want to be part of the scam."

Now here it was, once again, on Prince Street, the face with its subtle tease. Henry himself had said, at the celebratory dinner, that if a movie were ever made of his life, he could only be played by Michael

Gambon. Miranda had of course gotten the reference (in the course of a lifetime together, Henry had made sure that his daughter was well-versed in showbiz lore), but Philip, left behind as usual, had needed to be offered a list of Gambon's credits (Professor Dumbledore in the later *Harry Potter* movies was all he really needed), after which they agreed that Henry was perhaps right. The high insistent forehead topped with sparse gray hair, the heavy-lidded, almost reptilian eyes, jowls overstuffed with vague dissatisfaction—the suggestion, in the entire posed visage, that a better time was to be found elsewhere, somewhere to be sought after immediately, *right now. Come with me.* Henry had taken that gaze, that invitational, hips-forward stride, his imposing ex-boxer's body in good, soft, earth-toned clothes, out onto Houston Street after the heavy meal and found, right away, an incident into which to thrust himself. An altercation outside a taxicab, in which the driver was seen to be punching a man who was attempting to leave the cab. In the pause between the second and third punches, Henry had run forward, grabbed the injured man, jabbed the cabdriver in the chest to restrain him. Henry forced the man behind him and shouted to the driver, "Enough!" And then, "Now go. What does he owe you?" This angry young man, handsome and volatile and wearing a white shirt that shimmered in the humid night, accepted the wad of cash Henry handed him, got back in his cab, and drove off. Henry walked the injured man to a bench under the bus shelter, gazing toward his huddled, frightened family with an ironic "Observe my heroism" look. For all the irony, his daughter knew there was a genuine impulse at work here. Her father sought out such encounters to offset what he referred to, both in conversation with her and in his book, as "our infernal softness, our generational retreat from anything resembling *engagement*." Hence Haiti, which he publicly hoped would be dangerous.

"You're crazy," Philip said, all street smarts and handsome reserve. "You could have gotten killed."

"Where are the rest of your glasses?" Henry asked the man, whose glasses, half of them anyway, lay broken over the bridge of the man's bloodied nose.

Pasty-faced, with a head of hair like iron filings laid atop a potato, the man was nearly crying. "Thank you," he said. They all waited for something more from him, some declaration of who he was, while Henry went out into the street, stopped traffic, to find and retrieve the broken eyepiece. To Miranda, viewing him, there was, despite the foolishness of the action, something in Henry to grudgingly admire. Or more, to wonder at. Some banked ambition to own and dominate the city. To stop traffic by the sheer force of his presence. To do good. It was terrible to admire him. It only encouraged him.

"Here," Henry said, handing the man the broken piece. "Now we don't need to know what that was about, but are you all right?"

"I think so." The man stood. He would wander off somewhere. A bar? A dim apartment? Fights in the city, the casual violence: it was something Miranda had seen more in her childhood, when they had lived on the Upper West Side before gentrification, when there were muggings and break-ins and a lost, dusty, banana-smelling feel to the city, when their neighborhood had seemed more Caribbean than white—Comidas Chinas y Criollas on every corner—and her father had bestrode it like a colossus. It had only seemed that way, of course. She had been then the thing she sometimes worried she had never fully graduated from being: a daughter.

On Prince Street, she shook the thought off, regarding once more the familiar image of her father before turning away from it, late, on her way to the same Upper West Side where she had lived until the age of twelve, though morphed into unrecognizability now. She was on her way to see a man seeking to guard his own artist-mother's image as much as Miranda, in her ambivalent way, in these stoppages of hers, was looking out for Henry. As if to say to the wave of tourists in SoHo, the Asian and the blond girls with their bags from Sephora, their sunglasses and their constantly attended phones: *Observe this. Regard this. My father.* It was silly. She partly hated it. Still, she felt it, all that was at every instant of time waiting to be sucked under, the human as well as the physical essence of the city preparing to be buried by a wave, by sand, by the architecture of commerce. She picked up her tote bag, heavy with notes, and carried on.

But not before indulging one more memory. Under the bus stop cover, after the injured man had walked away, they had taken turns chastising Henry. "Daddy," was what Miranda said, sounding younger than she felt. Her mother had only stared at Henry. Her mother's eyes could make it seem like she were shaking her head when her head was in fact perfectly still. "Henry," she'd said, her sultry, low-slung actress's voice. "You utter fool." There had been fear and enormous affection in it, those two things at once, and it had briefly separated the two older people from the two younger. To be with these two was to watch them perform for one another, as they were doing now. Lily the chastising, half-admiring spouse, Henry the brave man. Something not entirely real in it, and within the moment, the old sense Miranda had that their marriage consisted of an ongoing sizing up of one another. Forty years in, it was as if they had still not quite made up their minds about each other.

They'd said goodbye to Philip, sent him off to his five-thousand-dollar-a-month one-bedroom, themselves gotten a cab. In spite of the new money coming in from the book, Henry always insisted, on these trips into New York, on staying with Miranda in her apartment on St. Felix Street in the Fort Greene section of Brooklyn. It was not convenient, for *her* anyway, to have them sleep on the foldout couch in what passed for a living room, but Henry, frugal as always in small ways, insisted. They were rising above the city, onto the Brooklyn Bridge, when Miranda's mind slipped away. Sitting between her parents, she looked out to the dark lights at the mouth of the river, the parties going on in dockside restaurants, the lights forming a Rubik's cube in the supposedly shuttered Wall Street high-rises. Who owned the city, precisely, right now? What force, or combination of forces, *held* it? She thought of all the young men who worked in these buildings, drawing huge salaries, and then coming home, late on a Saturday night like this one, to video games and online gambling, and porn. The enormous, brightly lit solitude that New York, in its brassy early twenty-first-century iteration, had come to nourish and cocoon.

Her parents were in the midst of one of their habitual, mildly bickering conversations.

"That was when you insisted on leaving me to go off and do *John Gabriel Borkman*," Henry was saying.

"I never appeared in *John Gabriel Borkman*. Furthermore, you know it."

"*Some* Ibsen."

"All right, then."

As they fought, or not really fought, Henry's hand caressed Miranda's knee. His ancient gesture with her, nothing "inappropriate" in it, to use the overused word, a touch that implied, that asked for, connection. Though I'm bickering with your mother, I have not left you. You are, as always, my witness, my audience. You've been chosen for this. She did not mind, or minded only a little. Let them bicker for my amusement. Above her, the lights of the great bridge, the enormous cably netting, the suspension, the delicate tension.

On Atlantic, that former receiving station that had become the center of the universe, courtesy of a man named Jay-Z, her father abruptly asked the cabbie to pull over to the curb. What had he seen? What was it he needed to get out for? When the cab was stopped, Henry forced open the door and vomited into the gutter. Nearby, the evening crowd barely noticed. One or two offered grimaces. Henry took his time, then reached back toward Lily, who offered him her own handkerchief, which he used to wipe his mouth. He apologized silently, while Lily retreated into her corner. "Oh God, Henry." It was for Miranda to ask, "Are you all right?"

She touched his neck, clammy and wet and exuding something— the stockpiling of the evening, the drinking and overspending at the restaurant, the forced charm and self-imposed self-mockery, the feigned heroism of stopping a fight on Houston Street. The performative requirements of her father's life were becoming too much for him. Lily would be there when he fell, but Lily would insist she not shoulder the burden alone. Miranda would always be called on.

"Dad. Are you all right?" she asked again.

"Perhaps," he said, wiping his mouth with the handkerchief, "perhaps lamb shanks and Barolo wasn't the wisest idea in the world."

His hand on her knee this time gripped a little harder.

2.

It was Miranda's habit to exit the subway at 103rd Street, rather than the more convenient (by one stop) 110th. The approach to her destination on 107th Street was better made from the south, because the vista of this section of the Upper West Side required, for her own needs, an ascent. There was something about the rising plateau holding, at its northern end, Columbia and Riverside Church that called to mind the great journeys toward shining cities in her favorite novels. Jude's approach to the city Thomas Hardy called "Christminster"; the view of Kew Gardens from the Thames while Daniel Deronda lazes in the comfort of his rowboat. It was her habit, a silly one, she had to admit, to impose on the new city an older version of itself, the one she had grown up in, the sweeter, more dangerous city, the city that had produced artists like Anna Soloff, the painter whose son she had come here to see.

It was still astonishing to think that when she'd been a little girl, walking with her father down their block of 107th between West End and Riverside, Anna Soloff had been living and working in her apartment in the corner building, a building whose good northern light allowed her to take in the buildings across the street, as well as the wide fork of Broadway leading northward. Had Anna perhaps on occasion glanced out the window and seen a young girl and her bearish, beloved young father conducting their everyday activities? The city Anna painted had died, but Miranda considered it a part of her project, should it come to pass, to restore the details not only of the artist's life, but of that lost world they had once, unknown to one another, shared.

Thus, the 103rd Street approach. Though it was heartbreaking. Where Gregory's Delicatessen had been was a French café. The awful Indian restaurant had become a wine bar. The Olympia movie theater, where her father had taken her on Saturdays (her mother so often busy at matinees), where she had seen all the benchmark movies of her childhood—*Star Wars* and *E.T.* and *The Secret of NIMH*—was now a high-rise, at the base of which was a branch of the Bank of America. The health food restaurant, so aptly named the Fertile Earth, where Henry had frightened her by complaining that a diet of cabbage and sprouts would lead him to an early grave, was now a restaurant called Mezzogiorno. Half the restaurants in New York seemed to be called Mezzogiorno. How many of the upscale diners even knew what "mezzogiorno" meant? It didn't matter, it was all code, it had become a city of codes, protective ones—*here you will meet only people like yourselves*—where once upon a time—her childhood—it had been impossible to impose a code, because the city, at least this part of it, had been all chaos, all *spill*.

This shouldn't have been allowed to happen. The infusion of vast amounts of money into a neighborhood that had once had a very different character. But it had. She herself had become part of the great diaspora—the exodus to Brooklyn. Was Brooklyn in 2012 the equivalent of what the Upper West Side had been in the seventies? Hardly. Even the bodega on her corner, no one's idea of a hipster mecca, offered no entrée into a significantly different world. Thirty-dollar bottles of wine and eight-dollar chocolate bars, catering to a crowd that didn't blink at such prices. In 1979, when her father had taken her into their corner bodega, there had been a smell like a deceased rat had taken up residence in the heating pipes. "Ignore the dead rat," he'd said to her, and patted her small head. (She'd taken him literally, of course.) He had had to negotiate the neighborhood for her: dead rats, boiled cabbage that could cause an untimely death, late-evening street-corner loungers who could easily have been revealed to be muggers. But to expect it to have been different would have gone against their own code. Her father had taught her that they were secret sharers here, living in a neighborhood that did not entirely belong to them. In Anna Soloff, the painter whose biography she hoped to write, she believed she had found the last guardian of that vanished world.

Aaron Soloff, Anna's son, would be waiting for her now, in the apartment he and his brother had kept after their mother's death. Miranda was already ten minutes late, which did not allow time to get coffee, which meant that she would be less than sharp in her questioning. And his demeanor, his responses to her questions demanded sharpness. He was not sold on her as his mother's biographer, not entirely sold on the idea of a biography at all. She was being tested.

At the top of the stairs, after buzzing her in, he was always waiting for her, some distrust implied by his having to witness her climbing the three flights. He possessed an air of lounging there, on the fourth-floor landing, as though this was where he entertained, drank his coffee, received guests. You could live a long, complicated social life in this city and never encounter a man quite like this. The city had its deeply rooted social pockets, its eccentric cul-de-sacs, and he belonged to one she had never been asked, or invited, to enter. Fifty years old. A psychiatrist with an office on Eighty-Sixth Street. None of this was unusual, though *he* was, his sense of secretiveness. He had taken on the manner of those who hold the key to private archives.

There was no voiced greeting when she arrived on the landing. His skeptical, handsome face regarded her shoes, as if that was the place to look, the shoes told you everything. She had worn sneakers, dark blue. He held in his judgment, gestured that she should precede him inside.

He and his brother had maintained the apartment, but sparsely. Not a museum to their dead mother, just a place to store her work. It was the enchantment of this that kept Miranda coming, allowed her to withstand his veiled but implicit suspicion. The stacked paintings, the ones that hadn't yet sold, or which had been withdrawn from sale, or left unfinished. They leaned against the wall, some of them covered with old canvas. They filled the bedroom where Anna Soloff had slept, there for any thief to steal, though it was unlikely the neighborhood thieves paid close attention to the art market, where an Anna Soloff had recently sold at auction for $1,900,000, the highest figure a Soloff had yet commanded.

"Sit down. Tea?" His hand was already on the kettle.

"Something with caffeine, please."

"Miss your coffee this morning?"

"Rushing. Yes."

He turned on the jet. His suit—sand-colored—seemed made of the softest imaginable material. There were men whose haircuts you just wanted to sit and study, like topographical maps. He wore his a little long, sweeping over the left side of his head, but there was a complex layering involved.

"What are we talking about this morning?" he asked.

"You're still interviewing me, I think."

"Am I? Well then, tell me the questions I should be asking you."

"How about why I love your mother's work so much?"

He was looking in the cupboard for the tea she'd requested, not finding it.

"Maybe I should ask you something less obvious. Fuck, I don't think I can accommodate you. There's only herbal."

"It's all right."

"Is it?"

There were these strange moments with him, where he seemed to be figuring something out by means of studying her earlobes, her chin. For very brief moments, she wondered if it was sexual attraction working between them, but that seemed too pedestrian to dwell on. They regarded one another as if they were each relics of a world unknown to the other; she must have seemed as strange to him—the unmoored young woman carrying a bag full of notes on his dead mother—as he was to her. The only advantage she had was that she had seen him naked, in his mother's painting of him as a child. *Aaron, 11* showed him as yet undeveloped, but willing to display himself nonetheless, posing for his mother in the doorway of this very apartment, hands on his hips, his head tilted just slightly, as if he were asking his mother when they would be done with this—it was embarrassing, and he wanted to play outside. Was there something strange in this, an eleven-year-old boy being asked to pose nude? Anna had the power to make you thrust such questions aside. The marvel of the painting lay in what the artist had been able to convey, in very few brushstrokes, about adolescent skin—its tensile strength, its smoothness, its gleaming, accommodating *stretch*.

"Suggest a more interesting question. Chamomile or peppermint?"

"Peppermint, please. How about isn't it time your mother found a biographer, and unless there's a line outside the door, maybe I'm the best on offer?"

"That's pretty pathetic." He smirked, and poured. "Though maybe true."

He sat opposite her. Watched her sip. Little more than a decade separated them, but he took on, at times, a fatherly air, as though in spite of his seeming impatience with her, he wanted to be sure she had a proper cup of tea.

"Listen, how many times have we met?"

"This is the third."

"And would you say there's been progress?"

"That's up to you, I think."

"Don't be so deferential. I would think it's your job to convince me. Be a little bit more of a salesman." He crossed one knee over the other. "Salesperson, excuse me."

"All right then. Just fucking let me do it."

"Whoa."

She smiled, tucked into her tea.

"She's beginning to fetch big sums. I don't know how much you and your brother care about that. I don't imagine either of you are mercenaries. So let's leave that aside, the fact that a biography would help in that area."

As he leaned back just slightly in his chair, she sensed a mild, *very* mild but still new, appreciation of her boldness. Or maybe of the argument she was pretending not to make.

"The thing is, her story needs to be told. And I'm the one to do it."

He allowed a pause before responding. She wasn't happy with the way that last had come out.

"Well, you've now passed your college interview."

"I don't like that," she said.

"No, it was condescending. But you can do better."

Something then seemed to shift, just slightly, in his attitude as he looked at her. A subtle lightening in his eyes. Unless she was deluding herself (always a possibility) she felt they were moving into a space she thought she recognized, a space she had only lately learned to be comfortable within. Eugene, her mentor at the auction house she had recently left, had tutored her in it. "There's a moment just before yes," Eugene had told her. "It's a lovely place. Nurture it. Don't rush it. Take a seat. Learn to *wait*."

"How much writing have you done?"

"Not much. I've been up front with you about that. Catalogue work. I've sent some of it to you, I believe."

"Yes, and I haven't had time to read it. But most of that stuff is obfuscation, isn't it? Let me throw around some words that leave you totally confused but make you feel the artwork is somehow important."

"That's more or less true. Unfortunately."

"Describe a Renoir. First, have some more tea. It's getting cold."

"I don't like Renoir."

He raised his eyebrows.

"I don't like the colors. I don't like the lushness. Or the women."

He waited for more.

"I prefer your mother's nudes."

She wondered if just then an image of himself flashed across his mind, one he felt embarrassed by. She thought she should probably distract him.

"Even more than the nudes, I love the cityscapes."

"Please don't use that word."

"All right, what word, then?"

His answer was a small, dismissive smile. "Cityscapes" had been the wrong choice, a cliché.

"Here's what's happening," she went on, riding right over that look of his. "We're all becoming very interested in the seventies. Right now, it's taking the form of nostalgia. For grunge. For the whole pre-AIDS, disco-ball, CBGB's atmosphere. But it'll get deeper. It's as though we're all waking up to how much we forgot about that decade, how different it was, how much was at stake. Not *all*. That's overstated. A segment—an important segment—of what you might call the—"

"The what?"

"You make fun of every cant phrase I use."

"Yes, I do."

"All right, let's assume you've already made fun of the next one. The 'intellectual establishment.'"

"Oh God."

"There."

"Does such a thing even exist?"

"I think it does."

"Show me, because I'd like to touch it and feel it."

She smiled, readjusting.

"It's Nero's Rome, but there are still books being published."

"And five people reading them. The money is drying up, or going elsewhere."

"All right, then let's throw up our hands and do nothing."

This, too, elicited a wry look.

"The 'cityscapes,'" he said.

"The way they captured something. The first painting of your mother's I ever saw was *The Opinionated Playground*."

"And it was a Eureka moment."

"I guess I recognized something. Something I didn't know I knew, or had forgotten. About this city. I looked at it and thought: Oh, that's what's disappeared."

Conveying the intensity of the recollected moment was not something she thought it would be wise to risk with him. He could diminish anything. He had eloquent lips. She had found Anna Soloff's great painting in a bedroom of the Park Avenue apartment of a woman with the beginnings of dementia, a woman whose late husband had been a serious collector. Eugene had taken her there, his visit part of the long seduction that needed to take place in order to win the woman's trust, and thus to win the competition that always went on when a serious collection was soon to be up for grabs. She had found the painting and had sat down in front of it and when she'd finally emerged from the room she had felt how diminished were the Léger and the Picasso that lined the entrance hallway.

"Listen," Aaron Soloff said. "It's a beautiful day, and you need coffee. Why don't I free you from this chamomile torture and we can conduct the rest of this outside."

"It's peppermint," she corrected, but he had already stood.

One of the advantages of living in a fallen neighborhood was, she supposed, the availability of good coffee. She was not ungrateful for this. The Upper West Side—the new Upper West Side—seemed able to abide the disappearance of everything that had once made it distinct so long as the corner coffee shop offered an impressive choice of roasts, and the presence, among the creamer selections, of almond and oat milk. Aaron made sure she was happy with all of this, insisted on paying. They walked a bit before settling on one of the benches bordering Riverside Park.

"You understand," he began, "that there are things I don't particularly wish to revisit."

"I do understand that, I think."

"Yet if you're a good biographer, those are exactly the things you'd want to probe."

It was not a question. She had the excuse of the coffee to keep from responding immediately. You could not look at a representative grouping of Anna Soloff's paintings without understanding at least a little of what he meant. It was delicate territory, she would have to negotiate it carefully. The first time she had seen *Aaron, 11* was at an exhibit in Baltimore. *Domestic*, had been the curt title of the exhibition. *Paintings by Anna Soloff, 1945–2000*. The title painting was from the period of Anna's first, and only, marriage, to a Puerto Rican artist. The painter's brick-colored buttocks were prominent, as she straddled her husband, visible only through the presence of a pair of testicles peeking out from under the straddling artist's bottom. As Miranda had wandered through the exhibit, the paintings hung chronologically, the presence of Aaron's father, Karl Rattner, began to emerge. The colors black and red became more prominent, the face of this man never painted without nearly invisible dark *x*'s crisscrossing his features. Karl Rattner had been aptly named, apparently. A Depression-era photographer who later worked for *Vogue*. In the most memorable of these paintings, *Rattner at Home*, he was seated in a chair, in a T-shirt and work pants, his deliberately outsize, unevenly proportioned head so prominent as to be almost frightening. A small boy (not Aaron, his older brother, Jonah) sat beneath the chair. Karl Rattner's heavy-booted foot was poised, ready to kick, and on the child's face was a terrible acceptance in anticipation of this.

"I suppose I should promise you I would tread very gently over that material."

"And you'd be lying, wouldn't you?"

"How do I know until I've done some exploring?"

He glanced at her quickly before returning to his inner consultation. She saw something then in his eyes, didn't quite know how to interpret it.

"It's my brother who objects more than I do. He's totally against this. But then, he *is* a bit of a dick."

Was she meant to believe this, that it was his brother alone who took issue with her delving into their mother's past?

"So you'd have to convince him," she said.

"Yes."

She hesitated, not sure of the wisdom of the next thing she intended to say.

"I could go gently in talking to him."

He was annoyed now.

"Stop. Don't undercut yourself before you begin. I won't allow you to do that. If you're going to do this, do it ..."

He did not finish. Already, on their third meeting, she understood him well enough to know that every phrase with which he might finish that sentence was a phrase he'd be inclined to reject. *Go all in. Double down.* Such phrases had been co-opted by news programs, by advertisements for casinos, and couldn't be spoken by people like him. She both liked and was annoyed by this heightened particularity of his.

"You've got to bring me something to bring to him. Something convincing."

"Tell me how bad he was," she said.

"My father?" He hesitated a moment, lowered himself slightly on the bench, hands in his pockets. He took his time, as though editing himself. "He was terrible to my brother. Largely because he was sired by a different man, I suppose. A fact he never forgave my mother for. Listen, I'm telling you too much. I'm doing your work for you."

She shook her head slightly, as if to collude in his stopping of himself. It would not serve her as a biographer to be this gentle, but for now, she knew she had to be.

After a moment, she asked, "Is this where you played?"

"What?"

"This playground?"

They were looking down on it, the edges of it, as it spread northward from its beginnings near Ninety-Sixth Street. The fountain and the large wading pool. Foregrounded in *The Opinionated Playground* were the children, looking busy but unhappy. The eye was drawn, though, to the women arguing by the benches that lay behind them, square at the painting's center, their wild frizzy hair escaping, their tight jeans, the new unaccustomed weight they'd taken on as a result of pregnancies. Women ignoring their children, arguing with one another as to what the world should be, how it might be shaped in the wake of all that had happened in the decade just past. The Upper West Side had been *about* that then—not about competitive arguments as to which were the best preschools, but about women figuring out how to make room for themselves in the new world that was inevitably arriving. If Miranda was reading into the painting, so be it: that was what paintings allowed. And it was, Miranda had to admit, what she wanted to see there, a witnessing of what she remembered, the energy and passion of the adults who had surrounded her as she herself had played in that park. She had wanted to become one of those women. Not become her theatrical mother but one of those smart, tough-looking women in jean jackets. And then, inexplicably they had disappeared. Vanished. They, and their world. The world of *Our Bodies, Ourselves*. Of women holding mirrors over their vaginas to study their own cervixes. The world of anti-nuke marches, of Kate Millett and Grace Paley and Marge Piercy. The world of female *fierceness*. She had gone to school on that world, only to find, upon graduation, that the discipline had evaporated. Her degree was worthless.

"Your father wrote that book, didn't he?"

It arrived as an unwelcome intrusion on her thoughts—a detour she did not immediately know how to navigate.

"It's your father, right?"

"Have you read it?"

"People have told me about it. It's strange. A couple of my patients have referenced it."

She felt a little cowed. She had not wanted her father brought up at this juncture.

"It's done very well for him," she said.

"I imagine it has. Do you get along with him?"

She wasn't sure why she took a moment before nodding in the affirmative.

"Mostly, yes."

"Oh, that's a telling answer."

"No, I didn't mean it to be. It was very good when we were here. When I was young. Almost too happy."

He waited. She wished she didn't have to say more, but there was a hunger to his waiting, and she felt that to give him more of herself— though just enough, not too much—was a necessary part of the sale.

"We moved away and it became complicated."

"How old were you?"

"Twelve."

He smiled.

"What?"

She allowed him not to answer, which he seemed not inclined to do anyway. She had given him enough.

"You have children, don't you?" she asked.

"I do. A daughter and a son."

He did not wait for her follow-up question.

"My daughter's a sophomore at college. My son is sixteen and the terror of my existence."

He wasn't. No. She knew that by his face. She also knew that "college" meant Harvard. With people like him, it always did.

"Anna painted my son when he was an infant. She was never one to pass up an opportunity to paint a penis. You've seen that painting. You're asking me questions you already know the answers to."

"Sorry. Yes."

He let her know he forgave her this small slip.

"And you? Children?"

"None. No."

"Never married?"

"No."

"Let me guess. Let me be really cruel. A succession of bearded young men in Brooklyn. Ambitious and remote. With well-tended *mustaches*. With each of them there was hope, and then . . ."

He opened his hand.

"A dearth of hope."

"Yes, you're being cruel."

But she let him know he was really not, at least not in a way that touched a live nerve. He had been mostly accurate, though not entirely accurate. The last bearded—actually, goateed—young man had been gone for two years. Those subsequent years had not been terrible.

He looked at his watch.

"Look, I do enjoy these little meetings, but I'm not sure we're really making any progress."

Here was a dip. Her feeling that they'd been moving toward yes had been wishful. Something more was required now.

"Listen," she said, "before you go, let me leave you with this. Your mother's going to *get* a biographer. That much is a certainty. But it shouldn't be somebody from the official world. It shouldn't be a curator, or somebody who writes for *ARTnews*, somebody who's going to want to fit Anna into a slot. 'Feminist Artist of the Seventies.' 'The Rediscovery of Portraiture as a Legitimate Form.' 'After Abstraction,' that sort of thing. Please do not allow that to happen."

She smoothed out one leg of her jeans, looked at the ground.

"Why not?"

"Because there's a better story. A fuller story." She hesitated before finishing, a deliberate move. "The one I see."

"Ah. You *see* one. One that may or may not be accurate."

"To be determined, I think."

He had turned toward her again. Impossible to imagine what he may have been thinking. Perhaps that she was naive, and attractive in a certain way, but not so attractive, and far too naive, to draw his attention any more than it had already been drawn. Still, everyone is a little bored. She knew that. Each of us is waiting for someone to come into our lives and say, in one way or another: you *fascinate* me, I want to know more. It is the everyday fantasy. He was likely as susceptible to it as the next man, but to draw him out would require an enormous subtlety.

"It's important to me to tell her story in its historical context," she said, feeling as she spoke that this was a little too art-historical for his taste. "Okay. I'm sorry for that. But as much as I want to tell her story, I want to tell the story of her time. She knew something about what was on the verge of being lost. She got it onto her canvases. And she refused to bow to any of the—well, I imagine the pressures, when representational art was the uncoolest thing. You were really poor."

"God yes."

"But she refused to let go, or bend. She stuck to it."

He nodded, but held something back. There was no full agreement.

"You know how Joseph Mitchell wrote that book, *Joe Gould's Secret*? I'd like to call my book 'Anna Soloff's Argument.'"

It seemed, even to her, schoolgirlish, the brightest girl in the class announcing the subject of her thesis, anticipating approval. Something in him brought this out in her.

"And what was the argument, Miranda? Do you really suppose you know anything about her, based on looking at a few of her paintings?"

She was stopped by that. It had been a presumptive move, and it might have lost her ground.

He slouched a little farther, looked again at his watch.

"Now I do have to go. About the rest, we'll see."

He stood. It was as though he did not even intend to say goodbye. His hands were in the pockets of his suit jacket, he was looking south to where his office was.

"Listen, about your father," he said. She had no idea what to expect, though she saw he was considering his words, not looking at her until the end. "It really is him who's left you stuck in the past, isn't it?"

It took a moment to get over the mild shock. She looked down at

the ground, summoning an answer. By the time she'd found one—
how did he *know?*—and looked up again, he had already begun walking away, like a man on a slow sensual jaunt through a city in which
he was entirely at home.

3.

At the airport in Port-au-Prince Henry worried, briefly, that the
country would, after all his preparations, be closed to him. It would
have been an embarrassment, following his high-minded declara-
tions about coming here, to be sent back in rejection. Customs was
like a holding station. The mass, of which he was one, looked less like
it was being welcomed into a country than held for delivery to some
obscure, unasked-for destination. It was overdramatic to think this
way, of course. It was just that everyone looked hot, and cheaply
dressed, and more than slightly anxious. He held his passport at
shoulder level as if to distinguish himself as an important American,
until he realized that was exactly what he had come here not to be.

The gray-uniformed customs agents passed him through, thank
God, along with the little church group he was traveling with. There
was a darkness to these Haitian faces that was not like the darkness—
a *richer* darkness, he thought—he'd grown used to in New York.
He'd forgotten every word of the Kreyol he'd conscientiously studied, and thus felt helpless, being herded forward, with his group, by
the Haitian nun who would be their guide.

The blast of heat that greeted them as soon as they were outside
they'd been told to expect. "It will be *hot*," the nun, Sister Beatrice,
had warned. The blast of heat was accompanied by the blast of horns
from oversize vehicles maneuvering rudely toward the curb, as if to
shoulder each other out of the way as violently as possible. New York
seemed a model of calm decorum compared to this. How was anyone

to know which of the black and gray and dark blue vans was there specifically for *them?* Sister Beatrice forded them through a crowd that had not thinned, and as she did, Henry experienced a sudden and surprising moment of exhilaration. There were two young men just ahead of them, college age or just past, perhaps young aid workers, and their quick movements, their air of being ready, even eager, to meet whatever challenges lay ahead for them in this madhouse, chastened Henry. *Don't be so old. Don't be so frightened.* Learn *from these young men.*

Sister Beatrice had, with admirable dispatch, found their vehicle. Their driver, a Chuck Berry look-alike, with the singer's identical baroque sideburns, hoisted their bags. In twenty minutes of driving, they managed to cover a mile. We are in a country without rules, Henry thought to himself. The others in the van were all simply breathing, taking it in. *We are in Haiti.* Yesterday we awoke in well-ordered American homes, and today we are in a land of rubble and strange, humpy, disk-shaped green mountains, and tall men with their shirttails out who walk inches from our car and occasionally bang on it for no perceptible reason. "Ignore them," Sister Beatrice said. "They want us to buy something."

There were six of them in addition to the nun. Sitting up close to the driver was their putative leader, the car salesman Frank Murphy. Frank had owned an enormous dealership, the success of which had allowed him to retire to a life of glad-handing philanthropy. What Frank had retained from his previous life of hustle was the mild unapologetic thuggishness of the high school bruiser made good. Frank's skin had developed a kind of crust. His thick silver hair was slicked back, full and almost always wet.

Next to Frank was the newcomer to the group, a youngish woman named Serena whom they barely knew. She had nosed her way into this project even after they had declared it closed. Dark skinned, with Arabic features, she spoke to the driver in a competent-sounding

Kreyol. Her eagerness to converse, to show off the fact that she had done her homework, made the rest of them seem lazy. Henry felt that they would very soon, or eventually, come to resent her.

Then there were the two older women, Karen and Joan. "Church-women," one might uncharitably call them, each in loose pale clothes. Henry sensed, in both of them, complications he couldn't wait to tweak. "I bet you've had a torrid past," he'd said once to Joan, a sharp-featured woman in her late seventies, when they'd been pretending to listen to their priest outline a parish plan in the church basement. "A *torrid* past," he'd repeated, until the woman, smiling and look-ing straight ahead, had elbowed him, hard, in the gut. Beside Joan, Karen was altogether more of a mystery. A decade younger than Joan, her dyed blond hair tucked up modestly, her hands carefully folded in her lap, she possessed the sort of pained seriousness that had to be treated with respect.

Next to Henry on the van's rear seat, young Jeremy consulted his complicated phone, searching for service. Of all of them, Jeremy was the one Henry would least have expected to sign on to a trip like this. A young father, he had what appeared to be a thriving business (digitalized billboards). Such men usually attended church only be-cause their wives insisted, but Jeremy frequently came alone, or with a child in tow, never pious but entirely present, and concentrated, in a way that made Henry, observing from a few rows behind, feel like a sloppy worshipper.

"The light," he said aloud, not meaning to have spoken.

"Hmm?" Jeremy asked, not looking up.

"Put your phone down and look."

He hadn't meant, either, the implied criticism in what he'd just said, and the light, while dazzling, was only one aspect of the country Henry felt demanded attention. The handmade commerce—fruit and vegetables spilling out of bowls, undifferentiated from what was being sold next to them (what looked, to Henry's eyes, likes bags of

cement). The hand-painted signs on the walls of the buildings—
BATTERY YUASA, SUMITOMO, KOBA—testifying to the way this
small island had been invaded and bled dry. The rubble of the recent
earthquake lying like stilled lava on the upward tilting paths. For
God's sake, Jeremy, *look. We have arrived somewhere.*

Jeremy dutifully looked.

"Just wanting to let them know we got here," Jeremy said.

After an hour's drive, they were seated at a restaurant filled almost entirely with diplomats and foreign businessmen. Sister Beatrice let them know that this would be their one and only elegant
meal; once they got to Les Cayes it would be catch as catch can.
From their table on the open deck they had a view of the Presidential Palace, collapsed on itself like a cake that hadn't made a
successful transition from the heat of the oven. Serena gazed around
the room in search of someone to impress with her Kreyol, Frank
Murphy settled in with his salesman's smile, as though this outpost
in a ruined country were just one more Rotary gathering, nothing
more socially complicated than that.

There was something in the air of the room to justify Frank's attitude. A subtle reminder that even in a devastated country business
went on. Briefcases were opened and shut. Large, glacéed-looking
shrimp arrived at the gassy port and made their way to these tables. Confident women in extravagantly patterned dresses and head-
dresses sipped foamy drinks.

By the time they were all back in the van, they felt ready to be
leaving the city, headed for the more primitive outpost where their
work would be done. But it took two hours to maneuver the van out of
Port-au-Prince. At one point a man attached himself to the carapace
of the van, hanging on for a quarter mile, his face plastered to the
thickly grimed glass. Sister Beatrice instructed them to ignore him.

They mostly slept on the four-hour journey to Les Cayes. Henry
opened his eyes as they passed through occasional villages in the

hills, live chickens hanging by their feet from poles, fires, the sort of life you became aware of in the late-night piazzas of Italy, except that here, in place of the central church and fountain, were makeshift shacks and a preponderance of rusty tin.

They arrived, finally, at the enormous villa-like structure where they would be staying, a Catholic monastery that had been built, they were told, in the early twentieth century, sometime during the period when the Americans had occupied Haiti. There was something about camping in such luxurious quarters that struck Henry— struck them all—as a little bit wrong. In light of what the country itself had recently suffered, they'd expected to be staying in shacks.

Sister Beatrice walked them down the long hall, lit by votive candles (by this time, night had fallen), past a huge portico where they could look out, from their great height, onto the dark Haitian plain, entirely unlit, not even by a moon. Beatrice began giving orders to the women—nuns, most likely—who waited in attendance. The monsignor who presided over this place was already in bed, would meet them in the morning. For now, it was for them to find their rooms and bed down.

Would they bunk together in pairs, the men? If so, he wished for Jeremy over Frank Murphy. Better to settle in and observe a young man's clean, fascinating habits over an old man's inevitably unpleasant ones. But each was to have his own room—really cells, monkish, unadorned. Henry's had a single window, walls bare but for the mandatory crucifix, a single bed tucked into a corner, a small wooden desk and chair. Saint Jerome could have completed his Vulgate translation of the Bible in this sort of room, accompanied by a docile lion. The room's starkness was enlivened only by the distant prospect framed within the small window. The Renaissance painters, with their penchant for the hinted-at vista, would have loved that window. He said good night to the others, closed the door.

An overhead light was the best they could provide. These Catholic retreats, so outwardly majestic, so extravagantly windowed, did not finally want you to forget that you had come here to be stripped and flayed, to see the world and its comforts as brothel-like, to grasp the understanding that a stiff bed and the contemplation of the cross were all one needed. *Ponder on your bed and lie still,* King David had commanded himself, in a no doubt depressive mood. Henry wished to obey.

But why, exactly? In the sudden solitude, Henry had to ask himself exactly why he was here. He recalled—dimly, it had to be said—when the idea had first been proposed, in the basement of Saint Catherine's, the parish to which he had attached himself in late adulthood, Catholicism having become, for him, what daily visits to the gym had become for other men: a practice, a toning, a ritual. *Go to Haiti, help fix a parish roof in a shipwrecked country.* At a certain age, provided one is physically able, such enjoinders become irresistible. To seek another world, another country, to not settle so easily for the comfort one had grown used to. The excitement, the fallen-for seduction, eventually led to these walls, this silence, this deep strangeness.

Among the things he had packed was his own book. He laid it on the desk, placed it on top of the small pile of paperbacks he had brought. The impulse to bring it here had been instinctive and a little prideful. He liked to have it nearby because he was in fact proud of it, proud of the *idea* of it anyway, proud of the money it was earning him. But there were things about it of which he was not proud—a glibness, a holding back on the sort of honesty that would have doomed it commercially. He had had to be *witty.* He had had to pretend it was all a joke, age. Still, it could not be denied, after a lifetime of near-successes as a playwright, and some outright failures, to have had a recognizable success was still a little bit thrilling. His face in bookstore windows! His name on the bestseller list! He had to put it aside in order to be here in the way he wanted, humbled, willing to serve. He had come here to find something other than self-affirmation.

He took off his khaki outerwear, clothes bought at REI as if he were going on safari. He stood there, a seventy-year-old man in his underwear, thinking there is, very likely, no sadder sight. Some part of him retained a physical memory of his much younger body, his mid-1970s body, when, perceiving the threat to his family involved in housing them on the then-dangerous Upper West Side, he'd taken himself down to a gym on the Lower East Side and started boxing lessons. They'd laughed at him at first, but underneath the laughter, he'd detected, once he kept coming, a certain respect for what he was trying to do, and, taking in his extreme limitations, they actually managed to teach him a thing or two. What he recalled now, with nostalgia, was the way his body had fallen out, collapsed within itself on the subway ride home after those lessons, and the taste of the beer he would buy from the corner bodega, guzzling it while Lily watched him with amusement. He still found himself, at moments like this, falling into the old stances, tucking in his elbows, but he stopped himself. The impulse of his life at this point had to be to embrace sadness, didn't it? Not to insist on the facile heroism of youth, but something else.

The room's bareness would help. He knelt over the bed, first checking underneath to be sure no bugs lurked there. He laid his head in his hands. It was never easy. "All right," was how he always began his addresses to the God in whom he could never quite fully believe. "I am here." His personal inversion of *Here I am. In the dolphin position*, he added. *Or near enough.*

"Your writing about religion, about God, is, to put it mildly, pretty odd," Terry Gross had said to him in the famous NPR interview, the one that had helped get his book a handhold on the bestseller list. He had thought it had gone badly, but others told him he had been hilarious. It was important to forget all that. To find oneself in the attitude of prayer in this strange place, thinking of *Terry Gross*, of all people, was to have brought the world along with him, and the effort here had to be to forget the world, to leave it behind.

The goal, he supposed, was to reach a state of nothingness. To simply breathe in these sheets, which smelled less of starch than of something vaguely bean-like, as though they'd been washed in close proximity to a pot of simmering beans. You waited, that was all, not for illumination but for the feeling of emptiness. That was as much as he knew of prayer.

Having prayed (because this was, after all, prayer—the severance from Terry Gross, from the expanded self, from magic), he stood and went to the window. Blackness. Such a black country, in every sense. A soughing through the leaves on the trees, and that was all. He had brought—had gifted to him—a contraption for the top of the bed under which you zippered yourself in to protect yourself from mosquitoes. He zipped in, settled into his makeshift coffin.

So odd. I have arrived. Here I am. A seventy-year-old man wishing for change. How much of that was willful, simply a pleasant idea to have? Did he really seek for God, or did he merely like the image of himself as a man seeking for God? He recalled then Saint Anselm's humble prayer to John the Baptist, one that Henry had recently written out and tacked above his writing desk at home, one that would be useful to remember now:

To you, sir, who are so great . . .
Comes a guilty, creeping thing,
A wretched little man.

That was more like it. Embrace wretchedness, Henry. If you can.

They drove the next morning in an open-backed truck to the parish where the work was to be done. They sat on benches that bordered the bed of the truck, and held to the bars that supported the mesh screens surrounding them on three sides. It was a patchy road from the monastery to Les Cayes that bumped and threatened them on curves. The road skirted a crevasse on the bottom of which was a nearly dry creek bed. Women used it to wash clothes.

The two older women sat in the most protected seats, deferred to. Frank Murphy, standing, posted himself like John Wayne in *Hatari!*, a bush hunter ready to snag a rhinoceros. In his element, or wanting to seem so. Serena was in a corner, intense eyes observing everything. In the opposite corner, Jeremy, wearing sunglasses, seemed gathered tightly into his compact body, less like he was on a humanitarian mission than as though he were preparing for a military exercise.

Père Felix met them outside the plaster house that served as his rectory. He was prematurely gray—a man who most likely had not yet reached forty, yet looked at least ten years older—and had the bearing and, in his manner, a hint of potential deviousness that reminded Henry of Clarence Thomas. But they had all very quickly determined there was nothing truly devious about Père Felix, after meeting him six months before. In small, exceedingly liberal towns like Grantham, Massachusetts, there were always men like Père Felix visiting, the invited guest of one or another group looking for a worthy project to help fund.

But this time had been different.

"I don't want your money," the priest had said to the assembled group in the basement of Saint Catherine's, "so much as I want your hope."

It was the sort of boilerplate they'd heard before, but the way Père Felix had opened his hands and adjusted his glasses had touched something in Henry, and in the others. There is nothing more appealing than essential seriousness. He had described for them the roof of his parish, the struts rotted out, holes in the overarching tin. "When it rains, we stop the Mass long enough for the parishioners to find a dry spot to stand. Then we continue."

A small project he was seeking help for. Those around the table sought a little more drama.

"This is a result of the earthquake, Father?" Frank Murphy had asked.

"It has nothing to do with the earthquake. We are far from where the earthquake struck. It is attrition."

Perhaps they were disappointed then. To help the earthquake-ravaged country had become, by then, a national obsession. But Henry thought "attrition" a beautiful word as Père Felix had said it. We are all suffering a little from "attrition." Something then had started in him, or been released.

"How much would you need?" Frank Murphy had asked, and Henry wanted to hush him for his crassness. An element more complicated than an appeal for money was going on. Henry's intuition had been right.

"You don't understand. Yes, money, but more than that. *Hope.* My people need to see you there. *Physically.*"

It was how it had come about. Why not? Why not go to Haiti? It was thrilling to consider. "Yes, I'll be going to Haiti in the fall" was a wonderful thing to be able to say, even as one took in the self-aggrandizement involved in announcing it. That was the silly part. The more serious part lay in the desire, the awakened desire for something more than the everyday repetitions of late middle age.

From there, from the initial, at first hesitant nodding of the group's heads, things had proceeded very swiftly. Sister Beatrice, head of the Haitian apostolate in Worcester, had arrived in Grantham like George Patton riding roughshod through Sicily. She had a solid-looking body that seemed essential to her work. Nothing slighter or less resilient would enable her to do what she did, traveling through the state collecting pilgrims incapable of resisting her.

They had not resisted her, had accepted her blandishments, her encouragements—"Of course you are not too old! Far from it!"—and now they were here. Sister Beatrice, who had ridden in the cab of the truck, with the driver, leaped out and embraced Père Felix.

A group of children had gathered there to stare at the rest of them. *The blan.* They were the event. The rich Americans who had come to repair the church's roof. The "hope" Père Felix had alluded to.

The church itself rose beside the rectory, makeshift, lovely. More of the white plaster seen in every building, a substance that looked untrustworthy. A bell tower. Ready to go to work, they were first invited to lunch in the rectory, rice and beans served out of an old pot by a woman without teeth. Père Felix's henchmen—other priests, all of them, though none of them wearing so much as a collar; heavy black men who resembled American linebackers, in striped cotton jerseys and dark pants—sat and stared at them as though waiting for an invitation to trust.

In the afternoon, they began the serious work, which consisted of a long dismantling. They climbed to the roof by means of stairs and pulled off the old tin. They worked cheerfully together, glad to be doing what they had come for. Below them, the children stared up, many of them in T-shirts sent from America in the first wave of post-earthquake charity. *St. John's Prep. Okemo Mountain.* Little scraps of privileged Americana draping their thin bodies.

At five, it was okay to stop. They were given beer—the local brand, Prestige—and sat in the shade under the colonnade of the parish school across the road. They were exhausted and happy, in small ways becoming familiar with one another in a way that simple attendance at Mass and at committee meetings at Saint Catherine's had not allowed. The older women showed surprising endurance. Frank Murphy was not quite the physical dynamo Henry might have anticipated. Henry and Jeremy became the indomitable pair, carrying and stacking tin. "I read your book," Jeremy said to him at one point. *"Really?"* But that was as much as he was going to get.

What they quickly came to love—to look forward to—was the drive back to the monastery, in late afternoon, in the truck. The wind that passed through their hair and clothes. Henry offered Frank his seat and held to the bars, loving the way the wind whipped up his sparse hair, imagining himself, for a moment, appearing romantic in Karen's eyes, then kicking himself for having the thought. The light was brown and thick and there were serious-looking soccer games in the long empty fields, the ball kicked into nets that seemed haphazardly hung, trees bordering the fields whose vegetation was limited to their tops, so that they suggested, at dusk, the arc lights in American baseball stadiums.

At dinner, they laughed about the day, drank beer Sister Beatrice had snuck in. "Presidente. From the Dominican Republic. Better than the beer Father gave you." Even after just forty-eight hours, Karen's color was starting to come back, some of the sadness that cast her face into a downward-tilting mold appeared to be lifting. It was as though they were all willing themselves toward something new. If what they were doing was only a cliché—privileged Americans off on a jaunt that was more about *them* than anything they might actually accomplish here—perhaps the answer was to embrace the cliché. Build a roof, have a good time while doing it. What else should they be doing? Bird-watching in New Guinea?

They would all be in bed before full dark.

First though, there was the sharing of the phones, Jeremy's and Serena's. Henry had not brought one, and had to be guided through the process of dialing his wife's number on Serena's extravagant device.

"Well, you're alive," was the first thing Lily said when he reached her.

"Did you doubt it?" He was standing at his little window as he spoke.

"Tell me," she said. He could sense, from the sound of her voice, her very characteristic languor. She was no doubt lying in bed, indulging in her favorite reading, the lesser Victorians.

"First you," he said.

"Nothing to report."

"No offers flying in?"

An old joke. Since they'd moved to Grantham, her acting career had become like a gentleman farmer's holdings. That is, she didn't work it very hard. Lily had been a staple of the old Circle Repertory Company on Sheridan Square. Some of the playwrights from that since-disbanded theater still asked for her for the grande dame parts. Everything else, she turned down.

"Seems strange to think of you back in the land of Harvey Fierstein, while I'm here in the world of the Tontons Macoutes."

"We're going to make this very dramatic, are we? My understanding is that the Tontons Macoutes went out with Baby Doc."

"Done some research, have you?"

"If my husband is going to go away to a country like Haiti, damn right I'm going to do a little research."

He rested inside the sound of her voice for a moment, savoring it. Savoring, too, while still a little annoyed by, the theatricality they assumed while talking to one another.

"All right, so seriously," she said.

"Seriously it's fine. We drive a truck to the worksite. We work. We bring 'hope.' No marauding bands of blood-crazed Haitians attack us, I'm afraid."

"And that's a bad thing?"

He held back from giving her the answer she expected. It had been up to him, always, to provide—to elicit—the tension that he believed marriage required. The necessary threat. In the chapter on love in his book, he had tried to write something honest about it, though he felt you could never really write honestly about love or about marriage, any more than you could write with real honesty about what went on in the mind in any given hour. (For one thing, no matter how orderly your mind, you would sound *insane*.) The couple that has stayed together will retain their essential secret—one they hardly know how to define even for themselves—regardless of what details they choose to spill.

"I'm supposed to give this phone back. Others are waiting."

"Then by all means, give it back."

Was she asking for more? Being married to an actress was to hear, in her voice, always, more than might actually be implied.

"I'm going to sneak a call to Miranda."

"Do. She'll be anxious to hear from you."

"Unlike you."

"Oh stop."

"No, you sound like you're dying to get back to the scene in *Villette* where the stable boy arrives at the house of the duchess and exposes his throbbing dick."

"That's exactly the scene I'm up to. Very exciting."

They both rested in the pause. A deeper familiarity had been reached, even if it was a superficial familiarity. An old joke to get them off the stage.

"Goodbye, my pet."

"You never in your life have called me 'my pet.'"

"Well, I'm starting now. Haiti is changing me."

"Good. Be changed. Just not much. Perhaps you could *simplify* yourself. That's all I really ask."

"I will work on that."

They hung up. Serena was lurking in the hallway just outside his door. It was Joan's turn next for the phone.

"One second. Five seconds. A very quick call to my daughter."

"Careful of the power. Not much left. And the outlets here are unreliable."

Serena offered him a little smile. She was growing on him. Her dark face with its schoolgirl's intensity.

"Darling," he said when Miranda answered.

"Oh. I didn't recognize the number. " She sounded startled. Had he interrupted something? Always the chief worry, Miranda's failure to have successfully coupled. A worry and a mystery both, around which he had to step carefully.

"Are you with someone? Have I——?"

A pause, then a distinct no, a hard push against the concern he couldn't help showing, despite having been told, countless times, that uncoupledness was, for Miranda's generation, not the curse it may have been for women of Henry's.

"It's me," he said, to deflect.

"As if I didn't know that."

"In darkest Haiti."

"And as always, at your most politically correct."

"How's your work coming?"

"Fine." There was another pause at her end, as if she were registering yet another source of his concern for her. He had cautioned her about leaving her comfortable job at one of New York's premiere auction houses in order to write the biography of an artist he had never heard of.

"Why don't you tell me about Haiti?"

"I can't. Not enough time. We all share a cell phone, and you know how these fucking bars keep going down."

A silly thing to say. And incorrect. He could see no bars on Serena's phone.

"Miranda?"

"Yes?"

"Seriously, I only have seconds here. You're well?"

"Yes."

"Just wanted to hear your voice. We'll have a longer chat when there are more . . . when there are more *bars*."

"Okay," he heard, and felt the ensuing silence like the measurement of a distance he didn't want to contemplate right now.

They were too close. He knew that. Or maybe it was truer to say that their subtext was too thick. Their history crept into every pause, every silence, like a water leak moving to cover more ground. What hovered over them, always, was a sense of something missed, something he couldn't name, a lapse of sensitivity, a failure to have taken her in fully, when she was younger, in some essential way. He knew she still resented him for it, though he knew as well that in the work she'd had to do in order to become herself, he'd been forgiven. Still, there was that part of him that wanted to make an ongoing plea: See me, please. See that I'm not entirely a monster, even a *forgiven* monster. He was not above thinking that some part of his impulse in signing up for this Haiti project lay in wanting to impress her. To show that some old, banked, not entirely forgotten social conscience had not died in him, even if it was now taking the form of an effort this small.

In hanging up, he felt a pang of loss he had not felt when hanging up with Lily. Still in the grip of that pang, he handed off the phone to a waiting Serena.

What struck him—or perhaps deepened in him—over the next days was the sensuality of the work. It had been a long time since he had done days' worth of manual labor in the sun. The heat and the constant need for water and the litheness of the young male Haitian bodies (a hired work crew had joined them). They were separated by language and by skill level and by something else as well. For all the forced friendliness of the work crew (they had names like Nickerson, and Cholzer and Levoy, and oddly enough, Basil), they maintained an unsurprising wariness in their regard of the rich Americans. Serena made her Kreyol-inflected attempt to penetrate their wariness, and though they were polite and friendly enough to her, they reacted to her pronouncements with barely detectable amusement.

By the end of the week, the crew had grown comfortable enough with one another—or gone deeply enough into a zone—that they began to play kompa music on the sorts of boom boxes that had gone out of fashion in America decades ago. On breaks from the work, a small group of the younger boys danced. The music encouraged thrusting movements, and it was impossible not to take in the way the dancing, thrusting boys noticed Henry and, beside him, Frank, watching them. A subtle taunting was unquestionably going on, an assertion, in the face of American wealth on display, of something else, something not to be pitied, as this whole roof project could be said to be an act of charitable pity.

Late in the afternoon on Saturday, they were given a hiatus from work and told there would be an excursion to Port-Salut, the beach at the far western end of the island. Another long, bumpy ride, then the cheapjack "hotels" common to every coastal enclave. On the long beach the sand looked unclean. The cove was framed by small mountains in the distance. Stripped to their bathing suits, the church group was not exactly transformed. They were given no new meanings by their exposed flesh, with the predictable exceptions of Jeremy and Serena, who dove immediately into the water and stayed there, playful with one another, beautiful in each of their ways; that is, in ways that had entirely to do with being young, with possessing flesh that knew no sag. The older group settled on a blanket provided by Père Felix, and watched. And wondered a little, if the playfulness on display implied an attraction. They had all learned more about Serena over the course of the week. She was married, had a daughter, worked as a translator.

Henry went in to join Jeremy and Serena in the water. Though they were friendly enough in greeting him, it was clear they were developing a rhythm that allowed for only two. What they were doing was perfectly innocent, wasn't it? Or was it? Were they using this endeavor as the cover for an affair? Shocking. Also, a little thrilling.

Back on the blanket, the elders resisted the approach of men hawking pots of some warm indecipherable fish. Others were selling small statues of men, like Christmas nutcrackers. Lift the lever behind and an erection popped out in front. Père Felix laughed the hardest at this. Frank bought one. "My wife'll appreciate this." They watched the young ones in the waves, and Henry felt a late-breaking resentment at the way they had rejected him, a sudden internal drop at being consigned to the blanket with the old ones. Frank and Père Felix were having fun with the erectile statue, while the women pretended to be coy, saying "Oh, put it away!" But why put it away? Why not be reminded of what used to be so *present* in all our lives? Did only Jeremy and Serena get to enjoy the presence of erections anymore, and that only by virtue of being so bloody fucking *young*?

That night, back in the monastery, Henry, taking his nightly walk, found himself hovering near Serena's door, then Jeremy's. Were noises to be heard inside? This was terrible, to be indulging his inner sneak this way. It was not the sort of behavior he'd expected to encounter on this trip. Yet here it was, and something in his impulse had to at least be acknowledged, for honesty's sake. Add this chapter to *How to Be This Age*: at seventy, we live for the thrilling possibility of watching—at least *hearing*—others fuck. How about saying that? How about just being out with it? Had he done so, would sales of the book have plummeted? Would Terry Gross have cut off his mike?

Such thoughts were stopped by the appearance of Karen, returning from the bathroom. She seemed perplexed to find him outside Jeremy's door. What are you doing here? *Hovering*, Karen. I am doing what every old man really wants to do every moment of his life. To get close, to get *back* to the lost, the once-possessed thing.

"You wander at night?" Karen asked. They were in the dark corridor. An intimacy existed, or wished to be teased into being. It was an invitation to make a joke, though he couldn't think of one. Or else to reveal himself, which he was not ready to do.

"Yes."

She was waiting for more. All he could think to say was, *Shall we put a glass up to the door and see what we can hear?*

As soon as she was gone, Jeremy opened the door. He was in a T-shirt and sweatpants, and held a toothbrush and a plastic container of water. Beyond him, Henry could see that the room was empty. No sated Serena lay on the bean-smelling sheets. No parted thighs, no wet bush, with the telltale dribble of semen left at the top in withdrawal. A stack of books, a candle, a neat pile of folded clothes. The inescapable Bible. Jeremy in his youth and ripeness was more ascetic than Henry in his hairshirted, wishing-to-be-transformed dotage.

"What's going on?" Jeremy asked.

"Nothing at all," Henry said. "Wandering in the dark, is all."

"Cool," Jeremy said, incurious, and then sauntered, straight-spined, down the hall toward the bathroom.

There it was, then. Go on a trip where your stated intention—your Note to Self—was *change yourself.* Was: *open yourself up to something new, you fool.* (With "something new" meaning, of course, something in the spiritual range.) And what did you find, but an attraction toward skin, toward sensuality, toward the great lost domain. Seventy meant nothing. You might as well be eighteen, the boy outside the candy store of the carnal world. At eighteen, you were often too timid to take what was there. At seventy, you had to hold your arms back from the impulse to grab.

Those were his thoughts, his tempering thoughts, as he sat in church at a celebration Mass the following Sunday. Not at Père Felix's church, still under construction and thus unusable, but at a smaller church out in what Henry continued to refer to as "the bush." They were to be the guests of honor.

Whatever Henry felt he had intuited about "the Haitian character" by watching the thrusting, mildly contemptuous kompa boys, he felt, as soon as he entered the little church, that there was something else to learn. The church—primitive, with open, unscreened windows, a membrane-like tin roof, and plaster walls on which you could see lizards crawling—had been decorated carefully, lovingly. Flowers and ribbons in the open windows. A huge cornucopia rested at the rear of the church—fruit and flowers for the offering. These people, having nothing, picked their gardens clean as oblations to a God who, in answer, had saddled them with an earthquake. The pews were filled, everyone dressed for a celebration. The guests from America—the "hope"—were seated in a special row near the front, nodded to. They felt their own want of brightness, encased, in their pew, in formality and sweat.

A choir had gathered at the side of the church; the hymns were in formal French. It was a mixed choir—boys and girls both—yet they were dressed uniformly. White starched tops, powder-blue bottoms. Skirts for the girls, trousers for the boys. Impossible to imagine how such clothes had gotten so clean, given the rarity of washing machines, of electricity itself, in this part of the country. Somehow it was seen as essential, and thus, achieved.

He regarded the choir. He regarded the boys, mostly, recognizing one or two from the work crew. However much they'd been transformed by the sound of kompa, they were transformed in an opposite direction—angelicized—here. One in particular. Perhaps fifteen. A sweet face, close-cropped hair. It was not appropriate to stare this way, yet stare Henry did. He told himself he wanted to understand. To comprehend the belief, if that was what it was, of a fifteen-year-old boy with no future, living in a hideously poor country, singing to "Mon Dieu" as if "Mon Dieu" was sentient and eager to attend.

That was, at least, what Henry told himself he was doing. But there was something else going on, and he chose not to fool himself about it. It wasn't dangerous, in any case. He told himself very clearly that it wasn't dangerous. In the sensual state he'd fallen into, this heightened alertness to what was ripe and alive, this was simply another manifestation: noticing a beautiful boy, wondering about him. That was all. Tonight, in his prayers, while kneeling in his stark room in the monastery, he would fold this moment in: Yes, Lord, I noticed a beautiful boy in church today. What are we to do with this, other than regard it as a blip in the day?

It had always been there for him, a mild, not insufferable draw toward the young male body, though never so demanding that it inhibited him from living what he considered a perfectly satisfying heterosexual married life. The times he had indulged it could be counted on the fingers of one hand, all in his twenties, and only once while he'd been living with Lily. He was not ashamed of them, even went so far at times as to pat himself on the back for his young boldness and courage in acting this out. But though these had all been in the past, what troubled him—what had the capacity to trouble him now—was the persistence of such feelings at an age where he had hoped they might have disappeared.

But no, they did not disappear. And why expect that, really? Wasn't this just another aspect of being this age? They persisted, always manageably, but still there, like the pullings around the skin of long-ago surgeries at certain instances of weather.

It was safe. Perfectly safe. His circuit breakers were in good working order. To notice a fifteen-year-old's beauty was like noticing the beauty of an art object in a museum. You regarded it from behind a rope.

The Mass did not seem to end even after the declaration of *Ite, missa est.* They all congregated in the churchyard. No one wished to leave, or had any intention of doing so. Across the churchyard, Henry picked out the boy he had noticed, looking slightly detached from the group he was with, the storklike choirboys. They kept their distance from *the blan*, while remaining keenly aware of them. Drawn, it seemed, not by simple curiosity but by a more complex force, a deep interest of their own.

"Why don't you introduce us?" Henry asked Sister Beatrice, when it seemed the separation was going to hold. This was all perfectly innocent, to ask to meet this group. She led the church group over, they shook hands. Some of the boys were only recognizable as members of the work crew when you got close. "This one is Jean," Sister Beatrice said, introducing the boy to Henry. "This one," as if he had no distinction at all. The boy nodded, as if bowing to Sister Beatrice's dismissal of him as only one of many. "Have I seen you on the roof?" Henry asked. The only word the boy seemed to understand was "roof," and he nodded, pouncing on the word with his soft, eager chin. "Travailles avec nous?" Henry asked, certain that he was getting the French wrong. But apparently the only French these boys understood was in the hymns. Henry mimed sawing and hammering. "The roof," he said, again. "Yes," Jean said, smiling uncertainly.

It was the end of their conversation, and the boy had not seemed to understand the question anyway. This would be the end of it, this noticing, this appreciative taking in. Henry likened it to a trip he and Lily had once taken to one of the hill towns of Italy. Every morning, in the central piazza, a boy would arrive on a motorcycle, and the girl setting out napkins in the café Henry frequented would stop her work, her body marvelously stilled in alertness to the boy's presence. She and the boy would embrace. Gorgeousness personified. You stopped and looked and marveled, and knew how much you were *outside* of what you were beholding. To not take in such beauty would be not to be alive.

Still, his thoughts as he rode in the truck in the late afternoons during the next, the final week of this sojourn, were of self-disappointment.

A damp blue light lay over the fields. Boys playing soccer, older men and women trudging, on their way somewhere, the obscure destinations that command our days. Ongoingness. He watched, and felt a keen wish to connect with something deeper than his own childish desire to catch sight of Jean.

That was what had happened. It had less the quality of an obsession than what he considered a minor fixation. He looked for the boy on their days on the roof, willing himself not to but unable to control his own gaze. Days when Jean did not come he regarded as disappointments.

Oddly enough, he had seemed to have ascended to the position of becoming his group's leader. Frank Murphy was undergoing a gradual collapse that required him to sit a lot. The others looked to Henry to be their spokesman. His energy felt undiminished, and he sensed, as the week had worn on, a hole in the social fabric of the group that had needed to be filled by his natural bonhomie, that part of him unaffected by what was going on internally.

The boy's appearances at the worksite that week had been scattershot. There one day, absent the next. On the days Jean was there, Henry worked hard to treat Jean like one of the others. Their task was to hand up sheets of corrugated tin to the crew straddling the rebuilt narthex. It took the more skilled to hammer the sheets into the wooden struts. They were like tightrope walkers; you waited for them to fall, and they did not. Jean was too young to be among the skilled ones. He carried and handed up tin along with Henry and Frank and Jeremy. He wore a red T-shirt one day that read *Garcia Farm*. His body took on a hopping movement as he worked, as if he were eager to do more than he was asked.

Henry rode in the truck and felt the wind and regarded Joan and Karen and saw how tired they were becoming. Another story might have happened here. Karen's loveliness had grown on him, a softness, a sense of her body as a soft, inviting pillow. Karen had not come here looking to have an affair, but he was certain Karen had come here looking for *something*, if only an alleviation of the sadness that seemed to inhabit her. How nice if the story that had unfolded had been a flirtation among two older people, drawn to each other and then drawn back, pinioned by the slow lava of reserve. But that was never what happened. Life didn't follow that pattern. It always chose a more disturbing turn.

On their final night in Les Cayes, a celebration was to be held in their honor. They were anticipating it. But the night of the celebration threatened rain. It was to have been an outdoor event—tables had been set up and laid out, electric lights hooked up to a generator, flowers garlanding the site—but for the final Mass (it was a Saturday night), they decamped to the second floor of the parish school. The rooms were bare plaster, the old wooden benches where the children sat pushed to the walls. Candles were lit, the entire village seemed to have shown up. *The blan* were thanked profusely, and thanked profusely again.

The same choir that had sung at the Sunday Mass sang again, this time led by a young woman, clearly their leader, their star soloist. The hymns were lovely, the rain pelted down, at first softly, on the tin roof. Père Felix made a speech, half in Kreyol, half in English, about how, at all subsequent Masses, the congregation would no longer have to hide from the rain. *The blan* were asked to sing, and sang badly. Sheets of plastic had been put up over the outdoor tables. They held the rain uncertainly. Everyone made up their minds to accept the fact that they would likely get a little wet.

Beers were handed out. The older members of the church group grew a little giddy, effusive. Serena made a speech in Kreyol, half-understood by her audience. Henry accepted the Presidentes Sister Beatrice handed him. Why not? He kept catching sight of Jean, in doorways, under the wet plastic, having fun with the other young ones, indulging in the closed, ritualistic behavior of young males.

Henry's presence here meant nothing to him. The choir had forgone the starched white shirts and blue pants of Sunday in favor of more informal dress. The boy wore a black striped shirt and black pants. He looked very pressed, and young. Henry watched him hovering over the table of wrapped candies the children had been told they could grab only after *the blan* had been blessed once again. There was an innocence, a simplicity to this young boy that Henry wished to honor. Tomorrow I will be on the plane. Tomorrow he will begin to fade. It was a relief. He stopped counting the beers he was consuming.

But effusiveness won the day. He cornered the young woman who was the leader of the choir, a girl in her early twenties, wearing a formal pleated blue shirt and a dark blue skirt.

"*Gorgeous.* Your singing is *gorgeous.* Were you to come to the United States, you'd be hailed as a wonder."

Credit the beer. The soft pattering rain. The electric lights. You could not go too far with these people. You never knew, anyway, how much English was understood.

The young woman blinked, leveled her gaze at him, taking in everything he said with utter seriousness.

"And if I could come?" she asked.

"Pardon me?"

"If I could come to America?"

He misunderstood her, half willingly.

"If you could come?"

"Yes."

"Would you want to?"

She hesitated—not her face, which was all muted eagerness—but the part of her that was crafting an answer.

"If my voice is so good."

It was as though she had placed a card on the table before him. Top that, please.

"Your voice is very good."

"Then?"

He flushed with falseness, tried to burp up his own mistake. They took you at your word. The too-easily tendered, inherently insincere American generosity. Unsaid was: I am only willing to give this much. Do not ask me to make an actual effort, much less a sacrifice.

"Why don't you give me your contact information?"

"My?"

"How would I get in touch with you?"

She looked at him a moment longer, perplexed.

"Do you have email?" he asked.

Layers seemed to be falling away, or else appearing. In a corner, the plastic covering collapsed enough so that it soaked one of the visiting priests. There was laughter.

"Listen. Père Felix would know how to contact you, yes?"

"Yes."

He took a card out of his wallet, searched for a pen. She had one. Where had she secreted a pen?

"Yvonne Blaise," she said.

Yvonne Blaise, he wrote, then showed it to her, to be sure he'd gotten it right.

"Just Yvonne. He will know Yvonne."

Her face would not release any of its holdings. He felt intensely, though, the stresses working inside her. Hope. He was hope. Entirely false, but still hope. They should never have come.

"Yvonne Blaise, I will do what I can."

She nodded, not picking up on, or disregarding, what was counterfeit in him.

It was then that, just beyond her, he saw Jean under the arch of a doorway, listening intently to their conversation. Jean, looking at the card Henry held in his hand, containing the name of Yvonne Blaise. Jean's face was the face of a boy on Christmas morning, one whose brother has gotten all the presents.

"Excuse me, Yvonne," Henry said.

She nodded her head, but did not move. He walked the three or four steps to where the boy hovered.

"What is it, Jean?" he asked, released into a new intimacy by the want displayed in the boy's face. Jean's tight expression was directed toward the card.

"This?" Henry asked, holding the card up. "This?"

The boy raised his eyes to meet Henry's.

"Do *you* want to come to America?"

A moment, and then, "Yes."

Some of the rain dripped onto them from where the plastic had caved a little. They moved out of its range. They shared a thoughtful moment, and the boy lifted the front of his black shirt to wring out some of the wetness. There was this to be surprised by: Sometimes they understood everything. Sometimes the language barrier was nothing but a ruse.

"How old are you, Jean?"

"I am seventeen."

Henry nodded.

"And you go to school here?"

Jean hesitated, then shook his head slowly.

The idea that this boy might be a candidate for an American education came to Henry slowly, like the punch line to a joke he had been late in picking up. He did not say anything. He let the idea sit. It was almost too packed, too crowded a thought to indulge; behind it was the attraction that would have to be squelched, if anything serious was to be done. *Had to be.*

Yet under these thoughts, something else. One's vast capacity to fool oneself. Turn away now. This is a moment. This is a challenge you do not need. Consider it a moment in the trip, something to consider, then reject. Go back to your safe life. Bask in the world's momentary approval. Get on the plane and go.

"Well," Henry said. "We will have to see what the possibilities are."

The boy looked at him again. He bobbed his head like a stabled horse does when he anticipates freer movement. He looked suddenly older, and asking for something. Henry understood in the moment what he had come to represent to this boy.

There was a private school in his town, and who knew? How did you forgive yourself for denying your power to make things happen? Was God involved in this? Was this the wished-for urge for change manifesting itself in the crooked way God always managed to offer his challenges? It did not seem, at the moment, an entirely stupid question.

"We will have to see," Henry said again.

"You will come back?" the boy asked, more English than he'd ever used with Henry before.

Henry took a moment before answering.

Two days later they were, as Henry had anticipated, on a plane, above the clouds. But he had imagined this moment would come as a relief, and it had not. The night before, their last night in Port-au-Prince, the church group had all eaten together at the restaurant of the hotel to which they'd been moved, close to the airport. Beer, and a fish none of them recognized the name of, and laughed over, and ate with some suspicion. They were going back to where they came from, trepidatious Americans frightened of a Haitian fish.

On the TV playing in the corner of the restaurant, CNN offered them a reintroduction to the concerns and obsessions they would be returning to. The renegade former son-in-law of Sarah Palin, famous only for having impregnated the vice presidential candidate's daughter, was being interviewed. His suspect fame sheathed him. In America, no one would question why he was being interviewed. But in a Haitian restaurant, it struck Henry as a travesty of something. *I am going back to the country where this young man has become, even if only briefly, a figure of consequence.*

There were jokes around the table. The fish. My God, the fish. And won't it be wonderful to get a good shower again? At the monastery, they had all bathed under a trickle. And to not worry about drinking the water! Yes, it would be good. They had all done this worthy thing, and now it was over, now they could pat themselves on the back and anticipate the comforts they would be returning to.

Above the clouds, then. He sat next to Frank, who was already moving on to other parish business. Henry nodded, his mood elsewhere. Frank was not dumb. Somewhere in Frank's conventional-seeming mind was the understanding we all possess. Which is that we are all, fundamentally, very strange. In the silences between him and Henry on the plane, Frank seemed to be acknowledging this. *Don't tell me about your strangeness. Please. I don't want to know. Just understand that I know it's there.*

Henry stared out the window. They were not so high above the clouds. A short trip, and they would change planes in Miami. Henry would part with the rest of them then, and board a plane for New York, where he had a meeting scheduled. Occasionally the clouds broke and islands appeared.

He consoled himself that he had made a promise to return, that this would not, after all, become a tucked-away adventure, something to talk about over dinner with people of his own class, stemware and old silver and sockeye salmon flown in from Alaska and reserved with the fishmonger for the Friday-night dinner parties in which travels were spoken of, silly jokes made, the people he had recently been among, and attempted to treat seriously, become the stuff of anecdote. Whatever the result of his new desire to try to help Jean— still a nascent desire, one he would have to mull over—he had at least determined that he would come back. Whatever had become of the political commitment of his younger years, there was still some small urge left: *Do something. Don't take the easy way out.* Perhaps this boy could be helped. Perhaps. Maybe it was too much to expect to educate him in America. Already, Henry found himself cautiously backing off from the idea. To "help" was as far as he would go.

"We did some good there, don't you think?" Frank said.

"Yes," Henry answered. "At least, I hope so."

4.

The restaurant Philip had chosen for their celebration dinner was deep in the East Village, in a neighborhood Miranda still could not enter without remembering a play her mother had appeared in, years ago. It had been on East Fourth Street. She'd been quite small, and her father had taken her to see it, over Lily's objections. The play had what would now be called a dystopian narrative. Her mother appeared in rags, with a dirty face and wild untended hair, and in the course of the play had to scavenge for food and, in a moment of desperation, licked the stage floor. The experience had been very strange, and her memory of it still affected the way Miranda felt when she walked these streets.

You had to climb a set of stairs to reach the dark, crowded restaurant. Philip was at the bar, and nodded as if to signal to her not to be distressed by anything she might encounter here. He favored such places, restaurants that had gained a reputation among those, like him, who made large amounts of money but wanted to be seen as living a life that sought out edges and culverts and shunned conventionality.

"Tell me, please, that you don't want a cosmo," was the first thing he said to her.

"I don't want a cosmo."

"How about a beer made from Australian hops. Melba hops. You like Melba hops?"

He knew the answer, was mocking his own hipster sophistication in a way that put her at ease. He leaned into the bar. His shirt was open at the neck, his dark, curly hair wet and thick with what was now called "product." He looked handsome and reckless in a way that defied who she knew he really was. Though "really was" was a phrase she could imagine Aaron Soloff scoffing at.

"How about just a glass of wine?"

"Sure. In about half an hour I should be able to get this guy's attention. We've got a forty-five-minute wait for a table. Even though I made the reservation for this exact time."

The stool beside him at the bar was technically available. A woman in a screechingly tight black dress had lain her bag and shawl over it, and was facing away from them.

"Excuse me," Philip said to the woman, and was ignored. He turned back to Miranda. "Shall we make a scene?"

"No. It's okay."

The noise was nearly deafening. The currently ubiquitous Meek Mill was on the sound system, though barely audible above the din. She regarded Philip as he apologized silently to her for a thousand small things: his choice of venue, the wait, the rudeness of the woman in the black dress. They were all part and parcel of the only social universe Philip would consent to inhabit. She would have been content to meet in some quieter, more sedate place, some restaurant he would mock her affection for by calling "Ye Olde New York." Perhaps, she thought sometimes, his need for this kind of urban experience was his way of making up for lost time. The unhappiest period of his life had been the years he'd had to leave his childhood home in New York to move in with Miranda and her family, after his father's early death and his mother's subsequent emotional difficulties. He'd spent those years making fun of everything in rural Grantham, then hightailed it back to New York for college, and seemed to have never looked back.

"So what are we celebrating?"

He had, in spite of his disclaimer, been able to get the barman's attention. The barman had the look of an actor who'd spent the day auditioning for an action film: big head, tight angry hair that clung to his skull like armor. His close-fitting shirt might as well have been a breastplate. Without consulting Miranda, Philip asked the barman to pour her whatever he recommended, so long as it was white. Had he given her the choice, she knew she would have embarrassed him with her, in his view, too-conventional selection.

"We're celebrating an email," she said.

"Okay."

Aaron Soloff had that day sent it. He suggested a meeting with his brother. In her mind, it was as good as a yes. The tone of Aaron's email, uncharacteristically upbeat and encouraging, sent her into a kind of swoon. When she told Philip, he only shrugged. Her ambition to write this book had not yet penetrated in a way that felt real to him. She considered them as close as two people could be, but a part of him remained as opaque as he'd been in high school, when they'd been schoolmates, a year apart, and passed each other in the corridors. He'd always lowered his eyes, resisting acknowledgment.

"How is it?" he asked, after she'd taken her first sip of the wine. "The Corsican selection."

She shrugged—she thought she could taste a little bit of earth in it, not her favorite thing to find in a glass of white wine.

He nodded toward the barman.

"Our friend Vin Diesel thinks the world of it."

"He's got too much hair to be Vin Diesel."

"Vin Diesel before he settled into being the guy we know and love. Once upon a time Vin was a sensitive young actor. With hair.

Once upon a time Vin spent his days praying to be cast in a John Hughes movie."

Their system of references had been worked out in their separate bedrooms in the house in Grantham. If there was an unwritten rule prohibiting their acknowledging one another in the high school, there had been a wild emotional freedom in those bedrooms. At night, they'd worked out dance routines to "U Can't Touch This" and "O.P.P.," making each other laugh hysterically. She sensed it was a part of his life he was now deeply embarrassed by, but allowed her to hold like a humiliating photograph from adolescence that nonetheless captured an undeniable truth.

"So tell me," he said, after they'd finally been seated. They were on a kind of balcony overlooking the main dining room. "While you pursue this project, which will make you not a penny, how are you going to keep yourself alive? Is this something that's going to be funded by Henry?"

"No. No, I'm not going to ask him for anything. I'm going to make it work. I don't care what I have to do. I'll be a barista if I have to."

She had left the auction house with some savings, had maintained a small income through the freelance work Eugene continued to ask her to do. Catalogue work, mostly. Sometimes he paid her just to wheel him to the visits he needed to make, to widows and divorcées who needed cash and had a spare Matisse to unload. His wheelchair was motorized, but they were each sentimental about the past, when he had needed her for the most basic things.

"Good luck," Philip said. "Just don't ask me. You know there's some statistic I read—something like four in ten people in this country, if they had to come up with four hundred dollars in cash, couldn't do it. I'm one of them."

"And yet you're in the Fortune 500 of people I know. In fact, you may be the only wealthy person I know. Under fifty."

"I'm not wealthy. I piss it away. Prostitutes and overpriced restaurants like this one."

The "prostitutes" part could have been true, but she suspected it wasn't. There had been girlfriends over the years, though they were ones she had heard about, rarely met. Once, long ago, they had vowed to one another that if they reached the age of what he called "Shit or get off the pot" and neither had a partner, they would marry and have a child together. Neither of them had been serious, but they'd each needed a safety net, and this would do until the moment had been confronted and gotten past.

"Okay, what's it going to be?" Philip was consulting the menu. "For starters. We've got Charred Yakitori Style Edamame. We've got Tuna Poke Wonton Tacos."

As much as Philip needed to dine in such places, he was also capable of noting their pretensions.

"You order," she said.

They waited then, and regarded the crowd below them. The opening beats of "Super Freak" came on and a visible ripple of happiness worked its way through the crowd. A woman sitting at a table below them, large breasted, vivid, possibly Central or South American, started to dance in her chair. Her boyfriend, Tony Montana, was consulting his phone.

She noticed Philip regarding the woman, smiled, teasing him a little.

"Philip, maybe it's time for you to go after one of those women. You're almost forty. What are you waiting for?"

"Look at her tits," he said. "You know what I think of when I see a girl coming toward me with tits like that? I think of her carrying a plate of some kind of food I don't really want, food that'll clog my arteries and kill me before I'm fifty. Those tits are like *fate*. That's how erotic it is."

"Did you ever consider that maybe you're gay?"

He didn't miss a beat.

"No, I leave the gay stuff to Henry."

Henry had tried to shock them once, at the dinner table in the summer house in Eastham, by telling them that, in his youth, he had enjoyed both oysters and snails. He had loved to drop hints about himself that way, hints that had only confused them until, later in life, they had been able to figure them out. The hints had only enraged Lily, who took him to task by telling him angrily to shut up. "They're *children*, Henry, and you're drunk."

Eastham had been the stage for Henry's most performative self, occasioned by the new opportunity of becoming surrogate father to an eleven-year-old boy. On the beach that stretched out at low tide before the rented house, he had organized epic wiffle ball games, purely for Philip's benefit. He'd gathered neighbors, people they barely knew, and assigned them positions in the outfield. Young, newly orphaned Philip had loved this. Young Miranda had been largely ignored.

During those summers, Henry had insisted on renting the largest, most rambling house—four or five bedrooms, more than they could possibly fill. It must have been expensive, but this had been the era of the TV show Henry had been hired to write for, after a play of his in New York had made him, briefly, a marketable commodity. The series was a contemporary Western he was fond of referring to as "Wagon Train." (Its actual title had been *Lawson's Bend*.) This from the period when Henry began disappearing for months at a time to L.A. The house in Grantham (similarly large and rambling) had to be paid for, though Lily and Miranda, abandoned there during Henry's absences, had felt a little lost at the beginning, Lily especially, when trying to conduct conversations with women neighbors who did not fully understand what being a stage actress in New York meant ("Have I heard of you?"). But for Lily, the move away from Manhattan had been a way of actualizing what had been until then only a voiced wish. "Enough with acting," she would say after every play.

The summers were when Henry tried to make up for his absences. Tutorials at the long fish-laden table (Miranda felt disgusted by the food half the time, refused to eat), the wiffle ball games, fishing expeditions for Philip's benefit. In spite of her adolescent disgust for fish, Miranda would have willingly joined them, but was not invited. "I need to make up to him for his father's absence," Henry had said to her. That Philip's father had been Henry's younger brother did not allow for any extravagant expression of grief on his part, but at night, after everyone was supposedly asleep, Miranda would watch him, from her high bedroom window, as he sat alone on the deck, smoking a cigar. It had made her wonder what adult grief was, how it manifested in the plume of cigar smoke, in his quiet staring at a spot that seemed only inches from his face.

"He comes back tonight, right?" Philip asked her.

"Yes." She had not quite forgotten, only put it out of her mind. Henry's little Haitian adventure was over, and his plane was getting in late. She knew he had a meeting scheduled for tomorrow. He would spend the night with her. It was not essential that she be there, in the apartment, when he arrived.

"What do you know? What happened to him there? Anything?"

She shook her head, sipped the last of the rough Corsican wine.

Later, on the rooftop of Philip's building, they watched the lights of the planes coming in over New Jersey and Staten Island, planes coming in from the south. Philip had bought a bottle of wine she liked from his neighborhood shop, to make up for the wine he'd made her drink in the restaurant. He'd lit a cigarette.

The view from his roof looked southeast over SoHo toward the harbor. Lights were not on in whole swaths of the taller apartment buildings. The dark apartments were likely the empty, ghostly urban investments of Russian oligarchs, Chinese billionaires. Some of them became occasional stopping-over points for these men's beautiful daughters, girls you saw in the bars Philip frequented. Parts of the city felt emptied out by this, decimated in a way, whorish: I am yours if you have the cash. There were occasional lights, and shouts from the street, and packs of NYU students, their phones held aloft like votive candles.

She wanted to say something to Philip now, something important. His hiddenness from her felt physically painful to her sometimes. The way he sucked in smoke. His beautiful hair, and the roughness his wide face and features were taking on as he, like her, began to age.

"So," he said.

"So," she replied.

"You have to get back to meet him, or what?" Philip asked.

"He'll be all right. He has a key."

"Sounds like you don't want to be there."

"Does it sound that way?"

What Aaron had said to her about her father leaving her "stuck in the past" still haunted her a bit. Perhaps Philip felt that, too, the way she was still connected to Henry in a way she should, by now, have grown past. It was undeniable that Henry's lessons had stuck, were with her still. Henry holding her hand when she'd been very young, leading her through the city, trying to teach her—*Those women over there, the ones holding signs, this is what they are protesting.* The closing of a school. A nuclear freeze. It had hardly mattered, it was all thrilling to her, to see the city that way, as a place where ideas were being forcefully debated, and Henry's teaching had been enough to allow her to worship him. "You'll join them someday," he'd always said to her.

At the end of this thought, and in part to push the mild wash of fear away, she chose not to resist the impulse to rush up to Philip from behind, and hug him hard.

"Hey, what's this?"

"It's my mad affection for you."

"Okay, but let's not forget we're on a rooftop. And I'm smoking a cigarette. I don't want to list the number of things that could go wrong here."

She turned him around to face her. Were he not her cousin, she could have loved him in another way.

"How about some music?"

He took out his phone.

"What do you want to hear?"

"MC Hammer, please."

"Stop."

"MC Hammer."

He found it. It was wonderful to hear those beats. It was adolescence. It was her room in Grantham, with the poster from *Say Anything* tacked to the wall, and the photos of George Michael testifying to her allegiance to the deep truths the singer was then in the business of unearthing. The way Philip's body would move, the only time she ever really felt he let himself go. She began the moves, on the rooftop, but he wouldn't join her.

"Idiot," he said.

"Come on."

He took in a drag of the cigarette and stared at her. The way he was able to tell her he loved her was by not moving a muscle, only taking her in, squinting a little, the sides of his mouth resisting movement.

Later, on the train, she realized that as hard as she'd tried not to be, she would likely be home before Henry arrived. The Q was—a little maddeningly, considering how much she had prayed for such a thing to happen on those occasions when she'd been late for something—waiting in the station when she got there, and moved with an uncharacteristic flourish through the depths of Chinatown, up over the bridge. She was at Atlantic Avenue before she knew it. Should she stop and pick up something for Henry? Would he be hungry? How essential was it, really, that she think this way about her father, that she think so *much* about him?

What, she asked now, had been the obligation placed on her, to live a life that took in, that *kept alive*, the high political fever of the city he'd introduced her to? Henry had professed himself happy when she'd taken the job at the auction house. But within his happy approval, she'd sensed some kind of dismissal of her. *So that's all you are to do with the hopes I have invested in you?* It was not, of course, Henry himself, but an internalized Henry, that had made her buckle at the excesses of the art market she'd come to serve. The new class of collectors who had come to the information sessions she'd been asked to conduct. Here's what you have to know in order to make a killing. Here's *all* you have to know. Some invisible Henry had been beside her during those years, forcing her out of a comfortable life. Like it or not, she remained loyal.

TWO

THE POLITICS OF
THE UNDERSTUDY
(2014)

I.

Henry's play *Third World* had been commissioned by the Manhattan Theatre Club on the heels of his great success with *How to Be This Age*. Never one to miss what she perceived to be a watershed moment in a writer's career, Lynne Meadow, the theater's producer (and an old acquaintance), had, after hearing Henry's idea for the play, come up with a tidy advance and, provided that they could get the commitment of a star, virtually promised a Broadway production. ("Virtually promised" was a phrase Henry had learned to read skeptically in the theater, but he liked the up-front money that was being discussed.) He went to work on the play during the fall and winter of 2012, just after returning from Haiti, had it ready by spring.

The private reading the theater set up that May to hear and assess the play had a starry cast. Sam Waterston, Stockard Channing, David Strathairn. There was a lot of laughter at the reading, a feeling that Henry had touched on a contemporary moment with wit and elegance. Before meeting with Henry and his director after the reading, Lynne Meadow cornered Sam Waterston to gauge his interest, and armed with the actor's own virtual promise, offered Henry a production at the Friedman Theatre for spring 2014.

It was a coup for Henry. He'd been on Broadway only once before. Most of his plays, small successes at best, had been Off-Broadway. His one Broadway experience had ended semi-disastrously, so the prospect of what he referred to, to Lily and to Miranda, as a "corrective experience" pushed the promised return to Haiti out of his plans until after the play had opened. That meant a two-year gap, at the least, between visits.

To a degree, this bothered him. As he'd expected and at times cautioned himself against, his experience in Haiti began to fade as soon as he set foot again on American soil and took up, or resumed, his life as a newly successful writer. There were invitations to give readings, and then the play commission. His publisher brought out the paperback of *How to Be This Age* early, as soon as a dip in hardcover sales was perceived, and there was a new flush of publicity. Whatever had happened to him in Haiti—his then-certainty that some change in himself was called for—gave way to the life of attention and flattery. Saint Anselm's call to wretchedness flew out the window, having no place inside the mild delirium of preparing a new play for production. Only occasionally did he think of the boy Jean in Haiti, the look of need he'd witnessed in the boy's face, his own mild and now increasingly dismissible commitment to return. It seemed far away, which was why he was surprised by the way it soon began to nag at him, a voice saying: *All right, do this, have your fun, produce your play, but I will be waiting in the aftermath. Have no doubt about that.*

What was that voice? Where was it coming from? There were times when he wanted to repress Haiti, push it away, allow it to become the anecdote it was fast becoming. But something wouldn't allow this. At this giddy moment, when so much was at last coming together for him, he felt an unwillingness to fully accept the world's suspect approval, the respectful smiles he was able to so easily elicit when he stepped into a meeting. The night under the dripping tarp outside the parish in Fonfrède had opened up an awareness in him.

The play he wrote that winter and spring had a somewhat misleading title. The main character was a composer of "new" music. (Henry had done just enough research to allow himself to throw in words like "serialism" and "atonality," to reference John Cage and Anton Webern, which he hoped would make it seem like he knew what he was writing about.) At the top of the play, after the audience had been treated, in the opening blackout, to an excerpt from what

Henry considered a symptomatic work (Ben Weber's *Fantasia*), the lights were to rise on the composer, alone onstage in the backyard of what was quite obviously an upscale summer lake house, listening, rapturously, to John Raitt singing Billy Bigelow's "Soliloquy" from the original cast recording of *Carousel*. As soon as others, offstage, are heard approaching, he turns off John Raitt and resumes, on his computer, and purely for show, composing music that sounded as atonal as Ben Weber's. The point—and even Henry worried a little about its bluntness—was that this was a man who had come to the end of his own rope writing music that appealed to only an elite, a man who hearkened back to the great Rodgers and Hammerstein moment where you could write a song capable of reaching, and moving, the entire world.

One of the things Henry noticed during the writing of this play was that he was having a bit too much fun. After carrying off a scene in his upstairs study, one that he felt had been particularly good, he would wrap himself up in an old parka and scarf and trundle off into the woods behind his house, awash in an air of self-congratulation. The path led down to a stream that opened into a pond, the surrounding land owned and managed by a conservation trust. They had been lucky, all those years before, in finding a house that bordered property that could not be developed. There had been decent snow that winter, abundant berries to be picked and tossed. He supposed that this was as close to happiness as he could reasonably expect to get in this life. He knew that when he returned from the walk and checked his email, there would be at least one or two items of interest, invitations from the literary world. He had developed a kind of pleasure in turning down such invitations, having spent the bulk of his writing life receiving so few.

As soon as he approached the pond, there was a dampening of the path, an incline that, in order to be forded, required him to sink two inches into mud. He did not mind. He had good boots. He wanted to go deeper into the woods. He wanted to have the capacity to track an animal. A fox, a lynx. To recognize the paw marks, the scat. Nearly thirty years of living here had taught him nothing. He could tell the difference between an oak and a maple, and knew a mountain ash by its orange berries, but every other tree baffled him. Such self-chastisement was a deliberate tactic; it opened the way to his elusive inner critic, forced him to stop having fun and grapple with where exactly he was going with this play. And there were, undeniably, things to grapple with, imperfections that gnawed.

He had conceived of a character—still not the answer to why he had chosen the title *Third World*, more a deliberate and, he thought, clever subterfuge—*from* the Third World. (Though he knew, had been informed by Miranda, that one did not use the term "third world" anymore, he had stubbornly gone ahead, wishing to milk the term for its irony.) A character from Pakistan. It might have made more sense to create a Haitian character, but he was not yet ready to dip into Haiti as source material—not ready to pull what was still very real and present for him into the realm of the imaginary. Though he knew even less about Pakistan than he did about Haiti, he managed to justify the choice to himself by creating a character, as he had always done, out of the shards of the quickly and cursorily observed. He knew he might draw criticism for such a move, but within the freedom of the writing table, such concerns went out the window.

The composer's hosts in the play were a pair of psychotherapists, and this couple's son had brought home for the weekend a beautiful Pakistani girl, a college friend, the son's lover. Henry had concocted a scene—one he was initially quite proud of—where the young couple come out of the lake after skinny-dipping and discover the composer spying on them. Previously, the Pakistani girl had eavesdropped on the composer listening to John Raitt, and wondered what he was so entranced by in the song. Now, left alone with him onstage, she asked the question again.

"Well, the sentiments are universal," the composer tried to explain. "The wish for a son. The confusion over the possibility of having a daughter. The sense that a daughter represents an added responsibility. The urge to do right."

At that point, Henry had written in a long, thoughtful pause, after which the Pakistani girl delivered what Henry considered to be his killer line: "I'm not sure I believe anymore in universals."

On the path by the pond, Henry stopped to ponder that line, complimenting himself and then stepping back from his own self-esteem. Was it true? Was it even original? Of course not. Someone had to have said it already. But true or original or not, he left it in. He was attempting to allow the experience of Haiti to infuse this work, but at his most self-critical, he understood that it could only infuse the work as much as it had infused *him*.

He tried to stay with these thoughts as he gazed up at the tops of the winter trees, the crooked, vulnerable pencil-sharp branches, and regarded all around him the Bruegel winter landscape of brown and black and white. He wanted, badly, with this play to push into a territory he had never visited before.

The notion of his title—of a "third world"—was yet another attempt at profundity. The male therapist in the play voiced at one point his belief that there are three worlds we live in, three worlds we pass through in our daily lives. There is the world of the everyday—our work, our habits, our preparing and eating meals, driving, walking, the ongoing existence. Then there are our attempts to transcend the everyday—our religious and spiritual urges. Our movement toward God, toward a higher consciousness, toward whatever we seek in groups, in congregations. But this urge had been so corrupted, over time, by the leaders of such congregations—priests and gurus both—that, according to Henry's imagined therapist, we are really only left, those of us seeking transcendence, with the more difficult entrance into a third world.

Which is emptiness. Which is nameless. Which is the place we sometimes inadvertently enter that has no defining essence, no credo, no limits. That terrifying, liberating place we only drop into when we are alone, completely alone, and willing, entirely, to detach. Henry knew enough to know that others would call this state Buddhist, but in his play, he was seeking to push all the names away. To call it "Buddhist" was to label it, and make it known, and therefore safe, another bourgeois affectation. "I'm a Buddhist" had often seemed to him, especially when hearing it from wealthy, comfortable friends, like saying, "I don't have the balls to believe in anything more difficult." Lying beyond, or perhaps to the side of the image of the Buddha, Henry had always thought, was something darker, more dangerous, a disturbance at the heart of existence that only the old faiths had the will, or the courage, to acknowledge. Often, sitting in church, listening to some of the harsher statements of Jesus, or Paul, he had a tendency to grind his teeth, to utter a quiet: *yes.*

It was this unknown and frightening state that Henry wished to enter as he continued on the path, much farther than he was prone to do at this time of year. Sometimes in the spring you might meet hikers at this point, but in midwinter it was rare to find anyone. The path grew muckier, his feet sank deeper, the pond widened but was marked by protrusions, stumps, fallen trees. *Let me push past the place where I can be pleased with myself,* Henry thought consciously, wishing it could be made unconscious.

He walked until he grew tired and wanted a place to sit. The pond was more enormous than he remembered it, an inland sea that widened and then narrowed before widening again.

He was, by now, more tired than he knew. Having begun this walk so high on himself and his work—the lunged-after profundity, which had so pleased him up in his study—he found himself suddenly assaulted by the opposite feeling, that he was writing shit, that he was no more than a journeyman writer, a second rater enjoying a lucky moment. It always hovered, didn't it, the north and south poles of a divided consciousness sending contradictory radar signals to one another. Be happy and content with yourself, and then turn a corner. There is always a corner. But he had come here for this, pushed himself on to achieve exactly this. "This is not fucking Buddhist," he said aloud, and wondered if anyone heard him, any woodland creature. He sat on the stump and closed his eyes and tried very hard to shut off his mind, and succeeded well enough. One of his hands went out. *Let whatever comes in such a space tell me something.*

The answer came in the form of a crash. It was so loud he was convinced a tree had fallen, and looked around, to see the evidence, to gauge how close it had come to him, how close, perhaps, to killing him. There was no evidence of a newly fallen tree. Nothing in these woods seemed disturbed. Where, then, had it come from?

He gazed out over the pond and eventually was able to see the ripple. It was coming toward him, moving slowly. Like the wake of an invisible small motorboat. He had been told once—he remembered now, by some naturalist acquaintance—that beavers, sensing their territory invaded, could be unfriendly, even dangerous creatures. Could the warning slap of a beaver's tail make a noise that loud? Best not to wait and find out. He stood and moved as fast as he could.

Still, as frightened as he was, it was thrilling to have summoned what he'd summoned, this encounter with the third world that lay beyond his own imagination, this world of hairy pelts and sharp teeth, and—let's face it—within this carefully protected-in-its-wildness sanctuary, a nameless malevolence that clearly wanted to send him a message.

It became a story he told his friends the next time they met. "The Beaver's Revenge," he called it. Once a month, he went out for dinner with three male friends, each of them veterans, as he liked to joke, of "the healing professions"—two psychotherapists, one internist. He had known them for years, since shortly after moving to Grantham—the therapists big, bluff, burly men, the internist a bit neurasthenic. He had known their sons and daughters and recently was getting to know their grandchildren.

Grantham's ability to support, even to enrich, such men as these came from the presence of the grand, eponymous private school that stood on, and spread out from, the large hill hovering over the town. Celebrities sent their children there, and the children, being the spawn of celebrities, often required therapy. So did the considerable staff. The surrounding communities—those former hippie towns along the Connecticut, two or three grown trendy and embarrassingly rich—also supplied a clientele. As for providing employment for the internist, a large teaching hospital had grown up in Springfield, a mere forty miles down the pike.

In spite of the brooding, intrusive presence of the Grantham Preparatory School, it had become a point of pride among the citizens of the town not to send one's own children there. Public school was the civic religion. An unmentionable, mildly shameful habit had developed over time, among the civic-minded parents of Grantham, to note the contrast between the Gothy, bleached-out students of the private school, seen haunting the town's single convenience store, no doubt in search of drug connections, and to compare them to one's own upstanding children, soccer and track stars, science fair winners, National Merit Scholars. When college acceptances at both institutions were listed every June in the *Grantham Gazette*, a certain smugness attached to the fact that acceptances at Harvard, Dartmouth, Brown, and Swarthmore from the public high school at least matched, and some years outstripped, those acceptances boasted by the private. Who needed to spend fifty thousand dollars a year when by means of endless meetings, fundraisers, school board candidacies, curriculum oversight, and a private endowment raised and maintained by the town's wealthiest burghers, the public high school could give Grantham's youth every chance that the supposedly more privileged had handed to them? It was through such exercises of civic virtue that Henry had first come to know the men in his dinner group. His own participation had helped land Miranda at Barnard, and Philip at NYU, exactly where each of them had hoped to land.

This dinner group had been the source of the much remarked upon chapter in *How to Be This Age* titled "Friendship." Henry had composed a moving paean to the virtues of having close male friends at a certain age, men with whom one felt free to discuss virtually everything. Over dinners at restaurants up and down the valley, they swam like bearded, heavy-gutted divers through the shoals of marriage, diminishing sexual capacity, occasional depression and illness, late-life attractions about which one intended to do nothing. It was a blessing to have this to look forward to, the four of them bellied up to the table, only two of them serious drinkers (Henry guiltlessly included in this subset). The friends' forays were occasionally to upscale bistros, but they tended to favor as often as not the Grantham Tavern, a cozy, genteelly decaying, firelit restaurant attached to the town's one hotel, a place kept alive by parents visiting the prep school. This was an old-school restaurant (no lemongrass or quinoa to be found on the menu), staffed by waitresses from the neighboring towns, ruddy women of a certain age who knew the four friends, joked with them, called them Romeos (which flattered them until they were informed it was an acronym for "retired old men eating out"). No matter. Part of the joy of old male friendship was the unalloyed fartiness of it, the lack of necessity to make oneself anything but what one *was*. He often wondered how it was possible to become a man of a certain age and *not* have this outlet, this unbuttoning among men, this laying bare of the psychic flesh in the locker room of the Aging Male Huddle.

Coming home from such evenings, warmed and slowed down by the amount of wine he'd consumed, he would usually find Lily stretched out on the comfortable old sofa in the TV room at the back of the house, watching one or another of the endless documentaries she was able to find on Netflix, all of them recounting the loves and adventures of various divas. Margot Fonteyn, Maria Callas, Edith Piaf, Maria Tallchief. "Which diva is it tonight?" Henry would shout, even before reaching the room where he knew he would find her. A kind of diva herself, albeit a reluctant one, Lily would lie stretched out, a glass of wine half drunk, various rugs and shawls around her, her extravagant hair, which she was just beginning to allow to go gray. His extravagant spouse, of whom he was inordinately proud, though he still harbored the wish that she would *do* more, get out on the stage more, allow herself to be celebrated as he felt she deserved. The other actresses of her generation—so many forgotten now, so many dead, only one or two (Streep, Close) truly famous, the stunning cadre who had once competed against one another for the chance to play opposite Christopher Walken or Tommy Lee Jones or James Woods in the old Off-Broadway days—occasionally one would show up on TV, playing a role so insignificant that Lily would say to him, "*That's* what you want me to be doing? Playing the nurse's drunken mother on *Grey's Anatomy*?" And he would have to admit to the dearth of great roles for women her age (he had offered to write in a role for her in *Third World*, but she'd refused), and that she seemed happy enough in her semi-retirement. But she had been so *good*.

He would sit and watch with her, the fire behind them, large windows opening into their deep backyard, a place for the sighting of animals, and he would snuggle. He had tried to write about this in his chapter on love, the highly satisfying act of Snuggle, of simple contact, the fact that whatever the issues that incensed the both of them, that retained the capacity to throw them into rages at one another, there was still the abiding fact of a companionable body, of skin, of contact. At twenty, it was probably difficult to appreciate how much this would come to matter. At seventy, it was what one had.

That, and a little more. Not often—perhaps every three weeks or so, which was often enough—they still had the capacity to arouse one another. Three weeks of utter flaccidity would be interrupted—and "interrupted" was, in fact, the proper word—by a sudden and surprising call to arms. On both their parts, fortunately. They would sink, with some deeply pleasurable murmur of acknowledgment, into the familiar unfamiliar, the state that retained the capacity to surprise. Don't analyze it too much, he would always say to himself, and then proceed to analyze it. Making love to Lily, he watched her face change, literally become younger. A woman on the road to orgasm is always a young woman. It was a nice thing to observe, this power they still had over one another, the continuing ability to reduce each other to grunts, to thrusts and parries and sometimes laughter. "Cover my face in cunt juice!" he'd shout in the midst of the act, wondering, in the aftermath, who exactly had said that? Not the silly-looking man he confronted in the mirror. Not the man still capable of finding himself drawn to a youth like Jean. Really, *him?* Doubleness was everywhere; in old age, you had to learn to see double on purpose, lest you be fooled into believing things were ever one thing.

In his dinner group, he chose not to talk much about this, though sometimes he wanted to. It served him better among friends, and for the persona he'd adopted in *How to Be This Age*, to align himself with the hopelessly limp. (Lily had chided him for it.) Yet in spite of all this—a living marriage, thriving male friendships, the writing of a new play that, as winter gave way to spring, Henry grew ever more convinced would add to his laurels—his post-writing walks led him ever deeper into the woods, closer to the outlying edge of the pond where he knew his nemesis lay in wait, eyeing him in his subaqueous, beaverish way, antagonistic, perhaps murderous, but in Henry's view, strangely intimate. He would rest on the familiar stump, and wait to be noticed, wait for the crash that would announce his unwelcome. There were days when he lingered there and it did not come. Days when he felt unseen, unwitnessed, disappointing days when the—increasingly to him—necessary connection was not made. There are men (and he knew he was one of them) who require a nemesis, a hound of heaven barking at their tail, in order not to be consumed by themselves.

In spring, the mud surrounding the pond made movement slow. Henry wondered whether, were the beaver to emerge and chase him, he would have the ability to get away. Still, he kept up the taunting of his presence, the invitation spoken aloud. One day, after a week of eliciting no response, he started to walk toward home, giving in to the awful sense that his presence had perhaps discouraged the beaver from building where he'd been building. It was a terrible thing to consider, and Henry was mourning his own abandonment as he slopped heavily through the mud. Then, from out of the void, he heard again, and almost at the last moment when he would have been capable of hearing it, the thundering slap.

No, I am still here, the beaver was saying. *I have my eye on you. Don't forget the promises you have made. I stand as your witness.*

For this, he felt grateful.

When, the following spring, rehearsals began in New York for Henry's play, he and Miranda found themselves in closer and more frequent contact. The theater had set Henry up in an apartment in a high-rise on West Forty-Eighth Street, a block from the Friedman Theatre.

Rehearsals were held a bit farther downtown, in a space on Forty-Third. Every morning Henry would stop at the same coffee shop, order a latte to go, then stand outside the rehearsal hall, smoking a single cigarette. Delicious. To be seventy-two and still doing this! To not have been sent off to the salt mines, as so many of his contemporaries had. His first play had been produced on Forty-Second Street—the old, Dust Bowl–like far west Forty-Second Street—in 1970. 1970! Richard Nixon had been president. John Lindsay the mayor of New York. Spiro T. Agnew had been a figure of consequence! The headiness of those days came back to him as he smoked his cigarette, the memory of how alive it had all been. Running into a very young Sam Shepard in bars in the Village, a still largely unknown Al Pacino encountered in the street. Al Pacino and Lily had had a flirtation, never (if she was to be believed) consummated, during a workshop of an Israel Horovitz play in the late sixties. My God. The cast of characters, the inevitable necrology that came with any serious recounting of those days. He sucked in on the cigarette, wishing to prolong it. I am seventy-two and still here.

Across the street from where he smoked and sipped his latte was an opening into a midtown garage, one that, very oddly, was plastered with posters from long-dead productions, all of them legendary flops. What was this? Some eccentric garage owner, perhaps a veteran of the theater wars, turning his garage into a memorial to the also-rans, shows like *Drat! The Cat!*, *Nowhere to Go But Up*, *Minnie's Boys*, *Flora the Red Menace*. Had any of these musicals run even a week? Yet the longer Henry stood vigil outside this garage, cigarette in hand, the more it made sense. Even failure in the theater amounted to a kind of immortality; there were always those who made a fetish of remembering. Here was the evidence: in the least likely of places—the opening into a midtown garage—a kind of Flanders Field of white crosses, laid in memory of efforts that had gone over the top and been summarily shot down.

Lily did not wish to decamp to New York. She showed up some-times on weekends, but Henry's weeknights were free, and, occasionally lonely, he prevailed upon Miranda to join him at a midtown restaurant for dinner. She was faithful—not always free, but more often than not willing to rearrange a previous plan in order to accommodate her father. He tried very hard to reach the chosen spot ahead of her, sensitive to the mild potential discomfort, on her part, of arriving there first.

There were times, though, when he was delayed at rehearsal—a vexing twist in the text discovered by an actor, requiring Henry to huddle with the director; the unannounced appearance of the publicity staff, eager to seek out venues for promotion of the play. He would approach the restaurant to find Miranda alone at a table. Some parts of parenthood were apparently never outgrown; it had always broken his heart to have arrived late to pick her up at school when she'd been very young. Every day in rehearsal when they played the John Raitt recording of "My Boy Bill" he revisited his old protective feelings, always knowing that they were mixed with the selfish and cruel sides of parenthood, that urge to be rid of one's children sometimes, to be free of the endless and so often distressing consideration of them. How many Henrys walked through the door of the chosen restaurant, his face lit up with genuine gladness and with apology, to sit across from his daughter and place his hand over hers? Did she see, or recognize, more than one?

"Trouble at rehearsal again," he said the second time this happened.

She had already ordered, and made headway toward consuming, a glass of white wine. Was this evidence of a potential revival of the drinking problem she'd had in college? *Stop.*

"It's all right."

"I'm *glad* you could meet me."

Followed by a silence. Where to begin? Where to dip the cup into the seemingly stagnant but in fact always fast-moving water of their long history?

Miranda had made progress over the past two years. She had wrested permission from the two sons of Anna Soloff, had gotten hold of a cache of letters, been given names and contact information of those acquaintances of Anna still alive. Most important, she'd gained access to Anna's diaries, kept sporadically since the thirties, when Anna had been a teenager. She'd been able to view the yet-unsold paintings, all but one. Through a friend, she had secured an agent—a woman of the old school, one who represented the estates of a pair of Anna's lovers, and, hearing of Miranda's project, expressed an interest in meeting her. Henry had offered to speak to his own agent, but Miranda had been resistant, and prevailed. Her chosen agent was, after a frustrating delay, finally negotiating a deal with a small publisher, based on Miranda's proposal and first chapter.

The "all but one" of Anna's unsold paintings was *The Remembering Animal*. It was Anna's final completed painting, a self-portrait, and for his own reasons (private, hidden), Aaron was coy about letting her see it, indicating there would be a "right time" to do so. As a result, an aura of mystery surrounded it.

"Here's to your contract," Henry said, lifting an imaginary glass while looking around for their waiter. "Done on your own, and done well, if I may say."

Miranda said nothing, smiled at him as though she were scanning his words and his manner, seeing a great deal to react to in both, and choosing not to react; at least, to say nothing.

When he had his drink in hand, he made the toast formal.

"And now tell me, though I'm not supposed to ask, how you're going to keep yourself alive until this magnum opus is finished."

Choosing the words "magnum opus" was a mistake. He saw that quite clearly in her eyes.

"I think you can probably remember similar moments in your life," she said.

His face, and the accompanying silence, offered her an opening.

"Times when you felt you had to do something that might not pay, and you worried how it might affect our well-being. Mine and Mom's."

"More times than you can imagine."

"Well?"

"Understand, Miranda, that my life has resembled no one's so much as Mr. Magoo's."

A slight smile from her, a raising of the eyebrow.

"There is a Mr. Magoo cartoon, I can't remember which one, where—you remember he's basically blind?"

"I remember."

"And he finds himself on a series of girders moving up in the sky at a construction site. Every time he's about to step off of one, and fall into thin air, another one magically appears."

She offered him the same hesitant smile.

"When you suggest you're using my life as a model, I shudder. You're following in the path of a blind cartoon character as if he's Moses." He leaned slightly away, opened his napkin in his lap. "Which is probably as perfect a metaphor for the parent-child relationship as any I could come up with."

She finished her wine.

"Shall I order you another?"

"Not if it's going to make you feel I have a drinking problem."

"I think no such thing. We should have ordered a bottle."

"One more will do me."

"Miranda."

He reached out and touched her hand.

She had grown—he had to take the time to acknowledge it—into a beautiful woman. Even the earliest sign of age—the slight reshaping of her face—did nothing to dispel the fact. At her birth it had seemed, distressingly, like she might become a clone of her hangdog father, but as she'd grown she had moved steadily in the direction of her mother. Someone had told him once that baby girls resembled their fathers at birth in obedience to some ancient belief that this would make the father more likely to stick around. But there was never any chance that he would not. Both smitten and terrified from the moment she had breached her mother's womb, he had felt locked into an allegiance with this child. Not that this had made him what was conventionally called a "good" father. Quite the opposite at times.

His appreciation of her beauty led—inevitably—to the issue of her uncoupled state. There had been great hope that the last of her serious young men—a saxophone player and erstwhile composer named Isaac—would be the one with whom Miranda might settle. A few years younger than Miranda, Isaac had had the doe-ish, beautiful face of a yeshiva bocher, with a goatee like a soft shaving brush. Isaac's music—they'd gone to hear him at a series of venues in Brooklyn and the West Village—was obscure, hard to listen to, and used silence as a bludgeon. You sat there and waited for the next note to be played, almost to the point of torture. But all right, this was what it was to be young, this was what was now called *jazz*. (Henry supposed that some of his own early plays were equally torturous to sit through.) Still, there had never been between Isaac and Miranda a palpable sense of destiny, such as the one he remembered feeling in his early years with Lily. Even allowing for Henry's sexual dividedness, and Lily's resistance to the idea of monogamy, it had been clear to both of them that each had discovered in the other an entirely necessary being. Was that no longer a part of the romantic apparatus for men and women of Miranda's generation, that sense of *necessity*?

"Tell me about rehearsals," Miranda said, perhaps sensing where Henry's thoughts might be drifting.

"Shall I be honest?"

"No. Lie."

"Well, Waterston's loss was a blow."

Two months before rehearsals were to begin, Sam Waterston had had to drop out. A perfectly reasonable conflict—a TV project he had committed to had to revise and delay its shooting schedule—which had left them scrambling for a new star. One they hadn't been able to find.

"Adam is very good, but he's not Sam Waterston, and I'm missing him. And, frankly, beginning to worry."

"It'll be fine."

"Oh God, Miranda, don't say that. That's the easiest thing in the world to say. 'It'll be fine.' That's what we say to cancer patients. Because what's the alternative? 'You're likely to die'?"

She took no apparent offense, though he had been a little harsh.

"Sorry. I'm actually having a wonderful time. But rehearsals are always cozy and wonderful and jokey, and even when there are fights you always feel like you're on the set of *All About Eve*, where everyone's a little larger than life and it's not ultimately the most serious thing in the world."

He gestured to the waiter to refill both their glasses.

"Except that ultimately it *is* the most serious thing in the world. When you get in front of an audience. When you see the worried look of the producers. And they *are* worried, by the way. Going up on Broadway without a star is a form of suicide. And then there's the verdict of *The New York Times*. Let's get drunk, shall we? Because talking about this is making me even more worried."

"It'll be fine."

"Shut up."

They had achieved their comfortable place.

"Now tell me who you're dating."

"Now it's my turn to say shut up."

The second glass of wine relaxed Henry dangerously. It always did.

"All right."

"I'm living like a nun," Miranda said. "Which is fine. I'm a writer now."

He ran his finger along the rim of the wineglass to prolong something. What he was seeing in her was something strong, something to admire, and also something to be alarmed by. Were she another man's daughter, he could have relaxed and congratulated her. Her ultimate collapse, should there be one, would not be his responsibility.

"Well, welcome to the world of terminal uncertainty."

"It's not so bad. I make my rent."

"Yes. You've become a *barista*."

She rode right over the slight disapproving tone.

"It hasn't been awful. Twelve hours a week is all I need. Everyone's younger than me and they tell me their stories. I come home and I feel clean. Coming home from the auction house, I used to feel—God, just sort of dirty. Or—soiled. By the greed. The insanity. I mean, to have to act excited that some hedge fund guy paid a fortune for a *Jeff Koons?*"

He leaned forward slightly, hungry for something. Her adult self on display. Holding back from saying: *But Miranda, you're forty-one.*

"At a certain point, I may want to interview you."

"About what?"

"About your life. About living on the Upper West Side in the seventies. What that was like."

"I'll tell you what it was like. It was scary. How many times did I have to run from muggers? Even after my foray into the boxing ring, which I quickly came to see would help me as much in an encounter with a knife-wielding thug as a course in Jesuitical persuasion."

She hesitated, smiled slightly, turning away from him. Something clearly going on in her.

"Miranda, what is it? Shall we order? Maybe the wine is making us both a little morose."

"No. I feel like I carried something out of that time. You know this. Our time on 107th Street. Something that's never left me. I feel silly sometimes. Everyone moves on."

She stopped herself. The waiter came in, sensing the interruption. They ordered the first appetizing thing each saw on the menu, and leaned back into one another. For Henry, this was always the exciting part—their ability to incite one another.

"I'm trying to follow."

"My biggest fear, if you must know—"

"And of course I must know."

"Is that I'm wrong. I mean, that my premise is all wrong. About all of you. That there was never something you were all trying to do. Politically, I mean. That it was all accidental."

He hesitated a moment, finding himself with nothing to say.

"Guide me a little more," he said.

"Remember that bookstore you used to take me to? The one on—was it Eighty-Ninth Street?"

"The New Yorker? Yes, Eighty-Ninth Street."

"That wonderful children's room in the back."

"Oh God, don't start me on the New Yorker. I need another glass of wine. Pete Martin, that insane wonderful man who ran it."

"Tell me if I'm wrong. They had a *communist* section."

"They did. Pete Martin was apparently the illegitimate son of an Italian anarchist."

"And people still gravitated toward that. Lenin and Marx and—"

"And Thorstein Veblen. And Antonio Gramsci and—oh, who remembers? God, you're bringing it all back."

"What drives me crazy is this sense that in *my* lifetime—and certainly in yours—there was still this possibility that we were going to take communism seriously." She laughed a little after she spoke, but he sensed something else, some attempt to crack him open. "I mean, I know, *communism*. But still, that some option was still there, still alive."

"Every play in those days was a socialist tract. *Every* play. *The Sunshine Boys* was a socialist tract. In disguise."

"Don't joke."

"I have to. Otherwise it will break my heart. We were all socialists. You're not wrong about that. We were all heading toward the barricades, with no actual idea where the barricades actually were. Socialists. Until we weren't anymore."

Henry had gestured for, and received, his third glass of wine.

"I keep thinking about those movies I've seen. Some of them you took me to, when I was way too young. Those foreign movies. I mean, what were you thinking?"

"Maybe that you needed to see those revival houses before they all disappeared. Before Netflix took over the world. The Regency. The Thalia."

"Yes."

"The Theatre 80 St. Marks."

"And there were movies like *La Guerre Est Finie*. And that other one, that wonderful one set in Budapest after the uprising."

Henry only had to think for a moment. *"Time Stands Still."*

"*Yes*. In those movies, there were all these people, sitting around their kitchens, smoking cigarettes and drinking . . ."

"Kvass."

"Or whatever. Knowing they were living after a failed revolution. Being able to *mourn* it. I feel I'm in a city that's living after a failed revolution that it doesn't even know happened."

He knew this part of her, knew something of what had taken her over in the last years of her once-promising career. If her uncoupledness was a fear, this was a perhaps even greater one, that she would end as one of those women you still saw haunting the Upper

West Side, having held on to rent controlled apartments—women with long unsculpted gray hair, insufficiently tended teeth. A vacant look, a seer's look. Stop and ask them for directions, and they would talk too long. People fell off the rails, because it became difficult at a certain point to know precisely where the rails were.

"Miranda, you've got to have another glass of wine."

She covered her still half-filled wineglass.

"No. No more for me. You've got to tell me if I'm crazy."

"Of course you're not crazy."

It was exactly what he'd been thinking—or fearing, anyway. But she was his beautiful, vulnerable daughter, and had to be consoled.

"There was—you probably don't remember—a communist meeting hall on our corner."

"Of course I remember. Right below Anna's building."

"Yes."

"I remember the men coming out of it. On Friday nights, when you and I were bringing home pizza from the V&T. Those men with gray ponytails and those *eyes*."

"Yes."

"She painted it. *107th and West End*, the painting is called."

It was one Miranda had grown increasingly fond of, a small canvas from the early seventies. The communists seen through a window in the basement, shadowy, insubstantial figures, outlines really, framed in a strong yellow light. But *warm* somehow, *heated*. Anna had captured a kind of political passion in the shape and movement of their outlines, the way they pressed into one another, bodies charged by their own intensity.

"She went there. She was one of them. Not a totally committed one, because it would have meant allowing someone else to control what she could paint. Still, a communist."

"Here we are, extolling them. Shame on us."

She simply looked at him, wishing for some encouragement he held back from offering.

"After Stalin. After all we know."

"We're not *extolling* them. It's just amazing to me that even thirty years ago that still went on. That we hadn't yet given up."

"Miranda, what are we talking about?"

In her eyes was the sadness of having gone in a certain, desired direction with someone who suddenly demonstrated an unwillingness to go on. He had let go of her hand. She was alone, being asked to cross Riverside on her own, while cars rushed past. She was forty-one, and needed to face how pathetic it was to have such a feeling at this age. Still, a part of her insisted that he could still be her guide, as he'd once been, on the afternoons when he'd picked her up at her grammar school in the west nineties. Standing at a distance from the overeager mothers, the cloddish, ex-hippie fathers. (Their baggy jeans, their mustaches.) Her father in a snap-brimmed cap and a raincoat, looking like a spy. His tiny wave to her, and his wink, his declaration of their separateness from these others.

"Didn't you all feel an obligation? You knew what didn't work. Where was capitalism going to lead us? Into more wars. Into these gaps between the incredibly rich and the incredibly poor. I know I'm being reductive. I'm not an intellectual. I'm in over my head, but do you know what I'm saying? It's almost as if you can only ask these basic questions if you don't pretend to be an intellectual. I feel like you all saw the horror of where we would go if we didn't fundamentally stop it, but you decided to go there anyway."

They shared a quiet moment. He tried to gather whatever thoughts were available. Very few were. Could he possibly ask for a fourth glass of wine? She was waiting for something from him, a resumption of something, an old dialogue he was now being reminded had been of great importance to her. It felt like a figment of the past he was being called back to, a place he had left, and was being chided now for having left. It made him think, if only briefly, of the boy in Haiti. Ought he to tell her? Would this give him a chance to burnish his leftist bona fides, this urge to help a boy in Haiti?

"I'm sorry. I think writing about her—or just *thinking* about her, reading her diaries—is starting to make me a little crazy. And I'm being a bore."

"You're the farthest thing from crazy, Miranda. Or a bore."

Again, she waited for more from him.

"You think *I* betrayed something?" he asked finally. They were interrupted by the arrival of the food, which he hoped would divert them.

"You. Your generation," she said, undiverted. "You saw that you needed money, you went along. You wrote for television."

Ah yes, the old argument. He knew it too well now. It had been a mistake to let her know, at the time, that he considered writing for that particular show essentially whoring himself out. The harder thing to convince her of had been the feeling that it was time—high time—to stop living marginally. There had been a guilt involved in watching Lily trudge up the steps of their walk-up after a grocery run, laden down with bags. A guilt in his awareness of the streets themselves, never allowing Miranda to be out on her own without extreme worry. What kind of father allowed his family to exist in such circumstances? TV had seemed like salvation at the time. A way to get them out of the city. They were no longer hippies. No longer urban pioneers. Age, and the new perspective of age, had made its intrusion. It was unacceptable—unthinkable—to imagine losing either of them to forces from which he couldn't protect them. It was the first of the obligations. Not to make them happy. (Who could do that?) But at least to keep them safe.

"Crucify me, Miranda."

"I'm not trying to crucify you. Only to understand. I mean, I know New York was partly a hellhole in the seventies, but why wasn't it enough for everyone to just stop for a moment, to halt the rush of things, to just work together to try and figure out what the next thing—the solution—was going to be?"

"I think the answer is Ronald Reagan."

"Don't be glib."

"All right. But the answer is still Ronald Reagan. A big cheery cowboy coming along and essentially saying, 'Hey, guys, we don't have to be depressed anymore.' Just loosen the financial floodgates, open it all up to foreign investment, and declare the seventies over. And suddenly everybody's rich and happy and forgetting there was ever a depressive moment in American history."

He leaned forward for emphasis.

"You can't possibly understand what it was like unless you lived through it. A decade where a night out consisted of *Network* or *The Deer Hunter*, or, God help us, *Apocalypse Now*. A night *out*. These were *popular entertainments*, Miranda, movies where you'd emerge into the night feeling you had to storm the fucking Bastille. Then the eighties arrive and, without any real *agreement* on our part, we find ourselves watching *Kramer vs. Kramer* and *Ordinary People* and suddenly it seems like the problem is not a derailed country but *us*. Tend to your emotions, be a good parent, and all will be well."

"I can't believe the movies were enough to halt the progress of an entire generation."

"Yes, well, think again, Miranda. It doesn't take much to turn a whole culture around. It happens in a nanosecond. The simple fact is we're not that smart, and we, most of us, have *zero* capacity to remember the past. Ask people about the seventies, and all they're going to remember is disco. And really, it has to be asked: *Were* we on the verge of a true reassessment, or did all the grunge just make us feel that we were?"

They looked at each other a moment, and both understood what was there. Every parent-child relationship is like a sea containing an iceberg. The goal is to avoid its vast underground shelf. But that was really the point, Henry thought: it is *all* underground, there is no avoiding it. Still the ship, even knowing the pointlessness of it, instinctively wanted to veer away.

"Tell me now," he said (was he dodging another question?), "why this is so important to you."

She regarded him with what he read as disappointment.

"I guess because I've got to understand her."

It came as a relief, the subject moving away from his failings.

"Anna painted her older son in the eighties. He'd become a lawyer. A corporate lawyer. She was very cruel to him—she hated what she thought he was becoming—so she painted him, hard to really describe, but almost like this *decaying* being."

He made no comment.

"Her own son. She saw the dangers, I guess, of the corporation."

"Oh Miranda, now you sound like you've spent too much time in the communist section of Pete Martin's bookstore."

She held back from anything further, saw that she wasn't being invited to continue. Her father was drunk. There had been a volume of such moments in her life, moments where they came to the edge of a desired intimacy before she noted something in his eyes, a retreat, a wish to be pushed so far and no farther. *I have this much to give*, he seemed to be saying. *Understand and respect, please, my limits.* It seemed silly, at forty-one, to still be looking for him to push past those limits. And he was right, of course. *She saw the dangers of the corporation.* Really? Had she become a woman capable of uttering such a statement?

They ate, each of them feeling something of an eclipse. The conversation would go on, they would try to revive it, but they would each feel the effort. "How's your broccoli rabe?" would undermine and replace the heat of their earlier exchange.

"I'm sorry," he said finally, when the bill had arrived. "I think you've probably learned by now that after three glasses of wine I'm incapable of sequential thought. Now I've got to go up to the apartment and rewrite a scene. God help me."

"It's all right. I think what you're basically telling me is that I've got to watch myself, not get lost in this."

"No, I'm actually telling you the opposite. If you don't get lost in it, you're not doing it properly."

He seemed sincere. She looked into his face to see if it was possible to resume what they'd started earlier.

"Get lost, but . . . well, the trick is to learn how to surface for air."

Henry paid the bill and she walked him to the entrance of his building on Forty-Eighth Street, him walking a little slowly, not as the result of age, but—was she wrong?—as if he wanted to prolong this, to return them to a simpler version of themselves. He took her arm, tugged it. He was wearing an old misshapen hat, and he pulled it down over his head. A part of him, she knew, loved looking like this, like an old man. He was humming one of his favorite songs, the ones he loved and had taught her to recognize. "These Foolish Things"? Was it that one? There was comfort in it, him trying to pull her back to the old affection, but she found herself resistant to comfort.

At the entrance to his high-rise, he asked if she wanted to come up.

"No. You've got a scene to write, don't you?"

"That's what I was hoping you'd help me avoid."

"Go up and do it. Make yourself some coffee."

Something in his eyes looked exhausted. He stretched out one hand to circle her face, then reached into his pocket, removed his wallet, and handed her a wad of bills.

"I don't like thinking of you on the subway. Take a cab, please."

"Now you're treating me like a ten-year-old."

"You'll always *be* a ten-year-old to me. Don't you see that?"

"Dad, no. Please. It's too late to be keeping me from the subway. I *live* here. Remember?"

"Yes."

He slipped the money into her coat pocket.

"Stop."

"Take it. It will help me rewrite my scene to not be worried about you."

He hesitated under the awning, unwilling to release her. A handsome young Latino doorman hovered near the entrance. He and Henry obviously knew each other, had a joking relationship.

"My daughter, George."

"I see," the young man said.

"She's beautiful, isn't she?"

"Dad, please."

"You should date her."

This was the place it had so often landed with the two of them, this embarrassing place where he went too far.

"I'm going now."

"George, you know she dates these young men—these *musicians.* And here *you* are, with an actual *work ethic.*"

George was laughing, but also looking at Miranda in a supportive way, more sensitive to her than her father was being.

"Okay, good night."

He followed her a little way down the block.

"Miranda, forgive me."

"You do this, you always do this."

"Yes, I know. See it as . . ."

"See it as what?"

"I don't know what the fuck it is."

Now she avoided his touch.

"Fatherhood. Drunkenness."

"Not every father seems to want so badly to embarrass his daughter."

"It's just *George*."

"George who happens to be a human being. Did you ever consider that you might be embarrassing him as much as you are me? Do you think—do you actually think—that everyone is exactly like you? That you can say 'It's just George' and dismiss him that way?"

He was chastened. In matters such as this, she had become his social conscience, and was not shy of asserting her authority.

"How many times do I have to say I'm sorry?"

She turned away from him, from a face that was now genuinely asking for forgiveness. She and her father on Forty-Eighth Street. The lights of two theaters facing each other on opposite sides of the street, the bright marquees and then something dingy and unclean about the theater entrances. It was just after eight and the shows inside must have started. There were things about the theater she had never really liked. The way you had to adjust to the lights coming up on a patently false world, one you were expected to make the effort to enter, then to actually *believe* in. Yet he had made it his world, he thrived here. She wanted now to release him into it.

"I'll let you go, Miranda," he said, seeming a little defeated.

"Go and apologize to George."

"I will. Promise me you'll take a cab."

"I will."

She waited.

"You first," he said.

He watched her go, feeling, once again, that he had blown it. Or avoided something. Or that, very simply, in any father-daughter relationship, there would be pain, there had to be pain, it was at the heart of things, in the DNA of fathering a girl.

Miranda turned, walked toward the urgent, digital lights of

Broadway proper. She did not turn around, but knew he would wait until she was out of sight before returning to his apartment.

The onslaught she was subjected to as soon as she turned onto Broadway had the effect of making her lower her head, as against a wind. As indeed it was—a wind. Everything possible coming at her at once, the world for sale. The M&M's store. Beyoncé. Jennifer Lopez. A number of women's faces she didn't recognize, young women in tight jeans in digital movement up on the giant billboards. Wet parted lips. *Fuck me but let me assure you I will be on top.* The digitalized men who wore their crotches like bow ties, like crowns. The Brooks Brothers world, where everyone was white, or might as well be. When actual blackness appeared in these digital ads, it was in its impenetrable form, a style choice of affected negation. U Can't Touch My Blackness. But you can buy some aspect of it at H&M and take it home to the Midwest. It had come to this, this horror, but you couldn't think about the history that had brought it about, because you'd wind up saying something like *She saw the dangers of the corporation.* Here it was, all around her, but to make such a statement—a perfectly reasonable one, she now thought—put you in the company of those men with gray ponytails and large sunken eyes coming out of the communist meeting hall on 107th and West End. Instead, you were expected to laugh. See what's become of it all. Sigh and move on, and take what you can. There was so much to take, after all. If you had the money.

She walked toward Forty-Second Street, trying hard to find some kind of acceptance in herself. She was already close to the subway when she remembered the wad of cash in her pocket. She touched the money, felt it suddenly, in this context, like ash in her pocket, like something burned and still intact, something that only a human touch could force to disintegrate. She was going too far, and she knew it. She was slipping, and had to hold on.

She rounded the corner of Forty-Second Street, found a panhandler, a woman with cracked lips the color of roof slate, and handed it to her. Then she stepped down into the subway, and in her own mind, disappeared.

It had been something—a challenge, to say the least—earning the trust (if indeed she had; there were reasons to doubt it) of Anna Soloff's older son. Jonah Soloff was less than two years senior to his brother, Aaron. Anna had hardly taken a breath between having one baby by the Puerto Rican artist who had no intention of sticking around and then another with the brutal photographer who had moved in with her and proceeded to knock everything over, her older child included, with his heavy work boots. Anna had had both boys when she was over forty. The last remnant of her faint loyalty to Judaism had gone into their naming. Jonah and Aaron, little big-eyed, often terrified shipmates on Anna's ark.

Jonah lived in an enormous apartment on Central Park West. It was where Miranda went to first meet him, and then later, for the series of interviews she had conducted over the previous two years. The apartment was always empty. He lived there with his second wife, a Japanese textile designer with whom he had two teenage daughters. What was it about the rich that allowed them to leave so little imprint of themselves in their own domiciles, other than the evidence of what was called "taste"? Teenage girls ought to have thrown things around, been a little careless, shouldn't they? Where were the sweaters, the empty plastic cups, the soccer cleats piled in the entrance? Jonah was stingy with the details of his family life. His daughters went to Dalton or Fieldston or somewhere. His wife was often in another country, doing whatever international business Japanese textile designers did. Jonah had left his early corporate-lawyerly life in order to take on the management of his mother's estate, a career shift that allowed him to be at home a lot. He was in the habit of greeting Miranda at the door with an unwelcoming expression, wearing bright white shirts, crumpled chinos, bare feet where his large and ugly toes made an unembarrassed show of themselves.

"Are you a bohemian?" he asked her the first time they met. "I don't care for bohemians."

It had been his opening gambit; deliberate, she thought, a bit crude. Where his brother—softer, more playful, if equally challenging—toyed with her like a young boy teasing a girl into acquiescence, Jonah had a harshness he was hesitant to drop. He wanted her to know from the get-go that he was only participating in the "vain hope, probably unfounded" that Miranda's book would promote his mother's "brand." (Miranda looked hard for the irony in those words, was afraid there was none.)

Already, in the two years since she had gained his tacit approval, Anna's work had taken off in the hyped-up, and quickly accelerating, art market of the 2010s. Eugene had gained access to *The Opinionated Playground*; it had been bid on by a foreign collector for two and a half million dollars. Somewhere in Belgium, or the south of France, the hungry women of the Ninety-Sixth Street playground made their pleas to one another—or perhaps only waited in a warehouse for their price to go up. Who needed to wear socks and shoes when your mother's work commanded that kind of international prestige?

"Sit down," he said to her. It was their fourth or fifth meeting. He often canceled at the last minute, though she suspected this was nothing but a power play. Unlike his brother, he never offered her tea. Or even water. She had taken to bringing her own. He watched her carefully to be sure she put it down on a protected surface.

"So you want to know what it was like being booted around the room by the asshole photographer. That's today's question. Am I right?"

She sat and sipped a little water and allowed him to nurse his aggression. In spite of his affect, Miranda did not dislike him. Had pity for him, in fact, though she suspected this was a weakness in herself she should work on. His childhood had been worse than Dickensian. He was handsomer—though in a blunter way—than his softer, more delicately sculpted brother. He had a large shock of black hair that hadn't a touch of gray, pillowy Middle Eastern lips, his father's limpid Puerto Rican eyes. He was like the boys—the football players— she had been secretly attracted to in high school, not being able to quite admit to herself that their black-stubbled chins, their thick arms, made furtive appearances in her dreams. It was this, her attraction to him, rather than what she considered his porous hostility, that made her feel a bit intimidated.

"I do want to get to that. I think what I want to know, though, is whether you've forgiven your mother for what she allowed. In your childhood, I mean."

"It's best to be bold with him," Aaron had tutored her. "I'm not sure he has any access to his emotions at all, so corner him there, and he'll be a little helpless."

Jonah did not look cornered after she'd asked the too-bold, perhaps mistimed question.

"Oh, that's stupid," he said. He held still a moment, then moved to the window, hands in his pockets, studied the view of Central Park, without, she was sure, really seeing anything.

"Are you deliberately setting out to write a bad book?" he asked her. "Because that's the kind of thing I'd expect to read in a really bad book. Whether Jonah Soloff 'forgives' his mother."

"It's important for me to understand her as a mother," she said, slightly embarrassed now by the need to justify having asked the question. She could never quite find the right lure to cast to him. It made her feel a bit of a failure. To not get him to open up would affect how she wrote the book. Anna presented issues as a mother that had to be dealt with.

"Let me shock you. I don't blame her for anything. She was a fine *mother*. She did what she had to do. She became a great painter, okay?"

"I don't disagree with that. I wouldn't be here if I disagreed with that."

"Well, write about *that*, then. Look at the fucking paintings and write about *them*."

It was the sort of line that made her want to push him harder, as his brother suggested. But she knew him well enough by now to know that in another minute, another two minutes, he would find himself in a whole other mood.

"I went down to Washington to see Karl Rattner's photographs," she said.

He had no response, though he had to know about the exhibition. Mounted on a lower floor of the National Portrait Gallery, *The Art of Fashion* had limited itself to magazine photographers of the fifties. Irving Penn. Avedon. Karl Rattner had only a few on display, not being in these others' league. Still, he had had a delicate touch with the gamine models of that decade, girls with wispy bangs and an air of early romantic hopelessness. Were the fifties always so heartbreaking? Henry had once described that time for her, for those women, as "the *Mary, Mary* world," referencing a hugely popular early sixties play in which a smart and attractive young woman spent two hours trying to win a man so dull you wondered why she bothered. Unspoken was the optionlessness behind such women's choices, and Karl Rattner's work seemed, paradoxically, to *get* that sense of existing within an unbearable tension, young women like Meissen cups waiting for some man to come along and smash them. Miranda had had to sit on a bench in the gallery, working to recall all the things she had previously learned about Karl Rattner, in order to offset what she found to be a new and inappropriate admiration of his talent.

"Yes? Were you impressed? He was good, wasn't he?"

"Yes."

He looked at her and waited. He was always doing that, setting her up for something, making her anticipate a revelation he had no intention of providing.

"I don't want to talk anymore about him," he said.

"You haven't said much."

"No, and I won't."

It had been up to Aaron to fill her in on the details, the way Karl Rattner had behaved toward the apparently detested older boy. Stepping on his hand while he lay on the floor coloring, throwing his crayons out the window, sideswiping him with his large hands, bringing home cartons of Chinese food and denying Jonah any. Rattner had been a big hungry man with a string of mistresses behind him, a number of previous children left in his wake. Sometimes, hearing the Rattner stories, Miranda envisioned an older Manhattan, a Grimms' fairy-tale Manhattan, full of apartments where lived discarded mistresses bringing up the children of creeps. Anna had once painted a view of the backs of apartment buildings in Spanish Harlem, where she'd lived when Jonah was born, and still lived when Karl Rattner moved in. In Anna's painting there was a window, a set of women's underclothes hanging out to dry, a few baby things, shadows against a beige wall. The unimaginative curator of *Domestic* had chosen not to include this work in her exhibition, but Miranda felt that was where it belonged.

Yet Anna had taken this man in, allowed him to impregnate her, looked away while he stole her older son's crayons and, one by one, dropped them out the window. Aaron had been dismissive of any explanation Miranda had tried to broach. "It was sex, pure and simple." Then he'd shrugged, as if that was all there was to say about sex.

Under this horrible man's reign, the little boys had huddled together. Big, bruisy, handsome Jonah had been the sickly one, the vulnerable one. Light, lithe, ethereal Aaron had been the escape artist—in Anna's early portraits of him, he had the weightlessness of Peter Pan. His father had kept his hands off him—the violence, it seemed, reserved for Jonah—but Aaron, witnessing everything, had created hiding places within the apartment for his brother, upended chairs the boys huddled under, places Karl Rattner had to struggle to reach. Hearing these stories made her love Aaron, and pity Jonah. Yet, in a way not easily analyzable, it was Jonah who was letting her in—who seemed to be *inviting* her in, in his way—while affecting the opposite. He had become her puzzle.

"I wonder," she said.

He gazed at her as if something on her upper cheek—an undiscernible flaw—fascinated him. It was a trick he used—perhaps a lawyer's trick to employ against women, to make them feel self-conscious. She had learned not to fall for it.

"She painted you, after you made the choice to become a lawyer. After you started working."

"I know what you're going to ask. Why did she make me so ugly and—what's the word, desiccated?"

"That'll do," Miranda said.

"Look, it's not saying anything against her *art*, which was great, okay? Let's agree to that, all right?" (She always noted the way he pronounced the word "art," like it was a word in a foreign language he had never fully mastered.) "But there were two things Anna was interested in in her paintings. Penises and vaginas and radical politics."

"That's three things."

"Is it? Okay. I mean, I have tried to understand why the nude is so important. To painters. The naked body. Really. I've read stuff. And it's not so hard. She used to say she *became* these bodies she painted."

"Right."

"Like it was *performance* to paint them. She said that once, in an interview. I don't really understand that, but maybe, okay, I understand it a little. The way she would look after she painted us. Me and my brother. My first wife. We were always naked. Take your clothes off. I wouldn't, after a while. I mean, come on. My first wife would. There were always naked people around the apartment. Not this apartment. Her apartment on 107th. And she always had this glazed, exhausted look after she finished painting for the day. Where's dinner, Mom? And she's stumbling around in a housedress."

It was what Miranda wanted, this glimpse into the dailiness of painting, this sense of what it must have been *like*. The housedress and the glazed look and the hungry little boys. She wanted more. The problem was that as he spoke he was picking at his toes, scraping away the skin, as at parts of himself he didn't like. It seemed he could not offer her something useful without making her go through a little ring of fire in order to get it.

"So when I decided to do a perfectly reasonable thing—go to Columbia Law, do something that had *reason* in it—it was like I wouldn't take my clothes off for her anymore. I'm giving you real insight here, aren't I?"

She smiled, as he had expected her to, and then she worried he would offer no more. She had to fight the urge to say *Please don't do that*, regarding his toes.

"*Jonah in the Corporation*. What an enticing title, right? Like, who cared, except for her? No wonder nobody wants to pay real money for it. All I had done was gotten a *job*."

"Yes, but she was against that sort of job."

His face assumed a kind of smirk, superior and defended at the same time. She wanted now some re-creation of the battle he and his mother must have had.

He had been sitting in a chair, in the painting. Anna liked to put her models in chairs, and then look at them, and watch what they did with their hands, how they posed. It told her something, the way they posed, what they thought of themselves. She spoke to them as they tried to make themselves comfortable, pretending to try to loosen them up, usually failing at the effort. But that was okay, was in fact what she wanted. The eloquence of physical discomfort.

In the painting, Jonah had looked bunched into himself, tight, defended, a little frightened of chaos. As how could he not? Cheap psychology might tell her that he had made his choice so that he could keep his crayons. Anna had painted his gray suit as if the body underneath was fighting to get out. His white shirt turned flesh colored in the region of his belly. She was brilliant with skin, and when she wasn't allowed skin, she made it bore through whatever was covering it.

"Didn't she try to discourage you? From going into that world?"

"And if she did, I was going to listen to her? A woman who lived hand to mouth until she was what, sixty-five? Food stamps and welfare checks. Exactly what did she want me to do, take after her?"

"I don't know."

It was one of the limitations of not having had a child herself, this inability to see what the moment must have been like for Anna, bearing witness to a child's unbold choice.

"Were you . . . ?"

"What?"

"Were you happy in that world you went into?"

His unspoken response to her was like a silent taking of the question and softly pummeling it, so that it had no shape left.

There had been an earlier portrait of Jonah, one that Miranda loved, and one she had to keep in mind as she regarded the man who seemed to be doing everything in his power to make himself hard and unattractive. Anna had called it *Jonah on the Cusp*. Painted when he was twenty-two, just graduating Columbia undergrad. Anna had possessed a genius, whatever form of poverty they happened to be living through, for making sure her sons were well educated. Fieldston and Columbia for Jonah. Trinity and Brown for Aaron. Scholarships. They would rise, no matter Anna's politics, and then she would be always a little disappointed at the forms their rising took. A corporate lawyer and a psychiatrist.

In the earlier painting, she had seated Jonah in a chair by the window, had him face three-quarters toward her, his strong shoulders encased in a pale violet sweater, wearing chinos. He had been extraordinarily handsome then, but in his chin something had started to gather, a weighing-in of the past, a felt resistance to his mother's view of him. The tension of the painting lay in this resistance, his fighting against Anna's attempt to force him to retain some of the fierceness or wildness or maybe just the plain innocence she had done her best to deny him. It was the recognition of this—Jonah's vulnerable face asking, *Do you think you can keep me here? Do you think you can* keep *me?*—that made it so moving to Miranda.

He seemed to be repeating this with Miranda, a twisting away from an assumed pose that left him looking, in her eyes, trapped there.

When she left him that day after the not entirely unsatisfactory interview, she sat on one of the benches bordering Central Park. As she could look up toward his apartment on the fourteenth floor, it was entirely possible he might just then have been looking down at her, watching her. Some part of her was always reluctant to leave him, in spite of the discomfort he put in her way, the questions he liked to throw back at her like refuse. Though he seemed glad when she announced that she was leaving, she saw something else. Something tiny. A part of his face seemed to empty, his mouth change shape. A memory of abandonment he couldn't help displaying. It was entirely possible she was reading in.

Two years into her work, the central thing Miranda felt she had learned about Anna Soloff was that the painter had not deceived herself. She'd seen quite clearly what her relationship with Karl Rattner was doing to her older son, the damage being inflicted by the violence and undisguised hatred. Jonah was right; Miranda needed to look harder at the paintings, to make her work more about *them*, but the ancillary parts of Anna's life (if children and domestic life could be called "ancillary") held too great a fascination. In her diary, Anna had written, "No one understands, I need a man like that." *Like that* was open to interpretation, of course, but in another sense it was entirely clear. In another diary entry, she'd written, "After the exhibition at the Frumkin, Karl and I had a good discussion about Philip Pearlstein's nudes. He read Aaron a story before bed." Intellectual harmony, and a sweet domestic scene. Peter Pan in the lap of Captain Hook, being read a bedtime story. Did it undo the other parts of the domestic scene, that Karl Rattner offered her moments like this one? No, of course it didn't. It only complicated things in a way the outsider—the biographer—had to take in. Anna's politics were unassailable, her work spoke for itself. It was motherhood that presented the problem, motherhood and sex. Was it essential that she entirely *approve* of Anna?

Something in Anna's self—willed destiny—to be a great painter—had required an apparent duplicity. Had required the negated saintliness of living with Karl Rattner. That was what Miranda had to figure out, in order to be true to her subject. The way Anna had endured this awful man—gotten something from him—without being broken by him. "I need a man like that," slung out in that Bronx-girl argot that Anna affected in her diaries. It was the hardest thing you could ever hear coming from a woman, because of course you knew what it meant, and Miranda got it, at least a little. The lure of the brute. She had fantasies of sleeping with Jonah. She had none of sleeping with Aaron, who was altogether too at ease in himself and seemed to need nothing. But Jonah fulfilled a different psychological requirement, the one that always got women into trouble, to find need in a flawed man, and to feel that you alone could answer it.

She took this in, on the bench, stared up once again at Jonah's apartment, half expecting to see him in the window, ghostly, entirely alone, strangely beckoning in his pose of incipient brutality.

She was due to meet a group of friends in Brooklyn that night. Miranda and her friends got together when they could, everyone busy (though one or two sadly, and unmentionably, not), the Barnard girls with whom she had maintained close friendships, all of them now just over forty, some with babies (having waited as long as they could), some, like Miranda, still not quite at the point where they had given up hope. Even with no man on the horizon, the eyes locked on the details in celebrity profiles, didn't they?—babies had at forty-three, forty-five, even fifty. You were ashamed of the way you noticed, and then fixated on, the details.

They ate in tapas bars, Middle Eastern restaurants. They drank a lot, laughing about their "drinking problem." Miranda was hugely grateful for these women—self-dramatizing though some of them were (one was an actress). Tonight, though, when she arrived, she couldn't help but feel a bit detached. Jonah Soloff always did that to her, created in her a space of difficult self-appraisal. The way he described Anna's look after spending the day painting a nude body. It was like that, in a way, being with Jonah. Like spending the day with a nude, studying its life, its angles and seams, its ordinariness, its meat-like essence, its collapsing muscle tone. She had the feeling of not being able to leave him, imaginatively.

One of her friends, Casey, was talking now about her husband's limitations as a father. The others laughed it off, they didn't really want to talk about men tonight (besides which, they had their own critiques of Casey's husband). They wanted to go somewhere else, or nowhere at all. To sink into one another's soft, comforting bodies, as they'd once done in beanbag chairs in the dorms at Barnard. Now there was the scent and sharp tang of zaatar, and berbere. The deep comfort of being six women at a table, in Brooklyn, in 2014. Miranda stopped thinking about Jonah. Forced herself to stop thinking. She dipped warm pita into a pot of hummus the color of what Casey called "baby vomit." "Stop!" one or two of the others shrieked (Casey's imagery lately tending to land, annoyingly, on the infantile). They laughed. Miranda, joining them, kept feeling little pulls of panic, indefinable. What if she couldn't make this book work? What if she failed? How would she talk about it with these women? The warm pita and the delicious hummus slid down her throat and she touched the friend beside her—Laura, the actress—and convinced herself it would be all right, she would get it, she would be able to line things up perfectly, and avoid the disaster that came from going too far into the rabbit hole of obsession. She would find a way to understand Anna's choices.

Yet even as she tried to be present here with her friends, her thoughts kept turning back to Anna, to Anna and motherhood, and to the sometimes brutal men who brought motherhood into being. The compromises that asked to be made. Say what you will, Anna had never fooled herself about the men she chose. Even in the midst of her poverty, she'd had the boys, wanted them desperately. "I guess I've got to be a mother," she'd written, the Bronx curtness you could almost hear coming off the page. "Got to." What choice did you have, when a man like Rattner came into your life, wanted to fuck you, big cock and force and Chinese food that would arrive in the midst of your poverty, even if there was none for your older boy. In secret you would feed Jonah, while Rattner was in the bathroom. Like a bird sneaking food into her baby's mouth. "Here. Quick." When the crayons went out the window, you turned away, looked at your canvas, the thing you were doing, the thing that, Miranda supposed, justified everything.

There had been a rain shower just before dusk. Now, outside, on the darkening Brooklyn street, there was a kind of tingly, post-rain haze that Miranda tried to see, through the window, as Anna might have seen it. Couples on dates, the boys with their wet, deftly piled hair, thick layers and buzzed parts, man buns (God, whose idea was man buns?) and the girls with them, girls who would have to subsume something in themselves if they weren't to break up with these beautiful boys, or else be destroyed by them. Boys who, in spite of their gentle affect, might be no different, when pushed to their limits, than Karl Rattner. How to see the world for what it is and not turn away? In the restaurant, the waitresses with their long exotic earrings, their huge thick cornrowed hair. It is as if we have all transcended something, traveled far from the *Mary, Mary* world. We are past that now. Now we will *see* everything, and will not be trapped. What visual detail did you have to land on to see the illusion, the self-deception in all this? How would you paint this exact scene so that you could *know* Brooklyn, know women and their choices and their sad compromises, in 2014?

Someone, one of her friends, was saying something to her. She had missed it.

"What?"

"Your father's play. When does it open?"

"Oh. Thursday."

"Thursday? My God. Are you excited?"

"Sure."

"'Sure'? That's all you're going to say? You've seen it already, right? In previews?"

"Yes. I've seen it."

But she said nothing more.

On the afternoon of the day of Henry's opening New York City suffered a torrential rain that lasted for about an hour and then receded, giving way to one of those oppressive late-spring suns that made you almost wish for the rain back. "Is this a good sign or a bad?" Henry asked, standing at the bank of windows in his apartment facing southwest over Hell's Kitchen. Miranda had gotten there early, was sitting at a table covered with congratulatory notes Henry had already received. Lily was in the bathroom, fussing.

Henry's suit was new, purchased at Barneys, beautiful and sleek and tinted in a range of colors—deep copper, green. He approached Miranda and asked her to touch it.

"What do you think?"

"Beautiful."

"Too extravagant? Too Beau Brummell? I may have to return it in the morning, depending on what the reviews say."

She offered encouragement, which required a little forcing.

"It'll be fine," she said.

"Shut up." He smiled at her.

Henry looked quite handsome tonight, had gotten himself a very good haircut, and Lily had touched it up with just the right amount of product to make him look slick and professional and confident. Michael Gambon not as Miranda was growing used to seeing him—as the heavy drinking reprobate father figure, somewhere between Magwitch and Mr. Micawber—but Michael Gambon as the head of the CIA, seated behind a desk, his finger pressed to his chin, seeing the world in its entirety as no less graspable than the prism paperweight on his desk. The only aspect of him that undercut confidence was the way he kept eyeing the small row of liquor bottles on the shelf that separated the kitchen from the living area. "If only I could have one now," he said. "A small one."

"You can't, Henry," Lily called from the bathroom. "I will not have you staggering down the center aisle of the theater."

"It's just what they expect," Henry said, looking suddenly glum. He squeezed Miranda's shoulder.

"Come hook me, someone," Lily said.

Henry gestured to Miranda that it should be her.

Her mother was wearing a black dress, lace around the neck reaching down to the bust, vintage—as most of her clothes were—with the most delicate of hooks at the back.

"Please don't let him drink," Lily whispered.

"I won't."

She attended to the hook, took in Lily's scent, wondered what this evening must be like for her, this woman who had triumphed in this world but held it now in such disdain. Lily's skin seemed full and rich to Miranda; her mother was letting herself get a little plump, claiming she didn't care. Regarding Lily's large, dramatic face in the mirror, Miranda thought she could step onto the stage right now, she had the size and the force. She was like the woman in Soutine's great portrait *The Old Actress*, all seeming kindness and repose except for the capering mouth, which stored an unsated ambition. And perhaps, Miranda thought, that was what this night was for her mother, a fulfillment of what was left of ambition, a waving to the crowd. Hello, yes, it's me. A great actress in retirement. I trust you haven't forgotten. I could still do this masterfully. That is, if I chose.

"Text Philip, will you, Miranda, tell him not to be late," Henry called.

"*You* text him," Lily shot back.

Their testiness with each other was opening-night behavior. The play was Henry's, but something of the drama of the evening would inevitably be appropriated by Lily.

"There," Miranda said, having worked the hook through the delicate thread, and watched her mother regard herself in the mirror. Would this do? Would this face do?

For Miranda, the evening would be something of an anticlimax. She had seen the play in a late preview. As with most of her father's plays (there had been at least seven she'd been old enough to see), she'd watched with a certain trepidation. She watched the audience more than the play, attuned to their rustlings, their coughs. When she'd been younger, she'd thought every male character in his plays had been him, every dark urge displayed on the stage a clue to who he was. She had outgrown that, but there was something in this new play to return her to her adolescent guessing game.

The composer in *Third World*—Henry's surrogate, she assumed— was staying, along with his wife, at the summer house of friends in the Berkshires. He was there to be honored at Tanglewood. The young musicians—the student orchestra—were giving a night of his music. A big dinner is laid out before they are all to leave for the concert. Deliberately missing is the daughter, the one child of the composer and his wife. A troubled child, the single issue of a clearly troubled marriage. The wife had wanted more children, the composer refused to have any more, all was to be subsumed into the effort required for his brilliant career, which amounted to this minor honor at Tanglewood—not the large venue but the small, not the BSO but the young people's orchestra, the students. At the end of the celebratory pre-concert dinner, everyone goes off, but the wife stays behind, saying she'll be right along. Then, just before the first act curtain, she opens a new bottle of wine and sits at the cleared table, puts up her feet. Her statement, her protest. She will not be right along. She is not even going to go.

It threw Miranda somewhat, this choice of Henry's. There was no way to find the obvious cause and effect, if indeed there was one. Miranda did not see her mother as having sacrificed a great deal so that Henry could have his career. During her childhood and adolescence, it had been she and Henry who had bonded, while Lily appeared in plays—busy, always busy, sometimes leaving for weeks on end to do a juicy role out of town. Mother Courage in Minneapolis, Arkadina in San Diego. She would return and need to retreat to her bed for a week afterward. Henry would take up the slack, time on his hands, his early plays not quite the successes he'd hoped.

So the mystery of the play, the question as to what, psychologically, Henry might be trying to work out through this onstage marriage, troubled her a little. Had her mother wanted more children? The subject had rarely come up, and when it had the answer always came down to Philip, whose surprise entrance into their lives had upended plans. Philip who had become the second child, the much-desired son. But as with all Henry's plays, it was not until she saw them for the third or even the fourth time that she could begin to ask such questions. The audience demanded to be attended to first. And on the night when she'd seen it, there was one particular member of the audience whose reaction to the play interested her, in a way, even more than her own.

Aaron Soloff had been her date for the evening, his long legs folded uncomfortably, one over the other, seeming alternately intrigued and a little bored by what was happening onstage. At one point, when he had taken out his phone, checked it for messages, she had turned toward him and whispered, "You're not allowed to do that." He had playfully put one hand over his mouth, in his eyes a look that said, *Those rules are for others, not for me*, before he agreed to shut it off. For her, something in his behavior had left a clear message: he could not take any of this seriously. And his reaction had its effect on her: you could be intrigued by sections of this play, made to laugh. But the great collective moment that a play was meant to be was not happening here.

Afterward, Aaron had invited her for a drink in his neighborhood. She was still not asked up to his apartment, the inner sanctum closed to her, the wife, the son who still lived at home. The bar he took her to was the bar of a restaurant in the west sixties between Central Park West and Columbus, elegant and quiet, a bar that seemed to have been there forever, and one where it was important to be known, to be nodded to by the bartender, an older man who Aaron said "used to be in musicals," the way he might have said, "used to crew at Yale," as though certain experiences were meant to remain proudly, nostalgically, but irrevocably in the past.

In a similar situation, Henry would have drawn this bartender out, forced him to talk. Aaron let things lie. They drank wonderful martinis.

"And now you have to tell me," she finally risked asking.

"Tell you what?"

"What you thought."

Aaron sat up straight at the bar, as if he'd been called upon to recite something.

"Well, your father doesn't know much about psychotherapy. That's the first thing."

He did not apologize for what someone else might consider, what her friends would call, a *dis*.

"And what's the second thing?"

Aaron said nothing at first, then spoke to the bartender. "Lawrence, sing something beautiful for us. Sing 'My Boy Bill.'"

Lawrence smiled in a minimalist fashion. He looked depressed, but settled comfortably into his depression, as though it were an unfashionable haircut he would never think to ask his barber to alter.

"You're not answering," Miranda said.

"No. I suppose it was a good play."

She ought to have felt encouraged.

"Suppose?"

"I don't go to the theater much."

He gazed into the smoky mirror behind the bar, took himself in, a small moment of narcissism she noted, and was unsurprised by. In the first flush of mild intoxication brought on by Lawrence's superb martini, she thought how comfortable this had become, how surprisingly comfortable she was to find herself ensconced in Anna Soloff's world. The little boy of *Aaron, 11* was sitting beside her, pushing his hair to the side, regarding himself. Some part of the life that she considered legendary—the life of the Soloff apartment on 107th Street—was here, breathing, alive beside her. It was a small but genuine thrill to consider this. Then in the next moment she thought that half an hour before they had been at her father's play, and now it might as well not have existed. *Third World* was fading already. She'd experienced a moment of terrible, painful loyalty. It should have been more. The whole evening should have been more.

She recalled that moment as she regarded her mother in the mirror. Her large, dramatic, gorgeous but inexplicably uncomfortable mother, looking at Miranda as if to say *What?* It was only another opening. Nothing enormous was at stake. Whatever the result of tonight, the Randos would go on being the Randos. Lily would return to her life, her clothes and her flowers and her books. Henry would write something else. Money would not be an issue, at least not a huge one. *How to Be This Age* continued to sell, and reruns of *Lawson's Bend* could still be seen on those little monitors that appeared over exercise machines in gyms, the face of the silver-haired, mustachioed leading man as indelible an image of the eighties as the MTV logo. Lily and Henry's world was not on the verge of being made or unmade.

All of this was true, but Miranda still experienced a moment of painful discomfort, recalling Aaron Soloff's dismissal of her father's work. Something she had always known, without being able to speak it, had been confirmed for her in that elegant bar.

Henry's first inkling that the evening might not go as well as he'd have liked came to him as he surveyed the opening night crowd in the Friedman Theatre. There had been photos taken outside, the theater's publicity staff making much of him, photographs taken beneath the marquee, Lily under one arm, Miranda the other. But this was all internal cover. The truth of the evening would come to him in smaller, less protected moments.

On the way to his seat, there were those whose hands needed to be shaken. His agent, a few old friends he had invited. But as he looked around, he noticed the telltale absence of celebrities. Who was there in their stead were the theater's rich backers, and this seemed a deliberate ploy on the producers' part. Anticipating failure, they had packed the house with donors so that in the morning they could say, "Well, we'll lose a small fortune on this, but you do see that it's *worthy*, don't you?" Checks would be written, costs covered. Had the play elicited buzz, the stir of a hit in the making, there would have been a different composition to the audience. Henry looked around for the familiar bald pate, the shiny Robert E. Lee–ish beard of Harold Prince, and did not find him. Nor did he see any of the well known actors who might have come, faces familiar from other openings. He could see no one but a few minor actors, veterans of some of his earlier productions. It did not necessarily mean disaster. But it did not presage success.

It took him a few minutes of such surveying to notice the black-and-gray head, the carefully manicured beard of Paul Livingston. Good God, Paul Livingston had come. Of all people. *Why?* And who was he with? A woman, someone older than him, which made her as old as Methuselah, as Paul Livingston had to be nearing seventy. He checked on Lily, to see if she'd noticed him. She clearly hadn't, was engaged in conversation with an actress in the row in front of her. He would tell her, he would not hide from her the fact that Paul Livingston was here.

Henry and Paul Livingston had very briefly been lovers forty years before, in the early seventies, when the actor had been cast in one of Henry's first plays. Already, Henry and Lily had been living together, happily and, Henry thought, quite romantically, so it was a surprise to feel such a powerful draw in rehearsals to this awkward, quirkily handsome young man. And of course, the "surprise," once it had led to their sleeping together, was something he had to confess to Lily, earning himself a large bruise from a picture frame she had thrown at his head in retaliation. It had nearly ended things between them, and had been the last such indulgence he'd allowed himself. Lily had forced him to choose, and when push came to shove, it was clear to him what he needed more. What he had needed was *Lily*, but in the heady days of the early seventies, he had believed that boundaries could be tested, that the door had not closed so firmly on the openness the late sixties had briefly promised. He could still remember the massive, days-long fight he and Lily had over it, could even remember that fight with a certain nostalgia, given how it had ended, with an explosive, tearing-at-each-other bout of sex on a park bench in Riverside Park, at dusk. But even given the distance of years, he found Paul Livingston's appearance tonight unsettling.

Thoughts interrupted by the arrival of Philip, looking dashing, dressed in the sorts of clothes Henry could never have envisioned for himself even when he'd been younger, that brilliant attunement to style that Philip had taken on in his early adulthood. Henry stood to greet him, relieved. "Well, you nearly didn't make it." Kissed him on the cheek, wished everyone in the theater might witness this. *This is my beloved son, in whom I am well pleased.* Clasping him in a way he felt might foment jealousy in the theater crowd, for most of whom family life was either a fantasy or an afterthought. Whatever the success or failure of this play, look what I have! Look how I am wrapped tight in this, protected! He did not catch the look on Miranda's face as she watched him greet and relish Philip's presence. It was too late anyway. The lights were going down.

From the beginning, the laughs weren't there. Not quite. At the reading the year before, Sam Waterston had made Henry feel that he was rivaling Noël Coward, but Waterston's replacement, a good workaday actor, seemed from the beginning cowed by the responsibility of a leading role, the need to shoulder the burden of carrying the play, drawing the audience in, all the things a genuine star does with the ease of splashing water on his face. A genuine star touches his ear and the audience leans forward, riveted. An actor lacking that quality has, instead, to sweat blood to draw the same attention. All of this had been evident since the start of previews, but Henry had still held out for a miracle. What it meant was that the play needed to do the work on its own, no happy tugboat assisting it.

Still, they pushed forward. Moments worked, undeniably. Then coughs came where they shouldn't have. Philip shifted in his seat. Henry recalled all the afternoon walks, the post-writing walks in the woods where he had been so convinced he was writing a masterpiece. It was as though his friend the beaver had arrived in this theater, had taken an aisle seat, and was regarding Henry with beady-eyed authority. *I tried to warn you.* In the aisle ahead of Henry, an old man was leaning forward, asleep, nodding awake only for the laughs. By the time the killer line arrived—"I'm not sure I believe anymore in universals"—the audience seemed unstirred. More coughing. How had it been that he'd thought he'd been writing something profound? Of *course* there were no more "universals"! Henry's poor composer looked like a fool for seeming crushed by the Pakistani girl's response.

Still, it was not all a disaster. The wife's end-of-Act-1 decision to skip her husband's concert seemed to surprise and intrigue the audience. The lights came up on a small buzzing—always a good sign. Henry made his intermission escape, not even checking with Lily or Miranda, not wishing to hobnob. He found his way through a side door down into the bowels of the theater, where a couple of stage hands nodded glumly to him. He opened the stage door into the alley beside the theater and lit a cigarette.

At a distance, down at the end of the alley, he viewed the

opening-night crowd filing out onto Forty-Seventh Street. From their movements, he could gauge nothing of their response. Cigarettes lit, texts checked. It seemed a silly business, this thing that had once been a dream, to come to New York and become a playwright. To have been a Newton Highlands boy, an Italian boy, adrift in the world of his father and uncles, the world of manual labor, trucks and small machines. He could feel sentimental about them now—could even feel the strength and honorableness of many of those men—but not then, not when he'd been very young, and plotting. Then, in his dreaming days, the mid-fifties, it had been the plays that had come into Boston in their pre- and post-Broadway runs, plays with titles like *Middle of the Night* and *Pipe Dream.* To see the names on the marquees of the downtown theaters, to stand outside and watch the crowds pouring in, had been like becoming aware of a Shangri-la just on the other side of the lobby doors. Now he stood in the alley of an actual Broadway theater, a man who had *gotten in*, but something was drifting down the alley, an old newspaper, a candy wrapper, a noise behind him suggested a rat might be rooting among the trash cans. When Henry peeked inside the stage door, he saw an old woman, one of the costume crew, carrying a torn shirt that needed to be sewn, shouting to someone else, "He ripped it!" He had stepped into the pages of James Joyce's "Araby."

It was a moment to bring Henry back, again, to the men of his childhood, the ones he had most respected, those few who had managed to make small fortunes out of the bric-a-brac of immigrant existence. Suppose they had been in the theater tonight, those heroic figures of his childhood, all dead now—Vinnie Lopez and Joe Defina and Freddie Tortolla. No doubt they'd have been dazzled by the unfamiliar "glamour" of a Broadway opening. But the play itself? Its concerns? Its removal (and, by implication, Henry's) from those basic things they considered central to life? Is this where his escape had led? To this etiolated work, these feeble jokes, this bird-seed tossed to a Manhattan crowd that, at heart, could care less? Had falling in love with the theater—those plays on Tremont and Boyl-ston Streets, the posters, the promised life inside—been only a way of avoiding the harsher judgments that had been placed upon him—silently, surreptitiously, but with ultimate clarity—by those men? The thought stayed with him. He could not easily brush it away.

The second act seemed to go a little better. It was shorter, for one thing. At the end, the applause was encouraging, with a smattering of standees. But when Henry stood, a few pairs of eyes glanced immediately away from his. Others seemed warily polite. His agent, a tall, somber man who could have stepped out of the pages of a Sloan Wilson novel of the fifties, whispered to him, "Even if they'd all been throwing their hats in the air at the end, we'd still be at the mercy of the *Times*." Yes, thank you for reminding me. And for pointing out that they *weren't* throwing their hats in the air.

When he turned to Lily, her face appeared drawn. It was the first time she'd seen the play; she'd read it, of course, and offered her usual severe criticism. Now, she wore the postcoital smile of a woman who had failed to have an orgasm and was trying, unsuccess-fully, to convince you that it didn't matter. Miranda did not quite look at him, which troubled him even more. Of the four in his lit-tle group, only Philip offered enthusiasm, clapped him on the back. "That was great, man." But he sensed Philip might only be trying to cheer him up, and though he was grateful, he was not encouraged.

There was, of course, the necessity to go backstage, to congratu-late the actors, to pretend it had all been a triumph. Henry's director, an angular young man, three decades younger than Henry and al-ready on to his next project, had only managed to see the second act, and wanted to know "How was the first?" A party was to be held in the basement of a restaurant taken over by the theater. Philip begged off, claiming an early-morning meeting. They waved goodbye to him on Seventh Avenue. "Great," Philip repeated. "Your best." They watched him disappear, his white silk scarf trailing in the light wind.

The rain that had come in the afternoon, then held off, reappeared in droplets only sufficient to annoy the three of them as they made their way to the restaurant. Henry summoned dignity enough not to beg his wife and daughter for comfort. There was no way to see the shape of the evening as anything other than an arraignment, followed by a sentencing. The *Times* review—there was no hiding the fact—would seal his and the play's fate. Lacking a star to sell tickets, they would be dependent on the regard of the popinjay who now held the seat of power. As soon as he entered the restaurant, Henry saw his agent posed by a door, behind which, he knew too well, the theater's publicity people were sitting before their computers waiting for the review to come in.

"Please tell them I'd like the strongest martini possible," he said to the theater staffer who approached him to ask what he'd like. "We'd *all* like one, the three of us. And after the bartender has handed you the strongest martini possible, hand it back to him and tell him to double the strength."

Henry considered it another not-good sign that the theater staffer seemed to have no sense of humor.

They found the table that had been reserved for the playwright. There was no great onrushing of enthusiastic congratulations, though there was, to be sure, some. The producers all huddled at a distance, but, significantly, he thought, not waving acknowledgment. Their martinis took their time coming, but when they finally arrived Henry thought he had never tasted anything so deliciously welcome.

It was Lily who seemed to be attracting the attention. Yes, well, that was understandable. No one had seen her for a while. When are you coming back? Glenda's doing *King Lear* next season, did you hear? You'd be a perfect Kent.

At such gatherings, Miranda tended, predictably, to fade, to give way to her glittering parents. Henry touched her hand. "Are you all right?" She nodded. She hadn't loved the play. He hadn't expected her to embrace it, though it would have been nice. "Don't worry," he whispered. "This too shall pass." They sat at their table like island dwellers, watching ships glide by. Had it not been for the martini—he had already asked for a second—it would have been excruciating.

And suddenly Paul Livingston's face, hovering above him, a face grown equine with age, distinguished, with a touch of career disappointment about him as light as the taste of marsala in zabaglione. "Henry, you've done it again," he said. "What have I done again? Sit down." "Well, yes, but look who I've brought with me."

Lily did not have time to react to Paul Livingston's presence, because the woman Paul had brought along, his date for the opening, was—Henry recognized her now—the distinguished octogenarian wife of a hugely famous British actor who had left her at the height of his fame. Having banked her own career ambitions for years (the children, the need to accompany her famous husband to the Academy Awards), she'd followed up his public betrayal by enjoying an extraordinary second act, playing dowager queens and Tennessee Williams's aging heroines brilliantly. She and Paul Livingston had had a shared success two decades ago in a revival of *The Milk Train Doesn't Stop Here Anymore*. She and Lily exclaimed at one another like schoolmates who hadn't seen each other since winning a field hockey trophy half a century before. "What are we doing?" the actress said, and sat next to Lily, immediately helping herself to a generous sip of Lily's martini. "Letting these men have all the fun. Look, next season let's do *Waiting for Godot*. The female version. It's high time."

"Fine," Lily answered, "except that I *loathe Waiting for Godot*. And don't think you can steal my martini. Paul, go get her one."

How comfortable it had instantly become, the man he had fucked forty years before having become so neutered and familiar, a pet Lily could order around. And Henry had so worried she'd be upset by his presence!

He turned again to Miranda: Was there any pleasure at all to be had in invisibility? In watching her parents perform?

"Henry, your play was brilliant," the actress said.

"Well, it wasn't. But it's nice of you to say. Now please do try and get my wife back on the stage. Suggest another project. Let's 're-think' the classics, shall we? I'm seeing you two in a lesbian version of *The Sound of Music*. Maria and the Captain."

The actress lifted her chin, assessed Henry's joke, deciding it was not quite good enough for laughter, only good enough for a smile. Looking at her, some gap in him opened. An awareness of an effort-fulness he would have to maintain until it was okay to leave, the weak jokes he would have to make, the affectation, the hahaha.

He turned and saw that the wait for the actress's martini might be a long one. Paul Livingston had been waylaid by a stout, attention-hogging publicist, a man ubiquitous at these events. Beyond him, at the door of the war room, Henry's agent was speaking to someone—Henry didn't recognize the man—his agent's head lowered somberly, nodding. He could not help but think that every sign was bad. He turned to Miranda and considered grasping her arm and taking her away from this. Lily and the actress were lost in conversation, inter-rupted only by the actress's übertheatrical "And this is your *daughter*." Miranda nodded, flicked her hair away, valiantly enduring all this. The surprise was to find Paul Livingston's return, the gifted martini in hand, sitting next to Henry, the two of them old men now, old men in suits, with careers behind them, in a city transformed under their very feet. Opening-night parties in the seventies, when they'd been young, had been raucous, held in Village bars, where they'd had to sidle up next to bikers at the bar in order to get a beer. And who, in

those days, gave a fuck what *The New York Times* thought? Except
that they had, of course they had, though they'd pretended not to.
As he'd said to Miranda at their dinner, they'd all been socialists.
Socialists until they'd caught a break. Socialists who wanted, deeply,
to be noticed and feted. Over Paul Livingston's shoulder, he watched
his agent going on sagely nodding, the report he was being given a
long and ponderous one, apparently. What did it mean?

He said to Paul Livingston, "You know my daughter Miranda,
don't you? Surely you've met."

"How would we have met?" Paul said. "You're absolutely lovely
and I'm sure you're accomplished as hell, and your father has never
introduced us."

Paul touched Miranda's hand, providing her with the name
Henry had not gotten around to giving. Paul, too, had had women
over the years—rumors always floated through this little world—
but he had come down firmly in his own camp. Now he seemed
to be flirting with Miranda. Was everything to be so vexing tonight? Henry scoured the crowd once again, the sea of those who all
seemed to be holding something back from him, some cruel judgment, some comment on the foolishness of his presumption. To have
forced them to endure what he now felt was a weak, flawed thing,
a piece of work that should never have been exposed to this unfor-
giving world. To have actually revealed his own feelings about the
third world of consciousness, something of real importance to him,
something that marked him out—as so few things did—as a seeker,
a man trying to claw his way toward something of seriousness. You
did not do that in this brassy world and expect to get away with it.
Or maybe—the thought crept in, and he was undefended enough
to allow it—you could only do this if you were a greater artist than
Henry Rando. He'd allowed himself to become known as the Erma
Bombeck of male decline—did he seriously expect this crowd to
suddenly treat him like Strindberg? He remembered his walks in the

woods, and as he did, glanced across the room and saw a woman in a black dress laughing uproariously at something the man beside her, a hawkish-looking little man, had said. They were not laughing, or even thinking about, *Third World*. And there he'd been a year before, wrapped up in his scarf, holding a makeshift walking stick, trudging through the snow like some latter-day Flaubert, not searching for but congratulating himself on finding, with such consistency, le mot juste. Oh Henry, what a genius you are! How they're all going to love this work!

"I think I need a cigarette," Henry said very suddenly, and stood. He was not sure what exactly had done it, pushed him over the edge, but to sit at this table a moment longer was not something he could endure. "I have to have a cigarette."

"Since when do you smoke?" the actress said.

"I smoke on unbearable opening nights," Henry answered. "As we all should."

The actress smiled again, as if this was another acceptable, not brilliant, joke. Before leaving, Henry caught Miranda's eye. He could not abandon her here. "Come with me," he said.

"Henry, don't take forever," Lily called.

"Oh don't worry, " the actress reassured him. "We have endless reminiscence to carry us through the night."

With Miranda on his arm, Henry managed to pass through a crowd of well-wishers, all of whom seemed to know exactly what the verdict of the *Times* was, and offered thinly veiled sympathy. A winding staircase would take them up to the street. Halfway up, he heard his agent call to him from below. He turned, noted his agent's unreadable expression, the man's extraordinarily proper tailoring, shouted "Later," and they were outside.

"I'm sorry, I could barely breathe down there," Henry said, his breath coming a little fast as he took Miranda by the hand and pulled her down Fifty-Seventh Street in the direction of Fifth Avenue. The rain, as if on cue, started to pick up. "Fuck," he shouted up to the sky, directing his words toward a God he imagined as taking a personal interest in tormenting him this evening.

A pair of passersby glanced at them.

For Miranda, this was familiar, a rage she had grown used to in adolescence, then convinced herself he had outgrown.

Henry turned—he wasn't proud of himself for this—back toward the entrance of the restaurant, imagining he might see his agent bursting out with good news.

"We'll just find a dry place, if one exists, a place where I can smoke." He tried to affect calmness, saw that he was not fooling her.

"Dad, are you okay?"

"We'll just get far enough away from the restaurant so that it's impossible to run into anyone."

"Dad."

"Ever. From the theater. *Ever* from there. *Again.*"

Even in the grip of whatever had come over him, he felt his own overreactive propensity. There was something so cowardly, so unmanly about what he was doing out here, this reaction to what he perceived, or maybe only feared—the theater's failure to wholeheartedly embrace him.

"I'm sorry," he said, and touched her on the shoulder, a gesture of apology. "I'm too old for this, Miranda. I'm just not up to it anymore. The fucking *silliness* of it."

In the entryway to a large, gilded old building, he lit a cigarette. He smoked with impatience, with a lingering anger at himself. Then he looked at her, saw how attentive she was being, felt ashamed of his own self-involvement. Drops of rain touched her forehead.

"Come in, come in out of the rain, Miranda."

He pulled her toward him. When she was close, he said, "It can't be easy to see your father like this."

He tried to smile, to adopt another attitude.

"I should have stopped while I was ahead. I should have stopped when I was fooling people that I seemed to have the secret. The key. I *don't*, Miranda."

"Do you expect me to be surprised by that?"

They smiled at one another. This was good. *Becoming* good. Just the two of them against the world.

"Your father is a terrible fraud. But then you've always known that, haven't you?"

"Dad, stop this."

"All right."

"First of all you're not being silly. I imagine this must be emotional."

"Yes," he said, and stopped there. Allowed her to see his real need and disappointment. No keeping her from it. Most men, he thought, are not given the opportunity to allow their children to witness their failures in the world. The stumbling. The public turning away.

In the grip of this, he looked past her—it was too difficult to maintain the direct gaze; she was being too kind to him—holding her hand tightly but looking up at the high-rises on Fifty-Seventh, feeling the city closing in on him. His blissful morning cigarette across from the parking garage where all those Broadway flops had been immortalized. He had just added one more to the list. And where had they all gone, the authors of those shows? He could see their faces, ones not unlike his own, still—hungry men (and given the theater's history, it would be mostly men) asking the question: You mean you're not eager for more of me?

At the end of this thought there was another, more of a reminder than a thought, whatever had come to him, or come over him, in Haiti: There was something else to be done, and he'd ignored it. He remembered the boy Jean's face. The words "You will come back?"

But it was Miranda's face that was before him now. When he looked at her again, he didn't know quite what to say, how to alleviate her concern, how to meet a kindness he didn't feel he fully deserved.

"It's okay," he said to her, and stroked her neck. "It's really okay."

"Is it?"

"I will survive this. I have survived worse. You need to tell me what you thought, Miranda. Be honest with me."

Her hesitation told him everything. They were suddenly awkward with one another.

"I need more time, I think."

He waited.

"You know I need to see your work a few times."

"Yes."

"But it was *good*."

He knew. The word "good" did not land anywhere in the region of deep meaning.

After a moment, he found himself shaking.

"Dad, what is it?"

"It's just the rain."

But that was a lie. In truth, he couldn't say precisely what had come over him, he only knew he felt suddenly very vulnerable to her. The feeling was like that of standing in very cold water.

Miranda seemed to have recognized the shift at the same moment he had, and took a step back. It was too much, his need, finally too much. She wanted to be free of this moment, free of the burden of him, free of the need to assuage failure. She understood that her duty was to stand by and comfort. Still, it felt too much. His endless need for recognition, his continuing need for reassurance. Yes, you are seen. Yes, you are taken in. Now let go a little.

She had never felt more grateful than she did when, turning away from him, she saw his agent standing under the restaurant's marquee, calling his name.

2.

It had come as a complete surprise, her agent phoning Miranda to offer her a month in the Wellfleet house. The house, owned by the agent's former long-term partner, would be vacant for all of August, her renters having found themselves, at the last minute, unable to take their vacation. The rent having been paid, and the owner unhappy at leaving the house empty, she had called and asked Miranda's agent if she knew a reliable writer who could use a free house on the Cape. The agent had laughed at that, then gone down her list of clients stuck in the city for summer's most sweltering month. Miranda had been fourth on the list.

"We're old dykes, and we're dykes of a certain generation," her agent had said on the phone. "We can't call up our kids and ask them to check on the property. So consider this your lucky day."

Miranda had no trouble subletting her own apartment for the month. Her money was dwindling, and the first half of her modest advance was going to have to last through the year. To be gifted with what would amount to a free month—her only expense would be food—was not something she had to consider for even a moment before saying yes. Not to mention the opportunity to work on the book, unimpeded, in a beautiful place. She was told she wouldn't need a car. The house was on an island that jutted into Wellfleet Bay. There were bikes in the shed, and the nearby general store, while it had gone in and out of business for several years, was open that summer.

"You'll finish your book," her agent said. "You'll be so bored you'll have nothing to do but write."

The largest expense was the train to Boston, then the Provincetown ferry. An Uber took her to the island—the only way to get there, she was told—but they arrived at high tide, when the wooden bridge connecting the island to the mainland was uncrossable. The driver—an older man, one who had been a fisherman in what he called "the good days" (he told her only as much of his story as he cared to), informed her there would be a two-hour wait until the tide was low enough to allow her to cross. He also told her the charge for sitting there for two hours, so she elected to let him go. She had the address of the house, but no idea how long a walk it might be. "The island's not so big," was all her driver told her before leaving her there with her suitcase and her two bags of books—heavy ones, a thick, newly published volume of Anna's early paintings from the forties among them.

There were families jumping from the bridge into the salty channel that had risen two feet above the marsh, leaving the road submerged. No way to cross and walk over without getting her luggage soaked. Foolishly, she had not thought to refill her water thermos. She would have to wait, parched and hot. On the other side of the bridge, alongside the long paved road, the high marsh grass resembled tufts of infant hair combed upward. She stepped toward the water that had covered the road, then took off her shoes, lifted her skirt, stepped in. The water was warm. She could feel the salt essence touching her shins and calves. The families on the bridge regarded her for only a moment before resuming their frolics. Big-bellied men with their sons. Women. The little boys leaped, legs wide. The moving tide carried them downstream a bit.

For someone who left New York so infrequently, there was a minor shock in considering there were still families like these, all-American families who seemed to exist outside the modernity of Brooklyn, that anxiety for perfection in the young families she saw on a daily basis. These people did not belong to the island but to the mainland—their cars and trucks were parked on this side. There would be wealth on the island, her agent had warned her—"It's all new money or families that have been there forever"—but for now these young families owned the bridge and the tides. Miranda stepped farther in and let the water reach her lower thighs. She realized she did not know the rules, of anything. A woman on the bridge, a blond mother with her hair pulled back in a tight bun, looked at her, and she thought she must seem strange, lonely, inscrutable, a woman who had been deposited here by a taxi, with a suitcase and bags of books. Like a heroine in a novel who would likely go through some self-inflicted difficulty before righting herself.

By the time the tide receded sufficiently for her to cross the bridge, the families were largely gone. The last one to stay did not even regard her as she rolled her suitcase over the bridge's wooden slats. The paved road—really a causeway—was puddled. On either side were shells and marsh grass and a sense of distances that lightened and affected the air. It felt like a world of crustaceans, shells opening and closing, gasping just enough of the air before retreating. Miranda was the interloper. She found herself voicing an apology, to no one, to the air. At the same time, she was thrilled. A month here. What would happen? Even if nothing, she felt the time ahead, in its closed-off, isolated being, as precious. The word "vacation" came to her in its literal form. She was vacating something. She was leaving a shell.

The paved road gave way to a dirt road that ascended, bracketed by pines. She saw the first houses, set far back, retreated, full of glass. She knew the address of the house she was looking for: 14 D Street. D Street. The name suggested an unexplored precinct of lower Manhattan, only bluer, saltier. D Street was the first named street she passed. It was not possible that the only house visible, a house that seemed to slouch over the marsh on invisible stilts, pale yellow wood—was the house where she would be staying. She had been told where the keys would be—in a jar under a large bucket on the deck—and there they were, and yes, they opened the door. Into an enormous room that took up the entire first floor. At a distance,

Great Island appeared across the water like the vision of Bali Ha'i in the movie her father had once forced her to watch, and then watch again, on the creaky VCR. She gulped enormous mouthfuls of water, sat on one of the stools surrounding the kitchen counter, and felt no wish to move.

It was not as though she hadn't known beauty. The summers in Eastham (and Eastham was not far from here, just on the other side of the bay). Even the grounds of the house in Grantham, and the wooded hills surrounding it. And her junior year had been spent in Florence. Beauty was not unknown. It was just that she had lived so long in the caverns of Brooklyn, where a liveliness, a mix of sound and smell, substituted for physical splendor. She went out onto the dock and lay on a chaise longue and found herself lulled into an eroticism composed of salt and wet light and pure solitude. Then she realized she had no food, nothing at all to eat. Perhaps July's renters had left something in the refrigerator, in the cabinets. It did not matter. It was a concern for another moment. From the deck she looked over the bay to a group of houses built on a bluff. Something here felt settled, unchanged for decades, the gables and the arches of the roofs seeming like the architecture of a more leisurely past, though she knew in a more logical part of her brain that the Cape was becoming like Brooklyn, a wealthy hipster element coming in, unconstrained, saying "Yes, we'll take this, too." She remembered the morose, homely face of her Uber driver, telling her he didn't fish anymore. The sea had been fished out, but for city dwellers like Miranda Rando, you came here and convinced yourself that for weeks, or months, the world was not a rushing, self-absorbed battle for limited resources but a place where you could still purchase timelessness.

What she found in the cabinets was a half-full box of pasta and a can of tuna fish. Also, Texas Pete's hot sauce and a row of condiments. She did not want to consider the disgusting meal she could make of such ingredients, but she knew she would not go shopping, not leave the island until tomorrow. She went down to the large bedroom on the lower floor, its windows facing the water, and lay down, exhausted. A row of shells lay on the sill. The paintings were not the traditional seascapes she might have expected in a house kept for summer renters. The owner's sexual tastes did not hide themselves—fuck the rich, conventional families who would come here for weeks, for a month. Make them look at the vaginal foliage of some Cape artist whose name Miranda didn't recognize, big red wet blossoms unfolding. The owner's tastes varied widely enough to include a homoerotic drawing—a bad one, Miranda thought—of two young men in a rowboat. It was comforting to sink into this room, this bed. She slept until near dusk. It was not until you left the city that you realized the weight of fatigue you carried. After waking, she walked down to the water, the beach at low tide, thick beige sandbars and a couple walking their dog, moored boats collapsed sideways into the tidal mud. She had been told there was a kayak here for her use, one marked with the owner's name, among the similar ones lined up like a row of crayons in the sand. She sat on a small rise, the marsh grass behind her, and found herself crying. Not sure why, except there was a power in gratitude. "Be careful of the ticks," her agent had warned her on behalf of the house's owner. She cried for her agent, her agent's generation, too, women who could no longer feel the way she did now, this openness, this idea—she was sure it would be gone by morning—that anything might still happen.

Dinner was to be gotten through. She made a concoction she didn't want to think about even while she was eating it. She ate like a sailor, only to fill her belly. Wine would have been nice, but could wait. Everything could wait. She lay on the blue sofa and dozed again, woke in full dark. In as few clothes as possible, she stepped out onto the deck. There were the lights of distant houses across the marsh, the sound of very occasional cars. The notion of stark isolation, of possibly entertaining a reason to be afraid, was not to be indulged. An emptiness surrounded her, bounded by lights.

The book containing Anna Soloff's 1940s paintings, published in concert with a well-publicized exhibition, lay open on the table the next morning. Miranda had begun the day by bicycling to the general store, buying coffee, milk, bread, fruit. She could think about dinner later. It had taken half an hour to get the shed open where the bikes were stored, having misread the directions, and she had forgotten as well the owner's instruction to bring her own helmet. She rode in a skirt. She felt the wild freedom of potentially exposed underwear. Who cared? On the bike path she noted the urgency of her fellow vacationers, their Lycra outerwear, the timers they wore on their wrists and consulted.

Now, the book open before her, she needed to force herself to concentrate. Anna had spent the forties trying to decide what to paint. Or, more likely, who to be. In her diaries, she admitted to a callowness, a *how dare I?* attitude toward painting. She'd been born in 1920 on Thieriot Avenue in the Bronx, her father a furniture maker, her mother a woman who limited herself, at the beginning, to mothering. There had been a succession of brothers, but Anna had been her father's favorite, the oldest, the only girl. As the thirties progressed, two things happened: her father's business thinned, and then failed altogether, and she'd been asked to leave school at fifteen. A job first in the garment district, then, as soon as she'd come of age, as counter girl at the Chock Full o' Nuts on Thirty-Fourth Street. She'd taken the subway. Her brothers were to stay in school. ("The old story," Anna had written later.) The other thing that happened was that word kept arriving from Europe of the fate of her mother's family in Poland. One after the other. Another old story. In her diary, Anna wrote, "My mother gets up, gets dressed carefully in a good dress.

She does her hair, puts on lipstick and perfume, then her energy saps. The day is over for her. She sits in a chair and sinks."

She had her first lover at sixteen, a neighborhood boy who had taught her how to ride a bike. ("Ouch," she had written in her diary, regarding the sex.) When she was twenty, her father hanged himself in the small factory where he'd gone to work. Up until then, he'd been chipper, positive, loving to her, but it was as if the mother's bad news from Europe had gotten to him in ways hidden, internal, finally unbearable. Also, failure had done its old number on him. He had used to hold Anna up on the mantel above the fireplace in the apartment on Thieriot Avenue, sit her there and say the single word "maidele."

Somehow Anna had found her way to the Art Students League. Her second lover was a tall, thin, affected young man she met there, a man named Arthur Messinger. She'd drawn him nude, and the sketches were still with her when she died, though they were not good. During the war, she'd found her way to the docks on the West Side, the Brooklyn Navy Yard, pulled toward the sidebar motions of the war. She'd painted men, workers, soldiers, her heavy influences all male: John Sloan and George Bellows, those driven painters of the twenties, their city figures leaning forward, as if into a wind, New York all hurry, all crowd, all tight muscles and blazing lights, and some nameless madness drawing them all. The only really good painting from the early forties, Miranda considered, was one Anna called *Adoration of the Magi*, a painting of three men on the docks of what Miranda assumed was the West Side, attending to a fourth, a man who had been severely injured in an accident. She was young and learning something about placement in painting, the important figures located off to the side, begging the eye to look there and not at the painting's literal center. A huge cargo ship dominated the right side of the painting, the men on board paying no attention to the small tragedy. ("About suffering they were never wrong, the Old

Masters," Anna had written on a postcard from around the time of
the painting's composition.)

The first sign of Anna's eventual greatness did not come until
the later forties, when she'd painted *My Mother's Remarkable Second
Act.* It was a portrait of her mother on the subway, colorful, Chagall-
like in its way, the subway posters advertising nothing but figures
of the painter's fancy, with simple words like "Cigarettes," "Face
Cream." Rosa Soloff had gotten a job during the war, a clerical job,
and had ridden the subway every day to midtown Manhattan. The
figure in the painting was tilted slightly to the left, wearing a small
hat with a flower on it, clutching a brown bag. But smiling in a way
that seemed brave and resolute, as if the woman—Anna's mother—
had reached the stage of life where all the available tragedies had
exhausted themselves, been used up without using *her* up. Three
sons were still away at war, hostages to fortune, but this woman who
rode the subway to work every day had found—had clutched from
out of thin air—an immunity. Rosa Soloff worked the clerical job
until she couldn't anymore, then moved into Anna's 107th Street
apartment and died there, attended to by Anna and the two little
boys.

Miranda pushed the book away, not ready for this, not ready—at
least not yet—for the required immersion in the succession of tragedies. It was almost too much, to reconcile the world of Rosa Soloff
with the clean, empty blond wood table on which the book containing her portrait lay. Miranda turned away from it, looked out over
the marsh. In her work on the biography, she had reached the late
fifties, the time of the blossoming of Anna's great loves, just before
the birth of Jonah. But she kept returning to those early years, the
thirties and forties, she hadn't gotten them right yet. How a Bronx
girl, a counter girl, a girl whose early journal entries showed no great
acuity, no lush sensibility, how that girl had learned, so vividly, to *see.*

Anna had joined the Communist Party in the early forties, encouraged by her early lover Arthur Messinger. ("Without Arthur I would not know politics," she had written. Though they had apparently stopped being lovers, he continued to tutor her in what she called, in one entry, "A Course Called the World.") She had attempted to convince the other counter girls at Chock Full o' Nuts to join the Party, but they were only looking for men, waiting for soldiers to come home, ready to move into apartments and fatten up and have their babies, girls hungry to go off and populate Long Island with the fecundity of poppy seeds. Though, from her teenage years onward, the Young Communist League in her neighborhood had been the primary site of her social life, she did not take the Party fully seriously until her early twenties. She asked some of the men, the leaders, if she could paint them, and this led to a series of workmanlike paintings of men with jutting jaws and deep-set, skeptical eyes, men clutching *The Daily Worker* and regarding the apprentice painter, the young woman attempting to capture them, with amusement. She was not yet good, only earnest. (It would take her own view of her mother to make her good.) One of these men, a novelist, became her lover. (Her agent handled this man's estate; his best-known novel, a proletarian thirties epic, had been filmed twice and was still in print.) The man had treated her badly, but taught her something. If Arthur Messinger had taught her A Course Called the World, this writer had taught her, apparently, A Course Called the Body. Anna went to school on men. When the soldiers came home from the war, she painted the scenes of homecoming minus the triumph. She had done a version of the famous *LIFE* magazine victory kiss in Times Square, only in Anna's version the sailor lifted the woman's skirt, grabbed her with a wide palm that wrapped itself all the way around the woman's exposed thigh and up the left cheek of her ass.

Miranda had to get this right, this development, this girl becoming a painter by looking hard and attentively. But perhaps not just yet, not in this light. Wearing only a bathing suit and a sheer blue shift, she walked down to the beach, feeling guilty for leaving the work-table, but not cripplingly guilty. The tide was at its median point, she decided to take the kayak out. The one belonging to the house's owner was dark blue, her name—BECKER—chalked in yellow. There was an honor system here, none of the boats was tied down. The paddles were back in the house's shed. She brought one down and eased the boat into the water. She hadn't used one of these boats in years, but found herself relearning the simple skills quickly. From her still point out in the channel, she regarded the beach, a couple with a child, a group of older bathers talking, academics from the looks of their gestures, men who hadn't been in business, thin chests tilted upward toward dominant heads. Men without mass.

Looking at them, Anna would have seen something more, seen the defining characteristic that made this moment a historical mo-ment, limned by its exact placement in time and space. Miranda, though, wanted to see it on her own, to train her seeing. She felt her own limitations, but not as a criticism; instead, as something that could be worked on. She dipped her paddle into the clean water. She would make this a daily practice. Then, as the heat became too much, she would go inside to engage with Anna and the forties.

She began the practice the next morning, waking early, making herself coffee, bringing it down in an old carrying cup she found in a cupboard. Sometimes she brought a book. The house's bookshelves were full of biographies, most of which tended toward strong-willed women whose romantic entanglements had not been crippling ones. (Was this a deliberate theme?) Jane Bowles. Lillian Hellman. Ame-lia Earhart. Djuna Barnes. Skipping through them, Miranda found herself less interested in the achievements than in the information about how these women had dealt with the problem of sex. Her own quickened interest amused her. She left the book and her towel on the sand, cast off in the early morning light, paddled downstream toward the grass-enclosed marsh. As the days went by, she found she had to pay stricter attention to the tides. The channel narrowed so much at low tide that if she were not careful she'd get stuck out in the middle of the bay.

The oyster beds began to emerge as she went out on the lowering tide. They were lifted above the ground, some of them hammock-like, others resembling miniature Potemkin villages, with sloped roofs. Hard, sharp poles protruded around the boundaries. She hadn't been warned (who would there be to warn her?), came too close on a couple of occasions, when the water barely covered them.

At lowest tide, the oystermen arrived, men in brown coveralls, men who made noise as they trudged through the mud. Their work seemed lazy, slow. If they noticed her, they offered no indication. They studied the raised beds, shifted them, made low comments to one another, pulled oysters out and deposited them into net bags. She allowed herself to remain in the emptying channel until there were barely two inches of water under the kayak. There was something she wanted to know about these men, their slow movements, their talk, these low-tide lives. An earnestness, a wish not to distract herself, propelled her to shore, to the work, the forties paintings, the love affair with the novelist, Anna's growing disenchantment with the postwar world, that world so willing, so eager to choose quiet and optimism, to ignore what had been opened and left gaping by the war. The work went on for Miranda, but she looked forward to mornings, to low tide, to the sight of the trucks that deposited the oystermen at the boat landing, their casual dressing and trudging, and the high voices shouting to one another. It was important to her that they not look at her and see just another rich tourist.

It seemed, in retrospect, inevitable, the day she got stuck. She had been playing it too close to the edge, making her way to shore when the tide was at its lowest. She guessed she had enough strength to drag the kayak over the exposed bottom. What she hadn't counted on was the sucking mud in this part of the channel. She stepped out of the kayak and felt immediately sucked down, her water shoes no help at all. It was difficult to move, took a large effort just to lift her feet.

After a short time, she became aware that the oystermen had noticed her. Their talk had ceased altogether. She saw their heads tilt toward her, then away, like shy boys at a dance. Finally one of them shouted, "You okay?"

He had to shout it twice before she was certain he was directing it to her.

"No. I don't think so."

Something inaudible passed between the men. Then she saw one coming toward her. Even with his high boots movement was slow.

"You misjudged, I guess," he said.

She noted that he was not smiling, not joking or flirtatious, was treating this with some seriousness, a problem in physics. He was tall with thick black curly hair, not a boy, but located somewhere in the long term between boyhood and the later, duller part of manhood. He pulled at one side of his coverall as he spoke to her.

"I can prob'ly drag the boat to shore if you want."

"It's hard for me to move. You're right. I misjudged."

He glanced down at her pathetic water shoes, smiled to himself in a way that barely registered on his face. He had strong lines around his eyes but the rest of him seemed youthful. One of the regular men, unremarkable, like the sort-of-handsome soldiers Anna had painted. He was probably thinking how ridiculous she was, how ridiculous they all were, people who didn't understand tides and mud.

"I'll pull the boat for you. See how far you can make it on your own," he said.

He was still not quite looking at her, which made her more embarrassed, as though to look at her would be to charge her with the full weight of her folly.

"It gets a little easier once you get a little higher."

He grasped the handle of the kayak and started dragging. She tried to follow but he was very soon far ahead of her. Her progress was slow and she was aware of the other men watching her.

From the shore, where he'd deposited the kayak with relative ease, the man waited. The mud underneath her finally allowed more of a grip. He waited until she was all the way onshore.

"Tide'll be up high enough in an hour or so you can get it back to where the others are," he said. "The others" stood out for her, like he knew everything, knew the habits of everyone on the island, knew that she was a tourist, nothing was secret. He seemed conventionally competent and strong, a self-effacing man in his late thirties or early forties, earthy and part of the island life that endured after the summer people left. But as she thought this, she considered that it was her own thinking that was conventional, she had no idea who or what he was, and determined to look harder at him but was too embarrassed by what had happened. It seemed only half her vision was available to her, she could not read his look, his face, but was convinced, afterward, that something mysterious had been there, something just outside the mechanics of the scene. There had been the tiniest attempt to pierce her with his eyes, before he'd turned away, an attempt to place her based on what he knew. And what he knew—or thought he knew—that small dark mystery that had been there for just a second, was what haunted her afterward.

For three days the tide was too low at daybreak for her to take the kayak out, and though she wanted to walk the beach, she was still embarrassed enough by what had happened that she did not want to be seen by the oystermen, and especially by the one who had helped her.

She set up a beach chair at a distance from them and read about Lillian Hellman's struggles writing *The Little Foxes* and looked up occasionally to see if they were watching her. She convinced herself after a while that it had been insignificant, what had happened, they had forgotten her already, so she moved her chair farther down the beach. It felt like a small act of defiance, powered by her own loneliness, and by something else, something she didn't want to examine too closely. The only people she spoke to during the day were the people behind the counter of the general store and at the package store, and occasionally when she biked all the way into Wellfleet Center to buy fish.

On the third day, she noticed him looking at her. That was all. She felt like a teenager, a girl who would go home and write in her diary, "He looked at me." It seemed that basic, people's movements toward one another never moved far, in subtlety or profundity, from the schoolyard. The fourth day, the tide was just high enough to support her in the kayak and he noticed her again but did not wave. He was alone at the oyster bed on the fifth day when she pulled the kayak up onshore and approached him.

"I should thank you," she said.

He looked up and there was a small smile that seemed a little too knowing, as if he'd expected this and was trying to manage his own expression, to master it.

"For what?"

"For the help. The other day."

"All you'd have had to do was wait. Tide'd come up, you'd be on your way."

There was something so matter-of-fact about him, it disappointed. There was a plainness, an unadornedness to certain lives—the flat voices and the uninflected words—that sometimes put her off. But she stayed there.

"How does it work?" she asked.

"What?"

"These beds."

He regarded her, still trying to figure something out. A man like this would probably expect to be flirted with. It was so classic it was almost boring, the lonely woman and the man of the earth, or in this case, of the sea. What protected her was that she was not certain. Why not simply talk to a man?

He nodded in the direction of what looked like miniature silos raised above the bottom.

"See those? Chinese hats?"

"Is that what they're called?"

He hesitated a moment, registering perhaps that she was from the world where such expressions were disapproved of.

"Oysters float in. Attach to a shell in there."

It seemed all he was going to say.

"And then?"

"Wait for them to grow."

He was standing over a large netted case suspended on poles. There were oysters inside. He lifted the case and shook it.

"Then they go in here. Till they get too crowded."

He continued to glance at her, then away, as though he were suspicious, or else questioning her actual interest in what he was telling her.

"And do you—what?—work just this part of the beach? Can anyone just come along and—?"

"No. We lease it. There's different farmers here. Guy over there buys seeds from Canada. You could ask him, we all do it different." He seemed to be growing more careful with her. "My father-in-law has the lease for this section. We do clams, too. You just walked over one of the beds."

"Oh." She was apologetic, but fixated on the words he'd just said. "Father-in-law" meant a wife. Of course. It was as if she hadn't heard anything after those words. But now she had to pretend to herself, as much as to him, that she was still interested in what he was telling her.

He was ready to walk away. There were pails and a net nearby, and a small boat that would carry him back to the landing.

"Can I buy some from you?" she asked.

"Sure."

He hadn't hesitated, and when he looked at her she saw that small, sly smile again, the one he had to manage, the one that indicated he knew this scene only too well, had played it many times before. But he was not—here was what was significant—yet bored by it.

"I can drop some off. Which house is yours?"

She told him.

"We're not supposed to do this. Before you sell one of these, you're supposed to have it checked. Make sure it's cold enough."

"Will they be cold enough?"

He hesitated, not looking at her, making himself busy, matter-of-fact.

"How many you want?"

She told him a dozen would do. Meanwhile there was this annoying thumping of her heart in reaction to her boldness. She wondered if he could tell. The light shifted slightly on the sand and on the low water, like a bedspread being pulled back. No, she decided she didn't like that image at all.

"Go and take a look at the Eastham house," Henry was saying to her on the phone.

She didn't answer at first.

"Why would I do that?"

"For nostalgia's sake. For *my* sake. Take a picture and send it."

"Yes," she said. "Sure thing."

The past. Of course. For Henry it was all about the past, though he would deny it, put the burden of past-fixation on her and ask what was wrong with her, that she dwelled there. Go and recover the past, Miranda, trace in the sand at low tide the wiffle ball games that were all for Philip's benefit. She was surprised by her own stored-up jealousy, the summers when it had been all about Philip, some male element in Henry that had had to be tamed in order to bring up a daughter suddenly loosened. Henry's ability to be entirely physical with Philip. From a corner, adolescent, she had watched, nursing her own quiet rage.

"Listen, never mind that," she said. "How are you doing with the—?"

"With the what?"

"You know."

"My deep disappointment, is that what you're referring to? My—oh God, here's where I'm getting old. I can remember nothing. What's the line from Thoreau? The famous—".

He was talking to Lily now. Miranda knew the line he was seeking but decided to wait.

"Your quiet desperation," Lily was shouting in the background.

"Yes, that's it. That's it exactly. Is it my quiet desperation you're referring to, Miranda?"

"Not so quiet, apparently," she answered.

Henry's play had failed, as he'd known—at least suspected—it would, the night of the opening. Lukewarm reviews, not terrible but indifferent ("a paean to male menopause," one wag had written) combined with the lack of a star's drawing power had led to weak box office and an early closing. About all this, Henry had joked. "Here's how God works," he'd said. "He gives you a nice little success, setting you up for the belief that you're in clear water. But God has indulged himself in too many viewings of *The African Queen.* Every time you think it's clear sailing, the next minute you're back in the water, pulling the leeches off your body."

Miranda had no idea what actual level of disappointment Henry's jokes were covering. She retained a sense of his mood the night of the opening, when they'd stood out in the rain, a sense of how complicated was his need for her. It had stayed with her, a heaviness. She was determined—it had become a necessity—to create a distance, a healthy distance from him.

Henry was planning another trip to Haiti. In September, almost as soon as Miranda returned from this hiatus, Henry would be leaving. "I've got to undo the bad feeling that opening left me with," were his words of explanation. She understood that his career was enduring one of its periodic silences, and that he was more hurt than he allowed by what had happened with *Third World.* "Haiti" had become, it seemed to her, a watchword for "healing," though Henry would never have used such a word. She only knew that he would be setting off in a very different mood. Terry Gross would not be waving a handkerchief from the dock.

Now, here, her month's sojourn already in the middle of its third week, these calls were becoming something of an effort. They had suggested coming for a visit, but Miranda had used the excuse of work to put them off. There was another reason, though.

Tonight, she had wine chilling in the refrigerator. It was near dusk, her favorite time. She would make another joke about Henry's "quiet desperation" and then hope she could get off. Henry did not want to get off, though, she could feel that.

She did, though, find a way to end the conversation, and then waited. Soon the truck would be pulling up, she would hear it from a distance, there were so few cars. He would be bringing her more oysters. It had become their joke, their flimsy excuse—"the oyster delivery," he called it. Though he no longer, not since the first time he had brought them, asked her to pay.

The first surprising thing she'd noticed about him—the evening when he'd first brought her the oysters—was that he wore worn, baggy jeans. It was late, she had waited for him, they'd been non-specific as to the time. If he hadn't come, she told herself, it would have been all right. Another man, a man of her own class, would have arrived in a pair of brightly colored shorts, snug-fitting, flattering. The men she'd most lately been with—Isaac the musician, Brian the arts administrator—had been like that. Bright clothes and un-shaven faces. Little straw porkpie hats, to declare their separation from the uncool world. But Armand DeSaulniers had arrived at the end of a day when it was clear he'd attended to a number of things before finding himself free to call on her. Work and perhaps a wife and perhaps children and then maybe a drink at a bar. His clothes were the clothes of a man who had done all these things and was not preparing himself to impress a woman. She felt like an afterthought, but was still glad he had come.

There had been an awkwardness arising out of their uncertainty as to what the terms were. Did she have a shucker? Did she know how to shuck oysters? Are you going to eat them tonight, or—? She wanted the oysters then, right then, when they were at their freshest. Careful, 'cause you can cut yourself, he said as he was shucking them. He had brought gloves for the work of shucking. After tak-ing them off, he showed her his hands. They were like the map of some thinly settled territory, big brown masses with red nicks and lots of dangerous-looking blue tributaries.

Afterward, she was surprised to find herself not ashamed. She waited for that emotion to come, invited it into the bed. It did not come. He had brought a condom, though only one, which could have meant he carried it with him all the time, or that he intended this to be brief and efficient and then back into the truck and home. Very little light seeped into the downstairs bedroom—no moon that night—and she waited for her eyes to adjust to what light there was, because she wanted to look at him, see him, see his body. He was, he'd told her, astonishingly, forty-eight. She had never slept with a man this old, and wanted to study a little bit what the differences were. Her last lover, Isaac, had been, comparatively, a boy, his body smooth and mostly hairless, but Armand had a body that seemed, even in the dark, like his hands, cut and marked and—she felt more than saw anything that established this—deeply *used*.

He'd slept and then awoke and wondered where he was. "It's me," she'd said, and understood that would mean nothing, she was very nearly anonymous. It had never been like this—never this unwary, this plain, a physical demand on both their parts and then no sense of what should follow, what should come afterward.

"You okay?" he'd asked, reminding himself of why he had come here, this house, the woman in the kayak, the unsubtle (she thought now) request. She felt like the greediest of consumers: I will have the house and the oysters and yes, the man, too, I'll take him. This is all my right. However much I want to detach myself from the rich tourists, I am finally and undeniably one of them. She'd watched him dress and thought: well, that's that. It was only at the last minute—she'd decided to accompany him upstairs, so that she could lock up after him—that he'd said "I could bring you more," and they had both laughed, indulging in the shared cliché, laughing at the fact that they were each willing to fall into it, drawing terms, making sure that it was fair enough, an understood thing. Like a handshake.

Armand. She could still not quite get over it, not even at the end of their first week together. That she was sleeping with a man named

Armand, a name that had the near-capacity to frighten her, it seemed so remote from anything she'd ever allowed herself to get close to. Her previous lovers—in addition to Isaac and Brian—had had names like Trevor and Gabe and Lucas, names given by parents intent on raising sons whose lives they'd hoped would not be too disappointing. They had been callow men, mostly, satisfying in their ways—some of them, anyway—but wanting in some essential substance. Being with them had sometimes felt like baking a cake in which you had left out something important, but couldn't name it until the missing taste was on your tongue, and then you thought: Oh yes, cardamom. Or anise. It was always the harbinger of the breakup, that naming of the absent ingredient.

Armand. None of those boys' mothers had thought to endow their sons with a clear and defining sense of belonging to a dying world.

What she came to enjoy almost as much as the sex were the conversations afterward, the way—after teasing him into it, working on his hesitation—he enjoyed being drawn out, sitting up against pillows pulled up to the headboard, like she were going to do something to him intensely pleasurable but requiring passivity. She had the sense—more than the sense, because he told her outright—that other women did not do this, did not ask him to render his life in words.

He was, he assured her, separated from his wife. She did not know whether to believe him. She knew it was the convenient thing to say, to claim that word "separation," because how was she to know for sure until a woman came to the house with rage on her face, and just possibly—why not?—a gun in her hand? He told her the saga of himself with one arm drawn up, his head resting against his big hand, amused at her wanting to *know,* still a little hesitant and careful, expecting at any minute that she would grow bored and ask him again for the more dependable physical gesture, the thing she had asked him here for in the first place. But as soon as she saw him leaning into that, she would say no, I want to know more. Then his sly smile would appear, him looking at her, saying: I'm not that interesting. And she, within the same silent exchange, saying, Yes you are. Of *course* you are.

All right, then. He claimed to have three children, two girls, fifteen and thirteen, and a boy, ten. A couple of nights later, he was willing to reveal the cause of his breakup with his wife. A woman who had hired him and a few of his friends to do renovations on her house (it was what you did after the oyster season ended in January) had gotten pregnant by him. She expected nothing (she lived in Boston, spent summers in Wellfleet), it could have been clean and without repercussions, except that his wife had found out and thrown him out. Another girl, this fourth child, and the child's mother wanted nothing more to do with him after the baby was born. He lived now, post-breakup, in a cheap rental, a room in a house owned by a fellow oysterman. He released these details almost in an attempt to minimize himself, to show Miranda how little his life amounted to, yet the wonder was that he seemed so unashamed. With his free hand he stroked her shoulder and her neck as he spoke. The essential thing in life was the sensual, was touch and texture and the near-constant surprises that came his way. A woman in a house whose walls were stripped, wiring exposed, saying: I want a baby. A woman on a beach who said, Come and fuck me and then tell me your story. In the bed he allowed gaps to follow the release of information, as if he had to newly consider the things he was telling her, as if he were surprised by, and trying to encompass, the fact that this string of events constituted a story that held and encompassed *him*. When she sensed this beginning to scare him, or simply confuse him by its system of heretofore unexamined links, she allowed him to fuck her again. No, "allowed" was the wrong word, because she enjoyed it too much. He was dorsal, a marine-like creature in the act of love. It was his element.

He was the sort of man painters like Marsden Hartley had gone up to Maine to paint, drawn away from the limitations of New York, gone up to where there were waves and rocks and young men— peacock men—lounging on piers. It was as though Armand were posing for her, one eye cocked, trying to determine what she wanted, still a little suspicious. He told her how, ten years before, a woman in many ways like Miranda, a woman from the literary/journalistic world of New York had come to Truro, bought a house, and begun searching for a man to get her pregnant. She'd found one, a local fisherman, legendary in that way; she'd had a baby and then been murdered. Something hung over this arm of the Cape that was like a Lorca play, a revenge tragedy. The pastoral gave way to something else. You could not share a bed like this, attempt to dig into a world like his, without summoning ghosts, horrors.

In the mornings, when she took out her kayak, she saw him less frequently; the tides had shifted. The oystermen came at different times of the day, most often when Miranda was at work, forcing herself, in the hot afternoons, to type and revise sentences, to try to understand the forties and fifties, to comprehend the choices of another woman's life. She suspected he told the other oystermen about her, that they gossiped in their way, that they referenced the dead woman, and the other woman, the one who had approached him in her pared-down house with the simple demand, to which he had acceded, as what man in his place would not? Sometimes he came in the afternoon, work ended early, the heat, the shore flies. One day she cut his hair, he stepped naked out of the outdoor shower and sat on a beach chair and she clipped away and thought of him there, making himself entirely available, with no future, no plan. There were stories he told her that she didn't want to hear, she covered his mouth, *No, don't tell me that*, waitresses who asked him to wait behind the restaurant in his truck, to wait for their ten-minute break in order to service them. He laughed when she professed shock. What do you think this

world is, Miranda? There is a world outside of Brooklyn, where people do this. On his belly and his upper chest were scars—she'd never
been with a scarred man before, a veteran of bar fights. He showed
her stitches in his head from where he'd been clunked with a glass
stein. At her repulsion, he laughed. Do you still want to know me?

What was hardest to take was the story he told her one day, a story
about a boat ride he'd taken with his three children. It was a simple
story, he'd told it simply. He'd borrowed a motorboat from a friend
and taken the three children out for a spin, and she could not help
but see that boat ride with a clarity that frightened her. The teenage girls, and who was this man, their father, at the helm? How did
he hold them, protect them, what was the chaos he presented them
with? It made her, strangely, want to cleave to Henry, who, whatever
his difficulties, had always established an order, an encompassment:
here is the place where you are held, here is the sustaining world.
But out on that boat there had been only the four of them, and Armand's inability to hold them in a state of cohesion. Miranda felt,
listening, an entirely new fear, because of the thought she'd begun
having, the thought that hovered at the edges of her mind, and was
pushed away, and kept coming back.

She was forty-one. It was her last chance. This was not exactly
true, but still it *felt* true. She lay in bed after Armand had gone—he
never stayed the night; it was as if it went against his code—and heard
those words and tried to close her mind against them. *My last chance.*
She held a pillow to her belly. They always used condoms but she
still felt an urge to lift herself up into the bridge position in yoga and
allow his deposit—whatever had not been held by the condom—to
travel upward. It was a sordid, ridiculous urge. "No one understands,
I need a man like that." She heard Anna's words, felt she got them
now in some way she did not want to admit. Her previous lovers felt
like water, like fluid, something passing; they had been permeable

men. Anna had understood that aspect of things. You met a certain unacceptable man, you fully *got* the unacceptability, and it still felt like touching granite. This was only a thought you could have while lying in a bed, on a promontory stretching into a bay, the air salty and alive, with the feel of something strange still on your body, a scent you weren't even sure you liked, like the fetid smell of deep low tide in the marsh. *Here is what it is.* You thought that, and resisted it, it was ugly, it evoked disorder, the antithesis of what was safe and enduring. You saw the three abandoned children on a Boston Whaler, waiting for their afternoon to be over, their dutiful afternoon with this man who was only chaos, only appetite, a force of unreliability. You thought these things, saw them clearly, and still lifted your legs and thighs up into the bridge posture to help the seeds swim in the right direction. Out of the millions produced, perhaps a thousand escaped the condom. If one reached home, it would be out of your hands.

She thought, too—in the late-evening hours—of what it might actually be like. For him to come to Brooklyn, to visit, become a part of her life. It was like a fairy tale she couldn't believe in even while in the act of creating it. Imagining Armand in the Brooklyn restaurants, the hummus and the spiced chickpeas, all the sorts of food that spoke to a certain self-selecting hipster element, and Armand wondering, Who do you have to fuck around here to get a cheap burger? And Armand, meet Casey and Laura and Cynthia. Meet Bree and Lauren. The way they would smile, and try to be accepting, and then what their eyes would look like. Miranda could see exactly the manner in which the assessment would go on, the way their looks would doom him as a partner: No, this is unacceptable, this choice reeks too much of desperation, Miranda. The only acceptable partners are the impossible boys, noses pointed toward their laptops, earbuds in their ears. Their beards, and their hats, and their ambitions. She could already envision the moment where she would decide, after Armand's first visit to Brooklyn, or his second, not to invite him again.

"Oh God," Lauren would say to her afterward. "I knew you couldn't really be serious."

Serious was the bridge posture she couldn't help but go into after he left. Serious was the calculation: even if it was not to survive as a relationship, could he possibly help her financially if she were to try to bring up a child alone? This is where it all fell apart. He was already supporting three, living in a cheap rental, surviving on work the income from which could be wiped out in a single bad season. A woman did not come to a man like this on the shore and say: Give me a baby, and also, could you help support it? That was never part of the deal.

Still, she searched for an opening, wondered at herself as she did so. Did you always arrive at this moment if you managed to put it off this long, pretending for too long that there would come a right, perfect moment, a respectable partner? That myth—the "respectable partner"—that Anna had known enough to smash through when the moment arrived for her.

The first of the fathering men in Anna's life—Enrique, Jonah's father—had been the essence of unreliability. Anna had known this. She'd left the decent man she'd been dating, a businessman, an artistic hanger-on, and gone back to the club where she had noticed Enrique sketching in a corner, hoping that he'd be there again. Brazen, wearing a red dress ("I felt like Ava Gardner in some movie I can't remember," Anna had written in her diary), she'd invited him up to the apartment in Spanish Harlem and seduced him. She'd been stunned by the indifference he displayed toward everything she offered him: the food, the wine, the paintings she showed off. Even her body, she wrote, he regarded like a late-evening cognac he could take or leave. She thought his sketches primitive, he would never succeed as an artist, he was full of himself that way but she could see from the beginning the manner in which he, like a lot of men, deceived himself. *Of course I will make it. It's inevitable.* Something happened between them. Anna was at pains to describe it, and then gave up. She knew a child would come of it, her time had come, and when Jonah came to pass, Enrique married her with the same indifference with which he ate the dishes she'd learned to make for him, endeavoring to please. They'd never divorced. The marriage meant nothing to him. Eventually he went back to Puerto Rico, there were photographs of him in a box Jonah had handed over to her, an old man, a white beard like moss on his face, leaning against the wall of a one-story house, his shadow against the wall. "My father," Jonah had said, affecting a perhaps hereditary indifference.

Lying beside Armand—he always slept after sex, emitting low snores, careful ones, curt, edited ones—she could imagine the same fate for him. To become an old man in a bar, white-bearded, eyes glazed from drink. Yet for now, for this moment, he embodied some truth she wanted simultaneously to embrace and run away from. The same truth she suspected Anna had perceived: If you want the thing to happen, here is the messy, unacceptable way it must happen. Here is the chaos you must embrace. On the beach sometimes she watched families: blond women wearing sun visors, tall men with short hair and glasses, the acceptable men, two or three children tagging behind, a dog from one of the approved breeds. Miranda had left that possibility behind, that neat life, that life shaped to resemble the covers of L.L.Bean catalogues. She could not imagine spending years with a man like these men, doctors or financial analysts, with rooms closed off inside them, men who made jokes and bought expensive bicycles and were fundamentally terrified. She could not have done that, lived that orderly life.

Was this all just a way of linking herself with Anna? She indulged that thought, in the bed, the way Anna had proudly embraced poverty, had two sons in succession with no idea of how she would provide for them, and when the time came, marched into the admissions offices of Fieldston and Trinity and demanded a place for them. That fierceness she'd had to carry, with Rattner gone, with her canvases and the two boys and the view from 107th Street, and the belief that whatever was stacked against women like her, it would all soon be toppled. Something was coming, it was the 1970s, the old go-go postwar America had run its course and something new was coming, for women, for poor people, for blacks. She went on the marches, she brought the boys, she picketed. Richard Nixon fell and New York City skirted bankruptcy, and in the dark corners of Pete Martin's Eighty-Ninth Street bookstore young men and women studied the old texts to see what needed to be recovered, what had been forgotten in the postwar glee that had produced so much deception. How do we *get back* to what we'd learned in the thirties?

In bed, Miranda thought all this, considered what it might be like to embrace such poverty for herself, to embody such force and belief, to hold the hand of the son or daughter of Armand DeSaulniers and march through Brooklyn, saying, *We must prevail, we must.* The world must open up and allow us to prevail.

And as she did, she had to fight the accompanying thoughts, the ones eager to destroy the fantasy.

It happened in the middle of the night one night, after Armand had gone, after she'd lowered herself from the bridge posture, after she'd settled into the silence of the house at two in the morning. She became, for the first time, afraid of it, afraid of the isolation, the loneliness, the fact of being a single woman alone on an island. Maybe she'd been half asleep, she didn't know, but what came to her was an image of Brooklyn, of the high-rise buildings going up, the sheer size of everything. She blinked against it, she pushed it away, as if she were pushing away fear itself. *Don't be afraid,* she wanted to say to herself. *Don't.*

She was remembering a Beyoncé concert she'd gone to at the Barclays Center, the wild affirmation, being surrounded by young black girls screaming and crying and nodding their heads at what they were being told, the freedom and strength they were being encouraged to embrace. Then stepping out, afterward, into the real Brooklyn, all the new buildings and the unwelcoming names on the buildings, names that were not Shaunelle or Trayvon but names that reminded you of who it was who owned the world. The hardness of those construction sites that wanted to push you out, and you tried to hold on to something—*yes, this is who I can be, something great*—but you knew, as you felt yourself being poured out of the tunnel of affirmation, *This is the world, this is the world that doesn't want you to have choices except for what to buy.* Another class of person would move into those high-rises, would embrace the affirmations that had nothing to do with them but which they would still lay claim to because they were there to be consumed, included in the price of the ticket. It was that simple, that cold. It was not a world where you could clutch the hand of the child of Armand DeSaulniers and expect you were moving into a world prepared to welcome you.

She closed her eyes. Of course it wasn't true. Of course there were things like strength, determination, fight. Of course those were real things. And even if Anna had not lived when she'd lived, in the dark, hopeful seventies, that time of marches and women's demands and the belief that *of course, of course* it would all change, it *had* to. Even if Anna had not lived then, she would have done it, had Jonah and Aaron, painted, endured, triumphed.

Miranda simply had to encourage herself, that was all. Of course this can still happen. It only requires strength, belief, the immense courage that Anna Soloff had possessed. She tried very hard to summon Anna's voice, to turn it into a command. *Do not. Miranda. Do not be afraid.*

3.

The first thing that struck him was how little it had all changed. Two years had passed, but from the looks of things it might have been two weeks, or, at most, a month.

On the street outside Toussaint Louverture Airport was a poster featuring Michel Martelly, the kompa singer who had surprised everyone, three years before, by getting himself elected to the nation's highest office. Before his presidency, Martelly had been seen mostly shirtless, or in drag, thrusting his pelvis on the stage like the boys had on the roof project two years ago. Now he appeared in a suit, his head shaved like a successful black American politician, like he had learned, in the years since his election, how to transform himself, rendering the sexually suggestive taunts he'd used to shout from the stage mythical and abstract. *Haiti is open for business*, the poster read, as if the foreigners decamping from planes didn't already know that.

Dr. Walter Mackey and his son, Nelson, who had accompanied Henry on the flight (along with Sister Beatrice and her large brother, Brutus) stared up at the poster as if it were a shield against the sun. They were standing with their bags, while Beatrice spoke into her cell phone and Brutus went off to find their driver. To Henry, the doctor and his son looked like classic models of hapless Americans, saps here for the taking. Dr. Mackey had the look of one of those nameless actors you saw in old Westerns on TV, a bland face seen behind the teller's grille in a bank, or sporting a deputy sheriff's badge. Henry had to fight the urge to offer guidance, and an entirely unearned cultural wisdom. This was only Henry's second visit, while the doctor had been here a dozen times, had in fact founded a medical clinic in Fonfrède. How was it one could be a veteran of this place and still manage to affect such apparent innocence?

Unlike the last time, they did not stop in a fancy restaurant for a formal lunch but drove straight off, on the still insufficiently paved highway, toward Les Cayes. This time, Beatrice did not need to coddle them, ease them into the chaos. The settlement camp, the one Henry remembered, built on a golf course, seemed to have been decimated, and Henry asked about it.

"Sean Penn moved them to another camp," Beatrice said. "Even worse."

"Big mistake," Brutus said from the front seat. "But at least he knows it."

"Sean Penn," Dr. Mackey said to his son, as if the actor's name would familiarize this place.

"I know," Nelson said, unimpressed.

Even the light, Henry thought, seems unchanged. The first time you come to a place, you look hard at things, but the second time, a false familiarity inhibits your sight. It is all as it was. Working on him, too, was the sense that he had no real purpose here, this time. No do-gooder project awaited him; only his own need had compelled this. He had tried to re-form the old group, but Frank Murphy claimed the excuse of tiredness and age, and Jeremy, when he'd approached him, had looked piercingly at Henry and asked, "What for?" Which was precisely the question. "Personal reasons" was what he had said to Sister Beatrice when he'd approached her.

This time, too, they were not to stop in the splendor of the hillside monastery but were to sleep, Beatrice announced, in humbler quarters. "You will live above the school," she said, "the school" meaning a woodworking shop she had established for enterprising young Haitian men seeking to learn a trade.

All right then. Whatever must be. The towns they passed on the road held the same desolation that had seemed so exotic to him two years before, when he'd believed that just by arriving here, he could make an offering of himself to Haiti. He considered the man who had gone on that earlier trip a more roughly sketched version of the man he was now, a man who had suffered a major career defeat. In the seat in front of him in the van, he considered young Nelson, seventeen, a boy with all of life before him, regarding the green fields, the foliage, the ramshackle houses, houses that looked abandoned even though people clearly lived there, houses whose chief lawn decoration was often a discarded tire, and thought he saw, in the boy's profile, a dismissal that reached beyond the immediate landscape.

That was cynical, of course. The dismissal was all his own. Fight that, the cynicism that had come over him since the failure of his play, a cynicism he was surprised and a little ashamed of.

They were nearing the outskirts of Les Cayes; small, shabby businesses lined up on the sides of the road, tiny arched stalls and caravans selling soccer balls, Frisbees, hats. The most prominent posters here were for Digicel and Voila. These people could barely afford to eat, but they owned cell phones more complicated than Henry's. Nelson was nodding asleep and his father nudged him. The boy blinked awake. What? What was so important?

"You're missing it," Dr. Mackey said.

Beatrice turned back toward Henry.

"Does it look different?" she called to him. "Does it look changed?"

Henry's answer was a small, indulgent smile.

"It never does," Brutus said. "Never will."

But it didn't matter, did it, whether or not Haiti had changed. He had another reason for being here.

He had come to see Jean, that was all. To keep a promise. The words "You will come back" had come increasingly to haunt him. There were obligations in life. This was simply one of them.

Before embarking on this trip, he had made inquiries at Grantham Prep, had sat in the office of the director of admissions, a man named

Evan Hatch. Evan Hatch—dun-colored hair, small, expensive glasses, the body of an athlete who had mastered one of those sports not requiring bodily contact—had regarded him with mild skepticism, answered Henry's questions as though there were something behind them he was attempting to probe. Yes, Grantham Prep might be interested in a Haitian boy, but one must be not too quick off the mark. There was a test to be taken first—something called the SSAT, a test no doubt being given in Port-au-Prince. The boy's skills would have to be assessed. And there was something else to be considered before depositing a Haitian in a competitive American private school. Jean might do well to first spend a year in the States, under Henry's tutelage, taking classes at the local high school. "Acclimatization," Evan Hatch had said. The complications hovered like smoke from an expensive cigar in the admissions office, the slightly dowdy but still privileged, cracked leathery air. And the boy was how old? "Eighteen by now," Henry said. "Maybe close to nineteen." The lifted eyebrows of the man sitting across from him. "Cutting it close," Evan Hatch had said. "But we have a PG year here." "PG?" "Postgrad. Thirteenth grade." The understanding Henry had been left with was that however eager Evan Hatch might be to "work with" Henry, the heavy lifting would all be his.

He thought of all this as they reached their quarters, and discovered that he was not even to have privacy. The three of them were to bunk together in a large room containing half a dozen beds.

"You choose first, Nelson," the doctor said, and Nelson, sour-looking after his interrupted nap in the van, threw his bag on the nearest bed.

"That all right?" the doctor asked Henry.

"They're all the same," Henry said. "So long as he's happy."

He had tried for a joke with that—Nelson looked so patently unhappy—but with such people you had to hold up a sign: THIS IS A JOKE.

The view out the window was deceptive. Les Cayes lay on a cove—the water was the same luminous azure color he remembered from Port Salut—but as soon as you leaned farther out the window you noticed that the shore was littered with refuse that stretched from the edges of the shoreline thirty or forty feet into the water, until it floated. Wood and plastic water bottles and who knew what else? It occurred to him here, finally, on this trip (it had never occurred to him on the last): This is a country that cannot be loved. But love it you must, like a child you have spawned who will always be a burden. He would have liked to kneel, to pray, he would have preferred darkness, but they had arrived early, in full light, and Brutus, who had taken the single, closet-like room adjoining this one, was making large, unidentifiable noises in their shared bathroom.

There it was, then. He would be living in the unattractive world of maleness, with its scents and its grunts and its perennial aura of a faint soiledness. Henry had escaped army service in the sixties by a lucky break: a post-college year spent studying playwriting at, of all places, the Union Theological Seminary. It had been the heyday of a certain kind of "religious theater," led by the Reverend Al Carmines at the Judson Poets' Theater, and burying himself in a graduate program had given Henry an out. After that year the army seemed to have forgotten him. Now the horror of what that might have been like came back to him. He announced that he wanted to take a walk, to acquaint himself with their new surroundings.

Les Cayes itself might have been a stage set for a film no one had yet gotten around to making. Filmmakers who chose to set their films in "third world" countries opted for a spareness, an emptiness, a whiteness suggesting abandonment, or else set them in overcrowded marketplaces more organized than any you were likely to encounter in the actual third world. Les Cayes lay somewhere between these two extremes. There was something haphazard, not fully thought out about city planning here: a storefront followed by a house followed by an indecipherable structure. What almost saved the urban landscape was the brightness and variety of the colors, but even this did not rescue Henry from an attack of vertigo. The cathedral, mammoth and impressive and European in look, rose at the end of the main street. Beatrice had promised they would have dinner the following night with the bishop. There would be an order imposed on his time here, but he felt none within.

That night at dinner, at a table in the small kitchen adjacent to Beatrice's vocational school, it was Dr. Mackey who took it upon himself to keep the conversation going. Beatrice had her laptop open; arrangements needed to be made. She was like a mogul checking on her holdings.

"Henry's a playwright," Dr. Mackey said to Nelson, hoping to rouse the boy's interest in something here. "Broadway, right? He's been on Broadway."

Henry, more sensitive to Nelson's boredom than the doctor was being, raised his eyebrows in order to downplay the magnificence the doctor was attempting to thrust on him.

"Such as it is," he said. "And it's not much."

He meant it. This little kitchen, closed in, its walls painted maroon, the appliances the sort he might have found in his own grandmother's fondly remembered kitchen sixty years ago, seemed more real to him than his memories of the opening of *Third World*, the laughter and the drinks and the theatrical faces. It was a small comfort to feel this way, to find himself not clinging to any identity beyond his current one, whatever that might turn out to be.

Yet Nelson was looking at him with, at last, a vague but real interest, an attempt, perhaps, to put together the disheveled man sitting before him with whatever glamour he might have associated with the word "Broadway."

"Nelson's named after Nelson Mandela," the doctor said to Beatrice, hoping to impress her as much with that fact as he'd hoped

Nelson would be impressed with the reference to Broadway. But Beatrice did not look up from her laptop.

Raymond St. Jacques.

It was the curse of Henry's life—*one* of the curses—to possess a stored memory of every actor who had ever appeared in a film, and to want to reference those actors in small societies such as the one where he now found himself, where no one would have the faintest idea of what he was talking about. Yet Raymond St. Jacques was exactly who the bishop resembled, as he dipped his spoon into a soup the color of boiled crab. Boiled crab might actually have been the basis of the soup, for all Henry could tell. Bits of shell floated up from the bottom, and the bishop, with St. Jacquesian distaste, fished them out and placed them on an empty dish.

Raymond St. Jacques had been omnipresent during that moment in the late sixties and early seventies when Hollywood seemed to have discovered a bevy of black actors who were not Sidney Poitier, and put them to work holding guns, and wearing flashy *Superfly* clothes. St. Jacques's face, like the bishop's, had been long and more gray than black, with prominent bags under the eyes. He'd been prone to conveying disdain, very good at it.

"I must apologize," the bishop said, "for the fish, fish, fish."

They had all, with the exception of the bishop, spent the day at the clinic the doctor had set up. They were still a little sweaty and rumpled, but the bishop had worn his robes to dinner, had greeted them with great formality when he'd finally entered the anteroom where they'd been asked to wait. He moved and spoke with a certain hushed elegance, forcing the listener—Henry thought deliberately—to lean forward to hear what he was saying.

"Judith has talent," he said, referring to the Haitian woman who was serving them, "but is limited by what is available here."

Henry, as well as the others, did not dare ask: And what exactly is it we're eating?

"I was in Italy," the bishop said. "In Rome. We're called there. It happens. I ate something called guanciale. You have heard of it?"

It so happened the others hadn't, but Henry of course had.

"Bishop, I believe that's pork cheeks."

"Pork cheeks, yes."

The bishop looked at Henry a little too long. With such men— the eyes—you always felt you were being reduced to some essence. They could be as corrupt and irreligious in practice as it was possible to be, but the long habit of dealing in "souls" nonetheless gave such men a gravitas that was disconcerting. It was as though, looking at you, he knew your exact spiritual purchase price.

Their surroundings—a long dining room, oversize for anything but a banquet—looked as though nothing had been changed or replaced in decades. The ceiling was very high.

Though Beatrice professed an easy friendship with the bishop, and though the bishop and Brutus spoke to one another with curt familiarity, it was left up to the bishop to lead the conversation. Deference to him created an awkwardness. Impatient with such formality, Henry stepped into the breach.

"How is Martelly doing?" he asked. "He'd just been elected when I was here last."

The bishop lifted his head just enough to indicate that Henry had perhaps made a faux pas. In spite of the poster he'd seen outside the airport, was it possible Martelly was no longer president?

If it had been a mistake Henry had made, the bishop made no effort to correct it. He pushed his plate of soup away and gestured to Judith that the next course should be served.

"He liked Aristide better," Brutus said.

The bishop glanced at Brutus as though he didn't appreciate being spoken for, but in this case would allow it.

Aristide, Henry knew, had been a priest who had represented a great hope for Haiti during his brief, interrupted reign. Foreign interference had doomed him.

"Yes, he's right," the bishop said, to cut off further probing, then turned toward Nelson, who had barely touched his soup.

"You will like the next course better," he said to the boy. "I can *almost* guarantee it."

It was the first time he'd assayed a joke, and Nelson once again failed to get it.

After a brief silence, the bishop turned to Henry. "Perhaps he does not know how things work here."

The "he" was confusing. The bishop was looking at Henry, but speaking to Beatrice.

"What do you know of our history?"

"Only what I've learned in one or two books."

The bishop allowed these words to settle.

"We have a history—I don't know what you've learned about in your books. There is an elite here. A mulatto elite. It dates from before the revolution."

Beatrice was looking at the bishop as though she were reflexively mouthing the words he was speaking. A strange thing to witness.

"But it is sometimes necessary to elect someone truly *black*."

He smiled slightly.

"*I* am very black. Sister is very black. And Brutus. Brutus is the blackest of us all."

"It's true," Brutus said, grinning.

"We have something here," the bishop went on, but he was stopped by the arrival of Judith, with a heaping platter of what looked like worms. Only for a moment, thank God.

"Oh, here we have it, more fish," the bishop said with mock-disgust.

Judith dished it out to all of them. Nelson stared at his plate, then at his father: Am I truly expected to eat this? The bishop looked at him with amusement.

"It tastes better than it looks, I assure you," he said. And to the others: "Conch."

"Ah, conch," Dr. Mackey said, as if he ate it all the time.

The bishop nodded to Judith, spoke in Kreyol, gesturing toward Nelson.

"'We have something here,'" Henry repeated the bishop's words back to him. Why did everything he tossed toward the bishop feel— from the man's facial response—like an affront the bishop was choosing, with some effort, not to take personally?

"Are you familiar with *la politique du doublure?*" the bishop asked.

"No, but from the sound of it, I feel I wish I were."

Again, the second's parsing hesitation, the bishop filing him under a heading: a man of foolish wit.

"The translation is, I believe, 'the politics of the understudy,'" the bishop continued. He gestured with his chin toward Beatrice, as if asking her to confirm this. Then he patted the wrist of Nelson, who was seated to his left, gestured silently that Nelson would not be required to eat conch. This was all done with the efficiency of a man used to doing two things at once, because he was not letting go for an instant the necessity of explaining the intriguing phrase to Henry.

"What it means," the bishop said, "is that we often elect someone truly *black*, as a kind of—well, *la doublure?*" He referred the question, again, to Beatrice.

"No, I understand, Bishop," Henry said. "I'm a man of the theater. I know what an understudy is."

"A man of the theater. It is all theater here. All pretense, I'm afraid. *La doublure.* He has no real power. He stands before the lighter-skinned ones who have power, *pretending*. And because he is so often very *black*—"(that strangeness of affect, every time the bishop used that word)—"the people are expected to trust."

Beatrice, Henry couldn't help but notice, was starting to look worried.

"Except once," the bishop said, "it didn't work."

Judith entered, this time with a brown mound on a plate. She placed it before Nelson.

"You will like this better. This is meat," the bishop said.

Nelson still looked hesitant.

"Go ahead."

"Go ahead, Nelson," Dr. Mackey said.

Nelson took a bite. His barely perceptible reaction indicated that it was acceptable. They all breathed a silent sigh of relief. The bishop allowed a tiny smile.

"Once it didn't work," Henry prompted.

The bishop lifted a forkful of conch.

"Once, yes. Papa Doc. Duvalier. He did not . . . *was* not willing to behave like an understudy. He wanted to play the lead part himself."

"Ah," Henry said, as if he understood.

"And the rest is . . ." The bishop patted his mouth with a napkin while he chewed.

"History," Henry finished for him.

"Ask them," the bishop said.

He meant Beatrice and Brutus. Beatrice looked straight ahead as if she were choosing, with some effort, not to speak. Brutus ate like an athlete, unashamed of his eructations, even proud of them, and unaffected by what was going on.

"They were children," the bishop said, "and the Macoutes came into their house and murdered their father before their eyes. Because he had opposed Duvalier."

Having said this, the bishop turned to Nelson, touched his wrist again, then gazed at Dr. Mackey.

"I do not want to upset the boy."

Nelson looked up as if he hadn't heard. Or, to be more accurate, as if he *had* heard, and wondered if he needed to make an excuse for being so unaffected.

"He can take it," Dr. Mackey said.

But the bishop said nothing more.

"I do not tell them this, Bishop," Beatrice said.

"Well, you should."

"It is not essential."

"History."

The bishop went on eating conch.

"We did not begin yesterday," he said. "We did not begin with an earthquake. Excuse me, this is not dinner conversation."

Henry said, "Please go on."

"No, I have embarrassed Sister."

There was a silence. Only Nelson was eating. Henry continued to watch Beatrice. She was not so much embarrassed by the bishop's revelation as seeking a way to move past it. In the instant, Henry admired her positive nature, which had to have taken enormous discipline.

"So, the clinic," the bishop said, turning to Dr. Mackey, indicating that this was to be the end of talking about Papa Doc, and the Tontons Macoutes, and the personal tragedies of those around the table. "I have visited."

"We're holding our own," Dr. Mackey said. "Clean water is a problem."

"Clean water is always a problem."

"We need to expand the cistern."

Henry had had it pointed out to him this afternoon, a huge cistern placed atop the clinic, holding filtered water.

"I'll be going home and looking for money to do that."

What came to him then—Henry had not expected it, and was

not fully prepared—was the essential seriousness of this man. For all Dr. Mackey's central casting dullness, his terrible *agreeableness*, he had come here on a simple mission and he was fulfilling it. Certain men, men like this, were born to be underestimated, just as men like Henry, with their theatrical faces and air of assumed force, were born to be overestimated.

"And you?" the bishop asked, turning again to Henry. "You are not here for the clinic."

"No, Bishop."

"Then what?"

It was like being called on by a teacher who had, until this moment, masked the severity of his dislike of you. But Henry had had enough of feeling cowed by this man.

"There was a boy." Henry touched his mouth with his napkin. "The last time I came."

He looked directly across the table at Beatrice, for whom this was news. He was not sure why he had kept the specificity of his mission from her. Fear of disapproval, he supposed.

"What boy?" she asked.

"He was in the choir. His name was Jean."

The bishop laughed for effect.

"Half the boys on this island are named Jean. What intrigued you about this boy?"

It was the strangest thing: Henry was being pressed, and at the same time he felt he'd been given a pair of wings.

"Well, I feel I made a promise to him. Two years ago. And that promise has haunted me for two years, while I've gone back to the United States and lived my perfectly useless life."

It was Nelson whose reaction to this statement Henry wished to gauge. But Nelson was intent on finishing his mound of meat.

The others were silent.

Dr. Mackey said, "I'm sure your life isn't useless."

"Well, I've just pronounced it so. And that's all that's important, I think."

"What was the promise?" Beatrice asked.

"Oh, that perhaps I could help him get into an American school." She looked surprised, but only mildly.

"There are others you can help. Tomorrow we visit the parish school."

"No. Actually. It's him I'd like to help. I'm hoping you can help me find him."

"Jean."

"Yes."

She opened her hands, gestured to the bishop.

"Perhaps Père Felix can help. But be careful."

"Why be careful, Bishop?"

The bishop made another of his ambiguous faces, directing his look toward Beatrice and Brutus. His long face became even longer, grayer. It was then that Henry remembered. Raymond St. Jacques had played one of Papa Doc's thugs in the film of Graham Greene's *The Comedians*. Of course. St. Jacques had been a master of the sinister. Perfect casting. He'd worn dark shades.

"So many boys to help," the bishop said, and pushed his plate away. "So many *boys*. It is a great mistake to choose only one."

But Henry, in spite of the warning, was determined, and the next day, when they visited Père Felix at the familiar parish, he waited for a chance to ask the question about Jean.

First, though, was the formality of visiting the church, observing the roof they had built two years before, to see how it was holding up.

"At every mass, we say a prayer for you," Père Felix said.

"Father, that seems excessive."

Once again, to feel himself constantly before an audience that failed to get his jokes. (But then, Broadway hadn't been much impressed by them, either.)

"Father, may I ask you something?"

"Of course."

"I'd like to be alone here for a short while." He pitched his face into a pose of polite excuse. "Where we are staying, there is no quiet place to pray."

The Father understood, of course. He nodded his head and disappeared.

Every church was different, had its own distinct character, trapped quiet in its own way. Henry sat. The notion of the "tropical," the "foreign" came over him, in all their tired, clichéd meanings, and he knew he had to work to move past this. He was disappointed by his own reaction to Haiti on this visit, his willingness to see it entirely through the prism of failure. So what if a lizard could clearly be seen skulking across the altar? So what if the statue of the Virgin resembled Carmen Miranda, with red lips and lush black hair that invited you to throw it over her shoulder and plant a deep biting kiss on her neck? His entry into places of worship was often accompanied by a sexual feeling, and there was nothing to be ashamed of in this. Perhaps it was the adolescent memory of waiting outside a confessional to admit to the sin of masturbation while simultaneously planning one's next masturbatory episode. Perhaps it was that, or something else, the feeling that sex was precisely what you were *not* supposed to be thinking about, and therefore couldn't help it. In these circumstances, sexuality became the tunnel you had to punch through in order to get to what was *past* sexuality, if indeed anything was. He closed his eyes, knelt.

Someone had once described the act of prayer as "interrogating silence." He couldn't remember who had said that, but the words were apposite. That was what you did, all you *could* do. Close your eyes and allow what was going to happen to happen. Often nothing did. Still, you waited. Close your eyes and allow the silence to talk back to you, to loosen its secrets. Sometimes if you waited long enough, there would come some brief internal plummet, like an elevator sinking, too fast, two or three floors. Then you would find yourself considering something you had not thought you were ready to consider. The vastness of your own selfishness and self-importance. The fact that the world was this enormous arcing structure, and you such a small helpless thing within it. You pulled away, you resisted that awareness. But there were times when, instead of doing that, you gave in. Became, briefly, nothing. Saw yourself, for a moment, as one might imagine God saw you: here is this individual, unimportant in the grand scheme, with his conflicts that he considers so large, so daunting. In God's view, of course, they were nothing at all, but they were what one *carried*, one's personal load. Cast them away. See them in their infinite smallness. At the moment of death, I will be able to see what a *little* thing they were, my demons, my difficulties.

In such a state, he thought he could stay here forever. He moved from a kneeling back to a sitting position. There had been times when he'd wanted God to strike him, to deal him a blow, knock him off his horse, à la Saint Paul. Of course it never worked that way. You received, at best, a nudge. You ignored it at your peril. God was ultimately a sly bastard, a comedian. He offered temptation at the exact moment when you convinced yourself you were past it. He said to the poor sinner: Never for a moment flatter yourself that you *know* yourself. Only *I* know you. And I will wait until your most vulnerable moment to reveal to you what I know.

In all of this, he thought of the boy Jean, closed his eyes, prayed silently: let me not be making a terrible mistake.

He heard the familiar steps behind him. Was there a special place where nuns' shoes were made, a factory in Honduras or the Philippines where hundreds of small women went to work making heavy, uncomfortable-looking shoes whose slightest creak spoke purpose?

She sat beside him.

"You have found a place to pray."

"Yes. Père Felix was kind enough to leave me alone for five minutes. And that's apparently all I'm going to get."

"You can pray anytime, Henry. We are here to work."

He looked aside toward her, his head still bent in the attitude of prayer he was reluctant to leave.

"And what is our work today?"

"The teachers are waiting for us. The students."

It would be a formality. Henry contributed to the upkeep of the school, himself supported four students in attendance. It was one of those meaningless American gestures requiring nothing more than the writing of a check.

On their way out of the church, he stopped, tugged at Beatrice's blue habit. When she turned to him, he pointed to the roof.

"*This* had meaning, Beatrice."

She looked like she did not know precisely what he meant. But then, why should she? For Beatrice, every act had meaning. Those *shoes* had meaning. The religious life conferred that. Forty or fifty years ago she had sat in her kitchen and watched her father murdered by thugs. Somehow this had led her to God, or perhaps only to service. Or perhaps there was no important distinction between the two.

The schoolrooms would have been an embarrassment in nineteenth-century America. Chairs that looked like they were only waiting for the right bodily pressure in order to collapse. A small chalkboard, a single drawing on the wall, the classic child's drawing of a tree where all the green foliage sat like a hat on top of the trunk. The expectant children, all enormous-eyed, stared up at him.

Beatrice said something to the children in either Kreyol or French (Henry was still having trouble telling the difference). The look that came over them made him think she had endowed him with some form of awe.

"What did you tell them?" he asked.

"I told them you are a saint. Saint Henry."

"Please don't do that," he said. And to the children: "Je ne suis pas un saint."

They all seemed to back away from that, confused. The awkwardness of the moment was terrible. He wanted badly to relieve it.

"Who—which of you drew this?"

He was referring to the single drawing on the wall.

Beatrice, seeking as well to salvage the moment, translated the question. None of the children raised a hand. The teacher moved toward one of them—a little girl—and touched her head.

Henry leaned toward her. "It's very good."

Oh God. Such moments. The saintly *blan* offering encouragement before jetting back to America to eat guanciale. He wanted to fight his way out of that. The little girl treated his faux-encouragement as if she saw right through it. Thank God, one of them has the toughness to understand a false moment when she sees it. Perhaps this will serve her in the life—whatever life—she was headed toward. It had never come to him with more force how little he understood what that potential life might be.

There were other classrooms to visit. As they moved about the school—the kitchen, the cafeteria—Beatrice seemed to be coming to the realization that Henry was the wrong ambassador to have brought here, that the sight of these underserved young boys and girls would not cause him to empty his pockets further than he'd already been coerced to do. At the end of the tour, Père Felix waited for them outside, a portrait of bland patience, pretending to have no idea of the sales pitch Beatrice had just concluded.

They invited him into the rectory. Two of the linebacker-priests who always seemed to be hovering here were at the stove, cooking something, or only discussing cooking something. A third was in the side yard, working on his motorcycle.

"The Father wants you to consider a new project," Beatrice said.

"What is that?"

"The kitchen for the school. You saw, it is inadequate. They're still required to cook with wood for fuel. We could use propane if there was a stove. Cheaper, better."

In French, Père Felix referred a question to Beatrice.

"He wants to know why the others didn't come. From your group. The group last time."

"It's difficult, Father. People's interest . . ." He shrugged. "Now look, of course it's a very important project, the kitchen. But Sister, may I speak frankly?"

"Of course." She folded her hands in front of her, one thumb and forefinger clutching the cross that hung from her neck.

"I feel the best thing I could do would be to bring just one of these children to the U.S. Give them a *real* opportunity."

She had asked him last night, after the dinner with the bishop, why he hadn't told her before about his intention in coming here. "I was afraid you would try and dissuade me," was his answer. Now she looked at him with the same disappointment with which she'd reacted to his answer of the night before.

He turned to Felix, hoping for more receptivity.

"Father, there was a boy I met here two years ago."

Beatrice began to speak to the Father in French, conducting a private conversation Henry was not meant to hear. Within the French words she spoke, Henry distinctly heard the word "Jean." He also detected a tone of familiarity. Had she been affecting a false ignorance when he'd spoken the name at the bishop's dinner table last night? Had she stored, like the God she served, an awareness of every hair on every head?

Père Felix shook his head slowly, shouted to one of the large priests in the adjacent kitchen. The conversation was closed to Henry, but again, the word "Jean" appeared in it. His pulse had begun to quicken.

It was the priest working outside on his motorcycle who had the required information. The conversation bounced from one priest to another, Felix to the cooking priest to the motorcycle priest, and back.

Finally Felix was able to report to Beatrice, and then she told Henry.

"He went with his father to deliver a generator to a church in Cavaillon."

Henry opened his hands.

"But he will be coming back, presumably. He's known? The boy in the choir?"

She nodded. "Yes, he's known."

"Well, can we find out when he's coming back? I'd like to speak with him."

Was it possible this whole trip might be a waste, that the boy might never know that Henry had come to keep his promise?

Again, the tag-team conversation, interrupted when the priest outside, still working on his motorcycle, couldn't hear the question. One of the priests had to go out, and when he came back reported that Jean and his father would be back tomorrow.

"I would like to see him," Henry said.

They stepped outside into the sun. The Father asked Henry where he was staying.

"Oh, Beatrice has us in deluxe quarters, Father. We're staying at Haiti's equivalent of the Ritz."

Would any of this be understood? He was surprised when they both laughed.

"You know the Ritz?" Henry asked the Father.

The priest turned to Henry. With some hesitation and effort, he worked what he wanted to say into English. "There is no reason you have to stay there. I have a house."

He pointed ceremoniously to a structure adjacent to the church. One story, in need of repair, but undeniably a house.

"Sister," Henry asked. "Why didn't you tell us there was a house available?"

She was laughing to herself, then aloud.

"Oh, you are welcome to stay there, Henry." Some secret knowledge was in her laughter. "By all means, be the Father's guest."

It could not be arranged for two more nights. Henry began to dream of a room to himself, though there was something undeniably sweet about watching the doctor and his son bed down each night, kneeling together in prayer before turning in.

They were used, at the end of their days, to coming back to the vocational school and noting either a silence in the workroom, or, at most, one or two older men idling near the benches where the electric saw and sanding tools lay. If the place functioned at all as a school, it must have been during the hours when Henry's small group was away. Which is why Henry hardly noticed, at the end of the next day, a single individual in the workroom. He would have gone right past if Beatrice hadn't nudged Henry's arm, and gestured.

Henry's initial confusion was understandable. The boy was taller, for one thing, having traversed the distance from seventeen to eighteen. Or was Jean now nineteen? Excessively thin, in basketball shorts and shoes that looked too large for him. He had grown a mustache, which dominated his face, as if making a declaration of its own wrongness.

There was, Henry felt right away, a relief to this. The boy's lessened beauty would make things easier. Easier, anyway, for Henry to convince himself he was doing what he was doing entirely for altruistic reasons.

"Oh," Henry said, feeling strangely becalmed. "Are you Jean?"

Beatrice had left them alone. The boy, affecting humility, nodded. If he was humbled, he was also clearly confused. Did he not remember Henry? It was entirely likely. Yet Henry was excited, as if, having just arrived at this moment, he had achieved something, fulfilled at least the most basic part of his promise.

"Do you remember me?" Henry asked.

"Yes," the boy said.

That humble tilting forward of the head that Henry wanted to ask him to undo. At the same time, though he was inclined not to fully believe the boy, he was touched. The boy's face revealed a mild confusion that still held in it a keen alertness.

"It's been two years," Henry said.

The boy said nothing and Henry was assaulted by a sudden feeling that this was not the boy he remembered but another, pretending to be the favored one. It was a strange feeling to have, and Henry turned away, looked out the window at the azure sea whose beauty, he knew, was deceptive. Look long enough and you would see the floating detritus. He chose not to.

"Shall we sit?"

But there was actually nowhere to sit. Henry leaned against a worktable. The boy remained standing.

"So how has it been for you?" Henry asked. "These two years."

It was a complicated question, the sort of easy shorthand Henry might have been able to use with Nelson, but clearly not with this boy.

"I mean, what have you been doing?"

The boy's smile—eager, and eager to please—was becoming annoying. Henry wanted to say *Please don't.*

"In school? Working?"

"Working," the boy answered.

"With your father?"

"Sometimes."

"I see."

You could not say—impossible to say—*I have come here, traveled across the hemisphere, precisely for this moment.* You had to pretend to small talk. You could not dig internally either—too much present-tense activity was required—at what had drawn him to this boy, caused him to imagine him, at odd moments, for two years. There was danger there, he knew. But to succumb to the danger, to back away from the potential good he might do because of a perceived danger, felt small, cowardly.

"And what—?" He stopped himself. He meant to ask *And what is the plan?* but that, again, was the sort of shorthand inapplicable to this room, this situation.

"Please tell me what you remember, from the time I was here before?"

It was not clear the boy understood that many words put together. While Henry waited for an answer, he studied the boy's face, its new roundness, the frizz of hair on top that had grown out some.

He was not certain why he didn't just come out with it, announce his plan about the school. It felt too soon, would be too overwhelming for them both. He must feel things out first. The boy hardly remembered him. Henry had held to a promise that may have meant nothing.

Beatrice was at the door now, which relieved Henry.

"Well, have you spoken to him?" Beatrice asked.

"We are only getting acquainted."

She was impatient. She did not like this at all. She said something in Kreyol to Jean and he nodded shyly.

"What did you tell him?"

"I told him you came here because you remembered him. That's all."

"He speaks English, Beatrice." Then, correcting himself, turning to Jean: "You understand English, don't you?"

Jean nodded, but seemed uncertain.

"He understands a little, Henry. That's all."

She knew this, too. She said something more in Kreyol, a longer question directed at the boy.

"Stop doing this," Henry said. "You're leaving me out."

"I asked him if he wanted to come here and learn woodworking. Maybe you'd be willing to pay for him to do that."

Henry acknowledged her. She was providing him with an out, and he knew he ought to be grateful. Paying for the boy's attendance at the woodworking school would perhaps be enough.

"Would you like that, Jean?" Henry asked.

"No," the boy said.

"Why not?" Sister Beatrice asked.

The boy looked at Henry. The conversation now was to be confined to the two of them. Sister Beatrice—with her sense of practicality, of limits—was to be left out. What had been the thing said, the line crossed, that had made this possible? The boy—stop saying *the boy*, Henry, he is *Jean*—seemed to understand that he did not have to answer, or defend himself, to Beatrice. He had found his patron.

It was something Henry had heard about, the Haitians' ability to find a wealthy American and, essentially, milk him dry. He'd been warned about it by others, back in Grantham, those who'd been to African countries, and to the Caribbean, to do "good work." There always seemed to be one particularly savvy one with an ability to read the American's guilt and wish for virtue, and to seize on it. He could neither fully believe, nor quite deny, that the boy in front of him might be one of those he'd been warned against. He had to caution himself against it.

"I don't think he wants it, Beatrice."

Still he couldn't say it, couldn't offer his plan. He had to talk longer with the boy.

Beatrice's phone was ringing. She stepped outside the room to answer it. They heard her loud voice raised in argument. Left alone, they smiled at one another.

"A life of woodworking is not for you then," Henry said.

Jean was no longer smiling. He nodded in the affirmative. It was a hard thing to take in, and Henry found his gaze deflected to Jean's mustache. But something was happening now between them that he couldn't entirely turn away from. When Henry looked up, Jean's face seemed to open, while at the same time guarding its own secrets, its own deep interiority.

Henry hesitated from saying anything more, felt such hesitation now was essential.

And still the boy went on looking at him, as if he had found something, and knew that he had found something.

The night was set when they would all be staying at Père Felix's house. At dinner, when he was told this, Brutus started laughing.

"What is it?" Henry asked. "Your sister had the same reaction. Is the house haunted?"

"No, it is not haunted." Brutus covered his mouth.

Such jocularity was no longer possible with Sister Beatrice. Since his meeting with Jean, she had begun treating Henry differently. It was as though he were a student who'd gone beyond the limits of what she wished to teach him.

"I only want to explore some possibilities for him," Henry had said in his own defense. "Listen, where I live there is a school, a private school. They offer scholarships. I've already spoken to them and I believe they'd welcome a boy from Haiti. That's all."

But she did not rise to the bait. The harsh look she'd sent him in the woodshop had become a permanent look. He could no longer make her laugh. He mourned this, but did not back down.

"We will discuss this," was all she would allow. "You take him on, he is yours, you understand."

In the evening, though, when he bedded down, after Dr. Mackey and Nelson's prayer, as he listened to their breathing in tandem, then the shift into a joined sleep—breath that was like a quiet, beautifully modulated chant, he considered that Beatrice was still trying, in her way, to offer him an escape hatch, and he would do well to consider it. "You take him on, he is yours" was a sentence to strike fear in the night. Not since Philip had he and Lily taken on a boy. Would Lily welcome it? With Philip, there had at least been a purity of intent, his dead brother's child. And a purity of relationship as well. But he understood too well there was something not entirely pure about what he was doing with Jean. He could admit to no designs on the boy. Perish the thought. One look in the mirror was all it took to remind himself of age, of decay, of all the things that made even the thought absurd. Never mind the whole moral question. But would he have gone this far if the boy's beauty hadn't been a factor?

The three of them were to spend the night in Père Felix's house, but on the afternoon of the settled-upon day, Dr. Mackey was called away to the clinic. Something serious had come up. So it was to be Henry and Nelson, at least until the doctor was freed.

Nothing here was a secret. It was a known fact that the *blan* would be staying in the house. In late afternoon, a group of boys arrived, to stare at them as they sat outside the rectory. Boys ten, eleven. After enough staring had gone on, Nelson took it upon himself to find a soccer ball and began kicking it around with them. Nelson had an ease with this, it was the first time it could be said that the boy seemed to be relaxing. He played with the boys in the soft reddish light of very late afternoon. Henry sat, content to watch. It may have been the moment he'd most enjoyed on the trip thus far.

After he had played with the boys long enough, Nelson came and sat with Henry on a bench. They were waiting for Père Felix to call them in to dinner. The boys Nelson had been playing with didn't want to stop. Like boys everywhere they had an infinite amount of energy and desire. Henry noted the way Nelson touched one of their heads, the easy physical bonding possible for those close in age.

Sitting beside Henry, Nelson placed his hands between his legs. They were comfortable with one another suddenly, Henry was not sure why.

"That was very kind of you," Henry said.

The boy didn't say anything, touched his own hair, shook it out, as though it had taken on moisture.

"What sports do you play, back at—?"

"Russell," Nelson said.

"Russell." One of those indistinguishable towns in western Massachusetts: the Protestant church steeple, the small town library, the marquee advertising a pot roast supper to benefit the volunteer fire department.

"Soccer. Ultimate," Nelson said.

Nelson affected modesty. They left it at that. But then Nelson seemed to want to say something to Henry. It took a moment for him to shepherd the words.

"My father," Nelson said.

He didn't say anything more for a few seconds.

"Yes?" Henry asked.

The adolescent male face was capable sometimes of taking on a pure, confused yearning that Henry had never seen—not in the same way—in adolescent girls. It was a dreaming-while-awake quality, an unselfconsciousness that was perhaps not possible for girls, who, at that age, became piercingly self-aware.

"What is it, Nelson?"

"No. He wants me to write my college essay about this place."

"Does he?"

"That's why he brought me."

Henry felt himself wildly amused. It seemed he always got people wrong. No wonder every one of his creative efforts except for the one where he'd admitted, full-throatedly, to his seventy-year-old cluelessness, had somehow come up short. The serious, dedicated Dr. Mackey had an ulterior motive in coming here, after all. He expected that all the colleges Nelson applied to would be wowed by this insipid adventure in Haiti.

"And you?" he asked.

"Doesn't seem right," Nelson said. "I mean, to come here just so I can write an essay." The look was back; he offered it to Henry, unembarrassed, as if they'd known each other a long time.

"Well, Nelson, I'm sorry if this seems too simplistic, but you know you *could* write your essay about something else."

Nelson nodded, a little too eagerly. He continued to scratch at his inner thigh as though he were trying to drive the itch inward. Then he said, "Like what?"

Henry laughed. It was the wrong reaction. Nelson looked hurt.

"I'm sorry. I *am* sorry. Surely there are other subjects."

"You're a writer."

"Yes."

Nelson nodded, as though that small, simple fact meant that Henry might offer him something here, now, a sword to raise against his father and the anticipated mini-masterpiece, "My Trip to Haiti."

"I would suggest, Nelson, that you think about writing about prayer."

It took a moment, but then it became clear that Nelson considered this the most outlandish idea he had ever heard. *"What?"*

"Prayer. I've noticed the way you pray."

Nelson had become very still. Impossible to know what he was thinking.

"I would imagine—I mean, I don't know where you'll be applying—but I don't imagine there'll be a lot of college essays having to do with prayer."

Nelson continued to inhabit that mysterious stillness. He glanced once at Henry, as if there were something inexpressible going on in him. Then he looked away, and it was as if Henry had insulted him and he wished the conversation was over.

"I'm sorry. Does this embarrass you, Nelson?"

The Father had appeared at the door.

"Dinner," he said.

"Father, could you give us a moment? Just a moment?"

Père Felix agreed, and Henry stood.

"Nelson, I'm sorry. I don't know what I said."

"Nothing," Nelson said, and stood as well. "I don't know what I'd say about *prayer.*"

There was something harsh in the way he said it, not as though he wished to disparage it but to protect it, and Henry understood the thorn bush he had walked into. "Prayer" was not something to be trifled with, or used to market oneself. It made for a new distance between the two of them that Henry regretted. He grew ashamed of his own reflexive irony. He was one of the grand population for whom nothing was truly serious. Only the self. Everything else was currency, exchange.

Dinner was mostly silent, polite. One of the large young priests joined them. They were waiting for the appearance of Dr. Mackey. Nelson, in particular, seemed on the lookout for him. Père Felix seemed to be waiting for another appearance, that of the jocular Henry. But Henry, feeling the aftereffects of having been silently reprimanded by Nelson, had fallen into a state of self-chastisement.

When dusk fell, Père Felix walked them across the yard to the house. It was dark within, and the priest turned on lamps. The walls were bare, the screens in the windows porous. Towels and sheets had been placed on the beds; they had been carefully prepared for. The priest indicated that Nelson and his father were to sleep in one bedroom, with a large double bed, Henry in an adjoining one, with only a single.

What was the secret of the house? What was it that made first Beatrice, then Brutus laugh at the thought of their being the Father's guests? Nothing looked suspicious, at least not glaringly so. The ceilings had large cracks in them, and gaps in places, but that was not unusual. The house seemed plain, functional, and Henry felt grateful for the solitude. It was clear, after Père Felix saw them settled, that he and Nelson would say nothing more to one another. The boy took to his room, closed the door. Henry sat on his thin bed, in the light of the lamp.

As soon as full dark came—it had to be close to nine o'clock now—he began to hear it. The sound came from above the ceiling. A scratching at first, then the distinct sound of running, scampering. Henry looked up at the ceiling and waited, with some small, disbelieving terror, for the appearance of what he suspected was up there. Perhaps the sound would stop. Perhaps they were all just settling down. But it did not stop.

He got up and knocked on Nelson's door. Nelson answered, sweatpants, T-shirt, a face that looked even paler than usual.

"Do you hear that?" Henry asked.

Nelson nodded, terrified.

"Oh dear," Henry said. "They did try and warn us."

Nelson nodded again, saucer-eyed.

"Perhaps we should call your father. Whoever drives him here can drive us back to the woodshop."

There was a sudden louder sound just above them.

"Oh dear," Henry said again, and Nelson nodded for the third time, with a bit more urgency. "In the meantime, if you want me to stay in your room, the two of us, strength in numbers. I could lie on the floor, keep a lookout."

"No," Nelson said. Henry's suggestion must have felt like cowardice. The boy could face this. Henry admired him for it.

"Okay, then."

He went back to his own room, first turning back to Nelson and saying, "It's probably a good idea to leave your light on."

Nelson agreed, but he felt he was abandoning the boy to something.

The scratchings and movements went on relentlessly. Henry anticipated a large snout appearing from out of one of the ceiling cracks, thought he saw one at one point. The legend—an urban legend perhaps (at least he hoped so)—was that Haitian rats were the size of dogs. He would gather the boy, they would go to Père Felix, apologize, ask for a couch in the rectory. Anything but this. Just as these thoughts became unbearable, the lights of a truck appeared alongside the house. Good, the doctor, he would run out, he would ask the truck to wait. Henry stood just outside the front door, put his hands up in a gesture of *Wait*, but the truck made a circular motion and was about to disappear when Henry shouted, "Stop!" The truck, having disgorged its passenger, did not stop, and it was only in its absence that he saw the figure before him. Assuming it to be the doctor, Henry said, "You won't believe this," but he knew already, before the words were fully out of his mouth, by the size and the shape of the figure that it couldn't be the doctor. It was Jean.

The boy stood there for a moment. What was that in his hand? Something large. Jean approached him. "You have seen the rats?" Jean asked.

"I'm afraid so."

Was Jean smiling? Yes. In his hand—Henry could see quite clearly now—was a baseball bat.

"How did you know?"

There was no need for an answer. Everything was known. The movement of the *blan* was tracked like the movements of battleships across the Pacific in the war rooms of World War II.

"Who drove you here, Jean?"

"My father."

That was that. Henry followed Jean into the house. The boy had an authority here. He knew the house. Nelson's door opened a crack, and Nelson's uncertain face peered through.

"It's all right, Nelson. It appears we've found our savior."

Jean entered Nelson's room first. He seemed larger than Henry had believed him to be. A strength across his newly broad shoulders. With great force he swung the bat so that it pounded against the wall. For a blessed instant, the rats were silenced. Jean looked at Henry and Nelson with a solemn, listening expression. The rats started up and Jean pounded the wall again, this time even harder.

In the ensuing silence, Jean said, "The main thing is to make noise."

Henry and Nelson looked at each other. Nelson's terror had not quite subsided.

"What songs do you know, Nelson?"

He had meant it, again, to be a joke.

"Perhaps," Henry said, "we should go and tell Père Felix that this won't work."

"No," Jean said. (Where had the boy's sudden authority come from?) "They will go away. Or at least be silent."

Jean sat on Nelson's bed. He seemed to be enjoying this, reveling a little in his ability to ease their passage through the night.

"Do you have a phone?" Jean asked Nelson. "iPhone? To play music?"

"No."

Henry, too, had brought only the most basic of phones.

Jean needed a moment to take this in. It was assumed the *blan* always traveled with the appropriate technology.

The rats seemed to have taken on a silence, retreated into a corner.

Jean went into Henry's room.

"You'll be all right?" Henry said to Nelson.

"Think so."

"Make noise."

"We've got to sleep, don't we?"

"Remains to be seen. When your father comes, have him take you back. I'll do the honors here. Père Felix won't be offended so long as one of us stays."

In his room, he saw Jean poking his baseball bat into one of the ceiling cracks. He banged around a bit. Then he sat on the room's single cane-backed chair and regarded Henry.

In Nelson's room, Jean had been full of smiles and authority, a boy flexing his muscles, enjoying it. Here, alone with Henry, he returned to something humbler, more serious.

"You're a lifesaver, Jean."

Jean seemed to have no reaction to this at all. He wore the face of a Buckingham Palace guard. Do not try to distract me.

"What is the school?" he asked.

"The school?" But of course Henry knew what he was referring to. A battle cruiser had traversed the distance from Peleliu to Saipan. A pin had been moved on the map. The rats chose that moment to resume shuffling. Jean shouted something in Kreyol and banged at the ceiling. Then he sat and waited, expressionless again.

"It is a school in Massachusetts. Very good."

Jean waited for more.

"Massachusetts is where I live."

In the ensuing silence, Henry said, as if he'd been made to understand the necessity: "Jean, I am afraid to make a promise I cannot keep. There are steps we'd have to take. A test you'd have to take. Some writing you'd have to do, to show them your—"

"What?"

"Your—you seem very intelligent."

Was the word understood? Jean gave no indication. His face remained set and expectant.

"Have you ever taken a test, Jean? One of those—?"

Henry tried to indicate the concept of a test with his hands. But how did you do such a thing? Jean watched him flail. He did not seem to have moved on from the notion of "a school in Massachusetts," where Henry "lived." It was enough. It would be sufficient.

"When?" Jean asked.

"Well, hold on," Henry said, trying to affect a lightness that was wholly inappropriate here, with rats huddling above them, with a human distance between himself and this newly serious, ambitious boy that seemed vast. "There is a procedure to follow."

The boy swallowed. Henry had the absurd thought that this conversation would be so much easier if Jean had never grown that mustache. The mustache had begun to feel like a kind of threat. He was not dealing with a child.

"Perhaps . . . now this is what I want to ask."

Why did it feel like he was a prisoner now, like he was negotiating for his own freedom?

"I'd like you to write something. Something very simple. Who you are, what you want, what your goals are. Why you want to go to school in America."

Jean's eyes narrowed. He was looking at Henry as though Henry were attempting to mislead him. But everything in a young face changes in an instant, like light. Like weather. Henry understood next that the boy was only scared.

"I'm sorry if this frightens you."

"It doesn't frighten me."

Henry didn't believe him. The rats had resumed a gentle, probing scuttling, and Jean, with his newly revealed authority, banged the ceiling, silencing them. After he had done that, he looked at Henry with a look Henry had not seen before, a look of male pride, even a bit of self-satisfied preening, as if the assertion of physical mastery had just established itself as the essential thing here. Writing statements of purpose to American academic institutions took on, in the moment, the weight of flimsy tissues dropped into water, instantly dissolving.

Then there was a shift, as subtle as could be imagined. Jean's face took on another look. Henry could not read it any more than he could accurately read any of Jean's other looks. The depth of foreignness had once again made itself known. But what he was afraid he was seeing now was Jean offering himself, as if this was the assumed, the expected payment. Jean's look was like a shrug: *So now this?*

Henry sat in shocked silence before turning away. *No. Not this.* When he turned back he forced his face to deliver as clear a message as he could manage, given his conflicted feelings.

"We will take the test," Henry said, as if to return them to an issue they had left behind. He felt behind his words a highly charged silence. Jean had seen him, and Henry had denied, or tried to deny, what Jean had seen. All of Henry's self-discipline could not undo what Jean had apparently seen. His heart was pounding wildly. Could Jean sense that, too?

"You will take the test. That's what I can offer."

Jean took a moment, then slowly nodded his head. They had arrived at some sort of clarity, if only the kind of clarity in which they had agreed to ignore what each had just learned about the other. Henry waited for the pounding of his heart to slow down. Then the boy, after regarding Henry once more, raised his head, as if the noise above, the noise of the rats, had alerted him.

THREE

DAYS WITHOUT RULES
(2016)

I.

Meryl Streep's young face, doe-ish, mildly startled, entirely unlined, repeated its gesture of resistance. She was sitting in the witness chair in a courtroom, defending herself against the assault of an unseen lawyer. A deep, staccato female voice, not Meryl Streep's, spoke the words "I would have gone out the window," and after a pause, continued. "I thought of it. Every day. Waiting until it was time to pick you up from school. I stared at the window. I thought how easily it could happen. All I had to do was give myself permission. That's why I had to leave, Billy. It was because of the window."

When Miranda looked up from the image—headphones over her ears—she saw three similar ones, on matching consoles. Meryl Streep's face in three other poses from the movie—in a bar, on the street, in the vestibule of an apartment building. You pressed a button to hear four separate monologues, each directed to the little boy, presumably now an adult, whom Meryl Streep had abandoned.

The exhibit, *The Joanna Monologues*, was housed in a small room on the main floor of the Schechner Gallery, in that corner of Chelsea so close to the river you expected to see sailors rolling down the tight streets, drunkenly singing nautical songs. Instead, women in expensive coats and precise haircuts roamed here. Men whose hair proclaimed an outsiderness that was the ultimate badge of insiderness. The neighborhood had become the province of Art. And money, don't forget money. The moment had arrived—had arrived long ago—when the two could no longer be separated.

Miranda was earlier than she'd intended to be for the event, being held upstairs, that she'd been scheduled to attend. Something would change for her upon entering the upstairs gallery, she knew that. Getting here before she'd wanted, she'd dipped into this room as a way of putting off a moment she anticipated with a combination of excitement and dread.

She'd been surprised tonight, though she shouldn't have been, to find the artist—a young woman named Cindy Auerbach—here. The artist was often present, acting as a kind of hostess, as though *The Joanna Monologues* were a private party she was throwing. She was thrilled with it, as why shouldn't she be? Tonight, she was sitting on the single wooden bench in the small gallery, being interviewed by a short, intense-looking woman who seemed to have something wrong with her leg. A recording device had been placed on the bench between them.

Cindy Auerbach wore her hair in spiked braids. She affected a Pippi Longstocking look that Miranda tried not to be critical of, her judgmentalism so clearly arising out of jealousy and competitiveness. Yet why did certain young artists feel compelled to dress so ostentatiously as artists? Cindy Auerbach had brought her baby tonight; he was strapped to the artist's chest in one of those contraptions that allowed the baby to look outward, not at the parent. The little boy—dark hair swept across his high forehead—bore a vague resemblance to Peter Lorre.

"Well, it was iconic," Cindy Auerbach was saying to her interviewer. "I mean, everyone saw it, and it created this new template for men, that they were going to be 'caring.' 'Caregivers.' And yet you watch it, and what does Dustin Hoffman actually learn to *do*? He learns to make French toast. He learns to fold clothes."

There were parts of this Miranda had heard before. She'd attended this show's opening, had read the catalogue copy. This room in the Schechner Gallery was devoted to "emerging artists," and not a great deal of attention was paid to what was installed here. It was the upstairs rooms that mattered, the upstairs rooms where Miranda was tonight expected.

"And the way the movie invited you to judge Joanna. *She's left her child.* As if no man had ever done that. As if—Jesus Christ—as if Lucian *Freud* never did that. And I thought—forty years on, we've got to examine that. Because—of course, cliché, cliché—'nothing's changed.' We're still judging women for the way they mother. And it was time—I thought it was high time—to give Joanna a voice."

The baby grasped the finger his mother offered him. It was an invitation for the interviewer to ask the next, inevitable question, the one about the stresses of being an artist and a mother.

Before answering it, Cindy Auerbach looked up at Miranda. She'd noticed her upon entering but was only now acknowledging her, as if it were a part of the interview, the moment where she wanted the interviewer to notice, and remark on, her easy approachability. No pretensions here. None at all.

"Hello. You're here again," Cindy Auerbach said.

"Yes."

Miranda lowered her earphones. The young artist seemed to be offering her an opening to comment on her work, but Miranda could think of nothing to say. She had had her hair styled for this event, she wore designer earrings and a dress one of her friends had helped her pick out, from one of those dress shops in the East Village where you were terrified to ask the prices. In the mirror in her apartment, her reflected image had spoken a kind of glamour. But here, in Cindy Auerbach's cutting-edge presence, she felt she'd dressed like a nun, and as though her hair had been cut in the deadly serious fashion of those who wished to declare their unavailability to anything but the library stacks.

She was about to answer—to come up with something—when the baby started fussing. A line of zinc-colored liquid spilled from his mouth.

"Oh, Paolo," Cindy Auerbach said, and reached into her bag for a Handi Wipe. The interviewer looked horrified, as did Miranda (she supposed). Yet there was nothing to it. Paolo was wiped up, the Handi Wipe quickly disposed of.

"My husband was supposed to take him tonight, but 'something came up,'" Cindy Auerbach said to the interviewer, and smiled in a mocking, not unduly troubled fashion. "And so much for *Kramer vs. Kramer* and the last forty years, you know?"

Miranda wanted to go now. There was nothing left to say, though she'd said nothing. Had she been asked to explain her presence here, she could not have done so.

She was at the elevator, pushing the button, when Cindy Auerbach approached her. Paolo, strapped into his carrier, wore the goggle-eyed look of a young boy who has just been sexually overwhelmed. Miranda smiled at him. You were expected to smile at babies.

"I'm *sorry*. You're Miranda, right?"

"I am."

"The opening upstairs. Anna Soloff. It's invitation only, right?"

"Yes."

Miranda could easily anticipate the next question. Cindy Auerbach's face brought home the memory of certain girls from high school and college, ambitious girls who would ask a great deal from life and inevitably get much of what they asked for.

The artist could not fully hide her air of annoyance at having to ask now. They were being joined at the elevator by two of the journalists who would be attending the opening, one wearing a jacket whose color—deep blue—Miranda would have liked to study. Distractingly good-looking men, each with a couple days' growth on his chin and face. Outside the gallery, there were more of them—women and men both—lingering, smoking a last cigarette before coming in.

"You'd like to come up, is that it?" Miranda asked.

Cindy Auerbach nodded, spinning her own affected girlishness into a protective layer of irony.

It would not be appropriate at all to have a baby upstairs, among the art critics and the photographers, with Peter Schjeldahl attending, with Andrew Schechner himself and his entourage. Paolo's spit-up would not be a welcome sight. But it was maybe for that reason alone that Miranda felt she had to offer her permission. This was Anna Soloff, after all, whom they were all here to celebrate tonight. A woman who had not been afraid to mix motherhood and art, who had no distaste for a baby's spit-up, who had brought her own young sons to gallery after gallery, in the years of her neglect.

This, at least, was Miranda's ostensible reason for granting permission. The elevator doors were opening, she had to step in.

"I'll put your name on the list."

But as the elevator doors closed on Cindy Auerbach's put-on grateful face, Miranda could not help but recall the image on the fourth and last console, the one marked *So I Will Not Be Your Mother, After All*, the one where the elevator doors close on Meryl Streep's face in its pose of renunciation.

The two handsome journalists leaned against the walls of the elevator as it lifted, heaving small sighs that carried within them the faint clovish scent of foreign cigarettes. One spoke to the other in French.

The essay that had precipitated this exhibit had been given the simple title "Two Nudes." It had been lifted from the chapter in Miranda's book about Anna's relationship with her early mentor Arthur Messinger. When Miranda had handed in the first 250 pages of manuscript to her agent, it was this section the agent had landed on with excitement. "We can excerpt this, sell it somewhere," she had said. *ARTnews, Artforum?* Miranda had asked. "Fuck those little ecclesiastical journals," the agent said, and after Miranda had condensed it into a freestanding eight-thousand-word excerpt, had sold it to *The New Yorker*.

And just in time. Miranda's bank account, perpetually nosing, like a downed jet, close to zero, received a lift. But beyond that, it put her on the literary map, as her agent said. (She was a woman who, when Miranda spoke to her on the phone, had to be imagined with a cigar poking out of the side of her mouth, like one of those tough-talking newspaper editors in thirties movies.) The essay drew attention, the agent was able to sell the forthcoming biography in three foreign countries, with two others making promising noises. The advances were small but welcome. Miranda was not becoming rich, only somewhat less panicked. And there was a bonus: the attention the essay directed toward Anna's nude paintings of Arthur Messinger led Anna's dealer, Andrew Schechner, to mount the show whose opening Miranda was attending tonight. *Anna Soloff: The AIDS Paintings.*

Miranda had been clever. She had to admit this, even to herself. In her diaries, Anna had had very little to say about her early sex with Arthur Messinger, the older man (he'd been twenty-six, she only twenty) who had taken her under his wing at the Art Students League in the early forties. More than the sex, apparently, Anna had revered Arthur's art, paintings of soldiers, paintings of a grim prewar city eating up its inhabitants, paintings that Anna had been influenced by as she arrived at her own dark urban renderings. Arthur Messinger's paintings had mostly been lost; Miranda had managed to see only a few of them. What had survived of him in Anna's life was his teaching, his taking Anna by the hand and pointing out that what had been opened by the Depression, by the thirties themselves, was going to be closed by the war. "We're going to forget everything we learned," Arthur Messinger had said to her. "Make your work an argument against forgetting." He had turned Anna into a committed communist, then, sometime in the late forties, he'd gotten a job teaching in California, and for a time disappeared.

The first nude painting Anna had done of him—the not-good one, the one from 1941—was of a too carefully rendered, thin young man reclining on a sofa. What Anna was later to learn—how little had to be made precise, how inexact you could be about the ana- tomical details as long as you got the essentials right—was en- tirely absent from the painting. She'd worked too hard on Arthur's knees, trying to get the bone structure perfectly correct. By the time she'd gotten to the face, she seemed to have lost energy, or will, and—in her essay, Miranda had been good about capturing her own response—you almost wanted to summon the older hand, the lighter, more decisive hand, to wish it to grasp the younger hand and *guide* it. But you had to allow Anna her apprenticeship. The only in- teresting thing she'd done in that early portrait was to drape Arthur in a scarf, a wonderful shade of purple, that wrapped around his neck and lay over his chest. One of Arthur's too carefully rendered hands clutched it.

Miranda's cleverness had been in superimposing the later nude painting of Arthur Messinger against the first, in making her chapter—then her essay—about the growth of a painter through the inception, loss, and later recovery of a complicated relationship.

It had not been easy to uncover the sequence of events that had led Anna to Arthur's bed in St. Vincent's Hospital in 1981. All that Anna's diaries revealed was, "Arthur is back. Visited him at St. Vin- cent's. Awful." Then: "Will bring my sketchbook next time. I have his permission."

Anna was sixty-one at the time. She'd failed to cash in on the great revival of portraiture, of representative art, in the seventies, though not for want of trying. Linda Nochlin, having left Anna out of her momentous essay "Why Have There Been No Great Women Artists?," had included *My Mother's Remarkable Second Act* in an exhibit of women artists she later curated, but it had attracted very little attention. Anna's progress had been piecemeal: she'd moved within the shadow of the bigger names—Alice Neel, Lee Krasner, Elaine de Kooning, Faith Ringgold—then coming into their own. When her work was shown, it was usually a single painting, relegated to a corner. In a 1975 exhibit at the Queens Museum, *Sons and Others: Women Artists See Men*, she'd shown *Aaron, 11*, and forced the then-thirteen-year-old Aaron to attend. ("Excruciating," Aaron had said to Miranda. "I wanted to stand in front of the painting, and tell everybody that my dick was, in fact, showing some signs of progress.") To hear Aaron speak of those years was to hear a history of humiliation. "All around us it was women, women, women, and Anna was saying, 'You know, I'm a woman, too.' And people would nod politely and start taking about Joan Mitchell and Agnes Martin." And then Arthur Messinger had come back into her life.

What was maddening for a biographer were those spaces where the huge events occurred and the subject retreated into a kind of radio silence. Anna's journals were full of details about relatively inessential things. Every conversation with the awful Karl Rattner had been recorded, every decent word out of his mouth (as if Anna were speaking to her future biographer: "Please be kind to me. Sometimes he was nice.") But about Arthur Messinger's momentous reappearance, virtually nothing.

"Sketched Arthur today. He mostly slept. Kept moving his legs. Couldn't get the outline right."

Things like that.

The energy then—Miranda's perceptive energy—had to go into the painting itself, the second nude. *Arthur, Dying.*

Little was yet known about the disease when Arthur went into St. Vincent's. Did it even have a name yet? It was hard to pinpoint the moment when Arthur had returned from California. Miranda had managed to contact Arthur's then-partner, a man now in his eighties, a survivor of the plague years, a hoarder who lived in a rent-controlled apartment in the West Village and was fuzzy about details and a bit resentful of Miranda's probing of his and Arthur's past.

It all—everything she had to say—had to come from the painting.

In the second nude, the sum of what Anna had learned was on display. Arthur's actual body might as well have been a blob of plasma, for all the hard detail. The toes, yes, large and ugly. The spots on the chest, the rust-colored eruptions. The chest itself seemed a thing out of a still life, a platelike shape rendered for its color alone. Anna had painted Arthur holding the hospital sheet off his exposed body, revealing himself with a kind of smirk. Anna had elongated and thinned out his penis so that it looked like a garden hose with a wad of gum stuck in the spout. Still, it allowed Arthur a last affectation of pride. Here it is, here I was. Ecce sexy homo. And in the smirk, the suggestion: I am still ready to fuck anyone who will have me.

Anna had enlarged Arthur's head, a painterly tic that had become a kind of specialty for her by then. Cast aside during the apprentice years was symmetry, exactitude. The human body always chooses its own place in which to fully express itself. In *Aaron, 11*, it had been young Aaron's hands on his hips. In *Jonah on the Cusp*, it had been Jonah's thick, sensual but ultimately withholding lips. In *Arthur, Dying*, the smirk was the defining feature, as if Arthur were addressing death: *Don't think you will have the last word.* And it hadn't. The painting itself made sure of that.

In the earlier nude, Arthur had had a full head of curly hair, a prominent nose, eyes advertising their own loucheness. He had been not a handsome but a prideful man. In the second portrait, only the pride remained, everything else stripped away. The hair was gone, the forehead become massive and articulate, a single blister on it, but what Anna had been able to express in Arthur's eyes was the undying vanity of a man who had come to live for his body, who did not deny its current decay but wished the viewer to see it as a chapter that had been preceded by other chapters. *Remember what I was. Because I do.*

Anna had brought Aaron with her to the AIDS ward. He was then a junior at Brown, but on his semester breaks, she took him with her to meet Arthur, and Arthur, on his hospital bed, had gazed at young Aaron as though reflexively trying to seduce him. "So this is the Infante," Arthur had said. "This is the Dauphin." Aaron had watched his mother sketch, and looked around the hospital ward, given a ringside seat at the inception of Anna's great, life-altering idea.

They were not all young men, but the young men were largely the ones Anna chose to paint. She had to work hard, with some of them, to get permission. And the hospital staff was not always happy with her presence. It was only Aaron's occasional accompaniment that provided Miranda with the details she needed, his description of the obsessiveness that had come over his mother. It was as though she had discovered in the AIDS ward her own *Bedroom in Arles*, her *View of Toledo*, her *Guernica*. Each of the paintings had only a name attached: Peter. Harold. Bobby. Jonathan. Jeffrey. They were young men, she painted them in poses she asked them to choose. "Don't worry. I will know everything I need to know about you by your pose." Peter, an actor, had sat on the edge of his hospital bed. He had covered his genitals with the sheet. Anna allowed this, though she preferred nudity. Bobby was another actor, a young black man who lifted one arm toward his IV drip and gazed at Anna as though she were not quite real, as though none of this was quite real, but perhaps, in rendering him to himself, she could *make* it real. Anna paid little attention to background in these paintings. "She became an artist of the single thing," Miranda had written. "'There is only one thing you need to know,' Anna's work by then had begun to declare. 'Here it is.'"

In one or two of the paintings, a secondary figure hovered in the background space. An absent mother hovered over Jeffrey's bed, a disapproving nurse over the body of Jonathan. By then it had become known that sex had landed most of them in this state, that sex, or drugs, explained the rashes, the dark red blisters, the mouth sores. Over the body of Harold she had painted a red-and-black cross. "I think he spoke to her about Catholicism," was all Aaron would say. "I don't know." But in the empty space between Harold's beseeching eyes and the cross was some larger internal reaching. Anna had painted Harold as she might have painted Saint Sebastian.

In *The New Yorker*, there had only been room for the two portraits of Arthur, and a sepia-toned reproduction of *Peter*. The others had to be alluded to, and because they were unseen—because they had not been viewed together in nearly thirty years—the demand for a show had grown. New York had to see these paintings, collected. Andrew Schechner had done a herculean job of gathering them together from the museums and private collections where they'd been housed. Only one or two collectors demurred. "Cocksucker," Andrew Schechner had said, after hanging up the phone on one. Miranda had been in the office with him. He'd wanted her there, his coconspirator. She'd been flattered, made important beyond her dreams.

Only a hint of Miranda's ambivalence appeared in the essay, an incipient criticism of Anna for what some might call an appropriation of these men's suffering. When she'd spoken to Aaron about it, he'd been silent at first. Then he'd said, "Of course," as if that were all that needed to be said. But he'd already given her enough to go on, describing Anna's face as she watched the young and old men admitted day after day, St. Vincent's soon recalling the received image of the operating rooms of the Civil War, groaning young men and besieged doctors. Let the other women painters have their second wave expressionism and their grids. Anna Soloff had found her late-career subject. And if there were something in this pursuit, in her use of these men's bodies to cause in her biographer a moral ambivalence, so be it.

One by one, the men began dying. Aaron wanted it made known that Anna had held their hands, mopped their faces, spoken into their ears, becoming, for some of them, a surrogate mother. Yet Miranda could not help thinking—*knowing*—that while with one side of her brain Anna had perceived the need to show compassion, with the other she'd allowed ambition to have its way. Was Miranda judging her this way only because Anna was a woman? Men had always done this, and not thought twice about it. Cindy Auerbach would not have judged.

Miranda understood well enough by then, you cannot write about an artist, you cannot inhabit her inner life and study her every move and come away *liking* her. There will arrive a moment when you come face-to-face with the momentous and necessary selfishness. You will have to accept it. The AIDS paintings did what they had to do for Anna's career; they also marked the boundary where the writing became painful for Miranda, even more difficult than it had when she'd been writing about the domestic compromises occasioned by Karl Rattner's presence. In *The New Yorker*, she'd had to tread delicately over her mild disapproval, to lace it through the sentences like inconspicuous punctuation, sometimes blotting it out altogether. I am a conventional, proper (for the most part), well-brought-up young woman who has been lucky enough not to have been forced into choices that might have morally compromised me. Forgive my presumption in judging an artist inhabited by a hunger barely comprehensible to someone like me.

Arthur Messinger was, as it turned out, among those who took longest to die. Anna had worked an agonizingly long time on the portrait, rejecting the first version, keeping Arthur alive (Miranda fancifully wrote) through the effort of trying to get him right. Having finally done that, she released him. It was 1985 when he died.

And perhaps by then, Miranda wrote, Anna and Arthur's initial connection—the tutorial laced with sex—had completed itself. Perhaps Anna finally justified her work with these men by seizing on the political impulse. Presenting them this way to the world might wake the world up. Perhaps. It was, at the very least, a way of thinking about it, though Miranda's background on this was thin. Anna had written nothing about it, the "Course Called the World" never again referred to in Anna's journals. Perhaps by then they had each left politics behind. Or else politics went so deep between Anna and Arthur that it didn't need to be spoken of.

They had, after all, come full circle. Forty-five years earlier, Arthur Messinger had taken a young girl by the hand, introduced her to art and politics as inextricably weaved things, assuming a shape new to him—the heterosexual male lover—in order to do so. Forty-five years later, he'd transformed into yet another unfamiliar shape—ruined, marked, wasted—in order to complete the lesson, and to give Anna's career the boost it needed.

This was, at the very least, a way to frame it.

The elevator doors opened onto a scene that suggested one of those splashy, double-page fashion advertisements that had begun appearing in upscale magazines. Ferragamo and Balenciaga and Versace had taken to setting up multigenerational gatherings on sundecks in Greece, and studiedly ruined dining rooms in Southern Italy. Everyone looked gorgeous, ageless (until you looked hard), buckled tight into the armor of fashion. Had art openings always looked this way? Of course not. Miranda had seen photos of the great MoMA openings of the fifties, where the men all looked like dull ciphers in thick black glasses and thin ties, and the women eschewed fashion, wearing boxy dresses, smoking cigarettes.

Andrew Schechner lifted his arm to wave Miranda over to him, which relieved her entrance anxiety. He was standing with a German critic, a man with a blockish rugby player's body, wearing eyeglasses with flesh-toned transparent rims. The critic looked Miranda over after they'd been introduced like he was reading, knowledgeably, the label of a bottle of wine he'd just been served. Andrew Schechner had referred to Miranda, in his introduction, as "the *cause* of all of this." The gallery owner had something faun-like about him, silver hair worked upward into points above his forehead, an ageless face that betrayed nothing of its owner's character (perhaps some work done here or there, but subtle, expensive, like careful erasures in painting). Miranda had been given no absolutely clear idea of the man's sexuality, though he was selectively intimate with her as they began their working relationship. Above his desk downstairs (open, just off the lobby, where he was there to be approached by anyone who dared) was a small photograph of James Coburn in the late sixties, the actor dressed entirely in black, groomed exquisitely, a transcendent image of cool that Miranda suspected Andrew Schechner modeled himself on.

When Miranda had surprised him by recognizing Coburn, Andrew Schechner had raised his perfect eyebrows. "You're too young to know him," he'd said. "Not if you grew up with the father I grew up with," she'd said, and told him Henry's name, expecting he'd know it. That he didn't—that his face remained blank—was the first of several warning signs as to the nature of the new and difficult territory Miranda feared she was beginning to tread.

Feared, but really *knew*. *The New Yorker*, the Schechner Gallery, small advances from Einaudi and Berlin Verlag, these marked her own ascension, and though they were, of course, things she mentioned to, even discussed with Henry, they were also things that marked a new, unspoken boundary. *The New Yorker* had never touched Henry's work, and *How to Be This Age* had not done significantly well in the few foreign markets where it had been published. Nor had any of the upscale journals taken note of it. Its success had only been of the popular kind. "It's all as it should be," Henry had remarked in one boozy conversation. "You're transcending me." "Stop it," she'd said, because she had to. She knew, right now, that if she looked beyond the artfully rough-hewn Germanic gaze of the man she was talking to, she would likely find Henry and Lily somewhere here, and she wasn't prepared to see them just yet.

The German, meanwhile, was boring in on her, asking her a question about Anna's time line, what she had been painting just before these works. In his eyes were signs of a hedged seduction: that is, he was asking himself the question, did he want to take the step? Miranda could almost see the questions mounting up: Wouldn't he really prefer waking up alone in his boutique hotel, indulging in a large solitary breakfast where conversation didn't have to be forced? Seduction was a reflex, he pulled back from it. Miranda was relieved; she wouldn't have given in, but refusal would have been awkward. Andrew Schechner had already gone off to talk with someone else, one of those impressive older women whose names were like the clicking sound that unlocked a safety deposit box held deep in the bowels of a centuries-old metropolitan bank. The German, excusing himself with faultless manners, moved on to a beckoning colleague. Miranda was briefly alone, yet it was not the aloneness of attending a party where you hoped you would be spoken to. She was as much the hostess here as Andrew Schechner was the host. It was, in a very real way, her party.

Her agent was approaching, tight silver hair, black outfit, a silver clip in the shape of a conch shell gathering in her shoulder wrap. "Everyone is here," her agent said in a low tone. "Get yourself a glass of champagne and mingle please, Miranda."

But no, perhaps not just yet. Before she surveyed the guests in the room, she wanted to survey the paintings. She had participated in the hanging, supervising placement along with Andrew Schechner, the two of them disagreeing only a little. *Peter* was clearly Andrew's favorite, and he had wanted Peter's boyish, mournful face to greet the viewer as soon as the elevator doors opened. So there was Peter, at the end of the long corridor. But Arthur was here, up front, right beside the painted words announcing the show, and the long, printed paragraph Miranda had composed, introducing it. She had suggested placing the two Arthur portraits together, but Andrew had been strict. "These are the AIDS paintings, Miranda. Everybody's read your essay, they already know about the early painting." And of course he had been right. The austerity of this show lay in its unwillingness to dodge what it was about.

"If only she had painted Roy Cohn," someone was saying, and there was laughter. Miranda didn't want to look, to see who had said it. She didn't much want to hear the remarks. A server offered her the requisite flute of champagne and she took a fortifying sip and found Aaron Soloff beside her. Even Aaron's hair looked different tonight, as if the invitation had read "Lacquered hair suggested."

"Well, look what you have done," he said, bowing in mock deference to her. "This, by the way, is Lydia."

She had not yet met Aaron's wife, all these years in. Miranda's first thought was to note how far this woman's looks and expression had retreated from the open, bemused pose Anna had painted her in twenty-five years before, a girl in a green man's shirt (and nothing else), sitting cross-legged on the ottoman in Anna's apartment. In the interim, Lydia had become a lawyer, and grown tight and a little startled-looking.

"This young woman, Lydia, came to me looking like the least likely suspect to jack up Anna's reputation."

"It didn't need much jacking up," Miranda said, and hoped that, in a minute or two, the champagne would do its work and she could begin to relax.

"No, but you've managed to jack it up nonetheless."

He touched Miranda's flute with his own, regarded her as he'd begun regarding her of late, as though he were simultaneously reappraising her on a higher scale, and congratulating himself for knowing in advance that she would rise to meet his standard.

"The family is very happy with what you've done," Lydia said, her voice a little too carefully crafted.

"Lydia's a politician, as you can see," Aaron said. "What she means is that we're ecstatic."

He spoke with his characteristic cool. Miranda wasn't meant to take this entirely seriously; at least, she wasn't meant to get very excited. For months now, she'd been asking to see Anna's still-withheld final self-portrait, *The Remembering Animal* ("I can't *finish* without seeing it") and Aaron continued to gaze on her, in response, from on high, as if one final test remained. She wasn't there quite yet.

"My brother, you'll notice, looks like he's getting ready to piss against the wall."

Aaron pointed out Jonah, at a distance, studying one of the paintings with an arrogant look. Aaron had been a little too exact. If Jonah had any favorites from among his mother's paintings, they were not these. His wife—whom Miranda *had* met, in passing, during one of her visits to the apartment—was with him. Both of the brothers had married women who, if they possessed any humor, worked hard to mask it. Jonah's wife, Yuki, regarded all these naked and seminaked men on the walls with faint distaste.

Miranda couldn't worry about them anymore. Not Aaron, not Jonah, certainly not their wives. She had moved beyond the place (at least, she told herself she had) where she needed their approval. It was a nice thing to have, but it had been a part of her pact with Anna—a part of her growing understanding of Anna—to see that, as they had been in some important way peripheral to Anna's working life, so they had to become peripheral to Miranda's.

She continued to sip champagne. She excused herself from Aaron and his wife, saying there was someone she had to greet. There was no one. There was the swirl—this one and that one—but no one but her parents was absolutely essential. She had not yet eyed them. Andrew Schechner was talking to Peter Schjeldahl, and with a discreet movement of his wrist, motioned Miranda over. Yes, she would be obedient to the dictates. Just not yet. Half a flute of champagne, and it was beginning to feel more justifiably her party.

She stopped before her personal favorite, *Michael*. She had not been able to find out much about the subject of this particular canvas, but he intrigued her. Anna had done a very small 18-by-12-inch portrait of him. Something in the quickness of her brushstrokes—she had used only black and blue—made him seem a kind of prelude to the master plan—*let me do Michael so that I can get on to Peter and Jeffrey and Harold, the big subjects*—but Michael had, in his own way, asserted himself. He was the only one of Anna's subjects captured smiling. (Arthur's smirk couldn't accurately be described as a smile.) It had been Miranda's too-conventional first reaction to Michael to think that he didn't really look gay, but what did that mean? He could have been one of the intravenous drug users, but Miranda didn't think so. No. Something in his pose made her feel she knew his story.

He looked like a laborer, a man who perhaps worked on the docks—thick shoulders, definitely mixed race, one of those beautiful faces whose ethnicity couldn't be decisively locked down. His beauty, as Anna had captured it in her offhand way, was like the surprising rough burnish on Cézanne's apples. There was a dusting of undiluted hope on him.

What Michael invited you to do, more than any of the others, was to imagine the narrative. A young man comes to New York, gorgeous, looking for pleasure. Perhaps Michael was who he resembled: a worker, a young man who spent his days with a wrench in his hand, a tool belt around his waist, laughing and telling jokes, pretending in an easygoing way to be exactly like the men he worked with, and enough like them that it was not even particularly difficult. The only difference was that at night, while the others went home to wives or girlfriends or to bars in Brooklyn and Queens, Michael went to bars not far from this gallery where his portrait was hung, and found his pleasure there, among young men like himself. And why should this not have been? Miranda had to fight a kind of sentimentality in herself in thinking about him, but it was a justified sentimentality. The honest pursuit of pleasure had met a moment in history when to do such a simple thing meant death. Something in Michael's smile, his pose like a figure rising out of a pool of rushing water—a place where, despite the danger, he enjoyed swimming— made Miranda understand the story Anna was telling in these paintings more than any of the others did.

It was moments like these—champagne-infused moments of perception in the midst of a party—that allowed Miranda to forgive Anna. Or, more accurately, to try to join her. It had been Michael, looking and thinking about Michael, that had led Miranda to her own, ultimately foolish idea.

When, at the end of her Wellfleet sojourn, she'd invited Armand DeSaulniers to visit her in the apartment in Brooklyn, and when he'd accepted—she remembered the grin, the enlivened eyes, the *What's this?* that had briefly inhabited his face—she made the decision to buy a sketch pad and some charcoals. It felt, at the beginning, too conscious a thing. She'd reprimanded herself, and then thought *Fuck it,* I am going to do this. I am going to sketch Armand DeSaulniers in the confines of my apartment. I am going to do what Anna did with every one of her lovers, just to see what that is like, and if that is an overly deliberate thing, so be it.

The first time, she had asked him to leave his clothes on. Like an amateur, she'd worked too hard on the lines of his shirt, a blue shirt he'd worn on the visit, crisper than anything she'd imagined him owning, as if he had an idea of New York, a wrong idea, that he had to clean himself up before going there.

She'd not been able to capture anything of him in that first sketch. What was it you had to know in order to inhabit another person's face, to find the truth there, the single true thing? She'd made Armand look generic. It was a talented college girl's sketch. She'd torn it up and Armand had wanted to see it. Putting it together, he'd nodded his head, clearly flattered by the image. "Not bad."

What did it mean now, to have him in her bed, the skylight above them, everything strange, even their bodies strange to one another, though everything worked, the sex worked. It was just that it had lost its raw scent, its sea-change aura. Who was this man when you took him out of his world? She would much rather have sketched him as he stood on the damp sand, in his coveralls, the utter confidence of his pose as he lifted and tossed oysters and stared out at a woman in a kayak who might possibly ask him to alter her life.

She had not told her friends he was coming, which meant she had to find an out-of-the-way restaurant, where they ate not-great food, where he looked more comfortable than she did, and afterward, on the street, put his arm around her in a way that made her self-conscious, as if Brooklyn were watching and judging her. The next morning she asked him to pose nude, and tried again, with no better results. She did not know how to *find* him, and it became yet another way of comparing herself unfavorably to Anna, Anna who had hauled men into her bed and drained them and made beautiful art out of what was left over, children included. But Miranda, it seemed, only knew how to take this man in in a remote place, an island separated from the world, a place dominated by mud and seagrass where a man like Armand could be appreciated like a minor god. In the confines of her apartment he was something else. He tried to coax them into small habits—what should they eat for breakfast? How about this, how about that?—as if they were getting ready to move in together. His wish to find a common domesticity put her off. So that when he got back into his truck, she knew all about herself, knew why it had never worked for her, and never would, the tiny network of compromises required to do the simplest thing, to accept a man's presence, to have a child. It was all romanticized for her, where to make it happen it only had to be simple and real, perhaps even a little boring and dirty. You had to want it more than Miranda wanted it. You had to have an operating part in you—call it blind will—that Miranda was too fastidious for.

Later, after she'd made her decision, when money started to become a bit less tight—after *The New Yorker* had "put her on the map"—she wondered sometimes what might have happened if she'd waited a little longer to decide. In her current situation, she might just have been able to afford single motherhood. It created a small ache to consider this, one that she knew would keep returning, perhaps for the remainder of her life. But she had made her decision, sent him home. When he called—yes, he did call, though only once—she made it clear she had decided against him. She was forty-three now, and though she knew that Armand DeSaulniers was not technically her last hope, the last man in America capable of getting her pregnant, there was something that made her feel *yes he was*. A possibility had arisen out of marsh grass and morning light over salt water, that was all. In Brooklyn's heavier light, it had evaporated.

Thoughts she was jostled out of by a hand at her elbow. Henry, his head tilted forward in mock humility. "Forgive me. I think I know you," he said.

Odd that he had caught her at this exact moment. What did her eyes look like? What did they inadvertently reveal?

"And I am a *big* fan," Henry said. His champagne flute was empty, and even in the moment when he was kissing her cheek, she sensed him looking around for the server. Behind him, Lily, overdressed for this event, in a shawl and a vintage ensemble, waited to greet her daughter with a look of unease that Miranda was unused to. Miranda, leaning forward to accept Lily's kiss, held back on a thought that felt cruel: Her mother had misjudged the nature of this event, dressed as though this were *theater.* There was something regal in the way Lily presented herself, and this was, well, another, different kind of theater, the theater not of large sets and costumes, but the theater of the sharp single gesture. Lily was not a queen here, and seemed to *get* that, if a bit late.

"This is wonderful," Lily was saying. "I *knew* some of these men, you know that."

"No."

"Oh God, yes. Peter in *Streamers.* Bobby in that Athol Fugard play."

Henry was nodding, still looking around for the second (or might it be the third?) flute of champagne.

"We didn't know them well," Henry was saying. "*Saw* them."

"No, I knew Bobby," Lily said. "It's extraordinary. A tribute. They're not forgotten."

"No," Miranda said.

"Ah, here we are," Henry said, finding the server and beckoning him near. "And one for you?" he asked Miranda.

"Yes, please."

"But none for your mother. She's liable to become embarrassing."

Good that Henry was socially at ease tonight, among people who didn't know him. Miranda chose not to inhibit herself. The second glass of champagne went down more quickly than the first. When she'd had what had been politely referred to as a "drinking problem" at Barnard, it had been Henry who had attended to her in her hour of need. Lily had been, if Miranda recalled correctly, in rehearsal for something, out of town. "You and I are just a couple of old drunks," Henry had said to her softly, in her dorm room, tucking her in after their visit to the infirmary. "But you know, the likelihood is, we'll be all right."

It was a relief to see Henry socially at ease because he had not been at his best since he'd returned from his last two trips to Haiti. There had been one eighteen or nineteen months ago, just after the opening of his play, and then another this past fall. He made only the briefest explanations for his continued involvement, something about trying to arrange a scholarship at Grantham Prep for a Haitian boy. Since the fall trip, Henry had seemed to have been suffering from something debilitating, his skin reflecting it. He never seemed quite *close shaven*. Miranda and Lily had whispered about it. Had Henry picked up a slow-growing tropical disease? He had never, though, become literally sick.

"You're coming to dinner afterwards, of course," Miranda said.

"Oh darling, you don't really want the old folks, do you?" Henry said.

"I do, actually. I want the old folks."

"Better we should go back to the Home. Let you shine."

"No. I want you."

And yes, there were these moments, still, when, even in the midst of celebratory events like this, she did want them to huddle, to gather in close, to assert a defense, an allegiance, a sense of their being an exclusive club. She and Henry, with Lily the peripheral but still necessary third. Without Lily it would be too difficult. Yet what complicated the moment was something new in Henry's eyes. What had made things between them safe, if frustrating, even in the days when their relations had been most intense, was the sense that he would always seek an escape when intimacy became too much for him. His work would call him away. Or ego. Or simple male discomfort. What was new—what was undeniable—was the recent absence of that self-regulating look. It was as though he wanted to tell her something that she didn't want to hear.

"Philip sends his regrets, by the way. He's off making his seventh or eighth million. He suggested we maybe put in a bid to buy one of these."

Then, Henry seemed to quite suddenly pivot. "Who's this?"

The elevator doors had opened, someone had entered the gathering, and there was something in the nature of a kerfuffle going on. Was this a celebrity entrance? Who, then? Miranda looked, and saw that it was Cindy Auerbach who had come in, and that something was going on at the reception table. Cindy Auerbach was clearly disturbed. Miranda had forgotten to leave her name.

"Excuse me," she said to her parents, and moved toward the table.

"I'm so sorry, I meant to leave Cindy's name as a guest."

The girl behind the table looked confused. Cindy Auerbach made no effort to hide her annoyance. "Don't you *know* me?" she said to the girl. "I'm the show downstairs."

"What's this?" Andrew Schechner had come forward.

"I told Cindy I would put her name on the list," Miranda said. "And I forgot."

"Well, of *course*," Andrew said, and didn't mean it. "And *Paolo*, of course. The more the merrier."

He was not pleased, but Cindy Auerbach had won her point. Having been granted entrance, she moved past Miranda and Andrew, found a young art critic who seemed to know her, and using that contact as a launching pad, began to survey the room for whom she might next approach.

"Extraordinary," Andrew said to Miranda, "how much space she can take up."

"I am sorry," Miranda said.

Andrew said nothing. He would not chastise her, he would allow his silence to say everything. They could only hope that the presence of the paintings, and the largeness of the crowd, would be sufficient to absorb Cindy Auerbach's intrusion.

Miranda returned to her parents.

"Who's she?" Lily asked.

"An artist," Miranda said.

In what subtle, or unsubtle, way had it all been ruined? Miranda was at pains to say. It was adolescent, it was beyond adolescent. It was childhood. It had been meant to be her party, and was no longer. All eyes—or enough of them to make a difference—were on Cindy Auerbach, or on Paolo. She had brought a kind of life, or energy, into the room; had made it, for the moment, about her. The men on the walls were all dead men. Focus would return to them, of course. It had to, this was an art opening, these were people who lived for this sort of thing, but at this moment they were also people capable of being distracted. Miranda felt it.

"Are you all right?" Henry asked.

"Yes. Fine. She's a little annoying, is all," Miranda said. And felt an effort she didn't fully understand, to draw everyone's attention away from Cindy Auerbach, and Paolo, back toward Michael and Peter and Jeffrey. She felt a strong wish for these dead young men that the world was still not fully prepared to grant. It had been at the edge of things for Miranda, but now, with Cindy Auerbach's career-focused entrance, her sucking up all the air in the room, it settled at the center. These men had become commodities, hadn't they? And she, in her way, had participated in making them commodities, "jacking up" their value so that to look at them was not to see them but something they had come to stand for, the late work of an artist whose value on the market was becoming astronomical. The ability to honor who they'd been as men seemed secondary to something else. What vast sums would Peter's and Jeffrey's and Harold's agonies now yield?

Cindy Auerbach's voice came to Miranda across the room—perhaps it was not the artist's, but she heard it as the artist's—and she understood, with an accompanying pang that affected her in the vulnerable area of her womb—that what she was seeing in Cindy Auerbach was what she had tried so hard *not* to see in Anna. Pure ambition, use of people, that ability to make a noise in the world that was essential if you were going to be noticed. And something else, the other, inadmissible, undeniable thing, the power of certain women to go after art and fame and motherhood all at once, to discount nothing in the quest for the fullest possible life.

She had not known she was still so vulnerable to this. Having made the decision as to how she was going to live her own life, she'd believed any lingering pain would be minimal.

"Darling," Henry was saying, taking her arm, picking up on something. Lily had started a conversation with another woman.

"No, I'm all right."

She excused herself, crossed the room, went into the bathroom. Two women were talking at the mirror, the subject was real estate. Not even to have quiet here. She closed herself into a stall. Why wasn't she up to this? It was so unbelievably stupid, this urge to run away at the same moment when it was most essential to assert herself. If she had had a child, if she, like Cindy Auerbach, were brazenly carrying the result of her full grasp and demand of life, would this event have been different? Would the *questions* be different?

In the stall she finally understood that the bathroom had emptied, the two real estate mavens had left. This was a relief. But it was ridiculous to think she could stay here. Perhaps she'd been overexcited at the beginning, overly impressed by her own importance at this event. Perhaps she only needed to breathe. It had been a moment of weakness, that was all. Now she needed to go back out. It is all right, she kept saying to herself, even as she saw, in repeated motion, the elevator doors closing on Meryl Streep's recanting face. "So I will not be your mother, after all."

At the dinner afterward, held at a restaurant just uptown, one that Miranda knew to be expensive and highly regarded, Henry and Lily had been seated at the end of the table, at a distance from Miranda. Andrew Schechner had arranged the seating. He was as strict about it as he had been about where certain paintings were to be hung.

Miranda felt protective, wanted to go and sit with them, but Andrew insisted that she sit beside him, that she talk up the biography with the people he'd gathered closest to himself, a gallery owner from Cologne, a museum curator from Houston, a woman who had assumed the late-twentieth-century position at the auction house that was the chief rival of Miranda's former employer.

So yes, she would talk it up. The book would be done, she hoped, in a year, which meant it would come out in two, which would be nice, because the woman from the Houston museum wanted the AIDS paintings then, in two years. Would Miranda come and speak? Of course. Andrew was convinced the show they had just left would draw glowing notices, and as he spoke, he broke something he hadn't intended to, a spelt cracker from the meager assortment that had been placed before them, and Miranda noted the microscopic anxiety rippling the man's perfect exterior. Andrew saw her noticing, and smiled, as if to say, *You will now kindly erase that from your mind.* She kept glancing down the table at Henry and Lily, and saw them consulting the menus printed on single sheets of good paper, though Andrew would do the ordering, and they ought to have known that. It would have been better, in the end, not to have invited them, to have allowed them to go off together to one of the old-school New York hangouts they favored, Shun Lee or the V&T on Amsterdam, places where they'd eaten forever, where they were known and courted by the waiters.

This was yet another form of separation Miranda had to deal with. Andrew had taken her to this particular restaurant once before. She knew the small plates he would order. She knew the quality of the stones in the impeccably laid-out trays that separated the tables, the fish in the small tanks that were the restaurant's nod to kitsch, as if the architectural group who had designed it knew instinctively how quickly clean, spare lines grew old, how you had to allude to corniness in order to transcend it.

As soon as she could, at the moment when Andrew Schechner tacitly allowed it, she went and sat with her parents. When she pulled up a chair from an empty adjoining table, a nearby waiter held up his hand. "Only for a minute, I promise," she said, before turning to her parents. "I'm sorry. Andrew insists I sell myself, and the book, and these people . . ." She didn't finish.

"Darling, do you think we don't understand? Your mother and I have done a lifetime of shilling ourselves."

She took the menu out of Henry's hands and placed it on the table.

"He'll order, you know."

"Of course."

It embarrassed her that she needed to instruct her father. She had to excuse herself for any diminishing thoughts she might be having about them. The reversal was too difficult. She remembered the night in the restaurant farther downtown, the celebration dinner where Henry had saved a man from being beaten up by a cabdriver. She wished for that Henry back.

"So when are you going to Haiti?" she asked him.

"In June," Henry said.

June was still three months away.

"If the weather there holds. If there's not a revolution."

"If it's safe," Lily said.

"Yes, that too."

He reached out one hand, and touched and pulled Lily's hand toward him. Their secrets seemed then, to Miranda, enormous. She had to bow out. A couple was arriving, the empty table would need the chair she'd taken. Miranda stood.

"It'll be very good, the food," she said.

"Oh, no doubt," Henry said.

One last look, then, and Miranda found herself done in. When she thought of it later, an image dominated. Henry as drowning man, his arm reaching out for her from the center of a whirlpool. She flinched, tried to keep her arm away from him, but at the last moment, he grabbed it. It happened that way in dreams. This was like that. She wasn't even certain why. There was nothing unusual going on. Nothing to justify her fear. Just his face, which she was able to read like code.

In turning away, she looked through the windows of the restaurant and saw pedestrians outside. It had turned into a drizzly March evening. Faces tilted toward the restaurant, a blankness. The kind of open, undetailed faces Anna had painted in her bleakest New York paintings. Hunger and mourning was outside, and here, inside, was a kind of glitter, was a curator from Houston who was inviting her to speak. She was being lifted. After a lifetime of striving, here it was. Come up, Miranda, come up to the level where it is safe, where food is served on small, perfect plates, where no one looks at the prices. Gaze down from this high perch, and what do you find but an image of your father clutching your wrist, his eyes large and red-rimmed and defeated looking. I am drowning, my darling. You must come with me. And as in dreams, you did.

2.

Nearly eighteen months had passed at that point since Henry's night in the rat-infested house in Haiti. His plan had been to return the following spring, to accompany Jean to the testing site in Port-au-Prince, where Jean would take the necessary test. No one else was available to do this, apparently. Henry had not minded that his presence would be required, though it was fraught. He knew that. Knew that the residue of what had nearly happened—or, more accurately, what had been *suggested*—in Père Felix's house would follow him.

Plans were made, a fee paid for the test, and then those plans had to be called off that spring when Haiti once again imploded. It was not an uncommon occurrence. Events like the one that prevented Henry's return had been given a name. Days without rules. Days when Haiti, normally just another loosely organized island chaos, gave in to the most melodramatic version of itself. Gunfire in the streets, sudden threats of kidnapping, buildings set on fire. A movement in the government was all it took sometimes, a promise broken, an agreement not popularly embraced. "It is not safe," Sister Beatrice had said to Henry on the phone. Their flight had been booked for early March.

"Well, then, when can we go, if not now?" he asked.

"If things calm down, we can go in the fall."

"But the fall—Beatrice, the plan was to get things started here for him. He's already nineteen, when will he be twenty?"

"Summer. August, I think."

Jean was not her first concern, but she knew his birthday. Every hair of every head.

"Twenty," Henry repeated dully.

"They will give the test again in the fall," Beatrice assured him.

It was extraordinary to find himself having such mixed feelings about it. He'd been given a gift. At least he could think about it that way. He'd been given time, at least. Time to think more carefully about what had happened. Time to convince Lily, who was not so far convinced at all. Who in fact hated the idea of a boy from Haiti coming to, at least potentially, live in their house for a year.

His hesitation went beyond Lily's potential disapproval. Jean's read of him lingered. From time to time, he considered dropping the whole effort, but was the fact that Jean had seen into him, seen the part that he was suppressing, enough of an excuse? Finally, no.

He needed only to take a step away, to see the task before him. If Jean could go to Grantham Prep, that was enough. The complications would then cease to matter.

None of this could he reveal to Lily. None of it. It would be cruel to foist it on her. Better to deal with it alone. Because there was no one with whom he felt he could honestly speak of it. Too much shame was involved.

His friends, the men in his dinner group, might have been the logical ones to discuss this with. They were professionals, after all, seasoned men, and he'd spoken enough about his same-sex attractions (all relegated, of course, to his earlier life, his youth) that they would likely not even be surprised. But it was too easy to imagine their assessments, the distaste, the outright disgust they would try very hard to keep from appearing on their faces. This boy was *how old?* And after their analyses, he could expect the too easy, even forced forgiveness, the camaraderie of the sexually forlorn, the *Who is to say what is* normal? and then the *You did the right thing, you held back, don't chasten yourself for the desire.* Those sorts of things would be said, over the overcooked plates of arctic char at the Grantham Tavern. He didn't want that. It was too easy to live in the world of anticlerical absolution. There was something, he was convinced, they would not understand. Something even *he* did not understand. He only knew that he felt resistant to the reduction they would no doubt offer. That the ambiguous offer had been made *mattered.* Never mind his strenuous resistance to it. The fact of it mattered.

He'd taken these thoughts with him on his daily walks to the beaver pond. In late spring the ground was barely thawed. Certain branches were still encased in ice, the ground muddy. The beaver himself was not to be found, no doubt hibernating somewhere, under the knotted cave of felled trees. There was a part of Henry that had always resisted analysis, shied from doing much therapy even when it seemed most called for. *Take it to God* had always been his mantra, but where was God these days? Hibernating, like the beaver. Left to himself, he could only wrestle as best he could with the basic question: Was his attraction to Jean something that would always corrupt whatever good he might do him?

He had prided himself on getting through the night in the rat-infested house, with Jean standing guard in his chair. He'd even managed a few hours' sleep. Jean had occasionally left him to check on Nelson. In his absence, the scuttling had returned, but Jean had always returned in time. In the morning he was still in the chair, watching over Henry. They exchanged a look, very different from the one they had exchanged the night before, but no more easy to interpret.

It was this second look that came back to Henry as he sat on a damp log by the beaver pond, musing. It was as if a bond had been sealed that night. What he had seen on the face of the sleepless boy who had guarded him was that the flexing of muscles, the sexual preening, the mastery of the Haitian physical world had all receded. The rats were gone. What was left was a vulnerable boy trapped on a small island, and before him, on the bed, rumpled, waking into consciousness, was what Père Felix had always encouraged Henry to be. Hope.

Henry then determined, so far as it was possible to do so, that what had happened was not enough to deter him from doing what he intended to do. He was not twenty-five. He was not even forty. Age would take care of a great deal, all on its own. You did not go back against your own best intentions just because a challenge was involved.

Meanwhile, as Henry wrestled with such questions that spring and summer, the underground movements of "career" began, unexpectedly, to nose up, like the green-headed shoots of nearly forgotten perennials. Since the failure of *Third World*, Henry had been unable to come up with another project exciting enough to bestir him. His agent suggested a sequel to *How to Be This Age.* "And call it what?" Henry shouted into the phone. "'Something I Forgot to Tell You the First Time'? I have shot my wisdom wad." The odd-sounding phrase caused his agent to pause. A "wisdom wad"? *Really*, Henry? But there was something else to consider. Though the show itself had been off the air for more than twenty years, the cast of *Lawson's Bend* was still miraculously alive. Henry received a call one day in summer, after the postponement of his spring trip to Haiti, from the friend in L.A. who had first lured him into his absurd but lucrative involvement with that long-running series. The beloved white-haired leading man—a "TV icon," as he was always referred to—had apparently grown bored with his current stint as the spokesman for a company hawking reverse mortgages. Viewers of the Hallmark Channel were used to seeing him walking with similarly white-haired couples, sagely counseling them on the virtues of handing over their hard-won home equity to a consortium of shysters. The "icon" of *Lawson's Bend* was apparently worried about his image, and thought a one-off return to his fictionalized Montana ranch—surrounded by his endlessly challenged wife, his larcenous brother-in-law, his rascally son and sexually rapacious daughter, along with the evil son-from-an-early-affair who had surfaced, Mordred-like, in season 3—would be just the thing to restore his fading reputation. Henry at least agreed to listen to the proposal from his former writing partner, one of those septuagenarian charmers hanging on by a thread in L.A., desperate for one last run at the table. Pitching the idea to Henry, he'd quoted Tennyson's "Ulysses" ("We are not now that strength which in old days / Moved earth and heaven"), making Henry laugh. "I think the only thing we moved in 'old days' was a few clichés." Still, he encouraged the man. There was something to be said, in the midst of his predicament, for indulging an old hustler. Why not do something absurd, return to Hollywood for a bit? The deal was dependent on the availability—and interest—of the actor who had played the rascal son, the only member of the cast who had managed to carve out a semblance of a film career. Summer was spent waiting out this actor's decision.

At the same time, Lily, whose agent had never stopped sending her plays to consider, finally found one that interested her. When Henry read it (she asked for his advice), he wasn't sure whether her interest had as much to do with the merits of the play as with a desire to get away for a bit from her morose husband. But she was fond of the playwright, whose work she had performed in years before, and whose career had endured a long and painful silence. Fond as well of the producer, André Bishop, who would be producing the play at Lincoln Center. She took her time, but finally said yes, surprising Henry, and instilling in him a bit of fear.

Because, though rehearsals for the play would not begin for a year, he knew that the lead-up would require Lily's frequent presence in New York, and to be alone in this crisis seemed more frightening than to be accompanied by someone with whom he could not speak of it. Then, how long would the rehearsals last? Four weeks, followed by an eight-week run. Henry would have to live in solitude for three months the following spring. A mild, at first manageable panic besieged him, his need for Lily's presence, her nearness, making itself known in the most painful way. As much silence as there was between them now, as much that remained unspoken, it was still his marriage, Lily was his life companion, and he depended on her. Needed her. Perhaps his proposed trip to Hollywood, should it happen, could be made to coincide with Lily's rehearsals. But life, let's face it, is never so kind. You have used up its kindness, Henry. That drawer is empty. At the end of the summer, the actor whose commitment they'd been waiting on dropped out. The TV project collapsed. He was booked to go to Haiti, to accompany Jean to his test, in late September. It was June, not August, when Jean had his birthday. Henry sent, by way of Beatrice, a card.

On the plane, he was accompanied by a small group from Leominster, all women, all women of a certain age. About Haiti, they seemed worried, and Beatrice had asked him to act as a reassurer.

How easily the role came to him, how little effort it took to slip back into the figure of the jocular bon vivant, the man who had done this so many times there was really nothing to it. The world was full of frauds, and he was ever willing to become, again, one of them. Were he to disclose to the apparently unamusable ex-nurse from Leominster who had been seated next to him on the flight the complexity of his relations with Jean, could her reaction be anything but suspicion? Yet he tried to imagine—she had taken out a book of crossword puzzles on the plane—that she might surprise him by revealing herself to be one of God's reported angels, those who walk the earth in human form, capable of infinite understanding and forgiveness. He imagined kissing her dry, aged forehead in thanks. "I think the word you want is 'aleatory,'" he said instead. The hint had been "depending on the roll of the dice." "Of course," she said, a little annoyed with him. "I think I'd have gotten that with a bit more time."

They were to stay in separate quarters, Henry above the woodworking school, the others in some sort of hostel Beatrice had managed to book.

Then, to find himself alone in the warren of beds. He bounced lightly, testing the springs on one bed after another. A gorgeous large silver-and-crimson-laced cloud hovered outside the window. It covered the canvas of the sky from just above the point where the cove reached its cuplike curve to the point opposite, where the rise of buildings to the east obscured Henry's view. There, in the water, was the familiar detritus, but the sun's rays penetrated just enough of the cloud to have created a small blanket of light in the water. Had he come to love Haiti? He was uncertain. But it was familiar now, like an old, not quite beloved friend in whom one sensed there were still depths to be plumbed. He lay on the chosen bed and waited. The words that appeared in his mind were "All right." All right. Here. Now. There is no longer any avoidance of what I have come here to do.

At the dinner Beatrice hosted in the hostel down the street, nearly adjacent to the bishop's residence, he listened to her tell the ladies from Leominster how, in the morning, Henry would accompany a young Haitian boy to the Lycée Français in Port-au-Prince to take a test that might—"fingers crossed," she said in her vowel-elongating Haitian accent—allow the boy entrance into a private school in America. The ladies murmured in response, the air full of goodness, as if just within reach were the acts capable of righting the world. Beatrice had made her peace with Henry's mission, apparently. She was not angry with him anymore, though she continued to evince a tentativeness with regard to the plan.

Alone in the large bedroom (Beatrice had instructed him in how to lock the building behind him), Henry knelt and attempted a prayer. Nothing he could say to the only half-believed-in God he was ostensibly praying to could be unadulterated. If there were in fact a listening God, He knew Henry better than Henry knew himself, knew exactly how much was sordid and dishonest about him, knew what was perhaps broken beyond repair, but knew, too—perhaps, perhaps—that beyond all the obvious dark evidence there was a strange, hoped-for purity to this moment. Was he being too easy on himself in thinking this? He lowered his forehead to the fist bunched into the position of prayer, the fist laid against sheets wrapped tight on this simple Haitian bed. He could not elicit—had no real use for—the established doctrine of the Catholic Church. All that had value was the humility implicit in the submission of prayer, the unvoiced words offered to God: "I do not know what the fuck I am doing. You know that, of course. Let's hold that truth between ourselves. Someday when we meet, should the fiction of an afterlife prove to be a reality, we will acknowledge that. Glancing lightly over me, among the massed dead, you will simply say, 'Oh yes, you were Henry.'"

That night, he slept well.

He had to wake at five to meet the van a half hour later. The drive to Port-au-Prince would take over three hours, the test being given at nine. He stood outside in the surprisingly chill predawn darkness. He had with him, in his satchel, the official documents Jean would need in order to take the test.

The darkness was deep blue, indigo, a color that had to be individual to the islands in the Caribbean. You did not see this color at early morning in the States. What you saw in Massachusetts was a uniform Puritan black, but here the sea and the vegetation seemed to inform the evening's palette. At a distance, a motorcycle revved, a truck raced down the streets, a hint of music. He waited. He was cold, but this was undeniably beautiful, to stand here, the white plastered walls of the buildings seeming classic, ancient. It was pleasant to indulge romantic thoughts about Haiti, thoughts engendered by his prayer of the night before. He found that fear and uncertainty had entirely left him. He was strangely willing to erase everything else from his life, to become only *this* man, waiting here, a little cold, hands in his pockets, picking up, faintly, a scent composed of some combination of sweet bread and garbage.

The van approached slowly. Beatrice had made the arrangements, he had only been told where to wait, so he was not certain this was his ride until it stopped before him. The driver was young, thin, nattily bearded, leaning forward, talking on the phone, a 5:30 a.m. urgency apparent. In the back seat, Henry saw only the outline of what had to be Jean.

He opened the van's rear door and swung inside. It was not Jean. Who, then? He had the brief old-womanish fear that he was being kidnapped. The dark eyes of the young man beside him took him in with a fullness, a knowingness. The figure bowed its head slightly. Of course it was Jean. How stupid of him.

Nineteen. In the year that had passed, something further had changed in the shape of Jean's face, which he could see only in the dark, illuminated by the flashes of streetlights. The mustache was gone, thank God. But there was a slightly heavier jowl. The hair on his head was longer, bushier. He had allowed himself to become a man. "Allowed himself." Another silliness, another wrong naming of the world.

"Hello, Jean."

"Hello."

He settled in. There were three of them in the back seat, Henry, Jean, and a strangeness not entirely uncomfortable. Outside, a yellowish light the color of a ripening mango was pushing up against the underside of the indigo.

"The driver knows where we are going?"

Jean spoke in Kreyol to the man, who continued to speak, with urgency, into his phone.

"Ya, ya," the driver said, and shifted, but did not give up on the phone conversation.

There seemed very little to say. It was not long before they were out of Les Cayes, the streets already peopling themselves in small clusters, vendors setting up their stalls, young men who had perhaps not slept the night before returning from revels, staggering a bit, an old woman awkwardly carrying what looked like a bass drum. The day beginning, the driver annoyingly intent on convincing whoever was on the other end of his call of something. A foreign language seems to render every argument trivial. "You are ready, Jean?" Henry asked. The boy nodded, stared ahead. Of course he wasn't. In the informational call Henry had made to Evan Hatch at Grantham Prep, he'd been informed that Jean would be required to write "Four or five paragraphs," and when Henry had asked what they might be about, the admissions director had said, "Oh, something about the environment, maybe. How do you clean up the world?" Had Jean ever had a thought about cleaning up the world?

At the same time that such a thought worried him, he could revel in the sheer beauty of this moment. The yellow light pressed upward, intruding farther on the indigo, and they were past the low buildings, into the thicket of trees. There was still evidence of life, men walking, white shirts, a scythe or a machete in hand. On their way to work? How could anything be known? This was why white people feared Haiti. How could you be freed of the melodramatic fear that the van would be flagged down, halted, the machete put to work on the murder of these three? But Henry had no fear. Even if the melodramatic turned out to be true, let it happen if it must. What better end? Beside him, he noted Jean nodding. The boy had fallen asleep.

The driver then, having signed off on the quarrelsome call, punched in music, something abrasive-sounding. No. Henry leaned forward, said the words, "Please, the boy is sleeping" and the man didn't understand, until Henry gestured, and the driver noted it and, unhappy, turned off the music. Wanting to pacify, Henry asked, "Kompa?" about the music, and received no reply. Kompa was the only thing he knew. No need for the driver to answer. Light was entering the vehicle, just enough to instill that feeling of endlessness, of hammock, that suggestion in certain movements forward that there is no necessity to name a destination.

Jean, in sleep, slumped toward him so that the boy's—but he could not call him a boy anymore—the young man's physical presence intruded into Henry's space. It was not so much the smell, though Jean had a distinct smell, copperish, not unpleasant but not entirely fresh. Not "fresh," that is, in the way an American would use the word: Dial soap, deodorant. Jean had worn his familiar basketball shorts, his long legs grew out of them, just enough hair on them to indicate some advance toward actual manhood that filled Henry with a combination of tenderness and repulsion. Jean seemed at this moment too *big* for this journey, his body too large to be funneled into the Lycée Français, where Henry imagined he would find himself among much younger boys, boys like the one Jean had been when Henry had first encountered him in the choir. The blue pants, the perceived innocence. No matter. Henry thought this both the strangest moment of his life and perhaps the sweetest, a moment blissfully resisting definition, as the boy, stretching back, shocked into wakefulness, blinked, smiled at Henry, said "Sorry," as if the intrusion into his space was an impoliteness. Left behind, it would appear, was the sexual tension of the night with the rats.

Still, Henry was not fool enough to believe that tension could be so neatly swept away. It seemed, though, to have been replaced by something else. Thomas Mann had named the feeling beautifully in *Death in Venice* (a book Henry had of course felt compelled to reread): what von Aschenbach had found in staying on in Venice, in casting loose from the rigidity of his former life, were "the boons that chaos might confer." Henry found that all the larger questions—the big New England questions of order and morality that had plagued him in considering this trip—were at a great distance now. Who could fault him for what he was doing? Didn't a man at his stage of life get to play a little bit with chaos and its potential boons, to allow himself to go for a ride in a van on a highway in Haiti, an act far from the rigidity of life as he'd known it to this point? Henry folded his hands. Welcome, chaos. I am prepared to embrace you. Jean retreated again into sleep.

But then it came—of course it came, the yin and yang of every radical act in a life—the opposite feeling. The potential that in indulging himself this way—in giving in to the chaos, the late-life indulgence of this ride in Haiti—he might be doing some damage. To the boy, to the boy's actual hopes. Was it all a game for him? He had done nothing to prepare Jean, had not even tried to find a copy of an old test to give him some sense of what might be expected. He was leaving everything to chance, and it seemed now, more than ever, a game he was playing, one with potentially painful results for this sleeping young man beside him.

They were in the outskirts of Port-au-Prince soon enough, the endless outskirts, the commercial road extending into the woods so that the actual separation of city and country was not discernible. The shipping, the high useless cranes perched heron-like over the water, the deserted-looking tent city.

Henry checked his watch and saw that there were only fifteen minutes to go before the test began. Even his limited knowledge of Port-au-Prince told him you could not get anywhere in the city in fifteen minutes, not unless you were a block away from it, and even then you were dependent on the streets being open, on there being no overturned vehicle in the middle of the road, on the weight of street life not inhibiting you with its blind force. He leaned toward the driver and pointed to his watch and said "Quinze minutes" with some urgency, but the driver only nodded, either not understanding or not caring, his brief regard of Henry like the regard of one species to another on a dirt path in the desert, the driver's face exhibiting a quickened, charged, troubled existence taking in Henry's aged whiteness, softness, this man for whom little should matter, the fight of life having already been fought and won. That was the tiny moment they shared, and Henry began to panic.

He touched Jean's knee, woke the boy. Jean rearranged his legs, saw where they were, blinked, scratched his own hair in a self-awakening gesture.

"Jean, I'm afraid we're going to be late."

Jean could not be made to panic. He regarded Port-au-Prince blankly (Henry had to wonder: Had Jean been here before?), then yawned.

It mattered more to Henry than to Jean, than to the driver. What was the degree of his responsibility? To be an American—to be an American who had managed to follow rules and achieve something in a competitive society—was to impose an importance on time and rigor that had no place—he thought now—in this van. They would get there when they got there. If they were late—if Jean had insufficient time to pass the test—that would be that.

In his panic (he was working on it), he turned to Jean.

"I feel I ought to have prepared you more."

Jean smiled without concern. Perhaps he felt that merely by entering the rooms of the Lycée Français he was entering his new, unprepared-for but still inevitable future.

"Jean, they may ask you to write something."

Jean nodded.

"I'm told, one of the things you may have to write about is—environmental issues."

Jean's expression did not change. The question seemed now absurd. Henry smiled as if to dismiss his own urgency.

"Jean, let's discuss this. If they ask you to write about the environment—"

"I will say stop cutting trees for fuel."

Taken aback, Henry smiled.

"Yes. That's good."

"It makes the landslide. The roots don't hold the soil in place anymore."

Jean was not even looking at him, but Henry offered him a smile of approval. How stupid to have underestimated him. Thought was here. Thought and intelligence, and perhaps all would be well after all.

As if spurred by Henry's new optimism, the driver began a series of quick turns, off the main roads, into neighborhoods Henry had not seen before. The city seemed all hill. On the terrace of a two-story house, a woman stood in a bright orange dress, brown skinned, full breasted, an image of health and beauty. He wanted to point her out to Jean, a perhaps-absurd impulse: You see, there is no reason to leave. There is beauty here. It is not entirely a place to be escaped. But beside them on the street was a man swearing at the top of his lungs, swearing at no one—at the air, the walls—and it was this man, not the woman in the orange dress, that Jean chose to regard. Jean's face reflected his sight of the man with a beautiful, empty passivity. Here in the city was the known world, heightened.

There were more sharp turns. The driver was showing his skill now, his knowledge of the city. They had five minutes to reach the Lycée, and Henry was encouraged to believe they might actually make it, though some unlucky pedestrian might have to offer her life in service of this goal. Whenever they were stopped in traffic, the driver leaned on his horn as if to awaken hell, a sound that affected no one, movement went on at the same pace on all sides. They continued to climb hills, the gears grinding, the driver swearing, until there was less life on the streets, a whiteness, occasional evidence of the earthquake all these years later, empty lots containing rubble that had not been attended to, small crosses, Catholicism making itself known in ways subtle and unsubtle, Catholicism and death holding a grip on certain neighborhoods, until, in the end, lest you ever think you could *get* Haiti, the presence of a bank, men in suits, women in stunning dresses and high heels, black wrought iron over arched doorways that looked only slightly crooked, a sophistication meant to transcend. Beside him, Jean took all this in.

Until they were stopped. The driver scratched his beard, made a small gesture with his hand. Of course. A line of boys approached the gated aperture, a line of boys who looked very young, in white shirts and black and gray pants, some of them wearing ties, some of them with glasses, boys who had been tended by parents, brushed and combed and with a slight hop in their steps, some of them pushing at one another. Was it an absurd gesture, to send Jean in among them? They were seven minutes late, but no matter. They would not be the latest.

"This is it, Jean."

"Yes."

The boy's—the young man's—wonderful lack of anxiety. Henry opened the door. The heat was extraordinary, he felt sweat instantly rising on his skin, but Jean stood beside him, he saw now for the first time, having grown taller than Henry. Taller than any of the other boys. The basketball shorts, the loose-fitting nylon shorts. Could someone not have told him how to dress for this? No, don't think about that. Henry touched his satchel and said, "I have it all here, Jean." He would go in with him. He would make sure all was in order.

First, though, he leaned in to speak to the driver. "You will wait here?"

The driver, touching again the fringe of his beard, made a gesture similar to the one he'd made to let them know they'd arrived.

"Not allowed," the driver said.

"Well, how long—?" Henry realized the driver couldn't tell him. "I'll find out how long the test is and have you meet us."

The driver offered a slow nod. Henry touched Jean's shoulder and motioned him forward.

The Lycée Français was like a hotel out of some Spanish epic, you could imagine thin-bearded eighteenth-century grandees plotting for a slice of the island here, over iced drinks. There were palm fronds. There were arches. The building dipped from its entrance level, revealing floors below. At the far end of a cool hallway, two nuns sat at a long plank table, signing in the boys, whose entrance noises gave way to something only slightly more restrained as they approached the table. Henry was pleased to see that not all of the boys were wearing white shirts. Two or three tall, handsome, blue-shirted Haitian men—men with the look of physical-education instructors at a well-heeled American high school—directed the boys as to where they should go. Henry had one hand on Jean's shoulder as he presented the documentation to a wizened-faced nun, a nun wearing surprisingly fashionable round eyeglasses. He fought the urge to make some excuse for Jean's tallness, his age. He glanced up at the handsome proctors, one of whom stared at Jean with a look Henry at first feared—as though Jean would be denied entrance because of his size—until he understood it was only the look of an older man assessing a younger man's potential, the look of a basketball coach studying the body of a young man at tryouts. He, Henry, was carrying a rigid sense of what was expected that had no place here. No one cared that Jean was tall, that he was older than the other boys. The nun shouted to one of the proctors the number "Dix-sept," and the proctor took Jean by the shoulder as Henry released him. What to say now? "Good luck, Jean," and Jean turned back to him, nodding shyly, for the first time with the sense of maybe not being up to the great challenge he was being handed. Henry lifted his hand like a father sending his child off to school for the first time, a father who suddenly realizes everything he has done to prepare the child has been insufficient. The nun wanted Henry to move, her harsh voice reaching him a little late. "What?" he said. She made a slicing motion with her hand. Go. We will do the rest.

The driver hadn't waited. There was no sign of the van, and Henry had neglected to ask how long the test would take. What then could he be expected to do? The heat was already pressing down. He could go back inside and ask, but he had become afraid of that little nun, embarrassed to go straight back in after she had so efficiently dismissed him. His cell phone was buzzing now. Beatrice. "Daniel called. He will meet you in three hours." Who was Daniel?

The driver, of course, who, more efficient than Henry, had managed to find out what needed to be found out. Henry held back from asking, but what will I do, Beatrice, in Port-au-Prince, for three hours?

Without an idea, he walked, reminding himself to make careful note of the streets he was passing, as he was quite sure that no one, even a block away from the establishment, would be able to tell him how to get back to the Lycée Français. Two blocks down the hill, he stopped at what passed for a café, really just a glorified bodega, a single small table, two metal chairs, set against stacks of what seemed like some sort of candy assortment, and then boxes of cleaning powder in a great pile. Only now did he realize he had not eaten, was famished. "Café?" he asked the tall young man behind the counter. "Pain?" He received a nod. The coffee was sweet, syrupy. The "pain" was packaged, with icing. But good enough. He ate, asked for more of the bread. He was not alone in the tiny café, men and women entered and stayed. He was pressed tight. A stranger to them, they disregarded him, this negligible force of whiteness, this old man scarfing down sweet bread, hoping for some sort of respite this café was incapable of offering him.

He saw across the street the opening to what had to be a small church. Yes, there was a cross above the entrance. A blessing if it was open. Simply crossing the street brought up more sweat. A woman was cleaning inside, conducting a loud conversation with some off-stage presence, perhaps the priest. She looked at him as he begged permission to enter. There were all these moments of noncomprehension; you wanted to negotiate out of your American sense of how things were done, but you had to jettison all that here and simply deal with a look you saw as faintly hostile, but was really just the surf-slicing fin of indifference. Without asking permission, he knelt. Her mop swished around him, as if his physical presence didn't matter.

Of course real prayer was impossible. Three hours. How would he get through three hours? He had neglected to bring a book, thinking that what time he had would be spent exploring the city, but he hadn't counted on his own exhaustion, or on the heat. The priest had come out, and even in the presence of a worshipper did not lower his voice as he berated the cleaning woman. He was one of those priests Henry had gotten used to here, men without visible sanctity, men who carried their bodies sensually, men no doubt used to fucking. He was young and indifferent to Henry, and when he left the small nave—only six benches deep—Henry stood and approached the row of votive candles lined up before the statue of an unfamiliar saint, a statue with the lean body and angular, bearded jaw of an El Greco. He placed a gourde into the slot and picked up one of the burnt-tipped lighting sticks. He would light a candle for Jean. But as soon as he picked up the stick, the cleaning woman started yelling, and when he turned, he saw that she was yelling at him. Incomprehensible. He opened his palms. Help me, please. Her yelling roused the priest, who came out of the shadowy transept and, after listening to her complaint, turned to Henry, and said, in English, "Five gourdes."

Five gourdes for a candle? It seemed outrageous, the equivalent of nearly five American dollars. No, the man was adamant. "I only wanted to say a small prayer," he said. The priest's face was unrelenting, and seemed to have risen out of some island-bound force that *saw* Henry, saw what he was doing here, saw and condemned his dilettante's motives and asked, unabashed, for more than he had anticipated giving. He emptied his pockets: Was this enough? The priest's face did not soften. What have you come here for? Henry lit the candle, expecting to be stopped in the act. He closed his eyes, said his prayer under the priest's hard observance. No indeed. There is no place that does not see you.

The reliable, the really *nice* thing about time is that, no matter how we worry and dread the endurance of it, it does pass. Henry managed to get through two and a half hours. He ate, he sweated, he drank profusely, he sat in whatever shade he could find. He needed desperately now to pee, and having no easy access to a receptacle, went back early to the Lycée, hoping they might take pity on him there. There was no one in the entrance. The place seemed newly abandoned. Had he misread the time? At the edge of the portico, looking down on the floor below, he saw two men, one a custodian, the other wearing the familiar blue shirt of officialdom, and shouted "Salle de bain?" The same Haitian indifference greeted him. Had he just asked them if he could take a bath? He gave in to something coarser, gestured to his crotch. They pointed the way.

In the dim, grime-encrusted mirror over the bathroom sink, he saw a face he hardly recognized. His thin, wet gray hair, the reddish sweating skin peeking through the top of his scalp, mottled. *I am mottled*, he said to himself. I have come to the point in life where I have to own up to the encroachment of mottledness. Mottledness was an old granduncle who used to visit his parents in the family house in Newton Highlands. As a child, you were always watching old people lean *toward* you, noticing their palsied hands, their skin. They are another form of existence, decomposing before your eyes. They are like sea creatures observed on the other side of a pane of glass in an aquarium. Then you are them. You become a sea turtle lumbering slowly, painfully slowly, through the depths. This is what has happened. A boy in a white shirt and tie had entered the bathroom, had not quite seen Henry, had not *needed* to see Henry, the sea turtle at the sink, and begun to pee with wonderful fresh force. That was lost, too. (Henry's own urination, whatever the urgency, had taken forever.) The boy did not wash his hands when he was finished but ran back to complete his test, and Henry wanted to call him back, ask him to wash. In his place, Henry washed his own large mottled face with cold water, careful not to let any into his mouth.

It was not long before there were more boys in the hallway. They appeared in small clumps, white shirts poking out of their pants, ties loosened. Mild hilarity seemed the order of the day. Many of them would have aced the test, no doubt. Who were they? The children of officials, the children of Haitian entrepreneurs, but unlike boys of a similar order in America, they lacked the haughty overconfidence, the air of sexual entitlement of privileged American males. Henry felt their life passing by him as he sat in the cool corridor, in a metal chair he had found and unfolded.

Jean was among the last. Henry might have predicted that. He was accompanied by one of the proctors, they were talking. There was something encouraging about this, that one of these men had taken notice of Jean, had thought to accompany him. Yes, they were distinctly talking. There was always the possibility—you had to work, in age, to keep this in mind—that things might go well. You must never allow yourself to go so far as to say *miracles can happen* (mostly, they can't) but you can allow into the darkened corridors of your aged cynicism the faint possibility of good fortune. It was entirely possible Jean was, in fact, as intelligent as Henry hoped. That he, like these others, had aced the test. Look at this, Evan Hatch! Look how easily Jean has adapted to this daunting environment. Surely he can do the same at Grantham. No need to have him spend a year as Henry's ward, under the watchful, suspicious eye of Lily. The proctor stopped at the entrance and Jean approached Henry. The boy—the young man—was smiling. Not a huge one, but still a smile betokening a certain confidence.

Henry stood.

"How did it go?"

"Good," Jean said.

"Wonderful." Henry looked back at the proctor, as if for confirmation. The man had disappeared. "Wonderful."

They stepped out into the heat, which affected Jean not at all. The van was not yet here.

"Jean, it occurs to me you haven't eaten. Are you hungry?"

"No. I'm good."

Some crest had been topped, a larger view taken in. Henry felt giddy.

"And tell me. What did they ask you to write?"

Jean blinked against the light. He was taking his time. He swallowed. It was as though he had to search for the answer, from a time distant.

"If I could change anything at my school, what would I change?"

"But—" For Henry it was like waiting for a sentence to be finished. "Jean, you have no school.

"No. I made one up."

"You made one up?"

"Yes."

"Jean."

Was there cause here for concern? Henry peered into the young man's face, asking him to get more serious.

"And—what school did you make up?"

Now the van was approaching. Daniel in the driver's seat, leaning forward, like a man arising out of some subterranean area, the darkness of the van seemed so deep. Daniel's face curious and withholding, partly absent and partly deeply present, carrying on him a look of mild suspicion, like a man witnessing a small crime he will choose not to report. Jean opened the van's door and swung in, and collapsed, like a boy after sports. Daniel handed him a cold drink, Ragaman, something like the Haitian equivalent of Gatorade, which the boy, the young man, swallowed in its entirety. There seemed, in the dark van, some collusion between these two that Henry could not understand, never would. The two spoke to each other in Kreyol, laughing at something they'd shared.

"What are you two talking about?" Henry asked, not expecting a full answer.

"His girl," the driver said, and looked directly at Henry.

It pierced him in an embarrassing way, the sudden fact of a "girl." This, his reaction, was not an emotion to be allowed. He nodded, as if affecting some hearty collusion. As they began to move again through the squalid grandeur of Port-au-Prince, Jean gazed out the window opposite Henry's, his body open and pushing back against the seat. There was one more word of Kreyol spoken by Jean to Daniel, the driver, who nodded deeply, knowingly, in appreciation.

He assumed he would not see Jean again. There was no need. The results of the test would be sent to Grantham in two or three weeks. Then they would know something. In the van, Henry had tried to communicate this, but Jean had not seemed to be paying close attention.

In the two days he had left before heading back, Henry planned to join the Leominster group. They would be filling backpacks with school supplies they had paid for, shipped separately from Miami to Port-au-Prince. Henry would be joining them in their busywork. He wished for nothing more than such quiet occupation now.

He found himself alone in the warren of beds the night after Jean's test. It was evening, not late. He had eaten with the Leominster group, but had grown bored of the conversation that went nowhere and excused himself early.

What had come over him was a strong dose of loneliness. To be here, alone, with hours to spend before he could expect sleep to come. Yes, he had a book, but the thought of lying on his bed in the company of Arthur Schnitzler was not what he wished for. He was not used to thinking of himself as a lonely man. Lily had always been there for him, even when, as had often been the case in their early years, she'd been consumed by rehearsals. But he could remember instances where loneliness had gotten to him, nights when Lily had been rehearsing late, when he would leave the apartment on 107th and linger at the bus stop where he knew she would eventually get off, not even sure which bus she would have taken. To be ensconced in marriage and still lonely had surprised him. And in part, as an adjustment, he had taken a step away from his own need, protected himself from it.

But then had come Miranda, his girl-child. His companion. Had he held her a little too close in those first years, needing something from her that she, in her child-wisdom, knew was a little too much? Had he, in fact, all these years lived a lonelier life than he'd ever supposed?

He could remember dancing for Miranda when she was a young child, dancing to the out-of-date records they kept, performing for her, and taking her on endlessly long walks to fill the days. No phone calls in those days to interrupt the outdoor life; cell phones had not yet been invented. He showed her the Upper West Side, like a kind of tour guide of the rhapsodic: look at the sky over the Palisades at sunset! Only now could he see that, yes, that had been loneliness, he could only now name it as such.

There was always, wasn't there, an emptiness lying in wait. The Buddhists knew that, and certain Catholic monks he'd read—Henri Nouwen—always encouraged the wayfarer not to fill time too assid-uously. Look out the window. Lie on your bed and be still. But it was difficult. And, Henry knew right now, it was complicated.

He went downstairs, opened the front door, sat on the stoop. Thank God he'd remembered to bring cigarettes. He lit one and studied the empty square, which just this morning had filled him with such happiness. What he wanted—he was able to name it—was for Jean to arrive. For the two of them to sit here and talk, perhaps share a cigarette. To laugh with Jean, to go over the day as if it had been a game they'd played, and could now replay. Something they had done together.

But there had been that small, additional bit of information that came back and haunted him now. The fact of a "girl." It ought not to have bothered him as it did. Of course Jean would find a girl. Of course he lived a full life here, not one where he was just waiting for Henry. Still, it removed Jean from him in a way that felt painful. To consider how much he had *invented* Jean. He had seen—or invented—a huge need there when there might well have been something else. Jean might only have seen Henry as an odd intrusion in his life, perhaps promising something but ultimately peripheral. How could he not have anticipated this?

As he sat, smoking, he retained a memory of Jean's beauty, the way he'd looked as he stood outside the Lycée, the boy's always slightly confused, hopeful stance. It was easy to see how it would dissipate, Jean's need for him. How, in the best-case scenario, Jean would become absorbed by Grantham Prep, would find friends there (his exoticism, if nothing else, would provide a draw), would find a girl. Would come to require Henry less and less, until he faded entirely. It would happen, and then what would Henry's life be?

It was not to be considered, at least not now. Smoke your cigarette. Allow the Haitian night to envelop you, to enclose your loneliness, your slowly eclipsing existence, the lifelong foolishness you have never been able to quite shake. Do not admit to the feeling rising in you now. Allow no admittance to the word "love."

Lie on your bed and be still.

3.

The German critic's name—an odd one, Miranda thought—was Botho Schaub.

"My parents are eccentrics," Botho said, when Miranda asked about the derivation of his first name. "But in Germany, it is really not such an unusual name." He was standing by the window of his hotel room—the exact boutique hotel Miranda had predicted he'd be staying at—blowing smoke out the window while simultaneously eyeing the blinking red light of the smoke alarm. He shrugged. He was wearing the most elegant pair of men's underpants she had ever seen.

It had begun with an email. "Of course I gave him your email," Andrew Schechner said, as if his gesture in doing so were the obvious one. He was going through a stack of slides on his desk. "You can always not answer an email, Miranda."

The fact that Andrew was not looking at her as he spoke—the fact that he was regarding this potentially intimate exchange as just another piece of business—unsettled her. Andrew had taken her on, was mentoring her. A fact—increasingly evident—she knew she should have been grateful for. The AIDS show had received glowing reviews, sales had been very good. The show would be mounted for another six weeks. Things between them might have ended there, but Andrew kept asking her to drop by. There was this and that to discuss. Mostly these discussions amounted to very little, suggestions as to where Miranda might try to sell excerpts from the book. A conventional guess would have been that he simply wanted companionship. She suspected something else.

"I would like to meet, have dinner," was the very simple message Botho Schaub had first sent her. When she told Andrew she was not answering it, he seemed annoyed. "Oh Miranda, what have you got to lose?"

A great deal, of course. There was always a great deal to lose, but in the confines of Andrew Schechner's office, she was made to feel that his mentoring came with certain requirements. Odd ones, to be sure. Why in the world should Andrew be allowed to determine who she dated?

"A dinner will not kill you, Miranda. He's an interesting man."

The second email read, "I understand if you are resistant. Hands off. I will not try and reach you again. Forgiveness, please." It was an email that seemed to have suffered its way through an awkward translation. This time, though, she gave in. It was only dinner, after all. She could do that much. Feel out his "interestingness" and leave it at that.

He chose a very small restaurant in the East Village, as boutique as his hotel would later turn out to be, tiny tables pushed so close to one another that intimacy seemed impossible. It felt as though they had to balance their plates on their knees.

All of which amused him. "This is New York," he said.

Yes. She supposed that was true. At forty-three, after more than twenty years here, she was finally entering "New York."

"I understand why you wouldn't want to answer my email," he said, and nodded, as if to establish a collusion that she saw at first as part of a complex plan on his part. But why see everything as a "plan," as something that needed to be defended against? They were two "interesting" people in their forties, habitués of a world she cared deeply about. It still took an effort to consider herself as "interesting." The "habitué" part she was also trying hard to get used to.

"Who am I, after all?" His smile was like a French actor's smile, as though his lips could not quite close all the way over a mouthful of delicious, as yet undisclosed secrets.

Little by little the secrets came out. He had a daughter, nine years old. It seemed to be the central fact of his life, his emotional locus. Less clear were his relations with the little girl's mother. He did not refer to her, did not say "I am married" or divorced, and it felt, at the very beginning, too crude to ask. His criticism appeared in the *Frankfurter Allgemeine Zeitung*, he taught in Frankfurt as well. Again, the questions she might have asked, the neat American questions—was he tenured faculty?—went unvoiced. They, too, would place her in too conventional a space. "You put it together," he said about his life, shrugging. He seemed peripatetic, one of those men equally at home in a number of cities. He wrote for *Artforum*, though his work for them needed translation, his English considered not quite good enough. He was scheduled to give a lecture in two weeks in Toronto.

Almost secondary was the question, was she attracted to him? She suspected she wasn't, though she admired his quiet, sloughed-off German authority, and his shoulders in the corduroy jacket he wore. His gaze at her was penetrative without being hard. Between courses he spoke, unembarrassed, about loneliness. Men like him, she supposed, thought of this as a selling point.

"So here is the awkward part," he said, when they were walking after dinner. Her destination was the subway, but he alluded to his hotel in the vicinity. The words made her smile. But no, no way. And he smiled in return.

"So I ask, do we do this again, or am I hopeless?"

She didn't answer.

"Without hope," he refined it.

"Sit with me while I have a cigarette," he said. "At least, do that. Washington Square Park. There are benches. I can walk you to Four-teenth Street after. The Q stops at Fourteenth?"

"It does, yes."

Though she felt, at base, that, yes, this was "without hope," she did not mind lingering. It was April, and New York was in one of those pockets of benevolent early-spring weather where you felt something was supposed to happen with your life. By summer, that feeling would have evaporated.

"Andrew says you are writing a good book."

"I'm glad he thinks so."

"He means it. He would not say." He had a way of smoking that seemed to require a full-body effort. His shoulders moved as he took in a drag. She thought of the way he smoked as being akin to the way he might embrace someone, a fullness, an entirety of carefully managed force.

"Which makes me jealous. I am trying to write one."

Another man with an ambition. She had had a lifetime of such men, the musicians and writers she had dated, then lived with, in her late twenties and thirties, men with insufficient talent or drive (it was always a known though unstated thing). Hearing them articulate their ambitions, late at night, often after sex, when they felt most accepted, was to sense both the effort within their self-presentation, and the belief that was being asked of her.

It had made them seem small, as Botho Schaub's admission, "I am trying to write one," revealed some small, vulnerable part of him, but one that endeared him to her—at least a little. On the bench, she had a sense of her own power. Whatever her self-acknowledged limitations and insecurities, she was doing the thing everyone seemed to want to do. She was writing a book that was being deemed "good." She stretched out her legs.

"They are nice," Botho Schaub said, as if she had done it just for him. "Now, the next thing, you look at your watch, you say, it's getting late."

He lit another cigarette and laughed mildly at his own joke, and stretched out his own legs.

"And look at mine. They are hams. They are ugly."

For the first time, she allowed in the possibility. The sense of "Why not?" She might sleep with him, if she chose to, not because she particularly desired his body, but because she liked the things he said, wanted to hear the next thing. It felt like another kind of power, to manifest an interest devoid of need. But no decision needed to be made, not yet.

At the subway, he attempted to kiss her, and she said no.

"Yes, that's awkward, too, isn't it? A man going for more than he should know to ask for."

"It's all right," she said.

"It's what we have to do, isn't it?"

There was that naked plea in his eyes that she always regretted seeing. Their need. The way it came down to something so basic. Under the sedentary rock of the sophisticated world, that sea of conventional lava always waiting to erupt.

"And now the final question. Do we chance another awkward dinner?"

She reached out and touched him on the back of the neck. A simple gesture of friendliness, like patting him on the head. He seemed more confused than encouraged. She enjoyed the feeling it gave her. But she would not take the next step, didn't need to.

It took two more dinners before she found herself in the boutique hotel. "You are making me crazy," he said at the second of those dinners. "Of course you know that. You are doing it all on purpose. I understand."

When he removed his glasses to massage his eyes, she received another strong hint of his vulnerability, separate from the one he had manufactured as a tool of seduction. The pale, tired-looking eyes, the little bags of self-doubt riding under the hood of physical and mental authority. It would be all right. She could handle such a man. Always a risk, but he would be something new for her, a man like this, accomplished to a degree and not simply yearning and hopeful. (All those Brooklyn boys, those Isaacs and Trevors with their full young lips, their journals and their baseball gloves, relics of adolescences they were unwilling to fully jettison.) It would be new.

As it was. He made love like an athlete of one of those sports requiring not litheness and grace but a kind of blustering brute force. To be coupled with him was like being in a scrum, an intimacy she felt was not always entirely, or solely, sexual. Was it satisfying? She could not say precisely. Armand DeSaulniers had spoiled her for normal flawed sex, had delivered a gold standard she suspected would not be superseded in this lifetime.

"There," Botho said, lying back against the sheets, as if orgasm amounted not to a completion but to a step in a process. As if to say: now that this awkward thing is over, now we can actually talk.

Beside his bed he kept a picture of his daughter. A little girl with braided hair, caught in a moment of delight, teeth that would need to be fixed someday but please not yet.

"She's adorable."

"Of course she is."

If there was a vulnerability, a sense of some internal barrenness that had drawn her to him, and made this moment in bed possible, there was also something about him that insisted on the first rate. The hotel, the restaurants, the daughter on the bedside table. (Of course he would only have a daughter who was endearingly beautiful, even in her necessary imperfections.) Out of the open suitcase, the clothes that spilled were superb, soft, his clinging underwear composed of a material that looked and felt like silk but was something else, a material that "wicked." The toiletries lined up on the glass counter in the bathroom were like small monuments to European ingenuity, the bottles and tubes like art objects she held back from touching. When he stood at the window in those marvelous underpants, he seemed to feel the need to make some kind of excuse for himself, gesturing disparagingly to his short, thick, overly muscled legs, raising his eyebrows as he saw her appraising his body: Yes, you see, Miranda, what I am, such as it is. And admit it, it is not so terrible.

On the tiny desk in his hotel room, he showed her the material for his proposed book. The Coenties Slip painters of the late fifties, early sixties. Abstractionists Miranda was not deeply interested in. Ellsworth Kelly. Robert Indiana. Agnes Martin. Lenore Tawney. A lesser-known painter named Jack Youngerman. "Look," he said to her, holding a glossy photograph. "On the roof. Coenties Slip. Youngerman was married to Delphine Seyrig. You know her?"

"No."

"My God. You should. French actress. Resnais. *Last Year at*

Marienbad. She met Youngerman in Paris after the war. He was studying there. Eighteen, she was. Look, this is their little boy."

There were photographs that brought you instantly back. New York in that late-fifties Ruth Orkin light. The hats ambitious young men and women wore, the coats and the slouching, withheld power. The ease, too. Redefining art, or coming close enough to it, in that cool way that masked naked assertiveness. It was sexy. They had come to the city and taken over, or were preparing to, and they all slouched on a roof, tending to the blond little boy, the young son of Delphine Seyrig and Jack Youngerman.

"You see?"

"I do."

"No. Why I want to write it."

"Of course I see."

"Wonderful. Yes. That moment."

He stroked her back the way a man might stroke a dog's back, ruffling the fur. He had not mastered the art of sensual gentleness.

They became a couple, known. They attended openings, they rode the subway to small, new galleries in Queens, in Bushwick. On the subway, he would never sit. He stood and held to the strap, eager, when the subway ran aboveground, to see. *What is this?* She was amused. All these old, dull neighborhoods being transformed. Sunnyside. Dumbo. He was fascinated by the clothes hip young black men wore on the train, the way they stood, their headphones, their sunglasses. She was seeing New York through his eyes. The city didn't tire him, didn't depress him the way it had some of her former boyfriends, who could only see it as a force that would never fully embrace them, and dreamed of moving to places like Rhinebeck, Beacon, eager to find a landscape more accommodating to unacknowledged failure.

The gallery owners always knew him. He adjusted his glasses and held back the approval they waited for. In the bed in the boutique hotel, he was a not entirely fulfilling lover, but in these galleries she sensed his power, the way he was lusted after, the hunger for a piece in *Artforum*. "Botho Schaub" less a name than a small, coveted brand. Afterward, he held her hand as they walked through deserted neighborhoods she would once have thought dangerous. "It's good, yes, what's happening?"

Did he mean them, as a couple? Or was he referring to the art scene? There were ambiguities that, were she to try to penetrate, would reveal how little she was able to read their situation. Was she still in power, or in the process of giving something over? That was what had been comfortable about the Isaacs and the Trevors, the romantic simplicity, and the mutual unwillingness to surrender to what New York was becoming, a resistance that kept them all from fully manifesting. For Botho Schaub, the city was like a fat bratwurst he wanted to sink his feral teeth into. Sometimes, in the deserted neighborhoods, he pushed her up against a doorway, thrust against her, bit her neck with a savagery that held itself back at the last moment and made a feint toward tenderness. "It's good, isn't it?" He was referring—this time, unambiguously—to the erection pressing into her. Here they were all alike, Botho and the Isaacs and the Trevors, they all needed this encouragement, this affirmation.

On the trains then, in the dark—he made them stop sometimes, get out onto a subway platform, in Carroll Gardens, in Astoria, to look harder at something that had caught his eye, a light display against the wall of a deserted building. "It's wonderful." He was forcing her to see the city in its new guise as a thing of beauty, of wonders. Never mind what was lost. When he had shown her the picture of the abstractionists on the Coenties Slip rooftop, she had thought they might be sharing something, a capacity to mourn the past that had defined her so long she did not even question it. But it was a false intimacy. In the postcoital moments when self-revelation was called for, she tried to speak of the deep motivation behind her Anna Soloff book. She felt the limits of his understanding—of his sympathy—in the way he did not stop rubbing her skin in that encouraging, fur-nuzzling way of his. "The book will do well, you'll be set," was all he said. She wanted to say that was not the point, but it had become the point, hadn't it? She was writing a book that would "do well," that would transcend its origins, and on the thickly threaded sheets of the hotel bed he was forcing her to own up to that, that the goal need not go any deeper.

"Let your work be an argument against forgetting," Arthur Messinger had said once to Anna, but there were things Miranda had to admit she was forgetting. The world lifted you, and you forgot. You stood on a subway platform in Brooklyn and watched the play of light against an old factory in Dumbo and thought the city had never been more beautiful, its ruins transformed. What was lost? You had to scratch at the question, you had to draw the blood of the an-swers' meanings. Maybe the progression of a city amounted not to a falling off but to a layering, and the layers had meanings as authentic as the original. Which was more authentic, the civilization that had produced the Trevi Fountain or the one that had allowed Anita Ek-berg and Marcello Mastroianni to wade into it? Meanwhile, a mildly crude but hugely self-confident German critic placed his fingers assertively in the cleft of your ass and rubbed and you slapped his hand away and said "Stop" and at the same time hoped he wouldn't.

Still, the questions did not go away, however much pleasure was to be had in sidestepping them. Had the gorgeous play of light against a deserted factory been paid for by Citibank? And how, pre-cisely, did that matter? Was there a woman in Frankfurt whom Botho Schaub would return to, the mother of the beautiful little girl? Did that matter either, or was she simply still too frightened to ask? It was as though he were convincing her—attempting to convince her—to step beyond the series of concerns that had kept her in place seemingly forever, Miranda Rando, onlooker, political neophyte, defined by a vague resistance to the changes brought on by late capitalism. It embarrassed her now, how willing she had been to retreat, in the early days of writing her book, to the position of barista, how soothing it had been to position herself as an outsider, teasing poverty while knowing she always had her parents to fall back on. Botho Schaub would not respect a move like that, and in his presence it was as though she were expected to jettison that old reduced self. Even her recent thoughts (they could not be described as anything so fully formed as a "plan") to have a child by herself, and to choose as the father a penniless oysterman, seemed to belong to the fairy-tale Miranda Rando, the girl who equated self-reduction with honor. It was not how it had to be. There was a world of men like Botho Schaub, like Andrew Schechner. If, with them, you were never fully invited to open into your deepest impulses and fears, it was because they wanted to convince you that the world was too interesting to retreat from. Seize it, Miranda. You have written a good book, or were close enough to that achievement to sense it. There will be rewards. They are not to be denied. Only a fool denies them.

She did, though, finally ask Botho Schaub one night about the little girl's mother. They were in bed, post-sex. There was a thing he liked to do afterward, run a finger along the slit of her vagina and lift it to his lips to taste. Like sucking the sliver of lemon peel out of an emptied espresso cup.

His answer was, "Oh, now you want to ask a question to make me sad."

"Why?"

He sat up in bed, as if he were preparing to be interrogated and had to find a mode of performance for it.

"I still see her, yes."

His falseness made her wish she hadn't asked.

"We have an—"

He waited for her to provide the precise word in English.

"An agreement?"

"Yes."

"Do you live with her?"

"Let's say I keep some things there."

"This terrific underwear."

She'd gone for a joke that he didn't instantly get.

"You don't like my underwear?"

"I'm in minor awe of your underwear."

"Good, then."

Where did this go? He lived with a woman in Frankfurt, they brought up a daughter together, they had an "agreement." It was the clichéd modern world they were sorting out on the bed. Women who allowed their men to consort with others. She could see this woman, could envision a certain harshness about her. She would look like a Teutonic Tilda Swinton, Miranda was sure.

"This changes things, this confession you have dragged out of me?"

"I 'dragged' nothing out of you. And no, it doesn't change things."

She supposed this was true. Still, she gathered the sheets around her and bunched herself into a tight ball. He waited her out, did not try to pretend. His strategy was the correct one. She would not reject him, or what they had established, because of this new piece of information. In the clichéd new world, there was no such thing as "the other woman." You could live in the world of fifties melodrama or you could accept that this was the way it would likely be for her from now on. Having rejected the opportunity to be a failed artist's or musician's wife, or the single mother of a child sired by a Wellfleet oysterman, what was left for her was a world of complicated, ambitious men whose commitments, or lack of them, were like sketches for a major work that might never come to fruition. As a seal on their pact, he insisted on making love again in his straight-on manner, a simple back and forth motion, as though he were planing her, a technique he had honed to the point where he fully expected the desired result would of course be achieved. But something held her back. In an odd and not immediately comprehensible way, she found herself thinking of Andrew Schechner while she was being fucked. She thought that this was what Andrew expected of her. As if there were a rule book. How to be the new Miranda Rando. The hip, respected biographer whose book would boost the asking price of Anna Soloff's paintings. She saw the steps she had already taken in fulfilling that role, and even now, seeing it with some clarity, did not fully resist.

When Botho left to return to Frankfurt, and to the woman with whom he had an "agreement," they shared a final breakfast in his hotel. He was distracted. He kept checking his phone. His expensive transparent-framed glasses seemed more than ever a kind of defensive weaponry, like the green-tinted glasses men wore when they walked into combat zones in high-end action movies. She wondered that she had never asked him about his exquisitely cut hair.

"Yes? You are looking at something with amusement," he said.

She shook her head. It was possible this was the end of something. Their last breakfast. She would miss the hard-boiled eggs with chicken and roasted kale the hotel served on cedar planks.

"When I come back, perhaps I will stay with you next time."

This she didn't answer either. The ambiguity in saying goodbye to him felt too thick an air to breathe.

"Maybe," she said, and he noted her holding back.

"You can save me a shitload of money."

"Nice," she said, and he smiled, like they were returning to the manufactured honesty of his initial seduction of her. "You put it to-gether." It was possible, in spite of the boutique hotel, the excellent clothes, that Botho Schaub lived fairly close to the edge.

"In any case, we'll see each other in Basel."

"How's that?"

"Andrew has invited you, yes?"

"To Basel? If he has, he hasn't told me."

"Well, yes, he's inviting you. I hope I haven't spoiled this."

Something vaguely unsettling had been placed between them on the small table. The collusion between Botho and Andrew had always been a mystery.

"For the great unveiling," he said.

He lifted his hand to ask for the check.

"And that—?"

He had removed a beautiful pen from his pocket. He was not answering her question.

"Botho, excuse me, I'm confused."

He put the pen away after signing his room number on the bill, seemed impatient with her.

"At Art Basel, they are presenting the final Anna Soloff."

The shock was too much, a part of her closed down. She felt nearly sick.

"Are we talking about *The Remembering Animal*?"

"I don't remember the title. It's a good one, though. Come, I'll be late."

He would take the subway to Atlantic Avenue, then the train to JFK. He hoisted his superbly weathered luggage, attempted to kiss her before he went down the subway stairs.

"No? So you are mad about something at a moment I don't have time to explain?" Again, he shrugged. "I'll call you." He hopped down the steps with that athletic grace he had, like a man being set free of something.

She walked immediately to the gallery, seeing nothing on the way, thinking nothing, tightened around a rage she chose neither to suppress nor explore.

Andrew Schechner was with someone. Of course. She sat on one of the white cubes in the lobby. Cindy Auerbach's installation had been removed and a new hanging was going on. The artist directing the hanging had receding hair and a scruffy beard and looked like one of the young men an earlier iteration of Miranda Rando might have dated. From what she could see of the work, he seemed a little too heavily indebted to Anselm Kiefer. Things protruded from the paintings, but she didn't care to look hard enough to define precisely what.

Andrew came out to answer a question the artist had posed. On his way, he glanced at Miranda with mild surprise, but his mind was on something else.

"To what do I owe the not entirely convenient pleasure?" he asked when he came out of the small gallery. He was dressed entirely in black—tight jeans, chest-hugging shirt—but he looked ruffled.

"Could we talk?"

"Not at the moment, no."

"You're inviting me to Basel?"

"Did that cocksucker spoil my surprise? Yes, Miranda, I'm inviting you. I'm in the middle of an interview in my office."

"The Remembering Animal." She spilled more than spoke the words. She felt like a woman coming to announce to a lover who has jilted her that she was pregnant. She felt she had no excuse for herself, nothing to fall back on. It was an extreme way to think, but irresistible.

The words stopped him. Something telling happened with his lips.

"Yes," he said.

Thank God. At least honesty had been invited into the room.

"Then you've seen it?"

"Of course I've seen it, Miranda. I'm Anna Soloff's fucking dealer."

"Why wasn't I told?"

"You're *being* told. Don't make me treat you like a child. I'm in an interview."

He left her then. She sat a few more minutes in her self-imposed bereftness before it began to seem silly, before the noise of the hanging, the studiedly cool voice of the artist, began to get to her. Then there was the entrance of the intern with harshly cut hair, a young woman like Miranda might once have been, one of art's uncertain acolytes, seeking validation, going for coffee, half-worshipping, half-critical of the youngish man who actually got to have a show. It all seemed, suddenly, like some depressingly repetitive thing she had participated in, the internship, the worshipfulness, the inevitable seeing-through. It had happened, would happen, to generations of women like her. She'd thought she had achieved something else, another step, another layer, but Andrew Schechner had essentially just told her that no, she had not really moved an inch from the young woman holding coffee, hoping she had got it just right for the artist, that he would acknowledge her, say: yes, you exist.

She went outside. It was difficult to cross the thick, heavily trafficked avenue separating the gallery from the river. A new commercial development had squatted on one of the last deserted outposts in this part of the city. She found a bench in the small park the city had constructed as an excuse for its commercial overkill. She sat and felt small and then told herself: *Don't*. Don't feel small. But to work her way out of it was difficult.

What was the essence of the rage she felt? That Andrew had treated her so dismissively might have been enough, but she wanted to analyze the feeling *before* that, the feeling that had started up at the hotel breakfast when Botho had told her what was to happen. No one had consulted her. Behind her back, Aaron Soloff and Andrew had decided that the time had come to sell *The Remembering Animal.* After the success of the AIDS show, Anna's asking price was at its peak. It made perfect commercial sense. Unveil it at Art Basel. Let the hungry collectors descend. Of course. Even Botho had apparently seen it. But she had been left out. No one had thought to tell her.

And really, closely examined, why should they have? Where was she, after all, in the food chain? She was the biographer who had published a piece in *The New Yorker* that had helped grease the wheels of a series of recent transactions that had netted Andrew and Aaron, and Jonah of course, their millions. She had been the worker bee, the intern fetching coffee. And why in the world had she expected that she be anything else? From what place had come her own sense of importance?

As she tried to bore down on an answer, she could hear Andrew's voice: Accept your place, Miranda. It is not a bad one. You are being invited to participate. You will fly, most likely first class, to Basel. We don't actually need you there, so consider this a huge favor. Imagine your hotel room. Botho will come and make his blunt, assaultive love to you, and the two of you will eat well and attend parties. None of this strictly needs to happen. It will happen as a result of a dealer's largesse. Because you have helped him, in your own small way, to make his millions. Whoever promised you a cleaner, purer world than this one, Miranda? On the park bench, she folded around herself, still not having probed to the core, the throbbing nerve still not isolated.

It had less to do with Andrew—the deal with him was always clear, or clear enough, occasional bouts of faux-intimacy aside—than with Aaron. Aaron and the painting itself. A promise had been made, hadn't it, in what she'd believed had been the true intimacy of 107th Street. "I'll show it to you when the time is right," had always been his coy promise. As if he were her collaborator, walking with her through the pages she was writing, reliving with her Anna's life. She had come to feel that she had a special relationship to the painting, it would be *her* mission to reveal it to the world. Now she was being made to see that it was, in the end, just an object, and Aaron had always judged the value of keeping it hidden not in personal but in financial terms. In some way she could still not yet fully explain to herself, she was being used, had been used.

Her phone was buzzing. It was her father, but she could not answer now. She had to see Aaron, had to talk to Aaron. If anyone could explain—if there was anyone with whom she could meet and sort through this moment—it would have to be him.

In the ten years prior to her showing the AIDS paintings, Anna Soloff had had a single solo show, at Montclair State College in New Jersey. Her work occasionally showed up in larger exhibitions, but when she sold a painting, it went for eight hundred dollars, at most a thousand. She continued to live on the margins well into her sixties. Reviews published here and there. Occasional teaching. Art classes given in a neighborhood "learning center." Handouts from Karl Rattner. In her diaries, she tabulated even the small checks she received from the communist meeting hall on 107th Street, tiny sums received for xeroxing and leafleting work. She paid $225 a month for the apartment. Her sons were both in college, courtesy of begged scholarships.

Karl Rattner had departed years before, having taken up with a wealthy woman in Connecticut. According to her diary, Anna spent her sixtieth birthday, in September 1980, sitting alone with a bottle of Almaden wine purchased for three dollars from the liquor store located on the other side of Broadway. Self-pity was a rarity in the diary pages, but it was here. Aaron had recently entered Brown, and was thus away. Jonah was dating a "hungry young woman I don't care for," and showed up late, and begrudgingly, to help his mother celebrate.

Still, you could not live this long, even on the margins, consorting as she'd done with the world of artists and patrons and curators, without making a few important connections. No dealer would take her on, and people like Henry Geldzahler and Jack Bauer at the Whitney gave her no more than a metaphorical pat on the head when she saw them at openings. By the mid-eighties, the time of the AIDS paintings, she had been more or less authoritatively dismissed, the little gray-haired lady stuck in the seventies, that decade of second-wave feminist art that had not found within it an important place for her. And if not then, when? But she continued to show up at every opening she could wangle an invitation to, and when she had enough of the AIDS paintings ready to show (she had judged their value, and highly), she invited a man named Mortimer Leavitt up to her apartment to see them.

The art world was full of men like Mortimer Leavitt, men who had made a killing in business (Mortimer Leavitt's fortune had come from retail handcrafted shirts) but who hankered after something else. Men who had a wish to be patrons, to nose in, by means of their money and their savvy. Anna had flirted with him at several openings, and he'd clearly been amused by her. At the time of his visit, Anna described him fully in her diary pages: he wore a bow tie, horn-rimmed glasses, very proper. He looked around at the AIDS paintings and then at Anna's other work and took off his glasses and cleaned them.

Waiting for his response, she asked if she could paint him. It was a tool of artistic seduction: Paint the wealthy and powerful and see where it leads. At worst, they might buy the painting from you.

"Would I have to be naked?" he asked.

"Not necessarily. But ideally."

"I see everyone here is naked."

He seemed amused in what Anna described as an "owlish" way.

"Yes. I like to do naked."

It was understood he was not agreeing to this.

"I think Benjamin should see these."

Anna wrote that, at that point, her heart started pumping in an uncontrollable way. "Benjamin" was the art critic Benjamin Weeks.

"I can see you haven't had it easy, have you?"

"No. I haven't."

There seemed a wonderful honesty to the exchange. Mortimer Leavitt in a beautiful blue suit with fine yellow pinstripes running through it, shoes that could likely be hocked to pay a year's rent on this place. Anna was used to the shabbiness in which she lived, but looking around now, seeing it through Mortimer Leavitt's eyes, she saw how entire it was. Only the paintings stood out against the shabbiness. She felt that, too. Pride not in herself, but in the work.

Would there have to be some quid pro quo in order to seal their exchange? No, apparently not. Mortimer Leavitt was gentlemanly, he had fitted a fine cone of glass over his coldness, so that it shone a little bit, and felt like something other than coldness.

"I'll tell you what," Mortimer Leavitt said. "I think I'm about to make you a rich woman." Then he hesitated. "Though, you understand, I can't promise."

The following week, "Benjamin" came. She had completed one more of the AIDS paintings, *Robert*. She asked Benjamin Weeks if she could paint him, and he said yes, but distractedly, his gaze having been caught not only by the AIDS paintings but by some of the others, the ones she had purposely left out on display, ones she was sure he had never seen.

"Be careful, she might want to paint you naked," Mortimer Leavitt said.

"Oh no," Benjamin Weeks said. "I never get naked."

He continued looking, holding back on something.

"Who's this?" he asked.

"My son."

It was an early version of *Jonah on the Cusp*.

"He's a looker, isn't he?" Benjamin Weeks said.

"He is. Both my sons are."

From behind another painting, she dragged out *Aaron, 11*.

"Oh dear," Benjamin Weeks said, and then he and Mortimer Leavitt chuckled together.

"No one gets away from you, do they?" Benjamin Weeks said.

"Not if I can help it."

Anna knew how to play herself. The tough-cookie Jewish broad who could not be defeated. She wanted to be told she was a genius. She understood she was playing the role in front of male power, and was a little disgusted by the necessity, but went ahead anyway. Benjamin Weeks continued to hold back, but looked very hard at the AIDS paintings.

"I think we should call Jerry," Benjamin Weeks said after a while. He had a fringe of wheat-colored hair that looked badly dyed.

"When can I paint you?" Anna asked. She would not let this moment slip by. There were moments, she knew, that must be recognized for what they are.

They made a date. The painting *Benjamin Weeks* became one of her late signature works. She sat him in her pale green armchair, dressed in a suit the color of a bruised peach. He could not be coerced into nakedness, and she accepted that. She painted him leaning slightly forward, as if getting ready to leave, or to say something, and in his face she had captured the look of a man who takes delight in everything that comes out of his mouth, the art critic who knows how good his mind is, and how delightful that the world has acknowledged it. Set against this, she had painted a short-fingered hand gripping one arm of the chair and, miraculously, that was what you looked at, that hand, the mystery of that hand, as if to ask yourself: So who exactly is this man when he's not talking?

"Jerry" was the gallery owner Jerome Spencer, who barely acknowledged her when he ascended the stairs at 107th Street, though he did accept a glass of iced tea. They had once had a nasty exchange, years before, and each made an effort not to remember it. The apartment was now filled with AIDS, with men's pale chests and deep-socketed eyes and tinctures of blood. Anna had added a painting of a nun who had come to the AIDS ward, a painting that would not be included in the show at the Schechner Gallery, a tall, masculine-looking, white skinned woman whose clasped rosary beads fell all the way down to her habited knees, the bright crucifix lingering there, the face of Christ sharply etched with a scowl. Jerome Spencer seemed to like that one the best, though, like Benjamin Weeks, he held back from saying so.

Anna liked to frame it as her own decision, to allow these men to make her a rich woman. (Women had had their chance, Linda Nochlin and the others, to help her out. The men might look through her, but they had their checkbooks ready.) The AIDS paintings, given rapturous press by Benjamin Weeks and others, were a little too strange, too daunting to sell right away. And there were still critics who held back, not quite ready to be told they needed to "rethink" an artist they'd previously dismissed. Jerome Spencer took her on, saying to her bluntly, "Look, I will stick with you, but I don't believe in quick killings." He had spoken so much in the tone of rejection that it took her a while to realize something very good was happening. An odd series of celebrities came to the opening, invited by Benjamin Weeks and Jerome Spencer: Lee Radziwill and Jasper Johns, Felix Rohatyn and Mike Nichols, Lindsay Crouse and John Malkovich. Anna wanted to paint them all, to get them up to the apartment on 107th Street and have them remove articles of clothing, to paint Felix Rohatyn in his T-shirt, with one suspender hanging loose off his shoulder. She was surprised when he agreed. Jonah and Aaron were both with her at the opening, looking handsome, Jonah in particular very ruddy, the two of them a little embarrassed, as always, by their mother's performance of herself. A gay art critic, on being introduced to Jonah, said, "Dink Stover at Yale, I presume," and Jonah had no idea what the man was talking about, no idea either that he was being flirted with until Aaron explained it to him. They were being newly assessed, Anna and her sons, and Anna loved the fact of showing them off, a show to set alongside the paintings themselves.

It was two years before the first big sale happened. That was in 1987. Anna was sixty-seven years old and finally solvent. She took on wealth and security, even minor celebrity, as if a deep hunger for these things had always been riding just beneath the bohemian exterior. She could not get enough. "We hardly recognized her sometimes," Aaron had said. "Who was this woman *performing* all the time?" She painted power. Felix Rohatyn in his T-shirt, John Malkovich allowing his pale naked dangling arms to define him, so that you understood, from Anna's rendering of him, the way he used his animal stillness to claw his way into your consciousness. She made money and was praised, invited to lecture, given shows in places she scoffed at in her diary. Des Moines. Tucson. She was being praised for the thing she had always done but had received little credit for in the first four decades of her career: finding the precise place you needed to look, the unexpected revelation every human body kept like its own well-guarded secret. Jerome Spencer held to his promise to stick with her, but ten years later, a rich woman now, she made the move to go with Andrew Schechner.

Miranda sometimes studied the early photographs of Anna and

Andrew, taken when they were setting up Anna's first show at the then still-new Schechner Gallery. It was a hairier, more hippie-looking Andrew Schechner in those photographs, a man with a loose, speculative, risk-taking face, a man who managed to see things no one else had quite seen, how extraordinarily much could be taken in the evolving New York art scene if you held out your hand in the correct way. In those photographs, Anna looked at Andrew with a kind of adoration. Had they slept together? In her seventies, Anna remained sexual. According to her diary, one of the men in the Broadway wine store, a Latino man she referred to only as "Charles," became, briefly, and only after she'd painted him, a lover. "He doesn't see me the way the others see me," Anna had written about Andrew in her diary, but had left it at that. It was as though she had no more time for the diary anymore, life was galloping now.

As for the earlier paintings, the cityscapes, the ones Miranda adored, a kind of mist came to surround them. A kind of "I used to think and feel this way but I don't anymore." It was as though Anna stopped looking out the window, took no notice of how the Upper West Side was changing, the SROs on her block falling away in order to accommodate the new people coming in, new people with a demand to be served not at the kinds of restaurants that had always been there but at their replacements, the ones that were replicating each other all over the city. "Mezzogiorno." Bland tortellini in some predictable sauce was now the acceptable thing; comidas chinas y criollas became the food of the recently bulldozed past. Only occasionally did Anna refer back to what was lost. "Whatever happened to the black man who used to stand at the corner and shout 'Hoot-ba!' every morning?" Where had he been transported, to what island of lost, no longer useful New Yorkers? Anna was too busy to linger over such questions. Power came to her apartment, and she painted power. Brilliantly, of course. But sometimes at night

Miranda lingered over the diaries, searching for some remnant of Anna's lost sensibility, finding it only in snatches.

Her sons married and she painted their pregnant wives, garnering a whole new realm of praise. Pregnancy had been the great neglected subject. Egon Schiele aside, who had really thought hard about the possibilities inherent in stretched, opaque skin, the way the fetus almost seems exposed under the mother's ballooning parachute-cover belly, blue veins popping like the juttings of a bas-relief? Her sons went off to their lives, law school, medical school. Anna painted their naked children: the curled leaf of a little girl's vagina, the popcorn sprout of a male infant's genitalia.

In the final diaries, and only in them, had Anna seemed to own up to something. "You paint the changes in the world, you paint politics in people's faces, their bodies." It seemed to Miranda an uncharacteristically flat, unconvincing sentence. In Miranda's imagination, it might have been the defensive sort of thing Anna wrote, late at night, when the apparition of Arthur Messinger visited her. Miranda envisioned the scene: late night, 107th Street, Anna in one of the cheap, sheer nightgowns she'd bought at Lamston's before the neighborhood decided a Lamston's was no longer suitable. Whatever money she had made, Anna continued to dress as she had in her poverty. So it was a pink nightgown, it was 2:00 in the morning, and in that dark 2:00 a.m. light, Anna wandered out to the living room that faced north and found the gaunt form of her old lover lingering there. "And what have you done with it?" he was asking. Not harshly. No, Arthur Messinger was at heart too gentle for judgment. "What have you done with it, this gift? How have you used it, Anna, my girl, my student (and then, his old, odd endearment), my budding little Jew?"

Miranda saw that scene as clearly as she saw anything, the light, the angle of Arthur's body. It was why she had held out so much hope in finally viewing *The Remembering Animal*. To complete Anna's story. How had Anna answered the question. What, indeed, had she finally done with the gift?

The apartment had by now been mostly emptied of Anna's paintings. A few lay stacked against the wall of the living room, the only fully visible one looking unfinished, ghostly, weirdly reminiscent of John Singer Sargent. Aaron had handed Miranda a cup, asked her to sit. He knew why she had come. His voice, when she'd called to make the appointment, had sounded distant, even a little chilly.

He was dressed as she was not used to seeing him: a crisp white T-shirt, a green cardigan so thin it seemed made of parchment. She was accustomed to seeing him in the more formal clothes he wore to his work sessions, and these made him look younger, looser. Richer.

"This is—I wish I could remember the name," he said, blowing on his tea. "Something with 'oolong' in it. Does that sound familiar?"

He was going for the sort of light joke (of course he would know what kind of tea he was serving her) that had always been a part of their encounters, as if from the beginning he'd assumed they'd shared something—an offhand irony, a similarly skewed view of the world—or else wanted to draw her to that place.

"You don't want any?" he asked, after she'd placed her cup on the floor, untouched.

"You know why I've come."

"I do. I was really hoping we could put that off for as long as possible. But you've always been a very direct young woman."

"Forty-three. No longer a young woman."

"I'm fifty-four, Miranda. I could almost say I'm old enough to be your father, but then, thanks to my mother, you've seen me at age eleven, and, well . . ."

He smiled mildly and tucked into his tea.

"So," he said when he'd finished sipping.

"Why haven't I seen it, Aaron? Why am I hearing that it's going up for sale in Basel, and you haven't even had the courtesy to keep your promise?"

"What promise was that?"

"Please."

"All right." He nodded, deciding not to waste any time on denial.

"The very first conversation we ever had—*one* of the first conversations—it was—I can't show it to you yet. I will show it to you when the time is right."

"Yes."

"Don't, okay?"

"Don't what?"

"Don't be *gnomic*. Don't keep saying yes."

"Am I being gnomic?"

"You are. Yes."

His little smile was becoming maddening.

"Apparently the time that was right was the time you could sell it for a gazillion dollars."

He put his cup down and considered her. She felt that she was being held within a frame. Made small. That was the recurrent feeling these days. Having started out with a certain boldness, a determination to define an artist for the world, she was now being dismissed. Thank you very much, we will take it from here. You have done what we needed you to do. Money will define her from now on.

"Have I been played, Aaron?"

He offered her a superior squint. They were back to an old way of being. *Use better words, Miranda.*

"Played?"

"Stop. That's a good enough word."

"Is it?"

"Yes."

"All right. Have you been 'played'?" He hesitated only a second. "There have been conversations, I'll own up to that. Between Andrew and me. What if she sees it and writes about it and, well—consider your power, Miranda—what if she writes something negative?"

She had received it like a small knife thrust, that "consider your power." Condescension in the form of a compliment.

"You don't have any idea what happens at Basel, do you?"

"Of course I don't."

"It's essential that things be *concealed*. You've got to create a hunger. No one has seen it until now. It almost doesn't matter if it's good, and of course it's good. The important thing is that it be *desired*. You have to protect—you have to nurture the conditions of desire."

"Oh stop. You're talking like a—"

"Like a what?"

She wouldn't finish, wouldn't give it to him. In any case, she didn't know the word she wanted. *You're talking like Andrew* was the only thing that came to mind.

"What you've got to understand—and I don't think you want to hear this—is that you've stepped into a world where things are very real, Miranda. All right? Money." He had lowered his voice in speaking the word, as if it required a certain hush. But at least this felt more intimate, more like *him*. "It's very real. It's like this quiet little man who enters a room and says nothing, but you always know he's there, and after a while you can't help referring everything to him."

"I'd appreciate it if you wouldn't lecture me about the importance of money."

"All right. Okay. But let's at least face up to the fact that in the four years since you first traipsed up these steps, things have gotten a little out of hand."

"And you couldn't have done something about that? Couldn't have protected her?"

"From what, Miranda?"

"From becoming what she's becoming."

"Which is what? An artist whose work commands a lot of dough? Tell me. You've been studying her. You've been writing her story. Did she resist any of this? This notion that you've been waiting to see the final painting so that you can determine who she was—that is, well, to use a word I try to never use, that is bullshit, Miranda."

His phone was buzzing. He looked at it only to check who was calling.

"My son."

"You can go ahead and take it."

"No. This is more important." He put the phone back into his pocket. "He's turning out to be a disappointment, this boy of mine."

She had no desire to probe.

"He wants to drop out of Wesleyan to do 'political work.'"

"His grandmother's influence?"

"Yes. Maybe. Or maybe Bernie is making them all a little crazy. Look, I can show you a photo."

"Of your son?"

"Don't be silly. Of the painting."

It was not what she wanted, not this substitute for an experience she'd anticipated would be very different. In her imagination, he would have led her to it. The two of them, in a room, a private viewing. An intimacy between them she only now understood she'd foolishly assumed.

He had gone to a table set up in the midst of the living room and opened a folder. He held up a 4-by-6 photograph.

"The great moment, Miranda."

"This is hardly the great moment. I need to see the real thing."

"And you will. But in the meantime."

He handed her the photograph. Something immediately blinded her to it. She almost pushed it away. She was not ready, and some childish resistance needed to be fought past, some sense of "If I can't have it my way, I don't want it at all." But this was foolish. She forced herself to look.

It was Anna at eighty. Paleness was the determinative feature, an intense paleness. Anna was naked, a mild surprise (she'd rarely painted herself, and never naked), seated, staring as one might stare at a viewer one had discovered looking in, surreptitiously, on a moment of privacy. Anna had made no attempt to flatter herself. In the few self-portraits she'd done, she'd always painted herself off to the side, one of the dizzyingly blue-jeaned mothers in *The Opinionated Playground*. Here, in this one, was a boldness that seemed new, but Miranda tabled her own perception. It was the wrong moment to have it. She couldn't look at it clearly enough.

"What is it?"

"Nothing."

"Disappointed?"

"I don't know."

He was attempting now tenderness, which she resisted as much as she'd resisted his earlier, more crafty-seeming self.

"I won't know until I see the real thing."

When she looked up, he seemed to be trying to penetrate her in some way she couldn't read. Was he being kind, tender, or was this only another form of condescension?

He pulled his chair around so that he was directly in front of her. Then he leaned forward and touched her knee, very gently.

"Is that all right?"

"No."

"Okay. Then I won't do it. I only meant to be friendly."

There was a silence then, an awkwardness. She gripped the photograph, attempted to look at it again.

"Here," he said, and took it in his own hands. He stared hard at it.

"I suppose I'm supposed to be moved," he said. "The last thing my mother finished."

He shrugged, the sides of his mouth lifting up into a loose grimace.

"What was that title you came up with, at the beginning?"

She couldn't remember at first. Then she did.

"'Anna Soloff's Argument.'"

"Yes. God, I can see that one moving off the shelves."

"Is that the point? To have it move off the shelves?"

"Would that be such a bad thing?" He was smiling at her now, a small teasing smile: don't be such a prig. "Maybe Anna's giving you a little gift. Maybe she's saying to you, look, it's okay to use me. Have a little success. Maybe that's what we're both supposed to do now. Let go a little. Take what she's given us."

"I'm not resisting success."

He leaned forward.

"You're resisting it tooth and fucking nail, Miranda. You came in here, and it was essential that you find in my mother some validation for a feeling you had."

"You're talking like a therapist."

"Then *let* me talk like a therapist. You had some idea about the past. That the proper attitude—always—is a pose of mourning. Anna Soloff's argument. What was it? That we should push all this away?" His arm swept out, as if the apartment encompassed the city, the changes in it, money, infiltration, loss. It was a virtually empty apartment. "Tell me, is that what she did? Every power broker in New York came up those steps in the last years. To the little old lady in the cheap dresses. Take off your clothes. No. Yes. Off to Jerome Spencer. Then to our friend Andrew. When she was seventy-seven years old, she made three million dollars. We were lucky to get a container of fried rice from the Moon Palace up the street when we were kids, and now Mom's making three million dollars. And did she spend her free time gazing out the window wistfully?"

"You resent her."

"Damn straight I do." He leaned back in his chair, as if to minimize what he was saying. "Was there ever any discussion with me and my brother? Gee, I'm sorry for making your early lives hell, but look at the nice rewards I get to enjoy now."

He continued to hold something back, perhaps embarrassed at this revelation of a feeling he believed he ought to have overcome by now. She had touched something in him.

"I don't think I need to confirm for you that I also loved her. And—wished her the best."

"I know that."

He had said enough. He picked up his cup, then hers, stared into it a moment.

"I have something for you, by the way."

He took the cups to the sink, placed them there, then went into one of the bedrooms and returned with a plastic bag, full of something.

"What is it?" she asked.

"We're finally getting rid of her old clothes. These are—well, a personal selection I made for you."

Having handed it over, he leaned back against the table.

"All right, so go ahead. Call Andrew and have him let you see it. If he hasn't had it packed already. Do what you need to do."

He seemed to settle in for a moment. Become quiet. He was regarding the bag of his mother's clothes, then turned, so he was looking out the window.

"The terrible thing is the way, after we lose them, they keep on reappearing. My mother dies, and then reappears as this great, attention-hogging artist. Gone, not gone."

He smiled a little bashfully. Indicating to her, she thought, that this moment of openness was some kind of favor he was doing her.

"Look how I'm being honest with you, Miranda."

"I'm noticing."

"This is what I get. I get for her to be this big thing. This sort-of giant. In death. Does that make it better?"

He stood then, seeming, for a moment, physically uncomfortable. As if he were telling her to go. He lifted the photograph.

"When you see it up close, take a good look at her eyes, will you? And then please tell me."

"Tell you what?"

"What she's remembering. I'd dearly like to know."

She had managed to make a date that night with her mother, unusual. Lily had been in New York, in rehearsals, for a month. Their meetings over these past four weeks had been brief—coffee, the occasional breakfast. They had brought back vivid, unpleasant memories of Lily in rehearsal. Going through the motions of domestic life. As a little girl, Miranda had wondered: What was the secret about acting? What was the psychic hole into which her mother disappeared? It ought to have come as a relief when Lily had gone into semi-retirement. But the newly promised emotional availability had never really materialized.

That tonight Lily had agreed to have dinner was only as a result of the play's rehearsals having moved into the technical ones, the ones, set just before facing a live audience, where Lily was allowed to take a break from acting, required only to recite lines onstage so that the lighting designer could set cues and the costume designer could make adjustments.

"Horrid. Torture," Lily said. They were at a window table facing Ninth Avenue, across the street from Lincoln Center. Miranda remained a little rattled by the conversation with Aaron. She noted how even seating herself in a restaurant was a dramatic gesture on her mother's part. The sense of always wearing too many clothes, layer upon layer. It could have been Miranda's own emotionally triggered response, but Lily's face always looked larger when she was rehearsing a play.

"If I'd remembered correctly how arduous this was going to be, I'd never have agreed to do this play."

"But you did."

"Yes."

For a moment, Lily seemed caught, vaguely hostile. I am not here tonight to be questioned.

"Yes, I did."

"And?"

"Well, it's strange," Lily started to say, but the waiter was already there, hovering. "The spinach salad," Lily said to him, neglecting the fact that Miranda had not yet had a chance to look at the menu. "Sorry," she said, and Miranda ordered a glass of wine, as a holding gesture. They found themselves again in that strange place that had always defined them as a couple. Where was Henry? Where was Henry with his jokes and his size and his willingness to always be the butt of their criticism, the male foil in their midst? They had, it seemed, needed his presence to facilitate their own bonding.

"I'm doing it—let me admit this—as a gesture to a man I admire. He was kind to me once. God, I'm sounding like a character out of Chekhov, aren't I? Or no, not Chekhov—"

Miranda held back from the feminine response of easing her mother into whatever it was she needed to say. She wanted to be asked questions, to be drawn out, and if that were to happen it would take time. The glass of wine arrived for Miranda. Lily was having none.

"The play—well, you'll see it, though I'm not sure I want you to."

"Why?"

Lily dipped a piece of bread into the tiny requisite bowl of oil and balsamic vinegar with a kind of savagery.

"Sur*prising*ly hungry," she said.

"Why don't you want me to see it?"

"Because it's ultimately so *private*, Miranda."

Now Lily smiled. It wasn't as though she were telling Miranda a secret so much as reciting a speech.

"It's always been private."

"How?"

"Do I have to tell you? Have you not observed me for forty years?"

"I have, yes."

Something then, between them, triggered by those words. Lily's smile frozen in place for a moment. They wouldn't go there. One of the other diners waved to Lily. "We have tickets for Tuesday," the woman called.

Lily's answering smile was sour, but the woman could not have seen that. You had to be up close.

"Now that woman is all I'm going to be thinking of Tuesday."

"Henry wants the two of us to come that night."

"The first preview? Don't even dream of it, Miranda."

"Then—?"

"You'll come to the opening and not before. The two of you. No, that's my iron rule. Look, what are you going to have? Decide. I'm starved."

Miranda obliged. What was traditional about this dinner was Lily's refusal to indulge in the emotional. To ask after Miranda's emotional well-being. To ask after her love life. Would Miranda have preferred a mother like that? No, of course not. Perhaps a little, that's all.

"I've had—" Miranda had decided to go ahead without waiting, to force this on her mother. She knew that Lily, once engaged, knew how to listen. What she did not know how to do was *elicit.* "—a kind of difficult afternoon."

"Yes?"

Give me the facts. No empathetic expression would precede the request.

"No, I've been waiting to see this final painting of Anna's, and today I saw a photograph."

She had already nearly finished her first glass of wine. Anxiety did that to her. Lily motioned for the waiter to pour a second.

"God, I envy you," Lily said.

"What?"

"Drinking. Go on. What, the painting isn't good?"

"No. I don't know. It may be. Should I be bothering you with this when you've got a play to rehearse?"

"No. You shouldn't."

Lily's smile was sly. An indication that whatever it was Miranda wanted to burden her with, she would handle it. That was how it had always been. High school. College. Miranda had never shied from coming to her mother with a problem, because her mother would know how to fix it. Do *this*, Miranda. No surging emotional wake need follow the boat. It was Henry who suffered with her, though Henry, for all his supportiveness, had often been ineffectual. Once, on a rainy afternoon in Grantham, Lily had demonstrated to her daughter how to summon tears onstage. Having done that, she'd wiped them away and begun preparing dinner.

"You shouldn't. Burden me. But you have," Lily said.

"How do you assess the end of a life?" Miranda said. It sat between them, like an emission that could neither be ignored nor undone. They both responded with self-conscious smiles, as though they probably should laugh at the portentousness of what Miranda had just said. "Anyone's life."

"Well, that's a rather large one," Lily said.

"Yes. It is."

Lily held something back, something she wanted to say but was deciding against. Miranda watched her in the act. Then Lily leaned forward and took a quick sip of Miranda's wine.

"That won't kill me."

"No."

The words Miranda held—*there's something you're not saying*—were ones she could imagine Lily's answer to. Lily would deny her own secretiveness. She would not be drawn out that way. She was defended from her daughter, the way all parents are who have not given themselves entirely, but have given just enough so that a surrendered vacancy exists.

"Well, I'll tell you," Lily said. "Between us. Something happens at the end of your life—"

"You're not at the end."

"Close enough. Please. Let's not pretend. Next year they'll start offering me dowager parts—the Queen Mother—and I'll tell them no."

"You're not."

"All right. You have to say that."

She reached out and touched Miranda's hands on the table.

"What is it that happens?" Miranda asked. "You were about to say."

"Fuck it," Lily said, and motioned to the waiter for her own wine.

Miranda had to wait until it was placed before her, the first delicious sip taken, before Lily would speak again.

"I will tell you this, Miranda, though I hesitate. There's something you've got to know. Maybe you *do* know. I hope you do. You ought to. When you *do* something—act, paint, whatever—you're always holding something back. From—well, *life*, for want of a better word. I can't even answer that question you asked me, for fear that it would take something away from me, something that I may need to *store*, something that belongs—somewhere else."

"Where?"

Lily smiled, disappointed.

"You really don't understand, do you? God, I sometimes wonder how Henry and I could have produced such a levelheaded child."

"I'm not levelheaded at all."

"You should have been a *mess*."

"I am a mess."

"Oh please. The very reason you're lost and wandering in this project is because you're trying to understand this painter who is so utterly unlike you." Lily smiled as though there were something obvious about this. "It's what's always amazed me about you. Your ability not to be as crazy as your parents."

"You're not—"

"Oh stop. Please. Will you? Why did you never marry, have children? Because you're fundamentally *sane*, Miranda. Because you believe in making *choices*, and when you approach life that way, nothing is ever going to be quite good enough, is it? There will always be a reason *not* to do something."

Miranda held back. They had not had this conversation before. Perhaps the play had released something in Lily. She was out of Grantham, in New York, in a restaurant where she was treated as a kind of celebrity. The domestic cord felt very loose.

"You probably wonder—why in the world did your mother stay with your father all these years?"

"I have wondered."

In order for this conversation to continue, they each had to pause, to reflect on the sudden turn it had taken, and to be sure they wanted to go on in that direction.

"There's a kind of madness at work, Miranda. People get together because they're insane. Needy. Blind. All of those things at once. They don't *think*. They don't *choose*."

A look had come over Lily's face—a dip into thoughtfulness, into privacy—that Miranda wanted to pursue. But then their food was arriving. Miranda hated that fact. It might stop Lily. She didn't want her to stop.

"Delightful," Lily said to the waiter.

Miranda also hated the fact that the waiter seemed to want to linger. A young actor, no doubt, in awe of Lily. *Go away, please.*

"Please go on," Miranda said.

"Yes. Well. You've turned forty, I don't think I need to hold anything back from you. I have endured an insane marriage for over forty years, and it is no more insane right now than it was at the very beginning. When I said *okay.* I mean, that is what you say. *Okay.* Like going under the fucking ether. Like you have no choice."

"Of course there was a choice."

"Not if I was going to be who I felt I needed to be." Lily spoke mockingly but sincerely of herself. "Henry was weirdly essential to that."

Lily then mouthed a large forkful of salad.

"He goes *on,* with all the insanity he brings"—Lily's face, though for only an instant, betrayed a certain bitterness—"being weirdly essential."

Again, Miranda wanted to pursue, but something in Lily's tone made her think better of it.

"There was a man," Miranda said.

"Okay. Good."

"A man I met on the Cape when I was there two years ago."

Lily ate ravenously; also, listened.

"I was thinking of having a baby."

"And making me a grandmother. I'd have liked that."

"On my own."

"And who was this swain?"

"An oysterman."

"No."

They were each smiling now, on the verge of laughter but not quite there, negotiating a tension from which laughter was looking for a place to escape.

"And what happened? No. Don't tell me. I think I know. You *decided.*"

"Yes."

"And I will tell you this, Miranda. If you were really like us, like your parents, *artists*, for want of a better word—though I hate that word, really—you would have done it. Closed your eyes and taken the ether and *done* it. But logic spoke, didn't it?"

"Yes."

"So here's what you have to know, which you seem not to have figured out. Artists do the insane things they do because something else matters. Not the life. Not the neatness of the life. Not the curtains or the bills. Not the way it *stacks up*. It sucks, really. It's terrible. The something else. Nobody else can have access to it. Nobody can know why you're doing what you're doing, because you don't even know yourself. It has no name, no—*identity.* You spend your life huddling over this small thing wrapped in a blanket, protecting it. God, I'm really going on a tear with this, aren't I?"

"No. Go—"

"Maybe you get to the end and you unwrap it, this precious thing you've been guarding all your life, pushing away everything *good* in life, and—there's nothing there."

Lily stopped. She wiped her mouth with the large cloth napkin. She looked away, out at the light on Ninth Avenue, the moving cars, the pedestrians. Miranda thought there might be tears in her eyes but then thought: no, those are not tears.

"Is that how you feel?" she asked.

"No. Unfortunately, no. We keep going on, believing in our specialness. We hold on to that until the very end. God help us. Something in us, maybe, as yet unrealized."

There was then a quiet moment, where Lily seemed to be peering very hard at what was on Miranda's plate.

"What is that?" she asked, as if she were only suddenly seeing it.

"A tuna burger. Didn't you hear me order it?"

"No."

Lily looked up at her and then they both laughed.

"I'm lost in this—I'm sorry," Lily said.

She clutched Miranda's hand.

Miranda understood that they would very likely never have the conversation that was always waiting to happen. The one about Lily's inadequate mothering. Even summoning such a phrase made Miranda cringe. What, after all, was "adequate mothering"? She recalled Aaron's face as he had expressed his resentment of a mother who had—what?—never properly apologized? Is that what we're to expect? It seemed childish. Aaron had finally come to know that; Miranda needed to know it, too. She found herself wanting to get a closer look at the final painting, to study Anna's body more closely in the light of what Lily had just said—the private thing always held close, not to be shared. Yet along with this desire came a sense of her own inadequacy. She heard, or took in, a little late the other thing Lily had said, the wounding thing: Miranda, you are not an artist. You are incapable of fully *seeing*.

Even before Miranda finished eating, Lily looked at her watch. "I'm due. The drunken harridan actress arrives at the tech rehearsal smelling of Tokay."

"It was chardonnay, I think."

"The hilarious thing is they all expect me to behave more eccentrically than I'm behaving. Everyone is on tenterhooks, waiting for me to throw a diva's fit. To scream about my wig."

"Do you wear a wig?"

"Something like a wig. It's to keep everyone busy, really. I feel like we should be doing this play in a tiny room. Spare. The words.

Let the words do it all. But if we did that, the Lincoln Center audience would feel cheated. So we have these sets. This elaborate lighting, this *wig*. Well, you'll see. Though I wish you wouldn't."

"No, I have to, don't I?"

"I suppose you do. Yes."

Lily paid, they crossed Ninth Avenue, they approached the Vivian Beaumont Theater, the pool before it with its Henry Moore sculpture, the colonnades, some 1960s idea of official art that had outlived its time and become, half a century later, strangely comfortable. Years before, Lily had appeared in a play here, in the same space where her current play was being performed, the tucked-away downstairs theater, the Mitzi Newhouse. Miranda could hardly remember that other play, it was from the years when Lily had appeared in too many plays, they blurred together, plays in which she'd dyed her hair red and affected an Irish brogue, plays in which she'd had to bare her chest in an affected mastectomy (Miranda had turned away: no), plays in which she'd believed she'd gotten *used* to Lily. But here, she watched her mother, seeming lightheaded after one glass of wine, traipsing across the plaza as if it were her playground, her familiar field.

"You don't have to walk me all the way."

"I want to."

In front of the high glass wall of the Beaumont, posters advertising Lily's play had been set up. The play was called *Pisces*. The artist who had rendered the poster art was very good, there was a Soutine feel to his work, the exaggeration folding in toward the real. Lily on a park bench, her eyes seeking something out in the surrounding dark while a man stood behind her, deeply green, his ears elongated and tucked back, a tail protruding. Lily's name, the other actor's name.

"Intriguing," Miranda said.

"Yes, we'll see."

Lily's kiss was light, her head dipped, resisting full exposure. She stepped down the side stairwell. Miranda had never seen her before. That, for a moment, was the thought.

There had been a scene that had preceded this one, weeks before, an encounter between Lily and Henry that had affected the way rehearsals had proceeded, Lily's approach to her role, the intensity of the work itself. A scene that had made her very glad to be apart from Henry, living in a high-rise on Sixty-First Street, a decent, if bleak, corporate apartment provided for her by Lincoln Center.

Lily was glad to return to the apartment every night, to eat by herself, a glass of wine. The high windows faced the river, a port where container ships docked. She was high enough that she was unable to view the details of New York City, people waiting for buses, the delivery trucks, the shouting, and what she felt, underneath all the activity, to be the city's essential torpidity, the quality that made her not sorry to leave when Henry had first posed the idea years before. In the mostly dark apartment, she turned on one lamp, sat on a sofa with her glass of wine, studied her lines, pushed the script away, tried not to think about Henry and what he had revealed to her just before she left for rehearsals.

She had been packing at home for the four-week rehearsal period when Henry came into the bedroom. It always took her a week to pack, the season was changing, who knew what the weather would be? But there was also the uncertainty of how she wanted to appear. Things that made her look ostentatiously younger? Reject them. But then there was the fear of prematurely accepting the dowager-self. Her clothes—far too many of them—lay piled on the bed.

Henry ought to have been amused by her uncertainty. He'd always been before, in the years of her out-of-townness, when she'd left him for one of the irresistible parts that could only be played in regional theaters. (When those plays were done in New York, the plum roles always went to the bigger stars into whose ranks Lily had just missed ascending.)

Instead, he looked morose. She might have asked him what was wrong, but didn't want to. There had been too many disappointments in their lives like *Third World*, and the answer to the depressed aftermath was always to just get on with it, to continue working. She had hoped that the ridiculous *Lawson's Bend* sequel would work out, if only because it would have gotten him out of the house, sent him to L.A., left her alone to prepare. It had been four years since she had done a play, and the fear—the one you could never quite shake—was that you would find you had lost it. Could no longer summon the thing that needed to be summoned. It had happened to a friend, fired after a week's rehearsal on a play that was meant to be her "comeback." (Stupid word.) You could not discount the same thing happening to you. Concentrate instead on the clothes.

"You pack for me," she'd said to Henry, "since you seem to have nothing else to occupy you."

"You know you wouldn't take my advice."

"No, I wouldn't."

"It's just nervousness, isn't it?"

"Of course."

He touched her shoulder, squeezed a little. "And here we are, still at this foolish endeavor."

She hadn't liked that. It cut too close to the truth. She was afraid, though, of the part of him that appeared to have given up. It was fine for her to give up—or to seem to, to retreat—but she had always counted on some boundless optimism in him, some willingness to keep going.

"Well, don't wear this," he said, lifting something that looked like a leotard. She could not remember having placed it among the possible selections. "Wearing this, you'll look like you're preparing to rehearse *Two for the Seesaw*. You're too old to play Gittel Mosca."

"Maybe I'm too old for this part."

"Oh hush."

"No, maybe I am."

He sat beside her, took her hand. "Nerves. You'll be magnificent."

She was staring into space, in the direction of the large bedroom window. Something sweetly green about this moment in early spring. Why was she leaving?

"It's just occurring to me. I'll miss the lilacs."

"I'll enjoy them for you."

"But you'll be gone, too." As if she were just remembering. "As soon as I open. Suppose something happens to you down there that forces me to leave the play?"

"Oh please. Don't let your melodramatic imagination run away with you. Nothing will happen."

He took in her fear—a default emotion, he was convinced. It was this way with every departure. She had called it that once, the onset of rehearsals, a "departure." Even when, as in the old days, the "departure" meant only a bus ride forty blocks south of their apartment.

But she was right. Henry would be leaving almost as soon as the play opened, returning to Haiti to talk to Jean. The test results had been inconclusive, but good enough that Evan Hatch at Grantham Prep had been surprisingly encouraging. "We can work with you on this," Evan Hatch had said. "A year at the local high school. As I said."

"So he didn't do badly?" Henry had asked. (Left aside was the fiction Jean had created, the "school" he had never attended, which he'd been asked to critique.)

"Not so great that we can welcome him in with open arms. But good enough. And these tests aren't the whole ball of wax. We'll want to meet him, see how he likes it here."

It was a victory, without question, both for Jean and for Henry. He had done at least this much, could present this to Jean. I have succeeded in making a place for you, however tentative. It was the interim year when Jean would have to be looked after that loomed uncomfortably.

"All right," Henry asked Lily, more seriously. "How can I help you?"

Lily was still focused on the not-yet-bloomed lilacs. "You can't," she said. "You know you can't."

What was wonderful and at the same time a little maddening about Lily was what Henry was seeing before him now. He had no doubt she would be, as he'd said, "magnificent" in the role she was taking on. And a part of her knew it. She would not have agreed to it unless she'd felt that capacity in herself. But this woman, who could be so efficient, so no-nonsense in so many aspects of her life, still harbored enormous doubts about herself. Seeing her like this made him think of her as a woman on the bank of a moat, one composed of thick, rushing water. Across the moat lay a large, glittering castle, a place that spoke of infinite welcome. But in order to get there you had to swim the moat. And she, in her wisdom, always spent a long, worrisome time studying the currents. Which pockets of swirling water might have the capacity to carry her away, to the point where she would be lost? He deeply admired this process, and his most self-castigating thought about his own artistic pursuits was that, instead of studying the moat and determining how best to make the deep swim, he was always looking out for the place where the drawbridge might be lowered.

"All right then, I'll leave you to it," he said, and got up off the bed.

"No." She grabbed his wrist. Then, after a moment: "Maybe I don't want you to go. Maybe I'm feeling if I'm going to make a fool of myself, at least you'll be here to reach out to."

"You've already said you don't want me in New York for rehearsals. I've given you that option. You could come back to the apartment every night and I'd be waiting with a soufflé."

"You don't know how to make a soufflé."

"No."

"Besides, that's when I want to be alone."

"Yes. I know."

"It's afterwards. After we've opened. When I have to entertain myself all day waiting for the seven o'clock call. I could call you then, and you could talk me through it."

"There are phones in Haiti."

"No, there are not."

"You know what you're doing? It's called anticipatory—"

"Why are you going?"

The shift in the conversation arrested him. He knew it was a way of pushing away her anxiety. But it was also something else.

"Seriously, *why?*"

"Lily, you're the one who is going."

"No. I'm just thinking about this. I haven't thought seriously enough about it before. I've been distracted. What do you need there?"

"Maybe I should start dinner."

"You're avoiding something."

"Will you please just *pack?*"

"No. Tell me why you're going. There's this *boy*. What's his name?"

"Jean."

"And you've been trying to do this thing."

"Yes."

"Without consulting me."

"It has nothing to do with you."

"Him coming to live with us?"

He had told her that much, suggested it, before backing away. He knew it wouldn't work. Someone else would have to be found, another household. This wouldn't be impossible, not in Grantham, though it would require some tricky explanation.

"He wouldn't necessarily—"

"This is important to you?" she asked very simply.

He appreciated the question, the seeming thoughtfulness of it.

"Yes. It is. I mean, I've gone this far. If I can do this much good for this boy, I'll feel very good." He touched her hand. "And I think right now I need a little victory."

Her face held an inner-directedness. He wasn't sure she'd been listening to him.

"What are you thinking?" he asked.

She shook her head. "About how we really do think sometimes— not sometimes, always—that this is going to sustain us."

"What?"

"Going on. Doing this. Acting. Writing. That it's going to be okay, make us safe forever."

"Yes."

"And it doesn't, does it?"

"No."

The light in the room had shifted, imperceptibly. Henry was more aware now than he'd been up to this point of where this might be leading, where honesty demanded it lead. Was it the light, or was it the strange intimacy of the question she'd asked?

"There's something, isn't there?" she asked.

Still resistant, he answered, "What are you talking about?"

She looked at him in such a way that he knew she would not repeat the question. The question had been asked, her intuition had spoken.

"Go away," she said. "Let me pack."

Having tiptoed up to the edge, she was giving him an out. She was saying it was not necessary for him to answer. She could live without the answer. It was up to him to continue this, if it needed to be continued. He could imagine not doing so, could already taste the falseness in his throat, the mild nausea of avoidance.

"Yes, you're right," he said, feeling a bit doomed in saying it. "This boy has brought out something in me." He paused, as if he were talking into a device, recording something she would listen to later. "Feelings."

"Feelings."

"Yes. Complicated ones."

"I see."

They sat in the silence. She fingered a few of her clothes, as if feeling for the texture.

"Go away, Henry."

He glanced at her, finding nothing in her expression to land on.

"No."

"I don't want to talk about this."

"We're so afraid of it. Why are we so afraid of it?"

She didn't answer; closed her eyes.

"Do you think for a second that this sort of thing—at *this* point—really threatens things?"

"This boy coming here. Of *course* it does."

"He won't have to live with us, Lily."

"Oh, then it's just fine, isn't it? Across town. In whose house? And will we never have him to dinner?"

"Of course we will."

"And you expect me to live with that?"

"So you're saying I can't do this—can't help the boy—because it would be too difficult having him over to dinner occasionally, knowing that I find him—"

He hesitated.

"Say it," she said with a certain harshness. "Make it *clear*."

"That I find him beautiful. That's all."

"That's not all," she said very softly. "If that was all you wouldn't have felt you needed to tell me."

She was right, of course.

"And *now*. You had to tell me this *now*. When I'm on the verge of something that's making me insanely nervous."

"You *asked*, Lily. You demanded. The timing is terrible, I know. But Lily—listen to me, I think it's only because you're in this state that you're reacting this way. Is it really such a big thing?"

"Yes. Yes it is."

Her face had colored, drawn in by her anger.

"I don't know who you are anymore."

He grasped her wrist. The violence in the relationship had always been hers—thrown picture frames, attempts to subdue him—but he was aware of his greater strength, and as much as it wanted to assert itself, he held back. Still, it was the flash point, wasn't it? Even in the holding back lay the measure of something, how close they came at times to the dangerous words and acts. He noted it in her face; she liked inciting this anger in him. It told her where they were.

"You have *always* known who I am. There have been no secrets. We have *done* this, had this life, with no secrets." He spoke as though, with the words, he was trying to hammer down a floorboard that had warped. "Nothing is going to happen."

"All right, so nothing happens. Does that take away from the fact that you're still lusting—"

"Not lusting. He's twenty years old, for God's sake."

"Whatever, then. Still capable—"

"And who isn't, Lily? You're telling me this behemoth on the bed next to you is all you could possibly desire?"

He was speaking harshly, perhaps more harshly than he needed to, and she seemed, at this moment, more vulnerable than he'd seen her in a while. He'd misjudged how deep the pre-rehearsal funk went. And who could ever say, even this deep into the marriage, just how they each affected the other, the agreement with oneself it took to go on loving another person?

"What are you trying to tell me, Henry? Are you telling me that you're capable of loving a *boy*?"

"'Loving' is too strong."

"Fine then. Tell me the word. Tell me the fucking word. You've never faced up to this side of yourself. You're not facing up to it now."

"I think I am. I'm admitting it, aren't I? I'm not hiding it from you."

"Why didn't you tell me? From the beginning."

"Is that what I'm supposed to do? Tell you every feeling I have, the minute I have it? Is that the obligation? We'd destroy each other if that was the case."

"No, just feel things in secret. While I think I'm married to this—"

"What?"

"—*person*. This person who has fought a whole difficult side of himself—"

"*Fought*," Henry mocked gently.

"What then, 'accepted'?"

"That's better."

"All right. Accepted, then. And I have *accommodated* it, whatever strangeness that has required. Whatever—well, has it poisoned things?"

"I don't feel things have been poisoned. Ever."

He wasn't looking at her. Couldn't, therefore, see her questioning expression.

"How can you think that?" he asked.

"Oh, I wonder. What an absurd thought to have, given what you're telling me."

"I would never have told you this if I didn't believe we could endure it. I am dealing with these feelings. They are not crippling."

"Wonderful. I am so happy for you."

"Stop. Just stop."

She looked up at him. It was time—he felt it very keenly—for him not to say anything. For a silence. In the old days of their marriage, it would be time for sex. For sex to allow them to articulate what could never be articulated in a fight, the brute truth of what one wanted—*needed*—from the other. But that easy slipping into the sexual dialogue had left them behind. All he could do now was reach out and touch her.

"We can handle this."

"If you don't stop saying that, I'm going to hit you. Don't tell me what I can handle."

"Okay, maybe I'm only saying *I* can handle it."

Again she looked at him, stopping just short of being accusatory. Something else. She was attempting to understand him in a way that felt new, as though she were seeing something new. Or maybe seeing something new in herself, a reckoning—or questioning—of how much she had perhaps deceived herself.

"I don't know, Henry. I don't know what to think. Maybe you should move out and live with this boy. Happily ever after."

"That's not worthy of you."

"Sorry. I'm not capable of your high-flown language."

"Yes you are. You're perfectly capable. Half of what I've written in this life has come from you. From listening to you."

"Don't try and flatter me."

She cast her eyes on him for a moment, seeking something.

"We've always been like the Lunts, haven't we, Henry? The theatrical couple. Delightful. Charming. Playing off one another. Making people laugh. And then there's this depth somewhere."

She stopped, looked at the floor.

"And we have to wonder, have we touched it? Have we lived there at all?"

"I think we have," he said, hoping it was true.

"Tell me. You've got to tell me."

"I'm not going to narrate our life."

"Why not?"

God, she seemed so young now. So vulnerable. So in need of something. He touched her again.

"I'm not going to narrate our life—*justify* it—because if you don't know what we've been there's nothing I can convince you of. I'm not going to let you go."

"Is it all up to you?"

She hesitated a moment, turned away toward the clothes on the bed.

"Choose, Henry. Just—choose. And then I'll let you know if it's okay with me."

When a play fails in New York, anyone can tell you, it sits on its side street like a stillbirth with a sheet laid over it, mourned by no one but its makers. It is as if it never existed. But when a play succeeds, when it is about to become a hit, it seems as though the entire city is present at the birth, hovering outside the delivery room, anxious to be given entrance.

So it was that Miranda was awakened by a call the morning after Lily's first preview. Her friend Laura, the actress.

"I hear your mother's terrific."

"Who said?"

A name given, someone who had seen the first performance.

"Standing Os."

"Doesn't everything get a standing O these days?"

"Yes, but no, she said this was the real thing."

It could be felt, then. In faraway Brooklyn, at the coffee shop where Miranda went for her morning coffee, she expected the talk at all the tables would be about Lily, about *Pisces*. She listened for it.

They were not allowed to see the play until opening night, though. Even Henry was barred from the theater. Philip was coming to the opening as well. A slight anxiety over that, because Philip had a serious girlfriend now—they had not yet met her—and there had been talk about his bringing her. Nouri. Philip spoke of her with an embarrassed lilt, like boys on a bench before going into a game might talk about girls, distractions from what is immediately before them. That Philip ultimately decided not to bring Nouri felt like a small failure to Miranda, as though he feared the family's potential disapproval, a way they all resisted his growing up and moving past them.

She called him on the morning of the opening, while she was drinking coffee on Bergen Street.

"Bring her," she said.

"Can't. Listen, I'm working."

"No. *Bring* her. You need to."

"Miranda, Henry said I couldn't even get an extra ticket if I wanted. It's the fucking opening."

"Bullshit. You can always get an extra ticket. It's Lily, for God's sake."

They held on to an ensuing silence. She could hear the sound of a sales floor in the background. Even over the phone, she thought she could smell testosterone.

"See you tonight," he said.

So it was the three of them, in the seventh row, on the aisle. A sense within the gathering audience of something to be anticipated. They already knew, of course they already knew. Henry looked haggard, which was the way he'd looked for months. He'd been sequestered in Grantham, on his own, while Lily rehearsed, and the experience had left him with a shadowy pallor lingering on his closely shaved cheeks.

"Are you nervous for her?" Miranda asked.

"Always. But it's foolish in this case, isn't it?"

Henry knew several people in the audience, waved to them.

"I'm feeling a bit like Norman Maine these days," he said.

"Who's that?" Philip asked.

Miranda and Henry had to smile, before Miranda turned to him and whispered, "*A Star Is Born.*" Philip's life with them had been a long tutorial, in which he was still catching up. Before Miranda could explain more, they were silenced by the houselights going down.

Then up again, on Lily, seated on a park bench. She looked theatrically haggard (as opposed to Henry's more authentic version of the same thing), a little bit stunning. You looked at her in that first moment and you understood—the whole audience seemed to understand, as one—that nothing else in the world was as important as what Lily was about to say.

"The silly thing is, I came and sat on this bench every day," were the first words.

Lily was talking to them, telling them a story. *Listen to me. We're going somewhere.* A woman whose marriage was dead, though her husband came home every night, expecting dinner. The children off, grown, distant. The clichés piled up. Lily's genius was to admit them, even as she spoke them. *I know I am not telling you anything new, but I am new.* And then a man showed up onstage, holding a newspaper. The audience gave him entrance applause. A British actor who had scored a success in a long-running series about royalty. They began a conversation. A slow flirtation. They were funny with each other. Miranda could imagine Lily married to such a man, and for a moment (guiltily, with Henry sitting beside her) thought how that might have been better, a second marriage, a man like this, serious, whiskey-aged in the way of certain elegant older British men, a man who lifted the fold of his trousers before sitting. All of this was familiar—two lonely people, two park benches—the stuff of a million similar plays—but none of that mattered. You watched it, transfixed, and part of it, a large part, was the way they looked at one another, the amusement, the sympathy, and the way Lily made you see her character noting, and beginning to attend to, her own haggardness, as if confronting herself in the mirror of the man's eyes.

In the next scene, Lily again alone onstage at the beginning, waiting, the man's entrance was marked by some small, at first undetectable change. "You look a little green," Lily said. The man smiled. "I *am* a little green, you'll find." Then he very skillfully shifted the tone by beginning a story about his own family, his wife, his daughter, and you knew before he got very far that death would figure in, a horrible death, and as you listened, the play's trick—there was always a trick, wasn't there?—began to tease you. The greenness was the tip-off, but you fought that suspicion, that burgeoning knowledge, because you were hearing a story of tragedy—the death of a daughter—and you wanted to believe it more than you wanted to analyze a playwright's strategy. *Give me the tragedy, please. Immerse me in it.*

"Yes," Lily said, when the man had finished his story, and it was a moment, shaped by Lily's listening, to hold the audience perfectly still. The old cliché—"you could hear a pin drop." Miranda took a second to glance at Henry, to note that he was watching Lily with a broad, hugely appreciative smile. Whatever was true about them, this was also true. His *going* to her in this moment, his cheering on of some part of her that had slept.

When the man came on again, after the next blackout, something had happened with his ears. They were tucked back, he'd been given gills. And so it proceeded, the man becoming ever more fishlike, piscine, and Lily initially not wanting to see this side of him, turning away before giving in to the fascination, finding the humor in it, asking, at first shyly, if she could touch his scales. He removed his shirt. The actor, in his late sixties or early seventies, had sagging tits, an Englishman's caved-in body, but the scales had been so brilliantly applied that you believed them. Or maybe it was the way Lily approached them, her touch, the sexual feeling in her uttered "Oh my" (a marvel, the way she allowed, even elicited complicit laughter from the audience). Henry whispered an appreciative "Yes." He was leaning forward now. Lily touched the man and said, "I'm sorry."

"Don't be," the fishman said. "Please. Don't be. It's all changed me, that's all." And for a moment Miranda forgot the play's too-obvious trickery and saw, and bought, the metaphor.

"It's that I haven't had one, isn't it?" Lily said. "A tragedy." And then started the action that would lead to her baring her own breasts. Miranda hoped this wouldn't happen, and it didn't. At the last minute Lily stopped. Full exposure was not necessary, would even have been wrong, though if she'd been asked, Lily would have been brave enough to do it. Her hesitation, her holding back, became the dramatic action. *I have nothing to display but aging breasts.* The clarity of her wish to have been given scales. To be a changed being, somehow equal to this man.

"Meat loaf," was what she said instead. Barked, really, like an accusation against someone unseen. Not a great joke, but the audience laughed, out of relieved tension and unexpectedness. "He brings me home recipes for meat loaf. He clips them out of magazines." Her marriage laid out, and the man touched her with scaly fingers, and they kissed.

So it went, six scenes, over the course of ninety minutes, and in the next-to-last scene, a tail, the man entirely a sea creature. The inference that they'd become lovers, that Lily had come alive in the green, watery sex that had become their surround. (The lighting, it had to be said, had become magical in the penultimate scene.) And then, in the final scene, the one where the fishman didn't come, the moment you knew you'd been waiting for, the moment when Lily turned away from the empty bench, looked again at the audience, suddenly bereft. "I made you up, didn't I?" Of course the audience knew by that point, had realized it almost from the first time the man had turned green, but had participated in holding that knowledge in abeyance, going instead with the sleight of hand, believing entirely in the play's alternate reality—*of course*, a lonely woman and a fishman willing to love her, that *should* happen—so that Lily's spoken realization broke the spell in a way that physically hurt Miranda. *Let us know it but don't say it, stay with the fishman please.* (She did not want to examine, though she had to, her regret about having left behind her own potentially transformative fishman.) It was Lily's face, in the moment of self-knowledge, that got to her. The way Lily, clutching her own shoulders, hesitated over the words, touching them like they were piano keys and this was the diminuendo. As if she were talking about every seemingly decent man, not just this one. "I made you up."

At the curtain call, the audience rose as one, screaming out their appreciation. Henry was among the first, nearly knocking into Miranda in his urge to rise, its suddenness, the meat loaf man applauding his own wife's disappointedness in him. It was as though this—the fact that she was now transcending him—was precisely what he wanted, even needed. Lily accepted the loud gestures of praise, seeming shy (an act, of course), as if asking the audience to hush, *enough*. Even the actor beside her, only halfway out of his fishman makeup, deferred to her, smiling, stepping back a little. As Miranda watched all this, her understanding grew, something she'd always known without fully allowing herself to know: her mother had always been the true artist in the family.

By the time the curtain call was over, Henry was sweating. He grasped Miranda by the shoulders, seeking a mutual recognition. "What do you think of that?" he said.

"Yes," she answered.

Behind them, only Philip looked less than overwhelmed. As they stepped out of their seats and up into the lobby, Henry besieged by well-wishers, Philip whispered to Miranda, "What the fuck was that? I mean, Lily was great, but—" Miranda understood, but the merits of the play itself seemed secondary to what she'd experienced. She clutched Philip's hand, as a way of asking him to keep quiet.

They made their way down to the dressing rooms, where they were only three of at least a dozen who had been granted this special access. Miranda recognized the other faces, well-known actresses who Lily had worked with, a TV celebrity or two. Their voices were all high in the corridor outside Lily's dressing room, waiting for her to come out, Henry's head rising above theirs, exultant, like a man in the midst of his own very good party. It was the British actor who came out first, out of his own dressing room. Even having had to re-move all his fishy appurtenances, he'd still taken less time than Lily was taking. The man who must have been his partner was waiting for him, natty, with a folded silk handkerchief in the breast pocket of his jacket. They touched each other's shoulders; the actor had his own small entourage to be acknowledged. Then he joined the crowd waiting for Lily to emerge.

When she finally did, she seemed smaller, a miniature version of the woman who had been onstage. She waved them all away. "Stop, please." She did not even glance at Henry, but Miranda received a corner glimpse, as if Lily were saying, *Of course these others are all going for this slop, but did you see any merit in it at all?* Miranda took this in, flattered, said yes in her silent way. In spite of itself, and in large part because of Lily, there had been merit.

They walked over the plaza to the restaurant where the party would be held, the same restaurant where Lily and Miranda had eaten dinner. The theater had taken it over for the evening. More applause as Lily entered, followed by the caravan of her admirers, the British actor in tow, brushing away the applause directed at him. "No, no, it's entirely her show." Henry seemed to be enjoying being part of the crowd, though there was something in his face, Miranda couldn't miss it, a high color, a bit of a desperate need to share this. He was waiting for something from Lily, who was making too much of her own continued "Stop, enough." "Give me a fucking martini," she said, and someone did, and Henry, too, and then they were beside one another, being photographed, though Lily was still not fully acknowledging him. (Had there been a pre-opening fight?) As he stood there, his arm around his triumphant wife, Miranda saw it again, the tightened, partially open mouth of mild desperation. *I would like a bit more.* And then Lily and the British actor were swept away by the publicity people, drawn deeper into the restaurant. The three of them, Miranda, Philip and Henry, remained near the entrance, celebratory drinks in hand, feeling at least a little abandoned.

"'I shall be sent for,'" Henry said, lifting his martini glass and eyeing Miranda over the rim, questioning her.

She only lifted her eyebrows, acknowledging that of course she got the reference, of course she knew Falstaff's self-soothing reflection at the moment of Prince Hal's ascension. Henry had made sure she knew it.

"You two are too much," Philip said, but he was looking out the window of the restaurant; he'd asked Nouri to join them there.

"Yes, we *are* too much," Henry said. Then he shifted from his own self-mockery to, "Is that her?"

Nouri was a stunning half-Iranian young woman, dark hair worn long, a nose like a statement of power. She made her way through the crowd inside the doorway. She and Philip did not hug. Miranda thought of the smiles she and Henry both wore as being too large, too theatrical, if anything too welcoming, and noted Nouri noting this.

"I've already read the *Times* review." She held up her phone. "Fantastic. I'm sorry I missed it."

"Yes, we'd have loved to have introduced you to Lily in a more intimate way," Henry said, "but as it is, you're going to have to meet her in the midst of her adoring throng."

"We're not staying," Philip said. It wasn't rude, they knew he hated this sort of thing, theatrical parties, emotional excess.

"I'd like to meet her," Nouri said.

They could no longer even locate Lily in the crowded restaurant. It was easier to find Barbara Walters, holding court at the bar.

"It would be ridiculously awkward," Philip said. "We'll check in with you guys."

Miranda walked them out. The night was deeply alive—a line of twentysomethings, holding up phones like lighthouse beacons, waiting to get into the rooftop disco next door. It was hard to believe that all this street life was not centered on *Pisces*, that there were other reasons to be out, and celebrating.

"He's told me so much about you," Nouri said.

She was the living definition of what people meant when they used the word "lovely." Something was in her, an articulated decency that alone could make someone fall in love with her. Philip looked more handsome in her presence, his hair longer, silkier, wetter; he looked like a man who has decided he can go another day without washing it, it will only improve things.

"Let's go," Philip said, and then turned to Miranda. "Listen, like I said, she was great, but the *play?*"

"I know," she answered. "But—" She left it at that.

She was no longer thinking, in any case, about the play. She reached up and kissed Philip on the cheek, tugged Nouri's hand in a farewell gesture. She watched them walk away, and then the night descended on her, all the emotion of watching her mother triumph onstage, and the realignment she'd taken in—her mother's artistry, her father's relative diminishment. Don't think about that. Just as they were about to round the block, Philip touched Nouri's shoulder, not to hug but just—what? The gestures of intimacy seemed so foreign to Miranda now. Had Botho ever touched her like that?

Of course he had. Dozens of times. But that all seemed now like an alternate reality. This was Philip, going away from her, touching a girl. Philip, who she'd always hoped could exist with her in some liminal space, outside commitment, outside what Lily had called the insanity of actually saying yes to someone. The last thing she saw before they disappeared was his hair, Philip's hair, a little bit of it flying upward.

Then she turned, looked inside the restaurant, found Henry in conversation with a short man, one of those types she knew must be a producer or a theatrical agent. Henry noticed her and held up his hand. His eyes seemed to retain a permanent startledness, like a man who has forgotten something, a man about to pat his pockets to locate a misplaced phone.

He came out and joined her, finally.

"What is it?" he asked.

She was wiping her eyes. She hadn't cried, but some evidence of how she felt must have been there.

"Nothing. Big night," she said.

"It is," he answered, not as if he were answering her but dissecting those bland, meaningless words.

"A cigarette, I think, would be just the thing. But I don't have one."

Henry looked at the line of twentysomethings, and Miranda thought: no, please, do not embarrass me tonight. Do not make yourself a clown on this particular evening. But of course, Henry approached one young man who was smoking, holding out to him a five-dollar bill, and the young man shook his head and handed Henry a cigarette and lit it for him, and the whole group around Henry and this young man started laughing. Henry was gesturing, no doubt telling them about the opening night, the party next door, charming them, insisting they see the play.

When he returned, he said to Miranda, "There are angels unawares, you know that."

"I think I do."

"And what are we to do now, the abandoned ones?" He kept sneaking glances into the restaurant, as if he really did expect to be "sent for."

"Oh," he said, his shoulders hopping, "something I've been meaning—" He blew out a long plume of smoke. "As if this isn't all enough, I got a call yesterday. A very dear uncle of mine passed away. You might remember him, my uncle Phil."

"I don't."

"Oh, you do. When you were little, when we used to visit my parents, I always took you to see him. Bald head."

"Well, that narrows it down."

"No, don't. We'd always find him sitting in his garden. The man lived forever, over a hundred. Oh God, wonderful man. I've got to go to his funeral."

Miranda nodded. It seemed inconsequential. Another, larger thing had happened.

But Henry continued to not so much look at her as bore into her. A moment passed. She could almost see the idea as it occurred to him.

"Come with me."

"Dad, I'm going to Basel in a week."

"Well, fuck that, I'm about to go to *Haiti* in two weeks. This is a *day*, Miranda."

He took her hand, held it tightly. Perhaps too tightly. Leaned toward her. "No, this is what we should do. Take a trip to Newton together. Your mother won't need us, we'll only be in the way. Look at her." He gestured inside, where they could still not see Lily. "We should do this."

"I can't. I've got so much . . ."

He continued to look at her, saying nothing. His eyes, though. The weight of the night in them. The intensity of his need. The way he was being ignored by the crowd coalescing around Lily. He was asking her for something else. The funeral was incidental.

She would spend this night resisting, promising only that she would think about it. Convincing herself that she could get away with saying no. But his eyes would go on making their plea, and soon enough the familiar guilt, the expectation that she still had to be there for him, would arrive.

Come with me.

In the end, she knew she would be coerced into going.

4.

At home, waiting to pick up Miranda from the train in Springfield (the train she had chosen stopped no closer), Henry found he could not concentrate on the funeral they would both be attending the next day. Could not focus on the triumphant opening night Lily had been gifted with, or on the thought of bringing his daughter back to this house, the day they would spend together, the gratitude he knew he should feel for her having gone along with his large request. No, what he was thinking about, what he found these days he could not stop thinking about, was Jean.

Impossible not to. He would be returning to Haiti in two weeks, to bring the boy some sort of news, and after the fight with Lily—the as yet unresolved fight (as how, in fact, could it ever be fully resolved?)—he could not imagine exactly what the message would be. *You've succeeded, Jean, and now, out of my own cowardice, I have to nullify your success?* No, he could not imagine saying that. But what? Weeks ago, Lily had laid out the choice. He was dodging it, dancing away from it, still not willing to fully face it.

Beatrice would not be accompanying him on this trip. "You've been enough times, you can go yourself this time," she'd said to him.

She would agree to arrange lodging for him, a pickup from the airport, a driver. Père Felix would arrange the meeting with Jean.

All right then. Henry wandered through the rooms of his house, trying to push all these thoughts away. Was it possible to indulge in a small, fortifying brandy before leaving? No, his fear of greeting Miranda with liquor on his breath was too great. He felt he had begun to appear weak to her in their recent encounters. He could no longer summon the old confidence, the old strength, the old jocular Henry. It had always been a performance, of course, and Miranda no doubt knew that. Still, it was important to maintain whatever remained of the illusion, to stop short of the full-throated admittance of how far into the well one had sunk.

Or maybe—the thought had only begun to occur—maybe it was time to show her something else. She had agreed to come to this funeral. How extraordinary was that? Perhaps he owed her, in return, some honesty he had thus far held back from.

He checked his watch. Five minutes. He could leave in five minutes, and that would prevent him from having to wait too long in the Springfield train station, an anteroom of hell. He chose a comfortable chair, turned on a lamp, studied, on the wall opposite him in the dimly lit room, a painting he and Lily had purchased in London years ago. They had long forgotten the artist's name. Miranda had suggested it resembled an early Celia Paul, blue and limpid, with a figure resembling a swan in one corner. But he found it hard to concentrate on the painting, or to sit still. He knew the technical term for what he was feeling. An "agitated depression." His therapist friends had labeled it for him. But having the label did not help much.

His phone pulsed. A text from Miranda. The train delayed outside Hartford. He would have to leave a bit later. He tried to remove himself from whatever panic this delay brought up. He had counted on the soothing effects of the drive. The highway largely deserted at this hour, NPR on the car radio. He might be able to lose himself in hearing about the pitched battles between Hillary and Bernie, the increasingly distressing prospect of Donald Trump.

Instead, he found himself studying these rooms more attentively. The settledness of his own house, these rooms containing his personal history. Art books he never opened, biographies purchased that he could not imagine picking up. (Benjamin Britten? *Really?*) On the wall, a framed letter from a theatrical legend who had written Henry after the opening of one of his early plays, a letter he had positioned so that guests would notice, only so that he could brush it away. "Choose, Henry. And then I'll let you know if it's okay with me." He still felt he could find a way around Lily's words, a way to have both. His marriage intact, and Jean here, in another house, then at Grantham Prep. *Have both.* If life taught you anything, it was that that was never in the cards, was it?

It had been something, though, Lily's opening. What it signified to him was that there would be more of it, the world would clamor for her now. And if he knew her, though she would claim a desire for rest, to be left alone, she would not be able to resist. Besides, what, anymore, could keep her here? A husband whose emotional life had proved to be so unstable, so unreliable, a husband who, were he forced to abandon his plan to help a Haitian boy, would be left with what, exactly? And even if he were to make that choice, her last words had implied that still might not be good enough.

What Lily wanted for him was to resume the old life, to be saturated again by ambition. But how exactly did you reabsorb ambition, when it had seemed to have so decisively left you? There was, in the end, no going back to what he had been. Still, if he were to lose this, he knew how much he would miss it, the comfort they had become to one another, the reference point they had each provided for the other, the physical comfort, the physical *need*. And what, he had to ask now, what had landed him here in this difficult place? What had been his sin? The wish to do good. That was all. Whatever the complications, was that in itself a bad thing? Call him what you wish—fatuous first worlder, virtue signaler—there had still been a decent impulse behind it all. Yet here, once again, was God's sly way. He will never allow the direct line. He will always provide a dangerous curve, a test. It is His way of forcing you to fully know yourself. How then, to win, except by losing?

Lily had been right about one important thing. If it had been just a matter of Jean's beauty affecting him, there would be no real issue here. It was that Jean had opened something in Henry that now had to be confronted. Something he couldn't, or still wouldn't, name. An emptiness, an availability; those inadequate words would have to do until he found better ones.

Who was it, which Greek philosopher had said that the three stages of a man's life were sweat, thought, and prayer? Cut it how you will, he had arrived at the Age of Prayer. Surprising himself, he knelt. And what did he have to say to God at this point? What exactly did God not already know about the travails of Henry Rando? Silence, then. His knees chafing against the floor, his head lowered. Say nothing at all.

Another text, the phone buzzing in his pocket. The train had resumed, Miranda's estimated time of arrival adjusted. He could leave soon. But he remained kneeling on the floor. He did not rush.

On the night before she took the train into Springfield, Miranda went to a gallery on the Lower West Side, just south of Chelsea, not far from the Schechner Gallery, a newish place that was hosting a group show. She'd seen the ad in *ARTnews*, and had made a note to attend before leaving for Basel. Included in the show—the part that drew her—was an installation called *The Last 8 Minutes of* Zabriskie Point. The artist was Cindy Auerbach.

The show—soon to close—was not well attended. An early summer evening, and everyone wanted to be outside. A group of college girls in startlingly short skirts was seated on a bench in a small park near the gallery, drinking, checking their phones, prior to attending some event at which they would no doubt arrive drunk. Glancing at them, Miranda thought of herself as a disapproving ogre. It was what she was becoming, apparently, a nose sniffing out scents that allowed her judgmentalism to surface. That she had once herself been a college girl who drank too much didn't seem to matter.

Cindy Auerbach's installation was in a room of its own within the gallery. You had to seek it out. The familiar Auerbachian tropes were on display: the monitors showing scenes from a film, the headphones that, Miranda knew even before picking them up, would feature voices reciting comment written by Cindy Auerbach. Had she come here simply to dismiss the artist? Was this what her life was going to become now?

The images, though, were striking. Miranda only knew about the existence of *Zabriskie Point* because of Henry. Of course. Antonioni's one American movie, from 1970, a legendary failure, largely plotless though undeniably gorgeous. A boy on a California college campus who's had it with sit-ins and aimless radical chatter steals a plane and flies across the desert. A girl who works in the corporate world is driving across the same desert, having been asked to deliver a folder to a corporate retreat. Boy and girl meet, pausing only long enough to make love in the sand. On the drive she has necessarily to resume, the girl hears on the car radio the news that the boy, attempting to return the plane, has been shot and killed by the police.

Miranda remembered that much, from the endless tutorial-by-VCR that Henry had conducted in the Grantham family room. "Oh you must see this," he would call to her, and then force her to endure one after another of the movies that had meant something to him in his own youth. All those dateless Friday nights of her own middle school and early high school years (Philip would often be out with his own friends, abandoning her to Henry). He had taken advantage of her aloneness. "Come here, Miranda, watch this with me." What had Lily been doing? The likelihood was that Lily had been away, rehearsing or performing somewhere.

Thus, she knew, without particularly wanting to, *Zabriskie Point.*

The scene Cindy Auerbach had chosen to repeat on the console was one Miranda had not remembered. Arriving at the corporate retreat in the desert, a modern wood-framed house, one designed to nestle among rocks, the girl had delivered the folder to a room full of leering men in leisure outfits. On her way back to her car, she caught glimpses of their women, the men's wives or mistresses lounging by the pool, women whose choices manifested in the clothes and hairstyles that had made the early seventies seem a kind of prison for the middle class, the sense that even when you were seeing people live, in the present, you felt you were gazing at a faded Polaroid. The dying, irrelevant world. Arriving at her car, the girl turned back and envisioned the house exploding. One shot after another, explosion and fire. And then an astonishing thing: Against an empty blue background, Antonioni had set up a model world. Under the music of Pink Floyd, the model world was blown up. The screen filled with exploding tiny patio furniture, dresses, refrigerators, frozen turkeys, Wonder Bread. Those were the eight minutes Cindy Auerbach had captured on the monitor. In a way, the headphones, the commentary, didn't feel essential. Those eight minutes were beautiful.

But she did put on the headphones, and recognized Cindy Auerbach's deep nasal voice, uninflected: "And of course, this is what we've forgotten. We were meant to blow it up. Don't you remember? Did that slip your mind? The Wonder Bread world. The world of *things.*"

Miranda removed the headphones. It was a bit much. Still, something was happening to her, she couldn't say what. She was glad to be alone in this part of the gallery, but still felt self-conscious enough to put the headphones back on, to hear the next snippet: "Now they own us as much as we own them. Now we buy better brands, hipper, cooler, we use words like 'synergy,' we do our yoga and we believe in the possibilities of *self*. But we are still in that world."

She took them off again. She watched the series of images through for a full eight minutes. What had she made of this as an adolescent, Henry beside her, Henry bringing her into what was at once a nostalgic trip for him, and a perhaps not fully intended political lesson? Perhaps men like him, men of the sixties, grew used to this, images of the world being blown up, a directive handed to them by the culture, by artists like Antonioni, channeling Antonio Gramsci: yes, it must all be destroyed in order for the new to emerge.

She looked around herself. She did not wish for this moment, had not sought it out. She thought of Cindy Auerbach, her baby, Paolo, her highly constructed artist's pose, and wanted to devalue her. But it seemed to her that Cindy Auerbach was getting to her in a way that felt nearly profound. She was back inside her adolescence. A bearish father touching her shoulder, running his gentle hand along her cheek—always stopping there—and handing her, with a terrible casualty, a directive. Just what Cindy Auerbach was suggesting here. This is what we need to do, Miranda. Blow it up. Do not love this too-comfortable world. It has to be destroyed.

Yet it had not been.

Before she knew it, she was sitting on a bench, in the same small park, now empty, where the drinking college girls had been. It had not been blown up. There had been feints made in that direction, but the directive had not been followed. The same overdressed women sat around the pool. Men with better haircuts than the awful corporate types from *Zabriskie Point* now consulted computer screens, but conducted essentially the same business. At night, some of them played in rock bands. *We are still in that world. It only looks different.* Something had proved finally indestructible, hadn't it? Here, in this part of the city, men and women were all on their way somewhere. Their clothes were stunning, their hair. On their way to galleries, parties, dinners. She felt, and was troubled by, her own distance from all of this. It has not been destroyed, so what then is the choice? She had believed Anna could help her, but Anna could not help her. Anna had herself accepted it all too easily, once the world had taken notice and begun to lionize her. The city in its gorgeousness rose around Miranda, sterling buildings, beautifully designed small parks, the well-integrated advertisements that showed just how deeply this neighborhood had been taken over, and by whom. The quiet perk of money bubbling up into an elegance of design. Who would want, anymore, to blow this up? This place of perfect coffee, of gentle architectural lines, this city of art?

The funeral Mass was being held in what looked like a cathedral, though it was only one of the cavernous churches built in the early part of the twentieth century to serve the immigrant populations then pouring into Newton. First the Irish, then the Italians. These last of the old breed of Italians, these scattered mourners, filled only the first four or five rows. Henry and Miranda were a bit late. Henry knelt and blessed himself, a couple of rows removed from the others, so as not to disturb. Always a minor shock for Miranda to witness the latent Catholicism in him, this obeisance to ritual. He had never insisted she follow him down this path, though he had tried to nudge her in that direction, albeit gently.

She was struck by the lack of facial subtlety in the depictions of the Virgin in these old churches. They made her think of other Annunciations, particularly one, possibly her favorite, a fourteenth-century Annunciation by Duccio she'd seen in London. The way the artist had managed to capture doubt and hesitation in the dark, Semitic face of Mary as she took in the uninvited, demanding angel:

No, please, do not ask me to do this, to give birth without the plea-sure of sex, to give life to a doomed son. In this church, as in all the churches of her youth, the very pale Virgin could only say, Yes, of course, why would I hesitate for a moment to offer this sacrifice of everything that is mine? I am a woman, my duty is to serve.

It was why she was here, wasn't it? Why she had agreed, in the end, to accompany that other demanding angel, her father.

At Henry's entrance, a few of the mourners had turned around. Wide smiles of greeting, tiny waves, then their remarking to one another that he had come. The celebrity author who had risen out of these humble parish beginnings. She wondered if this was what he had come here for, this hometown affirmation.

They surrounded him as they were making their way out of the church, as they got into their cars for the drive to the cemetery. The greetings were effusive. Small octogenarian women in their dark suits, hairstyles that had never changed, not since the sixties, the lacquered, important hair, the shoes, the authority that came from never having moved past a certain predetermined domestic sphere. Miranda looked at them and thought: no one has ever painted these women, no one has ever thought to capture this particular world on canvas. "My daughter Miranda," Henry kept saying, introducing her around to women and men she hadn't seen since her grandparents' funerals twenty years ago.

At the grave site it was "Of course we'll come," when he was in-vited to the home of one of the cousins for the post-funeral spread. "Of course. My daughter, Miranda, you remember." One after the other, the coffin left sitting on its hammock. "He lived a good life." "Yes, he did." "She's beautiful, your daughter." As if she wasn't there, wasn't forty-three, unmarried, a mother to no one, a biographer. What would that mean to them?

Henry took her to the grave of his brother, Philip's father, not far away in the same cemetery. He'd been buried—though he, like

Henry, had left Newton for New York—in the family plot, pur-chased by his then still-living parents. Miranda had little memory of her uncle Thomas, an energetic man, dark-haired, with a beard, an entertainment lawyer. He'd found his older brother hilarious. They'd gone together once—the fathers, Miranda, Philip—to an amusement park somewhere in Westchester. It was the only thing she could recall of him—her being on a ride (carousel horses, she thought), the fathers on a bench, laughing.

She watched Henry regarding his brother's grave, his hands folded. They had never talked about it, not deeply. It had happened too long ago, and she felt too self-conscious now to probe. When Henry turned away from the grave to regard her, it was with a very small smile, self-excusing.

There was a wonderful loud texture to the house in Newton Highlands where the gathering was held. It had been the uncle's house, Henry explained, a modest stucco structure built in the 1940s, bordering on a playground. In the back was a neglected grape-vine hanging over a picnic table. The uncle, Uncle Phil, widowed in his sixties, had lived here on his own as long as he could. Then his daughter and her family had moved in to take care of him. Only in his last years had he gone into a nursing home, at his own request.

Henry related these details on the way there as if he were telling her a story: This was the way it was done, this was the understanding, still, among these people. You took care of your father, allowed him to move in with you, or if his house was larger, you moved in with him. The accelerated rules of living, whatever liberating wind had arrived for Miranda's generation, had passed over this world without affecting it. Driving through these streets—nothing was the same, not a single store, it had all gone upscale—Henry felt a comfortable pulling back, a great relief after the agony of his thoughts about the upcoming trip to Haiti. This had been the place of safety, these streets. The family gatherings. The complete absence of self that a certain kind of tribal childhood entailed. You grew up *watching*. My God, the gift of that. All these extreme characters, the women with their unlocated passions, as if the fact of living and thriving in a new country unsettled them in ways they couldn't name, so that anger and love and desire landed on the near-at-hand in ways that had alerted young Henry to the human mystery. Watching them had been like watching a better play than anything he had ever seen in New York, those simpering reductions of life that had critics gasping and audiences paying their money for things—flat, dull emotions—that they would forget the next day. (Really? A *fishman*?) This was sour grapes, he knew. This was him licking his own wounds. Still, in the moment of approaching the house in Newton Highlands, he believed it. There could have been no better training for the life he would come to live than sitting at these people's feet and observing.

They embraced him without hesitation, these cousins he had hardly seen in the last ten years. The women especially. Fussed over him. Cousin Henry. Enormous platefuls of food thrust at both of them. Days of cooking had preceded this event. They asked Miranda about her life, these women in good funeral ensembles. She did not know how to translate it for them. "Brooklyn." Yes, some of the older ones nodded their heads. Relatives had lived there. A distant cousin had owned a garbage scow that had worked the East River. One woman in her eighties remembered riding with him on the river years ago, the smells, the backs of houses and factories.

"And your mother's in a play?" one of the aunts, Henry's contemporary, asked. "That's why she couldn't come?" As if Lily would ever have allowed herself to be dragged to this funeral. They did not know Lily. "It must be exciting," they said. Yes, it is. She grew tired of nodding her head, of refusing the next offer of a cannolo.

There were, too, in these rooms, contemporaries of hers, grandchildren of the dead man, with their own children, babies, toddlers, a couple of preadolescent boys in suits. They smiled at her, her contemporaries, she smiled back, but she didn't know them, and she had to take in the separation that existed. They were the ones who had stayed physically close, where Henry, for all his affirmation of the family-centric, had insisted on something else. New York, western Massachusetts, the realignment of self that came from living away from family. She picked up something subtle in the smiles of these contemporaries of hers. She was not like them. She had not followed the same rules. But wasn't she here, taking care of her father, exactly as they had done?

"Miranda, come." Henry was calling to her from a sofa, where he was sitting with an old man, white-haired, a man who looked like he were fading into the fabric of the sofa. She pulled up a chair and sat. The man's hands reached out, as if he couldn't quite see her without the aid of touch. His hands stopped in midair.

"This is a wonderful man, Miranda. His name is John Picone. I always called him Uncle John, but how, really, are we related?" He turned to the man. Henry was in his element here.

"I'm your father's second cousin," John Picone said. He was nodding, glazed-eyed, already seeing into the next world, in clothes that fell against dead air before reaching his body.

"He used to play the organ in the roller rink where we skated," Henry said. He was touching the man's knee, grasping it.

Miranda could only nod in puzzled agreement. The old man nodded in return, looking at her, perhaps not fully seeing her, but with still some life in his eyes.

"What were the songs you used to play?" Henry asked.

"'Mala Femmina,'" John Picone answered. The man was grinning slyly, but it was a grin taking its time to come into focus.

"Yes. You were subversive. I picked up on that. All these little boys and girls skating around the rink, and you're playing a song about the dangers of falling for an evil woman. Sending us a signal, were you?"

"I wanted you all to wise up."

They shared a laugh. Henry could escape into this. There was suddenly no world but this one.

"And you took your own advice," Henry said. "You never married."

"Never. Not me."

Was there a moment there of slight tension, of something unspoken? Henry rushed in to save it.

"Well, you know, you two have something in common. My daughter has never married. Not that there haven't been men seeking her hand."

It was Henry's reflex to unwittingly embarrass her, but the old man, sensing this, showed an unexpected sensitivity.

"She's choosy," he said.

They shared something then, the man looking deeply at her from out of those cataract-afflicted eyes. Some recognition. It both terrified her and did not. To be seen this way, in this room where she'd felt up till now entirely unseen—or perhaps wrongly seen—was not unwelcome.

But the room was growing stuffy. "I think I'd like to go outside," Miranda said.

"Yes, good idea. I'll come with you."

"No, it's all right." But Henry insisted.

They went out to where the grapevine had been planted. Henry broke off a branch. A group of smaller children were there, and a woman attending to them, one of Henry's nieces or second cousins.

"They were wonderful, these grapes," he said, and then turned to the woman watching the children. "Do you remember, or were you not old enough?" This much younger woman seemed less impressed by Henry than the others, the older ones, had been, and didn't answer. Henry took the snub in stride. "Cherries," he went on, this time to Miranda. "Up there. Look. That was a cherry tree that grew all the way up to the windows. Nothing in the world will ever taste as good. And this, here, was his garden."

It was not large, really just a small plot, neglected now.

"You could always find him here. I'd come by and visit. After my father died. I'd still take a drive, come to see him, just to keep something alive. The stories he told me." Henry was on a roll now, hardly needing to look at her. "No one told you these things, growing up, the betrayals, the whole epic thing of coming here, the deaths and the things they had to do to just make it. Of course, all immigrant stories are of a piece, I know that. But still, the things we take for granted. It's like a movie we've seen too many times, with music by Nino Rota."

He looked at her only to check. *Don't insult me*, she wanted to say. *Of course I know the composer of* The Godfather.

He leaned down to pull up what seemed an ancient root. There were still furrows in this little plot.

"We would sit here, he would tell me everything they'd had to hide. Which of them came over under a false identity they had to live with all their lives. The dead children. God. What you have to understand is they came here with great *shame*, Miranda. Terrible things had happened, and they had to deny, they had to move forward." He paused a moment. "Sometimes I think I never should have left. This is what I should have done. *Stay* here. Live in this world. Sit in a garden. Wait for the world to come to me."

"If you were going to sit in a garden, first you'd have had to learn how to grow something."

"Yes, there's that, too, isn't there?"

"You're being sentimental."

"I know I am. And I'm talking a lot of nonsense. But within the sentiment, there's always a tiny bit of truth, isn't there? I come here, it's always brought back to me. They lived the real values. I'm sorry, that sounds like such a cliché, but it's true. No one was left behind, everyone, everything was *absorbed*. Someone was sick, mentally—well, we used to use the word 'retarded.'"

To her critical look, he said, "Yes, I know, I know, we don't use that word anymore, but they were taken care of. The rest . . . what do we really get by going off, trying to make ourselves so large? So *distinct*? So *separate* from where we come from?"

"Dad, please do not do this. You know you don't mean it."

His eyebrows lifted, in acknowledgment that she was on to him.

"Indulge me, Miranda. Let me—" He was enjoying himself too much now to stop.

"You know, I don't think I've ever told you this. There were times, before you were born, I would go down to a certain coffee shop on lower Broadway, in the afternoon, at the ends of workers' shifts. Men like the ones I knew here. I would just sit among them, *getting* something from them. I don't know. Of course I'd had to get to the city, *had* to, but once I was there I found myself looking around, looking for the thing it could never fully deliver. I mean, where was the *thickness?*"

She had agreed to indulge him, or let him indulge himself, but this was becoming intolerable.

"Dad—how long do you think we're going to be here?"

"Oh, I'm having such a good time, Miranda. I'm indulging the hell out of myself. You can see that. Let me just have a little more. Look, why don't we just sit here, on this bench. I'll go in and get you something to drink. Coffee?"

"No thanks. No."

He took her hand. "Are you all right?"

"Fine. Yes. It's okay. Go in and talk to your cousins. I'll be fine."

"Ah, here he is. Come to see us."

The old man—John Picone—was moving toward them, slowly but with deliberation, moving as though he were wading through water. His head seemed sculpted, the corn wisps of his hair flying backward, the way the old Italians became all nose, faces like the prows of ships. He seemed to be heading directly toward Miranda.

"Did you come out to see us, John?"

The man sat, looking only at Miranda.

"I came out to see—your daughter."

Phlegm had interrupted the two parts of the statement. He wiped his mouth with a handkerchief.

"Well," Henry said. "Can I get you both a drink?"

"Fine. A little anisette."

"God, I haven't had anisette in years. Miranda?"

"No, thanks."

"Be right back."

He would not be right back. He craved the living conversations, the warmth of the cousins, the Nino Rota–inflected world.

When they were alone, the old man continued to stare at her, a small appreciative smile on his lips. Would he ever say anything? Actually, he *was* saying something. She had to lean forward. She thought she picked up the word "art."

"I'm sorry."

He made more of an effort. "Your father tells me you're studying art." His voice sounded unnaturally thin and high.

"Yes. Yes, that's what I do."

He did not reply. If he was doing nothing but probing her with his eyes, she thought she would allow it. She was not creeped out by it, though she thought she should be.

It was up to her to force the conversation forward. To ask a question.

"You played the organ?"

"Organ. Accordion. You name it. Everything. I studied from the time I was six. My mother wanted me to play."

After speaking, he seemed content to leave a long, seemingly endless silence. Then he resumed, imposing his own rhythm on the conversation.

"I liked—you know, the big bands."

Henry surprised her by coming back quickly, with anisette for each of them. She took one sip of the overly sweet liquid before putting it down.

John Picone tugged at Henry's sleeve. "She wants to know about—"

He left a gap long and wide enough that she felt she had to finish for him.

"He was talking about playing the organ."

"The big bands," John Picone repeated.

"Oh yes," Henry said.

"I wanted to—that was what I wanted. Harry James. Benny Goodman."

"Russ Columbo," Henry added.

"Russ Columbo was a *singer*," John Picone corrected, a little harshly. As was typical of the old, his face retained the posture of criticism long after he'd done speaking. (And, for Miranda, there was surprise in noting that Henry had revealed such a gap in his usually faultless cultural memory.)

"Columbo was a *front man*," the old man went on, not willing to leave it alone. "Sang with Gus Arnheim. Jimmie Grier." Then, an afterthought: "He had his own band later, but it wasn't much."

He allowed a chastening silence, having set the historical record straight.

"And why didn't you?" Miranda asked, feeling, instantly and regrettably, condescending in her politeness.

"Why didn't I what?"

"Try to play with them."

He didn't answer. Again, the unsaid. He looked vaguely disappointed in her.

"Well, there was your mother, John," Henry said. "Had to take care of her."

John Picone took a long pause.

"My sisters married, had families."

"I see."

Of course she didn't, or didn't want to. Here it was again, the branch cut off, the suck of obligation. Perhaps something else, an old secret never unearthed. John Picone continued to look at her, waiting for her understanding. Or perhaps she was deceived. Perhaps the old simply mastered a blankness that resembled gravitas.

"It's like I told you, Miranda. A man like John, a mother who needed care. I mean, you didn't leave. You didn't go off and get your own apartment."

John Picone made a minimal gesture, unreadable.

"Stop with that." He spoke softly, but shook his head. The subject was one the old man clearly didn't want to dwell on.

"Where—" he asked after a long moment, turning to Henry. "Where do you live?"

"Grantham," Henry answered. "We live in the wild west. The 'country.'"

Henry smiled, pleased by his own little joke, and then Miranda saw in John Picone's face a turn—she couldn't quite say what was coming, but it was something that made her concerned for Henry.

"You were a little squirt," John Picone said.

Henry looked at him, waiting for this to begin to clarify as a joke.

"Not serious. Never going to be serious."

"Serious?" Henry was still teasing out the joke.

"I saw you. I saw who you were."

"And what was that?"

A tiny, distant, discerning smile played around John Picone's features. He was enjoying the act of judgment.

Henry looked hurt now, waiting for some correction that was not forthcoming.

"John, I'm sorry you felt that way . . ."

John Picone needed to say no more. The tiny smile lingered. Miranda saw the way Henry was taking it in.

Thankfully, they were being interrupted. One of Henry's female cousins had come out and approached them.

"He telling you stories?" she asked Miranda. Overly friendly, with a bonhomie that felt practiced. "His wild past? Uncle John, we're giving you a ride home."

"Okay."

The light had already gone out of his eyes. Miranda wanted to call it back. A hush had descended on them, which this woman was attempting to fill with a liveliness, telling Henry he needed to come back more often, see more of the family. "Yes, of course." The old man sat quietly, having made his statement, while the woman spoke about his circumstances—the assisted-living facility where he was housed. "He does good. It's here in Newton, over by the Falls. He keeps his records there. Right, Uncle John?"

"Yeah."

"Ya, but we gotta go. Uncle John?"

He stood. Miranda felt compelled to stand, too. John Picone reached out and touched her in the place where her shoulder met her arm, a tiny poke, a gesture that spoke, very faintly, of collusion. He was warning her, unmistakably, against something. Then he began the shuffling movement that would get him to his niece's car, after which he would be driven to the assisted living.

"Goodbye," Miranda said, stopping him. She wanted more, she wasn't sure why. It was as if some story had begun to be told, and she wouldn't hear the end of it.

"You need to come see us more," the woman, Henry's cousin, said.

"I do," Henry said.

They watched them walk toward the parked cars, the niece's arm under John Picone's elbow until he pushed her away.

"Oh, we always wondered about him, of course." Dusk had fallen; they were in the car, on the haunted stretch of Route 2 between Erving and Millers Falls. "Was there a woman hidden away some-where? Was he gay? More likely that, I think."

Miranda, keeping it to herself, didn't think so. Something in the way he had looked at her.

"But give them all this, they knew how to keep their secrets."

"And that was a good thing?"

Henry smiled, his lips closed over an unspoken thought.

"Maybe. To protect themselves, and each other. I don't know."

It seemed to Miranda that they'd internalized, within the car, some of the outer darkness of the highway. She wrapped her arms around herself.

"Was that hard? What he said to you?"

"About seriousness?"

At first it seemed he wasn't going to continue beyond the question.

"I think he always looked at me that way. Most of them did. Who was this little boy, always reading books, always obsessed with plays? I was suspect. They did their part forcing me out, I suppose. How could I ever have survived there? I know, I know what I was just say-ing in the garden a few hours ago. When I would come back, with you, with your mother, these little visits, events big enough for him to show up at, he would always look at me in a strange way. Was he jealous of the life I'd gotten to live, or was it something else?"

Miranda became careful now.

"And what would that be?"

She could almost feel his process; his choice not to push this.

"Their judgments only land in old age, Miranda. At twenty, even thirty, I could have cared less about their vision of seriousness. Are you sure you're not hungry?"

"After all that?"

They laughed together, then allowed a silence.

At home, he opened the refrigerator. She felt she should tidy up for him, wash the breakfast dishes they had not gotten around to cleaning. His body, as he surveyed the contents of the refrigerator, appeared to her dangerously unfilled-out in a way she had not noticed in Newton Highlands.

On the refrigerator was a photograph of a full-bodied black nun dressed in white with her arm around a little black girl, also in white. Obviously a photograph from Haiti.

She was about to ask him a question about his upcoming trip when he lifted something out of the refrigerator, opened the container, and smelled it.

"Oh God," she said.

"What?"

"If you need to smell something before eating it . . ."

"No. Your mother hasn't been here."

"That's no excuse."

He settled on a beer. "For you?" he asked, and she shook her head. He sat before her, took off his tie, smiled at her as if they were going to have a good time.

"Do you suppose she'll ever want to come back here? I mean, all summer she'll be the belle of New York. You know the play's run has been extended."

"Yes, but she seems to have a disdain for it."

"Oh, don't believe that. You know your mother. She's lapping it up while pooh-poohing it. That seems to be the family skill. The way I was after—what was the name of that book I wrote?"

He lifted his eyebrows playfully, drank his beer. Then he reached out and touched her face.

"It's so good to have you back here, my darling."

She offered him a smile that must have had tiredness in it.

"And I know, I know very well, this is a terrible indulgence on my part. Forcing you to come here. I know I made you take time away from your—preparations."

There was, in his sudden turning away from her, a falling motion she noticed in his cheeks and neck, an unmistakable sign of advancing age.

"Basel," he said.

"Yes."

"I've never been."

"Well, why would anyone go? Except that it's the center of the world for a few days. This—limited world."

She felt, after speaking it, that she had shaped her words for his benefit. It was the sort of phrase he would use.

"Art. Money. Fancy people."

"Who you've become very comfortable with."

"Not really."

"You don't have to make excuses. It's become your world, hasn't it?"

She didn't know how to answer. In saying yes, would there be some infinitesimal betrayal?

"Thank you, by the way," he said. "For this. For coming. It helped, believe me, to have you there."

"It's okay. Not really. It's not really okay. I think you're lonely. That's why I came."

He seemed slightly taken aback. But only slightly.

"Your mother's been gone so long. And she'll be gone longer."

What was under that? What unspoken request?

"Miranda, are you sure I can't fix you something?"

"From a fridge full of containers that you have to sniff?"

"I'm sure there's something in there that won't kill us."

"No, I'm fine."

"And tomorrow morning you get back on the train."

Said as if the act would amount to a soft blow to his head.

"What will *you* do?" she asked.

He took his time.

"Pack for Haiti, I suppose."

"No work for you?"

"Your mother asks the same thing. Why aren't I burrowing away at something?"

"Why aren't you?"

"Not sure. The time comes . . ."

She waited for him to finish the sentence. It seemed he had no intention to.

"You don't think you'll go on doing it?"

"You know what I think? I think there's a time when life asks you to shut up. You've spent your life jabbering. *I* have. Look at me! Watch what I can do! Now this! How about now, *shut up*? Be silent. You've said enough. Except what the noise did—the self-assertion—was to push away everything about yourself you were supposed to be looking at from the beginning."

She studied him, simply taking this in. Impossible to know sometimes the actual depth of his seriousness.

"I'd like to know." She stopped herself.

"Yes?"

"I'd like to know what's really going on."

"With?"

"You."

That maddening smile again, in response. And again, her insane availability to him. The foolishness of the day they'd just endured. Cannoli and sentimentality, and then a certain harshness, provided by a white-haired old man. Her book was nearly finished, she reminded herself. She was going to Basel. There would be that lifting into a world—its now familiar tone of impenetrable brightness. A place had been more or less made for her in that world, should she be willing to do the work, to learn the rules necessary to inhabiting it. But within all this, her inability to fully embrace it. She thought of this old man sitting before her as a young man, going down to a coffee shop on lower Broadway to sit among workers at the end of their shifts. The quest for thickness.

"I think before I go away, before *you* go away, I want to know you're okay."

"What's that mean?"

"Don't be stubborn."

"No. 'Okay.' What's it mean?"

"I think you know."

"Health-wise, I believe I'm fine."

"That's not what I mean. Though you look skinny."

"Do I?"

He tapped the table. He was looking at her with an intensity she didn't recognize.

"It's something I've been noticing about you. Your pallor."

"My pallor."

"Don't just keep repeating me."

"It's sweet you're worried. That's why you came."

"That's why I came."

"It seems to me—tell me if this is true—you're at the age, you're forty-three, that it's important to move away from me. To resist me."

She would not have credited him with this insight.

"And here I am, pulling you back. Sucking you back into my difficulties."

She lowered her eyes.

"I mean, here's the thing," he went on. "We always expect a parent to stay in place, don't we? To lock into a pose. Become *Whistler's*

Mother. I guess the thing I have to say to you is that it's a false expectation. We go on—struggling a little, struggling embarrassingly sometimes—trying to figure out what we're supposed to do."

He turned away from her, looked at the outer space, the way the pool of light in the kitchen did not intrude into the room beyond.

"But it's my struggle, Miranda. I don't need to pull you in."

He looked at her again.

"What about you?" he asked.

"Me?"

"I never quite ask, do I? Your book. Your success."

"Don't overstate it."

"Why not? You're a source of pride."

It was not to be answered. She supposed he meant it, he was not being false, but it was like talking about something extraneous. Pride.

"Your love life."

She made a scoffing gesture.

"No. I never ask. I mean, I joke with you about it, but I don't *ask*. Am I not supposed to?"

"You can ask. There's a man. I don't think I fully respect him. Or maybe I just don't fully trust him. That's the problem."

"I see."

What was this space they had stepped into? She did not recognize it.

"Shall we go to bed? You seem tired," he said. "Shall we call it a day?"

It came as a shock, his willingness to subvert.

"Your train is at—?"

"Ten."

"So we leave early."

His hand reached across the table, grasped hers. He seemed to be reading something in her face.

"What? Should I be asking more questions?"

"About?"

"Him? This man? Your book."

"No. It's not so important."

"No? You're sure?" He seemed to be waiting for an invitation she held back from offering. "Okay then. Bed. Yes. I'm tired."

He got up. He began turning on lights. Odd, in that his stated intention had been to go upstairs. She watched him, trying to gauge something.

"This painting." He had stepped up next to it, turned on a lamp underneath it. "You once said it might be a Celia Paul."

"Yes."

"If it is, it would be worth a lot now. Hundreds of thousands, yes?"

"I don't think it's hers. I think you'd know."

He regarded it, turned the light off underneath it.

"You're the expert."

She did not know why she felt riveted to the chair, watching him. Until she was able to see it, what he was doing. The words "You're the expert," and the way he had asked about her love life.

"Shall we?" he asked.

He began turning off lights, one by one. She remained in her chair.

"I think I'll stay here a minute," she said.

"Really?"

"Yes."

It was an odd moment the two of them were having now. She knew no words—nothing significant—would come of it. He had left her openings—that little monologue about the way old age harbored its confusions—but she would not now pursue them. The moment had passed.

"Well, good night then," he said.

But before he went upstairs, he lingered a moment, simply

staring at her. It could have contained anything, that look of his. Impenetrable. But then he seemed to let her in. He opened his arms, shrugged with his face, his eyes. This is what it comes to, he seemed to be saying. This life we've lived together. This is the rehearsal for saying goodbye.

When he was gone, she tried to avoid what she was feeling by cleaning up after him, straightening the room. She went through the refrigerator and found a great deal to throw out. At one point, she realized her hand had inadvertently gone to her face. She was overcome for a moment. Then she went on throwing things out.

FOUR

THE REMEMBERING
ANIMAL

Andrew was not entirely pleased with their placement. He'd let it be known he'd have preferred the first floor, where the larger galleries were; they were on the second. Art Basel was like a big upscale mall, one designed so that every gallery stand had something a little bit daunting about it. At the auction house where Miranda had worked, they'd had a name for this psychological phenomenon: threshold resistance. The fear that, in order to be allowed to enter, you'd have to announce to an unseen gatekeeper just how much money you had.

The rush had not yet begun; the first collectors would not be allowed into the building for another fifteen minutes. For now, there was the very good coffee, a small plate of Swiss pastries, and the artificial but still beautiful light. The building, all black glass on the outside, felt, inside, like a huge cup into which light was being slowly poured. It was Swiss, but by afternoon, Miranda was sure, the light would turn melancholy, Scandinavian.

She'd had a wonderful time on the plane ride over, an exquisite breakfast served in what seemed the middle of the night, a good pillow, and her nearest neighbor a man with sleepy eyes who, thankfully, did not want to talk. The boutique hotel was an exceedingly thin one, squeezed between two larger buildings in the old town. She had a small balcony facing the river. Botho would not be arriving for another day, so she'd had a full day (having arrived in the morning) to sleep, to walk, to lounge on her balcony feeling beautiful and mysterious in a way that disconcerted her, as if coming here, simply entering this world, allowed for a severance from everything that had come before. The large envelope containing her credentials, handed to her by the desk clerk with a deferential smile. Others in the lobby, the international art collectors speaking mostly German and French, men with curly salt-and-pepper hair and untended bellies, expensive sports coats that looked to be made of crepe, wives, mistresses, the quick glances—who was she? Was she anyone important? Was she competition? To say "the air smelled of money" (the words had appeared in her mind) would have been to miss something. Every small society had a way of propping itself up, asserting in small ways its own importance. It had to do with something other than money, but the ability to land on the proper word for it eluded her.

She had packed the right clothes—Andrew had annoyed her by wanting to review her wardrobe with her before the trip, suggesting a couple of outfits he'd seen her wear—but she had left room in her suitcase for two of Anna's old housedresses. They were among the things in the bag of clothes Aaron had gifted her with the day she'd come to the apartment. Lamston's housedresses, thin and flowered, worn and washed to the bone. It had been wonderful to touch them when she'd taken them home to Brooklyn, to lay them on her bed and feel the way paint had stuck to the hems of the two she'd brought here. She'd hung them up in the tiny hotel closet.

"I need you," Andrew had said to her, "to be my subtle expert." His instructions were to make herself available in the booth, to dress beautifully but unostentatiously, and to let it be known that a biography was on its way. He was annoyed that Miranda's publisher had not come up with a mock-up of the cover. It was still too early for that. "I won't be able to talk to everyone at once," he said. "You'll be my lady-in-waiting. *Sell* Anna, but do it subtly, all right?"

"Am I expected to serve hors d'oeuvres, too?" she asked, mocking him.

"No, but it's not a bad idea."

She found, to her surprise, that she was not carrying Henry here, not carrying the residue of their evening in Grantham. If he had been consciously attempting to free her, she would make the commensurate attempt to accept that freedom.

There had been something superficially and quite wonderfully soothing about this voyage that helped that effort along. The look she had shared with the flight attendant (Andrew had not, as it turned out, sprung for first class, but the accommodations still seemed, to Miranda, plush), a young, beautiful girl, perhaps new to this job, the sense they both shared, looking at one another, *Isn't this wonderful?* To find themselves in the air, flying over the ocean, the jet propelled not by fuel but by some belief that it was possible to be lifted by will itself, will and beauty and smartness, that no force of gravity could pull you down once you had accessed this level of—well, again, not quite money, something else, what was the word? It was an *agreement*, that was all. We will not plunge, we are beyond that force. We have attained a kind of safety.

Unreal, was what it was. But she seemed to be accepting that, without effort, sipping coffee, watching Andrew with his assistant, a new one he had brought along. Claude. A very young man with a boy-band haircut from the sixties, a British Invasion look, a boy who would have looked perfectly at home playing self-effacing bass guitar for the Searchers, or Manfred Mann. Claude's only job was to fetch things, the pastries, the thin catalogues that had been shipped over, to be placed on the white cubes Andrew had transported from the downtown gallery, at enormous expense, in order to maintain a "visual coherence." Watching Andrew with Claude, Miranda had to wonder at herself for ever speculating that Anna and Andrew had been lovers. Here in Basel, Andrew was letting his gayness bloom in a way he never fully allowed in New York.

But then, all the gallerists seemed that way, overdressed, preening, waiting for the crowds that would soon arrive, pretending to distraction. "The one thing we can never be seen to be," Andrew said, "is *eager.*"

All right. Her instruction was to be aloof. What made this difficult was the presence of the painting *The Remembering Animal*, the most prominently featured of the four works Andrew was showing here. The others were by lesser artists, ones Andrew hadn't made up his mind yet to sell, younger artists he had brought along only to promote. It was *The Remembering Animal* he had come here to make a killing on. There were at least three potential buyers who had already met the asking price (overbidding was frowned on here), but Andrew wasn't ready to accept any of them. Not quite yet. No, let's wait and see.

It was the first time Miranda had seen Anna's self-portrait in good light. She had been allowed a private viewing in New York the week before (Andrew had acceded, grumpily, to Aaron's request that the painting be unpacked) but had had to sit with it in a storeroom, under bad light, and the experience had been more frustrating than illuminating. Here, under better light, the colors were softened, and the painting seemed, curiously, more gentle. Seeing it only in suboptimal conditions, she had thought of it as a harsh painting. But the light here brought out small, delicate things: the faint teal blue outline that hugged Anna's body and stopped just above the neck, a green vase of drooping flowers on the table beside Anna's chair, the pale rose tint in the skin of Anna's body, leading to a kind of dried-blood color in the extremities. Then the bright red nail polish, some declaration of—what?—undiminished sensuality? Miranda sipped her coffee and looked hard at it. This would be the last chance she would get. By the end of the fair, Andrew would have chosen his buyer. The painting would go off to a private collection, or to a museum. She might never see it again, at least not with this degree of intimacy.

Aaron had suggested to her that Miranda study Anna's eyes in the painting, but she didn't need instruction to know how to look at Anna's work. The eyes—but also the jaw, the set jaw—were of course where you would look, because the first thing you always knew about an Anna Soloff painting was where Anna *intended* you to look. Benjamin Weeks's small hands clutching the arm of his chair, John Malkovich's dangling, simian arms. Felix Rohatyn's vague public remorse located in the set of his chin, the place where Anna had found her opening. The tense shoulders of the young mothers in *The Opinionated Playground*, waiting for some world-signal to tell them it was okay to relax, the battle was being won. It may have taken you a while to notice what was outside the small window that always appeared in Renaissance or Dutch interiors, but Anna did not allow you such a randomness of approach. *Here it is. Look here.*

And, of course, the eyes were a mystery. That was deliberate, too. The withheld. The *I will only tempt you, I will not let you see my entirety.* Still, she looked at the eyes, as if to do so were to engage in a dialogue. I know so much about you. I have convinced myself I know so much about you. I know who you were at Chock Full o' Nuts, a teenage Bronx girl, tough, beginning her education at the hands of Arthur Messinger, reading communist literature without really understanding what it was about but feeling within it an *importance*, a way out, a view of life that might have saved your father from hanging himself in the small furniture factory that didn't provide him enough money to feed his family.

I know you, too, in the hand-to-mouth existence you lived in Spanish Harlem, seducing a Puerto Rican flaneur who pretended to be the artist *you* were, salving his ego, giving birth to his child, taking another man, a cruel one, owning her own sexuality enough to know that she needed "a man like that." Having another child, only half protecting her older son from the unannounced blows, the cruelties. And painting. Always painting. Allowing self-belief to propel her past what was tawdry. It was what made an artist different from everyone else, wasn't it? (How was it that Lily had put it in the restaurant across from Lincoln Center? Not caring about the curtains or the bills.) Being driven on by something indescribable but clear. Do the work, drag the boys along, make the money somehow. Jettison elegance and order, even a measure of what was conventionally called self-respect. They are to be thrown overboard in order to keep the ship afloat. Miranda knew that much, and knew that underlying it lay something hard. Anna might have flounced around and made a deliberate fool of herself, flirted with Mortimer Leavitt, seduced the power brokers by convincing them she was only a silly, charming old woman, a bohemian joke, but underneath this was something as certain, as ice cold as the numbers Felix Rohatyn balanced in his head. *This* is what a painting should be. A face, a body, a glance, a part of the body. A stance. A revealed secret. An interiority teased to the surface by the body's insistence that it be *known*.

This was all she knew about Anna. It would all be in the book. But she was coming to the end of her adventure feeling she was still confronting an absence. *Not getting* something, whatever was in those eyes, and in the jaw, too, the defiant jaw, the precision of what was being remembered. In spite of the wonderful coffee and the crisp pastries and the beautiful light, it eluded her. *Look. And then, keep looking.*

There was a sudden alteration in the air. Before the sound came, she sensed Andrew's tight face, at the edge of her vision, attempting to soften, to affect detachment. Oh, this? You're interested in buying *this?* As if his world, his very existence, didn't depend on the sale he had come here to make.

The air shifted, and then you could hear them. The gates had been opened. The hordes were beginning their ascent.

His driver's name was Shelove.

"I am Shelove, yes," the man said. Henry had received a text from Beatrice, announcing his imminent appearance, suggesting that Henry just make himself available and wait for Shelove to notice him. A tall man, blue jeans belted high, hanging very loosely on him.

A mustache and receding hair. An obsequious smile, the one Haitians had learned to put on in the presence of what they perceived to be rich Americans.

"Yes, I was told to expect you. Hello. I'm Henry."

As with so many others, as with Jean himself, Henry wanted to ask that the smile disappear, and with it the very thin and untrustworthy urge to please. *Do not be so kind.* It was hotter than he'd previously known Haiti to be, but then he'd never been here in June. Already, in the brief wait outside the customs building, his shirt was clinging to him.

"Yes, well, let's go."

But then the overly formal lifting of Henry's luggage and placing it in the boot of the van, and Shelove opening the door for him. He was alone in the van, and being treated like a dignitary. Everything at odds with everything else.

It made him recall the days of his success, still fairly recent but already deep in the psychological past, when he'd been picked up at hotels and driven to airports, flown to readings in Los Angeles, San Francisco, Seattle, Austin. The author of *How to Be This Age*, regaling his audiences with the amusing humiliations of approaching senility. Had he enjoyed it enough, taken it *in* enough? It had been so brief. And the drivers of those limousines, so often older Italian American men who wanted to chat, men whose lives had taken some turn that led to their driving limousines, a turn they didn't seem to mind terribly. Men with favorite radio stations they sometimes asked if they could listen to. Shelove did not turn on the radio, or seem very much to want to talk, but when Henry asked him a question there was the awful obsequiousness, the smile. Something felt amiss. Do not treat me as a serious man, Shelove. Have you not heard John Picone's definitive judgment of me?

The drive was going to be a long one. He would be staying again at the old monastery in the hills, the one he had stayed in on his first visit. The room above the woodshop was, apparently, currently occupied.

During the plane ride, Henry had managed to befriend a pair of young men, boys who looked like they could have been surfers, long blond hair worn under safari hats, traveling to Haiti to work on a water project. "Come with us," they said to him, "we can use an extra hand." It was tempting, but he had presented himself as a man with important business of his own, feeling a hint of his own fraudulence in doing so. "I'm seeing to a young man's education in America," he'd said, and they nodded to him, deferential. Had they wished to, these boys could have punctured his pose easily. But perhaps— why not give himself a tiny bit of credit?—it was not entirely frivolous, what he was doing. The test results had come in, hadn't they? Though Henry had not yet made up his mind how to proceed, there was this, at least: it could be made to happen. A significant change in one young man's life.

On the outskirts of Port-au-Prince, Shelove begged an apology. He had to make a stop. Outside a shop selling—well, everything, really, tires, tins of cooking oil, hanging medallions, variously tinted T-shirts with the words *Haiti Chérie* printed on them—Shelove asked forgiveness. "A minute," he said, and disappeared inside. Through the shaded windows of the van, Henry found himself staring at a woman stationed outside the shop. A woman with a large straight-up Afro, a pink T-shirt stretched over what might or might not be a pregnancy, a look of permanent anger on her face. Or disdain. They stared at one another. Henry resisted the impulse to turn away.

Shelove was back, the long silent white drive resumed. Henry was terribly hungry, but it was too late to ask to stop. The whiteness of the light seemed to consume the van. The *ongoingness* of Haiti, the way men still lined the roads in the countryside. But why should it have changed simply because he had been away? He would nap in the monastery. There would, he hoped, be something to eat there. Henry stared out of the window of the van and thought: Well, perhaps I have come here to die. It would be appropriate, wouldn't it? This last act uncompleted. Wasn't that what had happened to von Aschenbach, staying too long in Venice after the onslaught of the plague, just to catch one further sight of the ever-beckoning, ever elusive Tadzio? But then Henry smiled to himself: No, God is not a neat novelist, concerned with beautifully trimmed endings. God is a kind of John Cassavetes, an artist of the extended scene. He didn't even allow his own son a quick heart attack on the stones leading up to Golgotha. No, open yourself to Him and you can be assured of a protracted stay on the cross.

Perhaps he slept, that heat-saturated sort of sleep that didn't really count as rest. He opened his eyes to find they were ascending the hill leading up to the great white monastery.

Shelove opened the door of the van for him, stood with his suitcase, said, "I will wait."

"For what, Shelove? I intend to take a long nap."

As with so many others here, the uncertainty of knowing whether or not you were understood. A "serious" man would have mastered Kreyol by now.

But Shelove appeared to understand.

"No, they are waiting," he said.

"Who?"

"At the church."

"The church in Fonfrède?"

Shelove nodded.

"They expect me today?"

"Yes."

"Shelove, I've just gotten here. I need a rest. This wasn't to happen yet."

He was negotiating with the wrong man. Shelove had received his instructions. Henry had Felix's number and a reliable cell phone on this trip. He dialed, and paced. They were outside the back entrance to the monastery and his full and entire desire was to go inside, to sit in shade, to be alone.

"Père Felix?" he asked, when the soft voice answered.

"Henry. Yes."

"Père Felix, I am here and I'm told you're waiting for me."

"Yes."

"Father, I feel I need some rest first. I'm not prepared."

A silence. The heat, the strangeness, the desire to not fully engage yet. Let me have my little creature comforts, please.

"Jean is here with his father."

"With his father?"

"Yes."

"So today?"

Another silence.

"Father, may I have an hour?"

"Of course."

"I'd like to wash."

"Yes. Of course."

"You can take care of them?"

"Yes."

"An hour. I'll ask Shelove to wait."

He suggested that Shelove come inside, but the man shook his head. "Is not a problem."

Inside, at the top of the white marble stairs, he found a nun holding a stack of clean towels. Did she know he was expected? Where might he go? The nun shook her head, claiming ignorance, regarding him in all his strangeness. After a search, he found another nun, who brought him to a room. It was on the opposite side of the monastery from where his old room had been, facing a courtyard. Outside his window, a loud rooster was strutting about.

Perhaps he should go and find a place to pray for guidance. His fatigue felt enormous. One hour, then. He lay on the bed and closed his eyes.

It was two hours before he woke. He consulted the time on his phone, sat up blinking, panicked, sweating and probably stinking, and no one had thought to call. Shelove would be outside in the heat, Père Felix and Jean and his father waiting in the church, or in the rectory. Time did not matter here, he knew, in the way it mattered—or was said to matter—in what was once called the first world. But it mattered to *him*. He felt, already, that he was letting down those he had come, ostensibly, to help.

Shelove was exactly where he'd been left. The two-hour wait seemed to have affected him not at all. He opened the door of the van for Henry.

He ought at least to have changed his clothes. He had to imagine how he must look; the monastery was not a place of mirrors. Hair matted down, an air of unshavenness and mild decay. Well, so be it. The impulse to primp, what was that about?

They were soon crossing the bridge over the pale, khaki-colored river where women washed clothes. He leaned forward.

"Shelove?"

"Yes?"

"How do they get them clean?"

Shelove took a moment. Seen in the rearview mirror, he was, for the first time, *looking* at Henry, taking him in. Some quick analysis was going on. Then his face changed, became more conventionally enlivened, as he prepared to answer.

He did so by motioning with his fist, pumping it up and down.

"They *beat* the clothes?" Henry asked.

"Yes. *Beat*."

He sat back, continued to stare outside at the surrounding country. Familiar and unfamiliar. I *know* you, he wanted to say, but found there was a part of him that wanted to contradict himself. He was a tourist, that was all. Haiti's enormity, its immense privacy, kept him at a distance.

And there was the church. Children clustered near the doorways of the school, the same children who had greeted them four years ago, only younger now, ageless children. The repetitions. He had been the *blan*, the excitement, and now he was just an old white man who drew their attention for only a few seconds before they returned to their primary concerns.

"Inside," Shelove said, and pointed him toward the open door of the rectory.

On the balcony, in early morning, Miranda lit a cigarette. She was wearing as little as possible, a silk shift she had packed. She pushed her hair out of her face. The cigarette, her first inhalation, felt harsh. European. Thicker and coarser than she'd expected, the way sausages tasted here.

She had taken the cigarette from out of the pack she knew Botho kept in his jacket. Right now he was sleeping on the bed, half covered. Those legs of his, the ones he liked to make fun of, thick, unattractive, deeply masculine legs more appropriate to a locker room than to a bed, or a beach, or anywhere where one might want to show off. His hair was longer, and he had a few days' growth. Botho had arrived here as if in flux, in the midst of arrangements he seemed to have left unfinished.

The surprise was that he had no room of his own, intended to stay with her for the duration of the fair. "Andrew is paying, no?" he said, as if that answered every question, as if she could have no wish to be alone here, was happy to gift him with her company as often as he might want. It was a disappointment. Their sex the night before had been fast and intense, like a meal eaten in an upscale airport restaurant, while one kept an eye on the board announcing departing flights.

She continued to draw on the cigarette, pretending to enjoy it, and stared at the river, the wonderful light you could catch sight of only if you rose early enough, the mist on the water, the early appearance of the working world, boys on bicycles, and older boys on small motorcycles, women pushing carts, an extraordinarily well-dressed woman toting an elegant shopping bag over one shoulder. These little European cities with their secrets, and their ability to make you feel that even if you stayed here forever, you could never penetrate their closed systems. From another room she heard the faint sound of a television, the news from Europe.

It had been a challenging day, the day before, even prior to Botho's arrival. The collectors, their affect, their *not* seeing you—or maybe seeing you too clearly—their eyes darting to the side while pretending to talk to you. Who had just entered the booth? Am I talking to the right person? A woman from Miami with hair like thin black metal plates framing both sides of her face. The way they looked at Miranda's clothes, which were good clothes. The way they talked about their collections, and tried to suss out who she was: Was she a way in, or just floor dressing? She felt as much an alien here as she had in Newton Highlands.

And then the way they surrounded Anna's self-portrait like flies in summer. It was not theirs, but one of them would come to own it. One of these men who looked like elegant pirates (one even wore an eye patch), women whose voices betrayed Long Island or New Jersey and pretended to a lightness, a "What am I doing here?" while staring too hard at the gold chain around Miranda's neck, referring to "Anna" (Please don't do that, Miranda wanted to say to them) as though they'd been close friends in college.

There was nothing really so surprising about any of this, just the usual manifestations of privilege, of money and connoisseurship. She was used to such people from the auctions she'd had to attend in her previous life, the huge events that drew a certain crowd. The night Jacqueline Kennedy's mementos had been auctioned, she'd been asked (she'd been very young then, just starting out; her dress requiring approval from the woman running the event) to stand at the top of the stairs, a greeter. One man, sharp silver hair slicked back into wings on both sides of his head, had touched her ass for an uncomfortably long moment, and when she'd turned to him to say something, saw that he was not even looking at her, was waving to an acquaintance. It was his right to touch her, wasn't it? He'd paid the entrance fee. The same thing here. She had not known why she was here, what her function was. She was to act as a kind of frame around *The Remembering Animal.* She was to look, in a weird way, *expensive,* and of course felt that she was failing.

At the end of the day, Andrew sipped champagne and acted pleased. "Tomorrow, 3:00 p.m.," he said. "I will announce." Botho had arrived, in a hurry, and in a foul mood. He'd just learned he had competition on his planned Coenties Slip book; he'd discovered that someone else was nosing around in the same places he was, and he was furious that this other writer might beat him to the finish line. Miranda wanted not to have to console him. She'd wanted simply to go back to her hotel room and be alone, but Botho asked her if she'd been given a second key. He'd had to stash his luggage at Security. She had no choice then, or none she had immediate access to. The good feeling of the day before, the sense of being above the world, had entirely disappeared.

She had felt, at the close of the day, even her attitude toward Anna's painting shifting, subtly, as the light was shifting. It was necessary to objectify it in order to take her leave. A couple who seemed unassuming—their clothes the sorts of clothes you would see American tourists wearing in Florence or Venice, shapeless clothes, with too many pockets—entered the booth as if to gawk, like they were not sure why they had been invited to this party. They asked her questions. "She lived on 107th Street, yes," she answered, unintimidated by them, even basking a little in her expertise. "It was where this was painted." She described the apartment for them, preening on the fact that she'd been there so many times. The man nodded his head, encouraging her. These were people she could feel comfortable with, even a little superior to. Afterward, they went over to speak to Andrew, waiting patiently, even a little awkwardly, for him to be free. Once they'd gone, Andrew approached her, she expected they might share a little joke about these seeming rubes. "The Sheffleins," he whispered. "More fucking money than God. Built their own private museum in Tulsa." There was a kind of after-the-fact, lustful appreciation in the way Andrew watched them recede. Perhaps they would take away Anna. It was like watching your child choose an unattractive partner.

Claude announced that they were passing out complimentary sushi at the end of the hall, and Andrew sent him down for some. There were others waiting to talk to him. "Let me know, pay close attention. I don't want sushi rice showing in my teeth."

That kind of day. Then Botho's arriving in the hotel room ten minutes after she'd gotten there, still in a sulk, but just having interviewed Marlene Dumas. She did not want to hear about Marlene Dumas. She wanted a shower, silence, to lie on the bed and reabsorb the painting, make it hers again. She saw it as if it were floating away on a barge, carried down the river. Giving up a child must feel this way, carrying it and then giving it up to a couple who might seem "nice." But how much could "niceness" ever be trusted? And when, precisely, had the painting ever been *hers*?

Behind her now, she heard Botho rising. He regarded her briefly, then went into the bathroom. She did not want to see him come out. She did not want to see his naked body, or find herself subjected to his air of hurry, of presumption. She stamped out the cigarette, and there he was, regarding her, questioning. What had ever made her think this could be a viable relationship?

"You stole one of my cigarettes?"

"Yes."

He came out onto the balcony, amused by her, naked but thankfully not wanting to embrace, not ready to suggest another sexual encounter. He leaned over the balcony railing.

He sniffed himself under the armpits. "God, yes, a shower, I think."

Something she'd noticed about straight men: they were often weirdly proud of their own bad scents.

"Aren't you afraid of being seen?"

He turned to her. She was referring to his nakedness.

"No. Should I be?"

There was that feeling of his taking over, like everything she said to him ought to be taken as an affectionate tease. The charming self-effacement of Lower Manhattan was gone.

"You need that shower, Botho."

"Yes. I know."

He touched her neck, cupped it. Something was in him, in his eyes, in a strange way at this moment he represented the world, and she was contending with her own old resistance to giving in to the world's expectations. I do not need "a man like that." I do not need a man with this swagger, this body-ownership, this assumption of a sexual agreement that implies some sort of tacit acknowledgment, the negotiation of those in their forties, renouncing the possibility of family and domesticity and shared bank accounts. With a man like Botho, you were to accept the rules of hotel life, the tangled sheets, room service, the soiled towels thrown on the floor. He was questioning her now, and she turned away.

He went inside. She heard the shower running. She looked again at the river. Saw Anna, on the barge, accompanying her painting. No, I am not like you. I do not know how to use a man, as you did. What to take, what to discard, how to do it with dispatch. On the barge, floating away, Anna seemed to be smiling. Transcending something. Anna would never have had the moment Miranda was now having, this moment on the balcony. She would have known the precise value of everything. How to deal with a man, how to cleave to a separate purpose.

A line of poetry floated into Miranda's mind, something she could not connect to a specific poet, or even a specific poem. "Not to be a poet is the worst of all our miseries." Yes, you could negotiate it all if you had that place to go to, the artist's room, the closed door.

The mist on the river, she noticed, was lifting a bit.

Such was Henry's fragmented sense of time that when he saw the face of the man in the chair, he thought it was Jean's face. Thought, briefly, that enough time had gone by that Jean had passed his youth entirely, become a grizzled large handsome man with gray in his hair, wide shoulders, a big sensual mouth that looked to have been licked into shape by the experience of sustained displeasure.

The man stood. His thick body stood and he grasped the back of his chair. He looked vaguely embarrassed, at least uncertain how to behave. Not a man used to the gestures of obeisance. Not a courtier. Henry's sight grew clear enough to make out, behind this man, Jean and Père Felix, in the shadows by the kitchen stove. This, then, the man standing, had to be Jean's father.

What, then? To put out his hand and shake? There seemed a falsity to it.

"I'm sorry for making you wait," he said.

The man nodded. He looked Henry up and down, as if he were

assessing his fitness for some piece of manual labor they were about to undertake together. Then the man turned his head and looked to Felix to impose some form on this encounter.

"No problem," Père Felix said. "We are making tea."

Jean regarded him from within the kitchen alcove. Jean was dressed almost formally. A black shirt with some sort of design on it, dark pants. It was as though a packed bag might exist in a corner of this room, if Henry looked hard enough.

"This is Pierre," Felix said. "This is Jean's father."

There was a hat, Henry noticed, Jean's father was clutching a hat, the sort of hat the Italian men of Henry's father's generation wore, a snap-brimmed woolen cap. It was the world of Newton Highlands appearing in this rectory in Haiti.

They simply nodded to one another.

"Have a seat, please," Père Felix said.

Henry obliged. It was impossible, from the way the father and son were looking at him, to gauge their precise expectation.

"Shall we invite Shelove in?" Henry asked. "He's been in the sun all day."

"Shelove will not mind," Felix said. The priest seemed a little tired, a little—was Henry just reading this in?—less welcoming of Henry. Was it because this was the first encounter where Père Felix didn't *want* something from Henry?

The tea poured (Henry asked for some, yes. Also, was there a biscuit? There was), they sat in a semicircle. The father in his work clothes, the son in formal dress. Jean's long legs spread out before him. Shined black shoes.

"So, we proceed," Père Felix said.

Through the windows (Henry turned away), there was the wild greenness of June. Massive leaves like warriors' shields flapped against the screens. Shelove was smoking a cigarette outside.

"What have you come to say?" Père Felix asked.

"Well." Henry ate the biscuit and felt them all watching him as he did so, the sound of his crunching too loud a presence in the room. "Well, the first thing to be said is that Jean did well on the test. Well enough."

"Yes, we know," Felix said.

Henry was taken aback. "How do you know?"

Felix shrugged. The island without secrets. Beatrice must have told him.

Jean's father leaned forward, elbows resting on his knees, passing his cap from hand to hand as if he had an appointment to keep and wanted to make this potential handing over of his son as businesslike as possible.

On Henry's heart there was some new pressure. A deep sense of reality. These are *people*, you idiot, not projections, not figments of your imagination. It was as though he could hear the heavy gears of the world clanking into place. Say the word and life would change for these people. To stall, and gather himself, he asked for another biscuit.

No one got up to help him. He was expected to serve himself, as was right. Jean was looking at him with a look he didn't recognize: not exactly expectant, something else. He got up, went to the table, turned back, and saw that Jean and his father were speaking to one another in Kreyol. The father's words sounded harsh, but this could have been just the way men talked to each other here. Jean made a resistant motion with one hand, slumped away from his father. The priest, in the middle, became their referee. Henry regarded the window beside him. I could run now. I could leave this room, abandon all this foolishness, ask Shelove to drive me back to the monastery, rebook my flight. I could admit fully to my mistake, ask forgiveness. Cowardice was always an option.

"Henry." The priest was calling him back.

"Pierre would like to know what the possibilities are."

Pierre was leaning forward more intensely now and Henry, returning to his chair, had the unwelcome sense that this man wanted, expected, to be taken on as well, the two of them, father and son, brought back to Grantham. Their foreign scents, their thickening bodies, the food he would be expected to cook for them. Lily would fly away. There would be no more Lily. No more Lily, and no more Henry, either. He would disappear into servility.

"It's complicated," Henry said.

No one liked this answer.

"If Jean wants an American education, there are many hoops to go through. Many. He would have to spend a year in my town, going to the local high school."

As he spoke the words, it all seemed so unreal, his first impulse leading to this. The night under the dripping tarp. The boy's look at him: Jean's alertness, his holding back on what was really going on in his head. The lightness of initial gestures. Why not? Come to America, let me change your life. Why not? We act on wings. We *say* things.

But looking into Jean's eyes now, he saw something that caused him pain. It seemed that fear was appearing in those eyes. He saw it as the boy's ability to read Henry, as he'd been able to read him, mostly accurately, from the beginning. Now what he was seeing in Henry was hesitation, the great opportunity slipping away. And Henry, at this moment, found he could not deny him this. Impossible to weasel out at this point and still feel like—oh, welcome, John Picone—a serious person. Whatever it implied, whatever personal loss, he could not deny this boy his chance.

"We can arrange for Jean to come and take a look at this school."

He smiled. A part of him felt freed by having spoken the words. Fuck it, Henry Rando, you are doing something. Redeeming yourself, finally. In a life of utter selfishness. Finally.

But when he looked back at Jean, he did not see what he expected.

Did not see relief, or joy, or triumph. Instead, it was as though Jean were looking carefully at him now, taking in their history, and then—could this actually be?—dismissing him.

"You will tell him, Jean," Père Felix said.

Jean swallowed. Something seemed difficult. An embarrassment came over the young man's face. He turned quickly to his father, who looked unhappy, then back to Henry.

"I am staying," Jean said. "Staying here."

Henry did not at first know what to say. All the air seemed to have left the room. There seemed not quite a finality to what Jean had said.

Henry smiled, though he sensed its inappropriateness.

"What are you saying, Jean?"

Jean was a boy again, his face like the sky in the swiftness of a late-winter morning, when the clouds seem not yet to have decided how to arrange themselves. Henry's reaction was not to believe him. He wanted to get him aside, to achieve an intimacy.

"Staying with my father," Jean said.

Henry felt something drop within himself. He didn't like what his body was telling him now. How little he knew himself. He ought to have been relieved.

His father was speaking to Jean now, slicing with his hand. A name repeated, an unquestionably female name, spoken with disdain, the way only a sensuous older man who has distanced himself from his early sensual needs can summon disdain for the flesh. Jean pushed his father's words away.

"With the test results," Felix was saying, "Jean can go to school here. If he chooses." A pause, and then: "And you will help."

"But *will* you, Jean? And what—?"

He could not finish the sentence. He could not allude to the inferior education Jean would receive here even if, against what Henry suspected were the odds, he should choose to take advantage of Henry's implicit offer.

He stared down at the cement floor, then up at Jean's father, who was regarding him very strangely. This man, Henry was now sure, had *wanted* his son to go, and seemed to be begging Henry silently to convince Jean of something he himself couldn't. *Tell him to abandon the girl*, Pierre might have been saying. *Tell him.*

"You are sure, Jean?"

"Yes."

The silence thickened and Henry nodded. There was nothing to say. Pierre sighed again, unhappily. The priest was looking at Henry as if to be certain this all had sunk in.

"I suppose I should go then," Henry said.

"Shelove will drive you back," Père Felix said.

He noted the coldness of the priest's words and inflection. He had been called across a continent for this moment. Over the azure-blue sea. He had a small wish to point out to the priest the fact of the roof. We built the fucking *roof* for you, Father.

Then he looked back at Jean. At Jean's eyes. And he understood that he didn't know, would never know, what was in those eyes, what had ever been there.

"Well, if Jean chooses to go to school here, of course we will be in touch."

Felix nodded. "Of course."

He stood then. None of the others did, though Pierre looked to Père Felix for some direction as to what to do. The three of them sat in what Henry thought of as an emptiness. It was not an emptiness. Pierre passed his hat from one hand to the other and Henry had a memory. He and his brother, as boys, on the streets of Newton Highlands. It had to have been the early 1950s, that postwar moment when things were changing, when the hipster boys of the town were beginning to drive fast cars, to slick their blond hair back. No one wore a hat, only men wore hats, but he and his brother had been forced to wear caps like the one Pierre was handling. The sorts of caps that marked you out as the sons of immigrants when you didn't want to be seen that way. Henry's brother had taken his off, a gesture of freedom, of release, of wanting to be one with the blond boys in cars, and Henry remembered his own reaction: to rip the hat out of his brother's hand and force it back onto his head. An unusual moment for him, but a defining one. As long as we live in this place, let us be what we are. A tribal loyalty had surfaced, one he was himself surprised by.

Shelove was standing in the doorway, as if he had gauged the movement of the meeting and knew it was time to put out his cigarette and prepare. Henry nodded to the three men in chairs. He walked toward Shelove, who was not smiling, but wore a look of what Henry read as compassion, when in fact it could have been a look of anything at all.

Then they were in the van, moving up the slow, pebbly, sandy road, over the river where the women beat their clothes. He would not come here again. In the rearview mirror, Shelove was watching him, noting, with vigilance, his collapsed state.

"You are hungry?" Shelove said.

"Yes," Henry said.

"I will take you somewhere."

"Oh," Henry began to say, and did not know how to finish. "There will be food in the monastery."

"No," Shelove said. The word was definitive.

He took a right turn off the main road. On a dirt road even more primitive than the one they'd been traveling, they passed a series of what Henry assumed were dwellings. Small and tin, slapdash, one room. Shelove was taking him into the country he had never seen. There were occasional sightings of children, bare-chested boys holding sticks, staring. Puddles lined the road. They ascended a small hill.

At the top of the hill, Shelove stopped the van in front of a dwelling nearly identical to those they had passed, though slightly larger. A woman with wide hips and a floor-length skirt regarded Shelove and he spoke to her in Kreyol. At first she seemed not to have understood, but without anything changing in her face she began to gather wood and then she made a fire in the small brazier behind the house. From inside the dwelling, Henry heard children. Cautiously they came out, two boys and a girl, each of them between the ages of five and ten. Shelove did not smile at them or regard them with obvious affection, but in his simple allowance of their presence something seemed ordained. The woman was preparing to cook something and Shelove motioned Henry out of the van and lit a cigarette and offered Henry one. And why not? They smoked together. In the distance, there was a lush haze over the trees. There seemed dust on all the leaves.

"Oui-ped-i," Shelove said. He was not smiling at Henry anymore but looking at him with—the word could only be Henry's new favorite one—seriousness. "You lost him."

"Yes," Henry said, and sucked in on the cigarette. And how precisely did you know that, Shelove? It didn't matter. After the long journey, Henry found himself in the presence of—well, could it be called a form of grace? Why not? Before the descent into what he knew was to come—the report he would have to make to Lily, the resumption of some kind of life—there was this. This moment. Success does not give you such moments; only failure does. Accept, then. He had carried his impulse more or less honorably to its conclusion, and he had lost. He sucked in on the cigarette. Now be grateful.

Shelove spoke to his wife, barking at her, telling her to go in and get the meat. To Henry, it seemed overly harsh, but then he had never really known Haiti. And now he understood that he never would. The touch, the movement out of being Henry Rando, had been achingly brief.

Still, he smiled, and gestured to Shelove, offering a look of simple appreciation.

"Thank you," he said.

All right then. *This* is, apparently, how to be this age.

The Sheffleins were Andrew's choice to take away the painting. He announced it at three, as though he were summoning a press conference. Instead, it was only a series of phone calls. The Sheffleins had already decamped to Tulsa in their private plane. Andrew's announcement to the press—another phone call, which immediately lit up the invisible wires of the fair—was that the painting had sold for five and a half million.

"But I thought it was—" Miranda had understood that Andrew's asking price was five million.

"Oh hush," Andrew said to her. "This is always the way it's done. We jack it up a little. Just for fun."

And so it was done. Aaron had arrived in the afternoon, and there had been a series of tiny private conferences between him and Andrew. A lot of grave nodding to one another while Andrew was on the phone. During all of this, Aaron barely looked at Miranda. His eyes seemed larger, black rimmed and tired. In the years she'd known him she'd watched his clothes get better and better. Today he wore a shirt so soft-looking she wanted to touch it. A shirt that could have been made of distilled water, frozen and then warmed without losing its crystalline state. His hair had grown longer. Aaron had changed. Money had changed him. It was that simple and that profound a thing to notice.

The painting would go. It chilled her to think it. She stood in the emptying corridor before the booth. She had no more place here, nothing to do. No one was regarding her. She'd apparently served whatever vague purpose she'd been summoned here for. She was

ashamed of herself for having so enjoyed the prerogatives—the hotel sheets, the balcony of her room, the deferential nodding of the
female security guards outside this building as she'd entered each
morning—all the tiny, self-aggrandizing things she'd allowed herself to enjoy. She felt herself retreating to the old Miranda. The
woman who would return to Brooklyn, to the apartment that now
seemed too shabby, too small. She would write the last words of her
book, which would try to encapsulate this moment, an artist painting herself naked, revealing nothing—or nothing readable—and
gifting her two wounded sons their share of five million dollars. Is
that enough, boys? Enough for the pain I allowed you to endure?
What were the Sheffleins paying for, exactly? The gorgeous teal-
blue outline of Anna's body. That was all. That teal blue had been
determined to be worth five million dollars.

That wasn't true, of course. She told herself it wasn't true. She'd
grown more fond of the painting the longer she'd been with it. Of
course anyone with enough money would want to own it. But Anna
had hidden herself within it. The gesture, Miranda was certain, was
a deliberate one. The eyes had finally told her as little as Henry's
had, when he'd walked around the room in Grantham turning off
lights, then regarding her in his withheld silence. The old retain this
prerogative: you are not allowed to see all of me.

Claude had just returned to the booth agog at having witnessed
a Maurizio Cattelan sculpture, naming a rumored price that made
Andrew tell him to hush. Aaron finally turned to look at Miranda,
though his true focus was on yet another phone call that Andrew was
making. In the midst of the call, Andrew nodded to him and Aaron
looked relieved. He then approached Miranda.

"What are you doing for dinner?"

"Nothing. I'm not hungry." She amended it. "I have no plans."

"What about the German?"

The sides of his mouth lifted just slightly. It was enough to let her know what he thought about "the German."

"I don't think I need to eat with him. Congratulations, by the way."

"For what?"

"Five million dollars. What will you do with it?"

"I don't know. Do you have suggestions?"

When you were this rich, you could apparently afford to dip everything having to do with money in thick irony. They both turned back to the painting. It seemed a little larger than it had looked until now. Did money do that? There she was. Anna. Her body, Miranda was just now noticing, seemed a tiny bit bloated. You had to look carefully for the things Anna had hidden in plain sight, the slight sag of her belly, a couple of small folds rippling over one another. Anna might not have wanted you to look there, but honesty compelled her to be that brutal with her physical self. The accompanying pang, for Miranda, was: *If only I could look longer, what else would I see?*

"You told me to look at her eyes, Aaron."

"Yes."

She didn't have to respond. He knew exactly what she meant.

"You were looking for her to be the font of all understanding, weren't you?"

His question felt harsh, but of course true. She was reaching for something to say in her own defense, but Andrew was calling Aaron back. Another phone call, another last-minute adjustment, some further detail to be ironed out, a flurry of nodding and then two of Andrew's fingers going up. Once it had been settled, Aaron lifted the plate of today's uneaten pastries, found a small Art Basel tote, and put them in. He approached Miranda again.

"Let's go outside," he said. "Let's go outside and eat these things."

"You've just made five million dollars and you're stealing Andrew's pastries?"

"Miranda, the first thing you've got to learn is that you can never be rich enough. Come on. We need to say goodbye to her. Both of us."

It was almost ritualized, the way the two of them turned to look at the painting for the last time.

She had no idea what set of feelings might have been gathering for Aaron at this moment. She wanted to ask him what he had felt that day, on his way out the door, when his mother had asked him to take his clothes off and pose for her. Why had he said yes? It was a shocking thing to consider, an eleven-year-old boy agreeing to do that. He could have bolted. But no, he had submitted.

"Come," he said.

"No, I want to look just a bit longer."

"I'll meet you outside. Just outside. There are benches. Or—*blocks.* You'll find me."

She watched him walk down the corridor, his body's slight sag, the tote bag with the stolen pastries. She looked again at the painting. Anna had drawn her own head tilted to the side, as if deflecting the viewer's gaze. It was as if she wanted to smile but couldn't allow herself to. As if she knew she'd gotten away with something, claimed her own inviolable interiority. The artist's excuse.

"Tell that cocksucker he's the cheapest man in the world," Andrew was saying to her. "Stealing my treats."

"Yes, I'll tell him."

So goodbye, she said, without speaking, addressing the painting, and then walked down to the escalator and outside. It was not hard to find Aaron. He sat on one of the blocks, looking distracted, on the phone. There were women passing with suitcases on rollers, women who had been staff here, women who had helped in the greasing of the wheels of the great financial exchange that the fair had, in the end, been. These young women were like the girl in *Zabriskie Point,* they had perhaps been hurt or misjudged or made to seem valueless by their bosses during the past few days, girls who had come to see how much money came to dominate what they perhaps imagined had originally, long ago, been intended as a pure celebration of art. Miranda could envision them turning back to the great glass hulk of the fair and wanting to see it blow up, the world leveled and somehow returned to its unfallen state.

But Miranda suspected something else, too, a reckoning more personal. These young women (there were men, too, of course, but Miranda concentrated on the women) were like her. They were the former art students, the museumgoers, women who had looked at paintings and become enraptured and dreamed of painting themselves and then stopped out of—well, what? The ego had to be more ravenous than Miranda knew her own or most of these women's to be. The will to manifest had to supplant everything else. She remembered trying to sketch Armand DeSaulniers in her apartment in Brooklyn. He kept moving. The sketch would not hold him. He was too real to her, and for her to have captured him as she'd have liked, he could not be real, not quite fully human. The sketch had to be the real thing.

"That was my brother," Aaron said, switching off his phone. "He thought we should have asked for more. Greedy bastard."

He made room for her on the block.

"So where shall we eat tonight? The Bistro du Cassoulet? Der Potage au Sauerbrauten?"

"You're mixing languages."

"Yes. But we're in Switzerland."

He offered her a pastry. She shook her head.

"Go ahead," she said.

She would tell Botho to get his own room tonight. Perhaps he could bunk in with Andrew, but no doubt Andrew and Claude would be enjoying a celebratory fuck and would want to be alone. No matter. It was not her problem. She needed to be by herself.

"I vote for the Bistro du Cassoulet."

"Done."

"I brought this."

She opened her bag, the large one she'd brought along. Andrew had frowned when he'd seen her with it. She was expected to carry a small bag, tight and small and decorative. She'd been expected to be what Andrew required her to be, a kind of art object. Carrying in this bag had been her own small assertion of herself. The book would be another. It would have to do. It would be a start.

She took out one of Anna's housedresses.

"Sweet. You brought it here."

"Yes. The hem. There's still her paint on it."

They both touched the place where the paint lingered. Aaron brought it to his lips and sniffed and closed his eyes.

ACKNOWLEDGMENTS

My readers: Michael Gorra, James McMichael, Kelly Hogan, Jim Magnuson, Sherry Kramer, Josh Miller, and Eileen Giardina. My gratitude goes out to you for saying the difficult things, the things no writer wants to hear but needs to. Thanks for being brave, and kind.

To those who helped in smaller but still hugely important ways: Fred Richard and Bucky Avery, oystermen of Wellfleet, who gave me a tutorial in oyster harvesting, even putting me to work. Sister Judith Dupuy, Father Daniel Felix, and the group from Northampton with whom I went to Haiti in 2011. Martin Bonilla, Brother Benjamin of the Community of Franciscan Friars of the Renewal, Kaila Klapper-Binney, Adin Thayer, Ned Delacour, Hosea Baskin, Taylor Damron, Julie Flanagan, Linda Kampley, Robert Anasi, Ronald Blythe. The Benedictine monks of St. Mary's Monastery of Petersham, Massachusetts, who gave me space to write and taught me a little about prayer. The librarians of the Smith College Art Library, where much of this book was written. To Katie Liptak and Oona Holahan, for guiding me so sensitively through the editorial process. Chandra Wohleber, whose wide-ranging questions made copyediting this manuscript more fun than it had any right to be, and Janine Barlow, the excellent production editor. To David Rabe, for being a beloved partner in crime. Doug Hughes, for the listening and the deep friendship. And to Jan Maxwell, for being an inspiration to me.

There are some writers, too, to whom I owe a large debt: Phoebe Hoban, for her biography of Alice Neel; Katerina Dolejsova, whose story written in a Michener Center class I taught in 2006 became the spark for "The Joanna Monologues"; Amy Wilentz, for her superb books about Haiti, *Farewell, Fred Voodoo* and *The Rainy Season*; Jonathan Katz, for his invaluable book about the Haitian earthquake, *The Big*

Truck That Went By, Sarah Thornton, for *Seven Days in the Art World*; Christopher Mason, for *The Art of the Steal*; Peter Watson, for *Sotheby's: The Inside Story*; D. B. Wright, for *The Famous Beds of Wellfleet*. I am indebted as well to certain writers whose lines and phrases I have shamelessly lifted: Madison Smartt Bell, who coined the phrase "days without rules" to describe a very particular Haitian chaos; Francis Hope, for the poem Miranda remembers; Grace Paley, for her description of "the opinionated playground" in her story "Faith in a Tree"; George Mackay Brown, for his definition of prayer as "interrogating silence"; Philip Roth, for the phrase "the remembering animal" in *Sabbath's Theater*. W. H. Auden, it probably goes without saying, wrote the lines Anna quotes in her diary. Rachel Ingalls's brilliant novel *Mrs. Caliban* was the inspiration for the play Lily appears in. Drew Pautz's play *Love the Sinner*, produced by the National Theater of Great Britain in 2010, posited a moral quandary that started me thinking about the one Henry would come to face. Finally, a huge nod of gratitude goes to Nadine Gordimer, whose novel *Burger's Daughter* became a kind of North Star for me in the long years of writing this book in the dark.

Sloan Harris is, as always, the Man. He's never dishonest, he's never discouraging, he never doubts. I can't express enough the gratitude I feel for who he is, for the two of us having found each other thirty years ago, and for his sticking with me through some very rough patches.

Jonathan Galassi has stuck with me as well, and for this, I feel like the most fortunate of men. Someday I will figure out how a man of such erudition, such smarts, wears it all with such modesty, but I haven't gotten there yet.

Finally, my family. Thank you, Jesse, for being my surrogate son all these years, for trusting me and opening yourself to me the way you have. To my son, Henry, for your brilliance and your toughness and your exquisite, unremitting taste, which holds me to a standard.

My daughter, Nicola, for opening up the art world for me, for teaching me all you have taught me not only about art but about that most difficult of tasks, parenthood. To Anais, for giving me one more chance to love imperfectly but wholeheartedly.

And to Eileen, who is—there is no other word—magnificent.